A JANUARY STUDIOS NOVEL

A Little Bit Tempting

DEDICATION

If you've ever been forced to put on a mask in front of others, this is for you. Cheers to accepting your authentic self.

1

ANNIE

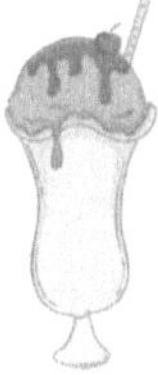

"I'm sorry, we are out of blueberry muffins."

Out of blueberry muffins? What kind of coffee shop runs out of the number one pastry in America at eight in the morning? Okay, maybe not the number one, don't quote me on that. But, on today of all mornings? It's fine. Everything's fine. I won't let this ruin my mood.

I straighten my back and offer Mary, my favorite barista at Flora Coffee, a polite smile to show how little I'm fazed by the fact that they are out of my favorite muffin.

"We, um, have blueberry scones." Mary has the audacity to hold out the item still in plastic wrap.

"Oh, is that it?" I wince, hating that I have to ask. My gaze wanders to the case, and sure enough, there are no other pastries to be seen.

"That's it, Annie. We should have more tomorrow, though." Tomorrow isn't as important as today, but I smile anyway.

"Oh, okay. I'll take my usual and the large drip." My usual being a large Americano to get me through my morning commute. I don't bother telling Mary today is a pivotal day, or that the blueberry muffin was supposed to be my good luck charm.

"Can I also purchase a fifteen dollar gift card to pay for anyone who comes in after me?" If I can't start my day right, maybe I can help someone else.

With my watered-down espresso in hand and an obligatory coffee for my boss, I exit Flora and walk to the curb to catch my Uber to the office. Today isn't *technically* my first day at Starlet PR. For the past three years, I've been an underpaid and overworked intern.

It's my first non-intern day, and to kickstart my career as a publicist, I get a trial client to prove my abilities—as if I haven't worked my ass off already. I've asked the universe for a short contract and an amicable client, fingers crossed she listens.

My purse vibrates in the leather seat next to me and I reach for it, already knowing who's calling.

"Hi, Marce!" I answer.

"Hello! Got your good luck charm for today?" Marcy, my best friend, asks.

We balance each other out and have since I first moved to Los Angeles five years ago. The first day I met her was the same day I learned how much Marcy hates mornings.

"Ugh, no." I groan and throw my head back to stare at the gray ceiling of the car. "Can you believe Flora didn't have my muffin stocked?"

"Wow, didn't they know it's your first *real* day today? Mary didn't save one for you?"

"Shut up, not helping. No, Mary didn't save one for me."

"What a bitch," Marcy jokes, laughing into the phone.

"That's exactly what I told her too. What a bitch for not having my muffin." I chuckle and drop my head in time to see the driver look my way in the mirror. Oops.

"You could always stop by the studio if you still want one."

Marcy works as the assistant director at January Studios alongside my sister, Cassie, her husband, Emmett, and a slew of their friends. It's because of them that I'm addicted to this damn pastry.

"I'd be late," I say as my eyes track the buildings as they pass. "Otherwise, I'd tell my Uber to take a detour."

The driver tries to talk to me, clearly only hearing the last part of the sentence, and I have to shake my head and mouth, *"No, keep going."*

"You should try to bake them. I bet you could recreate it with your fancy baking machine."

"My stand mixer? Marcy, that is—" I shake my head to no one but myself trying to contain my laughter. "One, that is called a stand mixer. Two, I could technically do that. But three, I don't have time to bake as much anymore." My job has taken over, and any semblance of balance is nowhere to be seen.

"You know, there's a way to solve that. You could—"

"Don't say find a new job," I interrupt.

"I'm serious, Anns."

"Maybe things will be different after this trial client," I say, my chest tight with dread that it will be the opposite.

"You say that, but—I already told you once—" Marcy's voice suddenly becomes muffled as she talks to what I can assume is an employee. "Annie, I need to go. Not going to wish you luck because you don't need it. You're a badass publicist and any client will be lucky to have you."

"Thanks, Marce. Be nice today."

"Not a chance. Love you." Marcy gets the last word in before the line goes silent.

A few minutes later, the car pulls up to the curb in front of the office while my discovery station blasts in my ears. I thread the handle of my bag up my arm and onto my shoulder.

I thank the driver, get out of the car, and breathe in the cool August air. If my stomach wasn't growling so loudly that I could hear it through my headphones, I'd be in a much better mood, but I can't win them all.

My feet clack on the tile floor of the lobby as I make my way to the elevators. Starlet PR is on the tenth floor and is full of large conference rooms and individual offices. I'm only in the office two or three days a week, but at least they keep the kitchen stocked with snacks.

By the time I enter the conference room where my boss (and CEO of Starlet) is waiting for me, I'm right on time—fifteen minutes early.

"Annie, good morning." Greg looks at me for a brief moment before returning his attention to his computer. He's dressed in his typical three-piece suit (today's is dark gray) and his barely-there brown hair is slicked back. He's your typical asshole CEO: always making sexist jokes and always has a laundry-list of items for you to do.

"Good morning. Did you have a good weekend?" I smile, even though he's still ignoring me, and place the large coffee next to him.

This is how every meeting goes. I show up, wait for Greg to finish whatever task he's doing, continue waiting as he tells me a random story about God knows what, then we finally talk about why we are in this room together.

"Oh, mhm," Greg says as he types, half-listening. "Oh, coffee." He smiles as he takes the cup in his hand. *You're welcome.*

I wait a beat longer before saying, "Any updates for me?" Might as well cut to the chase.

"Yes, yes." Greg sets his coffee down, then shuffles the papers that sit to the right of him. "We are going to meet your client today for an early lunch at Little Italy Bistro. I've booked us a private room." He babbles on about the menu and other unimportant items as I read the paper he slid over to me.

This *paper* should be a small binder with a brief about the client, as I was told I didn't need to prepare anything. I should have background information, recent articles, anything more than this sheet of paper. And what did Greg think was important to tell me? Is there anything on here I don't already know?

We only deal with actors, so that was known. The actor's location is in Los Angeles. No duh. And there's a statement about an NDA.

So, no. I'll be walking into this meeting blind. *Wonderful.*

Regardless of how I feel on the inside, I smile at Greg. "And do we know who this actor is?"

He nods. "You need to sign the NDA before you learn anything else about him."

A male actor, that's something not on the paper. Is he old? A teenager? What sort of problems has he gotten himself into? Why could they not send the NDA over in advance like normal? Did Greg already sign the NDA?

"Is this a last-minute client?" I ask, assuming that would be why Greg doesn't have more information for me.

"It is, yes, came in over the weekend. I don't expect this client to be too taxing," Greg says.

I don't bother asking what would have happened if this magical client didn't come through over the weekend. Instead, I nod like the picture-perfect employee while I jot down notes.

"I'll be keeping a close eye on this," Greg continues, "and step in when needed of course."

And by that, Greg means *if I lack skills or capabilities needed for said client.* Perfect. Three years here, and I'm still micromanaged. If I'm able to prove to him that I can handle my own client, I'll be hired on as a full-time employee when this contract is done .

This has been my dream since I was fifteen years old, sitting on my bed, reading gossip magazines and fawning over troubled actors that received their redemption arc. I fell in love with following their stories, watching how they turned their career around, and knew I wanted to have a hand in that.

After I gather the single piece of paper with the rest of my notes, I stand up from the table and push in my chair.

"Okay, Greg, I'm going to do a bit of recon before we head out if that's alright?"

He's back to typing, already tuning out even though I'm still in the room.

"I'll ping you when I'm ready to leave," Greg mumbles.

I hold back from flipping him off, instead turning my back to him and heading out the door to go to my office.

You'd think after all I've given this company, Greg would trust me. I've worked so hard, putting in long hours, weekends, not going home for holidays, and forgoing plans with Cassie and Marcy on more than one occasion. If this assignment ends poorly, I'll be starting over.

Sure, I'll have the experience as the intern, and some experience from when I "helped" Cassie with her publicity when she first became an actress, but who would trust me if I were let go from Starlet? I might as well be on a *Do not hire* list and toast to the end of my PR career if I can't help my first client.

My butt barely sinks into my chair when my phone buzzes on my desk. Cassie's name appears on the caller ID. She moved here five years before me, and it's been great to be in the same city. Although she's busy acting in movies or with Emmett when he directs films, we always find time to catch up.

"Hey, Cass."

"Hi! How's your first day going? I would have texted you earlier, but I had a late night with Emmett."

I roll my eyes, not wanting to know what 'late night' means. "Say no more. I just had a meeting with Greg about my client, and before you ask, no, I don't know who it is yet."

"Damn, still?"

"Yup, but I'm not worried. Greg and I are meeting him in a little for lunch," I say, fidgeting with a pen.

"Oh, a him. Maybe he'll be hot. And single."

"Cassie, I'm—"

"Married to your job, I know, I know," Cassie interrupts.

"No, I was going to say I'm not looking for anything. My last relationship was bad enough."

Cassie hums in agreement.

Dan Barnes seemed like a sound decision when we started dating. I was in my second year of college, nineteen years old, and ended up meeting him in the library. He was studying to become a lawyer, and had deep brown eyes I fell for immediately. Pair that with his smooth words, perfectly groomed dark brown hair, and rotating wardrobe of henleys... I was doomed from the start.

A year into our relationship, we moved in together. We were in love. Or maybe it was only me. For holidays, he would bring me to visit his family and they always welcomed me as one of their own. Between his two siblings, I bonded with his twin, Kiley, the most. His older brother, hot as he might have been, was never particularly nice to me. Dan did a lot of shitty things the last year of us being together, one of which was telling me I'd never make it as a publicist.

That was a little over a year ago, and I haven't dated anyone since. My entire memory of our relationship is like a stain that won't come out, no matter how many DIY methods I try. No amount of meditation or one night stands have healed that wound, so I'm stuck with this mindset that I have to prove myself to everyone.

I let Cassie know I'll text her later to get her off my back and to stop her from interrogating me. My mind can only take so many questions at once, and the Barnes family is the last thing I need to be thinking about.

There's a knock on my door. I hope it's not Greg. I swivel back around in my chair as a familiar redhead pokes their head in.

"James," I greet my one and only friend at the firm. If it wasn't for them, I wouldn't have lasted through Greg's bull-shit. They've worked here for over a decade and have been teaching me all they know.

"Heard about your meeting with Greg." They grimace, then slump in a chair in front of my desk.

"From who?" I bet it was Nancy. She works at the front desk and is always stalking calendars and trying her best to overhear conversations she's not a part of.

"Nancy," James confirms.

Fucking Nancy.

I nod in response, then say, "You don't happen to know who my client is, do you?"

James shakes their head. "Not a clue. No one knows, which is surprising because Greg likes to brag on the big clients we land. So, maybe your client needs minimal help with the press?"

"Maybe," I drawl as my focus lands on a band on their left hand. "Um, James, what is that?" I point to the new jewelry.

James brings their hand to their face, as if the ring has always been there and I'm reminding them of the fact. "Oh, this thing?" Twisting their palm to face them, they give me a better look at the golden band slipped on their ring finger. "Todd and I eloped this past week. Just the two of us."

"I should scold you for not inviting me since I am the one that set you up, but I kind of figured when you two were ready, you would elope and not tell anyone."

"Ah, yes, I remember you introducing us like it was yesterday," James says, crossing their arms as they lean back in their chair, a smile blooming on their face.

"We were both at Flora..." I start.

"You were with Cassie, and I was there by coincidence."

I smile, remembering the memory vividly. "Todd had just brought me my muffin, you walked over, I introduced you, and you slipped him your number on the way out."

James chuckles. "Oh, right, that is what happened. What can I say? I can't resist a man in glasses."

"He always wore those damn glasses, even though they were fake." I shake my head and laugh. Before Mary, Todd was my favorite barista. He quit a few years ago to work as an event manager at some company I can never remember.

"That's accurate. But I didn't care, I fell in love with him anyway."

"And you didn't invite me to the wedding…" I tease.

"It was an elopement, Annie. The only other person there besides the officiant was my mom." We both laugh at that. "Anyway, we're hosting a party this Saturday and we expect to see you there."

"It depends." I shrug, looking at the papers in front of me from this morning's meeting.

"You can take an evening off, little bird. You don't need to overwork yourself."

Little bird. James has been calling me this since I started and they've taken me under their wing.

"Easier said than done," I say with a thin-lipped smile.

"Too bad. I've already told Todd you could go."

"Of course you did." I try to glare at James, but I can never be mad at them.

They're too nice to me and they're lucky I love them.

James stands from the chair, grabbing their bag they previously set on the floor. "Maybe you can bring your new client. Give yourself a neutral place to spend time getting to know them."

I tell James I'll think about it once again, not being able to commit to something like that when I don't know who my client is in the first place. They wave me off and leave me alone in my office to get work done prior to this meeting.

For the next few hours, I catch up on emails and local news. Calls from vendors blow up my phone, wanting to send me updated material for their fall and winter specials. Reporters reply to my inquiries, but I send them to my voicemail so I can deal with that tomorrow. I don't get up from my desk until Greg finally pings my computer and tells me we are leaving for lunch in ten minutes.

Here goes nothing.

2
ZAYN

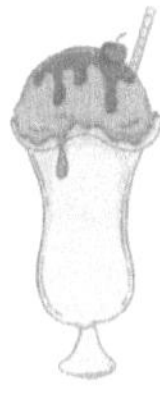

"You've gotta be fucking kidding me." My heart beats out of my chest as I pace the same ten steps in my trailer. My right hand threads through my freshly faded hair. This was supposed to be my *I've accepted the job of my career* haircut.

Ed, the director at January Studios, remains still, perched on the arm of the couch, letting me stew in my anger. After the year we've had on set, he knows it's best to give me a few minutes to collect myself. This has been a recurring meeting for Ed and I.

"You need to calm—"

"Don't tell me I need to fucking calm down, Ed. I'm fucking calm," I huff. Placing a hand on each hip, I lean back into the kitchen counter, stopping the pacing. "Sorry," I mutter, peering to my left to catch Ed offering me a thin smile.

"The answer isn't no to the role, Zayn," Ed says.

The role that he's referring to is the lead male in an action trilogy. I've been pining and searching for a lead role for the last two years. It's a role that will move me from B-list actor to A-list actor. I need this. I've been acting for nearly a decade, five of those years being here at the studios, and I haven't had my break. Most of the actors that film here have, but not me.

Instead, I've been in various movies and short films, but nothing blockbuster worthy. People recognize me around the city, mostly from the last movie I did, and only because I was the token lifeguard who saved the lead characters from a near-death situation.

"I know I haven't had the best year, Ed," I say.

"You broke a reporter's camera." Ed glares at me.

"He asked a dumb question." I shrug. The reporter should have seen it coming when he asked about my ex-girlfriend of twelve years.

"You also cussed out the news reporter. On live TV."

I just nod, no excuse for that one.

"And then don't get me started on how you've been treating the staff here," he says.

"I don't talk to the staff," I argue, holding up both hands.

"Exactly. You need to improve your image, be friendly again, be the Zayn you were a year ago before all this started happening."

He means the old Zayn, when I was twenty-nine, had myself together, and had a promising future with what I thought was the love of my life. When I hung out with other actors on set, volunteered to help run lines, and donated time and money to a local organization that helps young actors.

"What if I don't want to be friendly again?" I grimace.

"Look, Zayn, I'm going to be honest with you, if you don't fix your image and attitude toward the media, I won't be able to offer you the role."

My chest sinks and my gaze follows, making its way to the floor. There's a part of me that wants to quit, walk away from all this. But what would that mean for me? If I didn't even try to fix myself? If I didn't give this an honest shot before it all likely goes to shit?

"Got it," I mutter. "Any ideas on how I'd begin to do that?"

"Yes, two. And they aren't ideas, but things I need you to do." Ed grins, flipping the papers on his clipboard until he finds the one he's looking for.

"Hit me." I return my focus to him.

"Great. Okay, one, I need you on set three days a week to help run lines with new actors."

I grumble. Not what I want to do with my spare time, but having experience with coaching beginner actors and the possibility of Ed not giving me this role, I can't say no. I nod for him to continue.

"And two, for help with the media, I've been talking with Logan, and he hired Starlet PR over the weekend."

Logan, my agent for the past decade, kind of my friend. "And by hiring, you mean?"

"You'll have to ask him. I don't have all the details."

I slowly move my chin up and down. This isn't going to be fun.

"Alright, kid. I need to go chat with Emmett for a few minutes before the day gets away from me. Listen to Logan, okay?" Ed asks.

Emmett, an actor and writer here at the studio, is a few years older than me, but we hung out a time or two before my life flipped upside down.

"Yeah, Ed. I will."

Ed leaves the trailer and I'm grateful to have a few moments alone. My eyes close and I inhale deep, letting the air travel in my nose, down my throat, to my lungs. I hold it for a few seconds before opening my mouth to exhale. The rock in my chest loosens as I do this a few more times.

I could use a few minutes outside, so I take a walk before meeting Logan. He's the only person I talk to besides my younger sister Kiley. I take the long loop around the studio so I have enough time to give her a ring.

"Z!" Kiley's excitement instantly brightens my mood.

"Hi, Kiki. What are you up to?"

"Just studying."

"This early in the morning?"

"Z, it's nearly noon." She scoffs, and I can picture her shaking her head at me. "I have finals for my summer classes."

"I still don't understand why you wanted to go back to school."

Kiley and my younger brother, Dan, are twins. They both went to school twice.

Dan's the lawyer, Kiley works in marketing. She wanted to go back to get something—a certificate, maybe?

"I need it for my promotion. Not all of us can use our good looks to get the jobs we want," she says.

"And abs."

"Right," she chuckles. "How can I forget your best feature? You did spend the last film with so few clothes on that I thought Mom was going to pass out from covering her face with a pillow for most of it."

"Kiley, I was a lifeguard. I had on swim trunks."

"Still."

"Well, anyway, enough about me... I just wanted to call and check in," I say.

"Everything's good on my end. I'm hoping to make it over to your place soon, it's been a while."

"Sure, Ki, I'll be around. Well, hey, I need to go, okay? I have to meet with Logan," I say, seeing Logan waiting for me in the distance.

"Yeah, sounds good. Love you!"

"Love you."

Kiley never asks about work. Maybe it's because she doesn't know what to ask or maybe it's because I've told her to mind her business one too many times. Either way, it's always a relief when she doesn't ask me to explain my vague answers. Maybe I should. My family tries to be supportive of this career, even though it's not the most stable or predictable. Kiley also never brings up my ex, Marissa. We were together since high school. She became family, and everyone loved her as much as they love me. When we broke up, it broke my relationship with my family. They didn't ask me about my grief, or about what happened. The only person I talk to is Kiley, even if I don't open up to her.

After the one person you love the most decides you're only holding them back, it's easy to decide you don't need to trust anyone. I don't need to open up to others, wail about my own personal story and struggles.

"There he is!" Logan looks up, puts his phone back in his pocket, and starts jogging toward me.

"Hi Logan, sorry I'm late."

"You're not sorry." Logan glares my way.

"No, I'm not." I shake my head. "Ed tells me you hired some PR firm?"

Logan nods. "And we're going to be late to meet them if we don't leave."

"Right now? We're going right now? Can't you do this without me?"

"Yes, right now. And no, I need you to meet them. I'll catch you up on the drive over. This lunch should be fairly quick and painless. Try your best not to be grumpy, okay?"

"I'll try my best, no promises." I smile wide, making it painfully obvious that this is not what I want to be doing right now, then I slide into the car.

The ride over to Little Italy Bistro is a short, fifteen-minute drive. Logan does his best to fill me in, even though I find my-self zoning out for half the conversation. I don't need someone to help fix my image. What I need is the space to figure out what my next step is and do it myself.

The driver pulls up to the front curb at the restaurant. As I step out of the car, I marvel at how packed it is. It's always been like this when I've been here in the past, which is why I try to avoid it. All seats are filled, there are servers running back and forth between the patio and inside, and smooth jazz blares over the speakers. My mouth waters as the smell of garlic and tomatoes hits my nose.

Logan walks in front of me, leading me through the crowd of people. I keep my head down, which I figure is better for my image instead of glaring at everyone out of habit. See? I don't need a publicist to tell me that.

"Zayn," someone calls from behind me.

Fuck. I ignore them and keep walking.

"Zayn, just one question," the voice irritatingly says, reminding me of their presence.

My gaze lifts from the ground at the same time I almost slam into Logan. He's since turned to face the mystery man, sporting an oddly happy smile and raising his brows at me to oblige the reporter. I simply roll my eyes at his silent request.

"Sure, one question," I say through gritted teeth as I turn around.

A short, stocky man stands in front of me with a pen in one hand and a notepad in the other. He's wearing a matching striped suit, which is unusual for this August heat.

"Aren't you dying in that?" I ask.

"Huh?" The man asks, looking around the room as if I wasn't talking to him. I point a finger to him.

"Oh." The man chortles. "No, no, I'm cool as a cucumber."

He giggles at his own joke until a few beats later when he realizes I'm not laughing with him. His laughs slow until they die out.

"Your question?" I ask.

"Oh, yes, right," he rambles. "Will we see you at the upcoming gala for the Young Actors Association?"

"No—"

"He will be there," Logan chimes in, throwing an arm around my shoulder. I jab at him with my elbow and smile as he mutters "ow" and removes his arm.

The short man writes down what I can assume is "yes" in his small notepad.

"And will you be bringing a date?" The man meets my stare and for a moment, I think about grabbing the pad of paper from his hands and ripping it before throwing it back in his face.

"That's two questions," I reply, then turn on my heel to continue into the restaurant while Logan apologizes to the man on my behalf.

I find a server who directs me to the back room, finally giving me the privacy I was told I would get.

Inside, there are four chairs and a buffet of food in the middle of the table. I'd rather have the advantage of seeing the people from the firm, so I walk around and sit down in a chair that's facing the door. Light jazz music plays as I wait for the others to join me.

Logan walks in a minute later with a look on his face that I'm familiar with. His eyebrows are scrunched in tandem, his eyes nearly slits, and his mouth is pushed together in a way that you just want to laugh at because of how ridiculous he looks.

"You're angry," I say as a statement of fact.

"This is exactly why we are here."

"This firm?" I ask.

"Yes, a publicist will be good for you."

I groan, throwing my head back. "Do I need someone to tell me what to say and what not to say?"

"Yes," Logan says, shuffling a few papers in front of him to make way for the pasta. "If you want that role in the trilogy, you will do as she says."

I nod. My knee bounces, the panic of losing control already starting to set in. I close my eyes momentarily, taking a deep breath to try and calm my nervous system. Control is something I need after losing everything. My future was set: get married, get the job, and be happy. Now, I have none of that. The only thing I do have is the control of my day-to-day, and now I'm going to give that up to some random stranger.

"You need to chill out." Logan pipes up. He's already loaded a plate with a mound of alfredo.

Choosing to ignore him, I start to do the same, opting for chicken parmesan. If the firm is going to be late, I'm not going to let that hinder my lunch.

As if on cue, the door swings open to our small room. I glance up to find the server first, smiling at whoever is outside the door. A man, who I assume is the boss of Starlet PR, enters first. He smiles and takes a seat across from Logan.

"My associate will be here in a moment. Thank you for meeting us here, we love this restaurant. My name is Greg."

Have I mentioned how much I loathe small talk? Luckily, Logan does his job and talks to Greg about his day.

"Ah, here she is. Annie meet Logan and Zayn," Greg says a few moments later.

That name makes me pause. There's only one Annie that I've known in my life, or at least only one I care to remember. She was never mine, but every so often the image of her face graces my mind. Soft brown hair, crystal blue eyes, a dimple on her right cheek when she smiles. Her laughter fills the air, enough to get high on. Except, this can't be that Annie, can it? The one that dated my brother.

The one that likely hates me because of how I treated her two years ago when I met her.

I glance up from my plate to find the same pale blue eyes looking back at me. And from the looks of it, Annie is my new publicist.

3
ZAYN

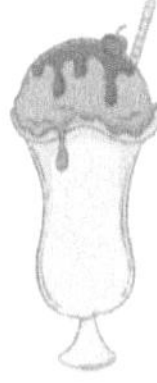

THE AIR IN THE room is electrified, and I can't seem to look anywhere else but at Annie. She's wearing a white blouse cut low enough to draw my attention, and her brown hair frames her face. Her lips are a deep shade of red, and it's not until Greg speaks that I find it in me to tear my eyes away from her.

"Annie, take a seat," Greg commands. There's one left next to Greg, so she takes that, sitting across from me.

I glare at Greg out of habit before remembering that I shouldn't care about her.

Her chair squeaks as it moves back. "Sorry," she mutters.

Instead of her focus being on me, her eyes are on Logan. Why is she looking at him, not at me? Does she not remember me? No, that's impossible. The flush in her cheeks tells me she does, as does the way she's fidgeting in her seat, as if she's fighting to keep herself from glaring at me.

"Annie, this is Zayn Barnes. Zayn, this is Annie Mitchell, your new publicist." Logan chimes in, even though we've already been introduced.

"I know," Annie slips. Her eyes widen and bounce between Greg and Logan, never once landing on me. "I mean, what I meant to say is, I know who you are and I'm happy to help."

She finally drags her gaze to meet mine, and there's a sense of familiarity in it. I hold her stare, my tongue darting outside my bottom lip for a brief moment.

"Nice to meet you, Annie."

She dips her chin to say the same, and her eyes briefly shoot to my mouth before the mask returns. A smile replaces her momentary scowl and her eyes shift back to Logan.

For the rest of the meeting, I find myself stealing harmless glances at Annie while the details of the contract are laid out in front of us. It'll run from the beginning of August to the end of December, which will hopefully be when I sign the contract for the trilogy. Five months is plenty of time to smile at the cameras and fix my image.

"Alright, let's get down to business," Greg says. "We propose one event a week for the next five months, with a few of those being more large-scale events. You're already aware of the gala on Saturday, which will be your first event. Before then, we suggest you two meet to get to know each other." Greg looks at me. "We will need to start small and reintroduce you to the media. Annie, here, will help with all the logistics and what to say."

"I don't do public events." Leaning back into my chair, I cross my arms.

"What he means to say," Logan glares my way before he comments, "is that he doesn't feel prepared to do public events."

I give him my best side-eye, ignoring the fact that he's supposed to be on my side and help me do this the way I want to. I've only attended two events in the last six months. The first didn't have a ton of media attention, but it was large enough that I cussed out two different reporters. Marissa was at the next event, with a man on her arm, and that was when I almost punched a photographer for telling me to smile. Logan saved me from that disaster. I haven't been to another event since.

"I'd be willing to meet tomorrow, for us to start preparing," Annie suggests. "In private, if you'd like."

I glance at her, assuming she'll look away immediately, but instead she locks eyes with me. My cock twitches, reacting to her challenging my gaze. My own body doesn't know that she is off limits because not only did she date my brother, but she's also my publicist. Oh, and I don't date, not even casually.

"He'd love that," Logan says. Annie's attention on me never falters.

"Well, that settles it. We will begin tomorrow," Greg exclaims, jotting useless information down in front of him.

For the last few minutes of lunch, Annie signs all the necessary paperwork. Whatever happens between us is now protected by a legal document. Her having relations with my brother won't be a conflict of interest, as she knows so little about me.

Because of that, I'm still able to have some control with this situation. Even though she's the puppeteer, telling me what to say and who to say it to, I'm still going to control the overall narrative. And that alone eases the knot that's forming in my chest.

Logan and I walk over to meet Greg and Annie on the other side of the table. We shake hands, alternating between the pair.

"I'm looking forward to our partnership. Let me know in the meantime if there's anything I can do for you. I'm just a text away." A soft smile appears on Annie's face, a mask of professionalism. I reach out to shake her hand, immediately regretting it when I feel her warmth and watch the red rise in her cheeks.

We drop each other's hands, and I clear my throat as if that'll help me forget the feel of her skin. The first time I touch a woman since Marissa and my pulse radiates through my entire body. Fucking pathetic.

Logan comes to the rescue again, filling in the words I lack. He graciously lets Annie know we will be in touch and thanks them for helping me. A load of bullshit, in my opinion. I don't need help improving my image, which I've told Logan multiple times. I can do it alone. I can talk to the media, say what they want to hear, smile for the cameras, and be the guy everyone wants me to be. This year may not have been great, but if Ed needs me to be more personable to offer me the role, I'll do it.

What I don't need is a distraction, which I almost guarantee Annie will be. With our past, I already know we will butt heads. No one with that amount of energy and optimism will get along with someone like me, especially when she already has a foul taste about me.

Where she radiates sunshine, I darken with clouds.

I'm going to keep my head down, do the work, and land this role. Seems pretty straightforward to me.

4
ANNIE

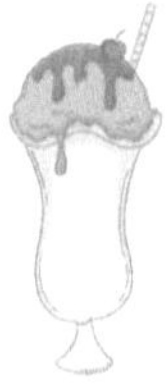

IF I HAD A pillow, I'd be screaming into it. I cannot believe Zayn Barnes is the client that will make or break my career. Of all people in Hollywood, it had to be my ex-boyfriend's older brother.

"Annie, sweetie, you okay?" James is standing in my doorway, an exact replica of this morning. I can smell the coffee from the extra cup they're holding. Rushing over to them, I offer a weak smile.

"Oh, yes. I'm okay. Just a long morning." My lips turn up into a grin. Fake, but they won't press me for more. I grab the drink from them and turn around to walk to my desk. "I met my client. He seems nice." I remove the lid and take one deep breath, the fruity smell of coffee somehow grounding me as I take a seat.

"Thank you for this." Snapping the lid back on, I take a sip.

"And who's the lucky guy that you get to spend a bunch of time with?" James asks.

"Zayn."

"As in *the* Zayn? Zayn Barnes? The hottie with the beard?" James is practically drooling over the man.

I shrug and smile because they are not wrong. "The one and only."

It's taking everything in me right now to hold back spilling everything to them. The only person that knows the full story about my ex is Cassie.

"Interesting. And you're supposed to clean up all his latest media drama? That guy knows how to upset reporters." James leans casually against the doorframe. They tend to have all the easy clients. The ones that just need notes for an upcoming interview or some pointers on what to say for a speech.

"I'm supposed to help move him in a better direction, yes. The entire lunch was spent talking about events coming up and contract details. Greg wasn't able to brief me about the client because of the NDA."

James just nods, taking it all in before they offer advice like they do every time. "Ah, an NDA, you should have told me that this morning. Well, be careful. I've heard that guy doesn't have a great reputation."

"You mean it's not great that he dropped some guy's camera in a lake?"

"I thought it was just a trash can."

I laugh. "Regardless, I'll be fine. It's what I'm best at. Remember the client I helped you with last summer?"

"The woman who couldn't stop crying about her dog whenever someone asked her about it?"

"Yes, James, the poor woman *grieving* her dog."

"I remember," James says, nodding. "You ordered her a keychain replica of her dog to carry around and somehow that made her stop crying whenever someone brought up the damn thing."

"You *could* be a little more empathetic, James. But see, I'm good at taking someone's negative image and helping them remedy it."

"You were made for this job. Just be careful, little bird. He seems like trouble."

"You're just saying that because he's attractive." I glare at them, knowing I've spoken the truth.

Jame's giggles. "Just text me if you need anything, okay?"

I nod before James exits my office and closes the door. Since I know little to nothing about what Zayn is up to these days, I need to spend the rest of the day researching.

For typical clients, I would have done this already. I would have been prepared from day one. Around the office, I'm known for being the over-prepared employee and the one that's always willing to help. It's why I've taken on extra hours at the firm, helping out when I can. In return, people compliment my work ethic and say that they'd be lost without me. Ever since Dan told me I'd never make it and belittled my career, I chase external praise. It's one thing that keeps me going when my belief in myself starts to waver.

My computer dings, and a new text banner appears in the upper right-hand corner. My heart betrays me by flipping and beating quicker once I see who it's from.

Zayn

Meet me in two hours at Dave's Diner.

I did say I was a text away, didn't I? Two hours doesn't give me long to start prepping for the gala this Saturday. It would have been better if Greg would have told me who the client was, to give me proper time to research and document our course of action. Everything that I know about Zayn is surface level.

I know he's thirty years old and doesn't like me. And as I've already established, the older brother to the man that mentally scarred me for life. Where his brother was my type on paper, Zayn is the complete opposite. His hair and beard are a harmonious shade of dirty blond, with subtle hints of brown and grayish undertones, giving him a rugged and natural look. He towered over me today when I stood next to him as I tried not to picture myself nestled under the crook of his arm.

I didn't expect him to take my breath away, like he did when I first met him two years ago, before he stopped acknowledging me when we were in the same room or when Dan tried to get him to say hello to me on FaceTime calls. Yet, here I am, curious about what's going on in his head, feeling a pull toward his grumpy demeanor.

I still don't understand what his end goal is, why he needs a publicist. We should have talked about that during our meeting earlier, but Greg wouldn't shut up about the damn movie

Zayn was last in. Zayn doesn't have a great image, but knowing January Studios doesn't work with just any actor, he has to be pining after a specific role.

Redirecting my attention to the computer, I figure I have enough time to do a bit of googling before I leave the firm to meet him. By my phone's estimate, it'll take roughly thirty minutes to reach the diner. It would have been nice for him to find somewhere a bit more in the middle, but he was presumably only thinking of himself. The diner happens to be across the street from January Studios and is notorious for kicking out anyone who looks like a reporter—it's probably why Zayn wants to meet there. The more private, the better.

My search turns up what I expected. Most of the articles written on him are speculations or rumors. The interviews published recently are short, two or three questions max. I scribble down a few questions to remember to ask him, then switch the browser to look at images. I was hoping to see photographs of him with family or friends, to get a sense of who Zayn has been since I last saw him over a year ago. I should not have ventured into the images tab because *holy shit*. Looking at Zayn, you can tell he's muscular. His shirt clings to his biceps, emphasizing that he maintains a healthy physique. But, let me tell you, shirtless Zayn... that's something else.

"You dropped something."

My eyes flicker up to see James, who has once again returned to distract me from doing any actual work. Closing my jaw, I press the x button on the browser tab to exit out of the gallery.

"I wasn't doing anything."

Bless James, who simply smiles, oblivious to the fact that I was ogling at a man that I dislike with every fiber of my body.

There was a time that I liked Zayn. That was before I met him, when I saw the way Dan lit up when he talked about his "older brother who is the best actor he's ever seen." A year into our relationship, after we'd been living together for two months, Dan asked me to come home with him for the holidays. I said yes, obviously. And I was excited to meet his family since my own mother lives halfway across the country.

The moment I walked through the Barnes' front door, Dan's twin sister Kiley enveloped me in a hug and we hit it off immediately. She told me stories about the boys and hung out with me while Dan was helping his parents in the kitchen.

Zayn must not have expected me, because the moment he walked into the room, he stopped. Kiley asked where some girl Marissa was, and Zayn replied that they were on a break. No one introduced me, but Zayn's gaze never left mine.

"Are you leaving soon?" James pulls me from the past memory.

I nod. "If I want to beat traffic, yes. Plus, it'd be nice to get there before him. You know, get a booth and all. I don't want to leave a bad impression." I add a shrug and let out a sigh, then pack up my items from my desk.

My laptop goes into the case, then into my bag, followed by a notepad and a few pens.

James walks me to the elevator, wishing me luck, which I take since I desperately need it.

I plan to write down a few more questions on the way over, hoping Zayn doesn't mind if I take this first meeting to do an informal interview to try and get to know him.

Bias aside, I need to help him. If I help him, he will probably land a role, and I get to work at Starlet full time. It's an "I help you, you help me" sort of situation.

The car ride to the diner took longer than expected, and I'm ten minutes late. Thanking the driver out of habit, I exit the car and walk toward the entrance. The parking lot is practically empty, but when I step through the front door, the place is packed with people. The smells of butter and onion fill my nose as I survey the room, looking for Zayn. I've been here a lot. It's where Cassie and Emmett met, so they tend to pick this place if we meet for dinner. Even though rock music blares on the speakers and there are likely one hundred movie posters hung up on the walls, I like this diner. It reminds me of when Cassie and I used to go out to eat at a local diner back home in Indiana and order a giant stack of pancakes to split.

I find Zayn in the back corner booth, my attention immediately drawn to him. He's staring at his phone, a scowl painted on his face. Everyone that walks near the back looks in his direction, curious about what's hiding beneath that mask. It's what I'm thinking as I stare in his direction, wondering when the light went out inside him and why he remains to himself.

"Hi, sorry I'm late," I say as I reach the table and slide into the other side of the booth.

Zayn peers up from his phone and a shot of electricity runs down my spine as I stare into his dark green eyes. "I only have…" Zayn glances back at his phone before looking back at me, "thirty minutes before I need to be back on set."

"Right, right. Again, so sorry. I can place an order for us, if you'd like? I come here quite often." I whip around to try and find a server to no avail.

"I already ordered for us."

"Oh." Turning back to the table, I bite my lip involuntarily and my cheeks flush from the heat of his stare. Zayn's eyes snap to my lips, but they're gone instantly with a shake of his head.

I reach into my bag and rummage around, trying to find the journal that I know I put in there. I finally find it nestled under the computer, so I pull it out and place it in front of me.

With a deep breath, I look up to find Zayn staring. His left hand palms his beard, drawing my attention to the stubble. My clients in the past have never left me this flustered and at a loss of words. Could it be the way he's looking at me that causes me distress? Does he remember me? And if he does, does he still not like me? And if so, will that affect how he acts around me? Who will bring Dan up first? My head spins with millions of questions, not one of them helping the tightness in my chest.

Zayn and I had a moment, which I'm not sure he remembers. I do. Vividly. A late night snack run to the kitchen turned into his hands on my waist. Nothing happened, but sometimes I wonder what would have if I was single and not with his brother. Maybe in another lifetime I would find out.

"So, I have some questions, if that's alright." My gut bubbles with anticipation and nerves as I remind myself why I'm here. Zayn answers by widening his eyes, no words escaping his mouth. I let out a nervous giggle. "Right. So. Is there a reason why you stopped doing interviews? There wasn't a whole lot of information in the packet I was given." In addition to the single piece of paper Greg gave me, Logan provided two more sheets which only told me what movies and shows Zayn acted in. All things I could have easily looked up. What I don't know is why I'm needed or how I can help him.

"It's personal." Zayn grabs the water in front of him and raises it to his lips. He notices me as I watch his movements, his throat bobbing, then his tongue as it darts to catch a drop of water from his bottom lip.

I need to get laid. Drinking water should not be this sensual.

"Right, and I respect that, I do." I smile, trying to keep my emotions in check before I continue. "In order for this to work, it would be great if you thought of this as a partnership."

"Not going to happen." He takes another sip.

God damnit. Is he distracting me on purpose?

"It needs to happen. I know what's at stake for you." Or at least, I have a hunch.

Zayn leans forward, resting both elbows on the table. "Well, Princess, if you think you know everything, please enlighten me. What's at stake for me if I don't go along with this little partnership?"

I hold back a grumble from both the nickname and the way he talks about my work. So, in response, I lean back in the booth and cross my legs.

I flip my notepad open to a new page, giving him an extra beat of silence. He thinks he's going to be in charge? No. This is my court, my game, he's just playing it.

"I think there's a role you want," I meet his glare, "and if you don't work with me, you won't get it. You need me, Zayn."

"If you must know, there's a lead role that I'm in the running for. Ed and Logan believe I need help, but what I need is for you to simply tell me where to show up, and I'll do the rest."

I was right, it is a role. A lead role.

"You'll do the rest? You'll handle the media? The inter-views? All by yourself?" I scoff, annoyed that I have to deal with Zayn for the next five months. "Okay, Zayn, fine. We can try your way. And when it fails, we will try mine."

"You'll come with me on Saturday," Zayn demands, taking a bite of his burger. At some point during our bickering, a nice server slid our food between us and left without saying a word. She's smart and able to stay out of this. I, on the other hand, am stuck dealing with this grump.

"What do you mean by I'll come with you? What happened to handling this on your own?"

He lets out an annoyed sigh like I'm supposed to already know, followed by an eye roll, which I find to be a bit excessive. "You'll put on a dress, ride with me in the car, give me pointers on who to talk to and who to avoid, and be my date to the Summer Gala downtown."

"I don't need to be your date to the gala. This is a small event. Only a few reporters will be there. It's only dinner and an auction." I try to argue, try to insinuate that he would be better without me, hoping he takes the bait. I was mistaken. Zayn is not the type of person to back down from what he wants.

"My way, Princess, remember? Wouldn't your boss want you to help me?"

The feeling of dread hits my stomach like a fifty-pound weight. He's serious. Having to go to the gala never crossed my mind. I thought I'd prep a few notecards for him to help with any media interactions. And I hate the fact that he brought up my boss like he knows what's at stake for me. Two can play at this game.

I grit my teeth and say, "Fine," knowing that I won't win this argument. Not when Zayn has a giant stick up his ass.

"Great. Glad that's settled."

"As long as you join me at a friend's party beforehand."

Zayn's eyes narrow. "No."

"It's a non-negotiable. We stop by for one hour, minimum, before the gala." I cross my arms, trying to border the line of professionalism.

His eyes drop to my chest for a moment, and I remember I'm wearing a v-neck dress, so sitting like this draws his attention to my now-raised breasts, but instead of dropping my arms, I tighten them. A slight smirk appears on Zayn's face before his lips form a thin line, but for that fleeting moment his grumpy demeanor drops as the slight tinge of red blossoms on his cheeks from being caught checking me out.

He clenches his jaw before sighing deeply and muttering, "Fine. I'll pick you up. 4 p.m.?"

I nod in response, keeping my arms crossed tight.

Zayn just mumbles, or maybe it's a growl, but he stands up, gives me one last look, and then leaves the diner.

Once I see the door close behind him, I drop my arms and gaze to the table. He already paid, which is the least he can do after forcing me to attend this gala as his date. I'm not sure if this goes against company policies, but it'll be harmless. It will be better to be by his side anyway, to see how he handles the reporters and photographers and be able to report back to Greg if necessary. If I'm able to see him in action, maybe I'll be able to give him better tips. Because right now, I have nothing to go off of.

Dishes are being picked up by the server, which is my reminder that I need to leave this diner. I stand up from the booth and smile at others as I wind around the mix of chairs on my way to the front door.

I can't tell if my irritability is from being in a packed diner or if it was influenced by Zayn's mood. Either way, my chest hasn't lightened. I feel like it's going to explode any minute. The need for a quick yoga session or a moment of silence is imminent.

Besides the need to over-please the person I'm working with or for, I often find myself burnt out from overcommitment. I say yes to everything: order catering for a luncheon, write the extra paperwork, make the decks for presentations. Normally I can recognize the signs, snapping too quickly or feeling an immense amount of dead, and step away, but I can't do that with Zayn. I don't have an option but to push through.

I wanted to have time to prep him, but no, he had to insist we do things his way and, with the way he was looking at me and how persistent he was, I couldn't say no. I hate that he has this effect on me, but I hate that I find myself eager to get to know him even more.

Once I'm in the Uber, I dig my phone out of my bag to send a text to Marcy to meet me back at my apartment. If I'm being forced to go to this gala on Saturday after stopping by James' apartment, I'm going to need her help figuring out what to wear. My day-to-day wardrobe is a simple pairing of jeans and a blouse. Sometimes I spice it up and pair it with heels or a light blazer, but I've never had to dress for an event with so many watchful eyes. The thought alone reminds me of the awful pit in my stomach.

The car slows to a stop at the curb in front of my apartment. Marcy is standing outside near the front shrubs looking at her clipboard. She brought her damn clipboard. Clipboards are the way they live and breathe at January Studios, so I shouldn't be surprised, but I thought her work was slowing down since filming was wrapping up.

To her left is a giant duffle bag, full of what I can assume is dresses she's worn to previous red carpet events she was invited to because of the studio. I'm lucky to have someone to mooch off of.

She looks up as I walk toward her, dropping the clipboard to her side. I pull her into a hug, already feeling lighter from the earlier meeting.

"I cannot wait for you to update me on your client. I've been waiting all day for you to text me." Marcy heads to the building in front of me, guiding the way to my apartment.

When I graduated from college this past spring at a fresh age of 23, Marcy helped me find and move into this apartment, which happens to be directly across from her complex. It's between the firm and the studio, so location wise, it's central to everything I need. I would have lived here forever if the building's owner didn't suddenly decide to sell the plot to a local developer. It's going to be torn down soon, but I'm not sure when. Marcy's offered I stay with her, but her studio apartment is not big enough for the two of us.

"Well, you're not going to believe who my client is," I warn.

Marcy peers over her shoulder. "It's someone I know?"

I give her a big nod. "Yup."

"Who is it?"

"Zayn."

"As in actor Zayn? Asshole Zayn? Zayn, who doesn't know how to smile?"

Marcy places a hand on her hip as we reach my apartment door.

"You don't smile much either, you know." I scrunch my face.

"I do if you're not a complete asshole." Marcy grins now, trying to prove her point. Except all it makes me do is chuckle as I unlock the door and open it for us.

Marcy drags her bag of dresses inside and sets it on the couch in the living room.

"Lucky me," I tease.

"Why did your boss give you him as your first client? Why not someone… easier? I mean, I don't work with him that much directly, but I've heard about his attitude."

She's not wrong. I would have loved an easier client. Someone who wouldn't talk back and would answer my questions. Someone who saw what we are doing as a partnership instead of a business transaction. Especially someone who isn't related to my ex. Instead, I'm stuck with grumpy, yet awfully sexy, Zayn. My heart is torn between reminding me of the past and reminding me the pull toward him never left.

There's a part of me that wonders if Greg wants me to fail. Maybe he doesn't see any long term plans with me and figured he would assign me an unwilling client. Then, if things blew up, I'd be to blame and he wouldn't have to hire me. I'd be forever known as the girl who wants to be a publicist but can't even maintain her own public image. I shudder thinking about Dan, and his words. "*You'll never make it Annie. You're too nice, too much, no one will take you seriously.*"

I close my eyes to center myself before joining Marcy by her stack of dresses.

"I'm not sure why Greg gave me Zayn. Maybe because it was last minute and I was the only one left." I shrug.

"You know you could do a lot better than Greg and his shitty firm."

"That shitty firm is the top firm in the area. I'm not qualified to work anywhere else. Plus, I do like it there. They get all the best clients, and I never have to travel far."

"Okay, well I won't argue with that. I like you here. I can't stand to hang out with Cassie and Emmett alone anymore." Marcy puckers her lips.

I stifle a laugh. Cassie and Emmett tied the knot one year ago, a year after her debut movie premiered. The sun shone on a late summer evening in July, and they were married alongside a handful of their closest friends. It was the month after Dan and I split, and I thought maybe all love was useless. Now, I see Cassie and Emmett challenging that everyday. They found their dreams, while finding each other, and I wish that one day I'll find my person that supports me the way that Cassie and Emmett support each other.

"Don't worry, I'm not going anywhere," I say.

"Have you found a new apartment yet?"

I shake my head. "Still looking."

"How much longer until you get kicked out?"

"They have to give me a sixty-day notice since I've been there for longer than a year, so I expect that will come any day now. If I still haven't found something by the time they decide to tear the building down, I'll have to come crash with you while I keep looking. I will also not be choosing to spend alone time in Cassie's apartment." I would rather live out of a hotel than stay with my sister and her husband. Those walls are not thick enough.

"You could still live with me, you know."

"The only open space in your apartment is if I slept on your couch or threw out your dining room table," I argue. "I'll figure it out, don't worry."

I can see Marcy is about to push me, to keep asking me questions, but the longer she hesitates, the more sure I am she's going to drop it. She's the best friend I've ever had, being able to read my moods and know when I feel like talking about something versus dropping it. This is one of those topics that I don't need to talk about. I know I need to find a place to live. I'll figure it out and I'm glad Marcy trusts me enough to know that if I need her, I'll tell her.

"Okay, okay. Well, how about we try on some of these dresses?" Marcy holds up the first garment.

I spend the next two hours trying them on, a few more than once. Eventually we start taking videos of me twirling in a circle so we can dwindle down the selection. I thought she'd bring two, maybe three. No. She brought ten. Who owns that many fancy dresses? Apparently Marcy, who instead of donating them or choosing to rent, hoards them in an extra closet in her apartment. She jokes it's her version of *27 Dresses,* except there isn't a punchline. She just likes them all too much to get rid of them.

"That's the one." Marcy looks me up and down, twirling her finger to encourage a spin.

I indulge her, spinning once more, letting myself forget about the weekend ahead, about the grumpy man I need to find a way to break, and choosing to let myself have fun in this moment.

"I think you're right."

5
ZAYN

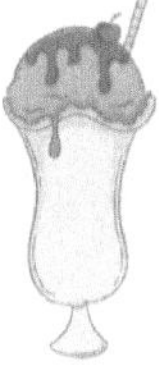

By the time I eat breakfast Saturday morning, I have already opened up my messages with Annie ten times, contemplating canceling our plans for tonight. But then I'd have to think of an excuse, and I'm not creative enough to make something up. Thinking about the people I will be forced to meet and talk to creates a queasy feeling in my gut and reminds me I'm not prepared.

Could I have texted Annie and asked for help? Well, sure, that's her job. But I'm not about to be vulnerable to someone I barely know when I can't even open up to my own sister. Picturing tonight, I imagine myself sitting at a table in the back, away from everyone else, and avoiding anyone with a camera. I don't plan to dance, or go out of my way to talk to people, or do anything besides attend the event. The PR firm never stated I had to do anything, just simply show my face. Get in, get out.

This all would have been fine, or at least manageable, but then Annie asked me to attend a party for a friend. She wouldn't have pushed me if I said no. The way she eyed me after every answer lets me know that she's letting me have this win. She's choosing to be her people-pleaser self and give me what I want. That's one of the only things I know about her. That and I'm still painstakingly attracted to her.

Out of the corner of my eye, my phone lights up, causing my focus to shift from my now-empty coffee mug, that I should refill, to the notification on my phone.

Annie

What are you wearing?

Tonight. Not right now. I don't care what you're wearing right now, to make that clear.

Can you match me? If so, can you wear a green tie?

dark green

like a forest green, not olive green

I wait a minute to see if any other texts from Annie come in, but they stop. I palm my neck, trying to relieve the knots that have formed as I let out a low sigh. Then, I type a quick message back.

> I plan on wearing what normal people wear to galas. Isn't this information you should already know?

Annie

> Hard to know when you haven't been to an event in months and you wouldn't let me ask my questions.

> Don't forget forest green

> I'll be there at 4. Don't keep me waiting.

I'm finding it hard to take a deep breath as nerves overwhelm me.

When I asked Annie to come with me, I didn't anticipate having to look so... "couple-y." I didn't fucking think. The way she responded to my tone made me want to push her buttons. That's the only reason why I invited her. I thought she would push back harder, give me more of an excuse to let up and agree to be peppered with questions. The fact that I wanted her to fight back leaves me disoriented. And to top it off, now I have to meet her friends.

I wonder if they know about me, or about my brother, or if she's kept those memories locked away. My mind flashes to when I was momentarily single, when Marissa and I were on our millionth break, and Annie took over my thoughts. I could never understand how my brother managed to land someone like that, someone as beautiful as her. Even though my brother and I had a decent relationship at the time, he's never been the best partner. He only cares about himself, which is likely how he lost her in the end.

After I plop my dirty dishes in the sink, I head toward the living room to decompress. There are still a few hours before I need to call the car to go pick up Annie, which leaves me time to call Logan and ask for some pointers for tonight. If I'm forced to attend this gala, I need to know what I'm getting myself into and what my exit points are.

Luckily, he answers on the first ring.

"Zayn, what's up?"

"Tell me about this gala tonight. What am I getting myself into?"

Logan sighs on the other end of the line. "Annie didn't brief you?"

"She—"

"You didn't give her an opportunity. Did you?"

"Well I—"

"Zayn, we talked about this. You need to let the woman do her job."

"You are fucking infuriating. I am letting her do her job," I say.

"Telling her she has to be your date for tonight is not letting her do her job. You're overstepping, and it's still the first week."

It's my turn to sigh as I take a seat on the couch. I need to sit down to have this conversation.

"She's making me go to a party beforehand."

"Is that supposed to make it better? She's helping you, you know. You should try and be less grumpy," Logan says.

"Just tell me about this gala," I say, changing the subject. Annie is helping me, I know that, but it doesn't mean I'm happy about it.

"Well, you already know it's for the Young Actors Association. People are happy you are returning and might ask you questions about getting involved again."

The groan that comes out of my mouth should be enough to tell Logan how I feel about the event.

"It's a good first event back for you," Logan continues. "They *are* the ones that helped you land your early roles."

And played a pivotal part in my career. And helped me gain access to hundreds of industry connections. But over the past few years, my involvement has slowed. Each year I give back less and less. I haven't stepped foot near their headquarters for over a year. I couldn't bring myself to talk with others and explain what happened between Marissa and I.

"Great," is the only reply I have for Logan.

"Don't worry so much. You'll have Annie to help guide you since you forced her to come with you."

I grit my teeth. "I didn't force her. She said yes."

"Regardless, I give her three weeks of putting up with you."

I laugh. "You've put up with me for the past decade, maybe you can give her some advice."

"My advice would be to you, not her, as you're the one in the hot seat. She's there to help you. Remember that. Have fun at the gala, try to stay out of trouble."

I huff and disconnect the line. This past year may not have been the best, I'll admit that. My attitude might be a slight problem, but I've been like this for so long at this point that it's hard to see where the light at the end of the tunnel is. It's not that I don't want to improve my image, I do, I've just been trapped in this darkness, with no one to shine a light on the way out.

Will Annie be the light? Or will she find that I'm not worth pulling out of the dark?

6
ZAYN

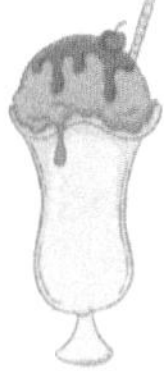

THE CAR SLOWS IN front of Annie's apartment a few minutes prior to four. Lifting slightly off the seat, I take my phone from my back pocket to send a text to let her know I'm here.

A few moments later, the sound of the door handle clicking open breaks my attention from my phone. I'm about to say hello, except my words get stuck in my throat.

She alluded to the fact that she was wearing a dark green dress, but for some reason, I didn't picture *this*. Maybe I didn't want my mind to wander, to let thoughts of her invade even more. Thinking back to earlier, I could have asked her for a picture to prepare myself for the way she looks tonight. The dress is tight around her hips and flows, with a high slit on her left leg, toward the floor. Only held up by a pair of skinny straps, the front of the dress droops in a low swoop, giving me enough of a view of her chest that I feel the front of my pants tighten.

Get a grip.

I've seen plenty of beautiful women in dresses. None of them caused my breath to hitch like Annie does.

From first glance, her hair appears to be a shade of medium-roasted coffee beans, but when light shines on it, you realize between the shades of brown, there are tones of caramel and raw sienna. And her eyes. Don't get me started on her eyes. They're a deep blue, with specks of gold, and remind me of mornings spent at the beach, when things were better.

Annie slides in beside me, and I'm overwhelmed with smells of cinnamon and honey. She smells like a goddamn bakery and I'm trying hard not to wonder if she tastes like one too.

"Hi, excited for tonight?" Annie asks. If she notices me lost in her aura, she doesn't say anything. She tugs down her dress, shifting back in the seat, but keeping her hands by the slit of fabric. Her bottom lip is lost under her teeth as her focus remains on her leg, which is now bouncing up and down.

"Not really," I answer honestly.

"It'll go by fast. We just need to stay at James' house for an hour, and then we can head to the gala."

The car remains silent as we drive over to her friend's house.

"Is he a close friend of yours?" I ask.

"Their pronouns are they and them, just an FYI. But yes, more like a mentor and a friend. They've worked at Starlet for over a decade."

"Got it."

Does Annie have other friends? Or does she spend most of her time at the office? She seems like the type of person to let herself be overworked, tied to her job more than she should be, which would explain why someone she works with would invite her over.

"They got married recently and it was kind of my doing, them meeting, so I'd be in trouble if I didn't make an appearance."

I open my mouth to ask a question, but shut it, not feeling up to conversing at the moment. We stay silent for the rest of the drive until we reach James' neighborhood. It's nestled on the north side of the city, away from the hustle and bustle of downtown. As we drive down the main road toward the house, cars line the street on both sides.

"How big is this party?"

Annie rolls her eyes. "Knowing James and Todd, they invited the entire city of Los Angeles. They love welcoming people into their home."

Not exactly the kind of event I was hoping for before the gala. I was wishing for a quiet evening. Instead, I'm walking into a home where I'll know no one and be forced to make small talk.

Wait a minute.

"Did you plan this on purpose?"

"Hm?" Annie's gaze snaps to mine.

"Did you know it would be busy and force me to practice small talk with people? Is this supposed to help me prep for the gala?"

Her eyebrows narrow for a moment. If I blinked, I would have missed it.

"Maybe," is the only word that leaves her mouth as we pull up beside the house in question.

"Stay there." I scowl at Annie as she reaches for the door. "Wait for me." She glares back, then opens the door.

This woman.

I exit the car, not bothering to thank the driver, and step in front of Annie.

"What was that?" I ask, my tone a little louder than I intended.

"I don't answer to you, Zayn."

Fuck, her attitude. I clench my hand and let it go, then follow it with a deep breath.

Annie, on the other hand, doesn't seem bothered by this at all. She beams at me, then turns toward the house and starts walking. My attention is on the concrete as we approach the door.

"Annie, I was so happy when James told me you were coming."

I know that voice.

My eyes snap to a man that I've spent a lot of time with. Someone that was a mentor to me before I fell off the face of the earth and stopped answering his phone calls.

"Todd, I wouldn't have missed it." Annie steps over the threshold as Todd pulls her into a hug. I look at the bunches of flowers by the door.

"Todd, this is—"

"Zayn," Todd interrupts, and it catches Annie off guard.

"Todd." I nod. I didn't think anything when Annie told me about James and Todd. Todd is a common name; it could have been any of the million Todds in the world. Of course it had to be this Todd, the event manager of the Young Actors Association.

"You two know each other?" Annie asks with a look that I can't quite read. Worried maybe? Definitely surprised.

"Why don't you two come in and grab something to drink?" Todd takes a step back, avoiding Annie's question, and opens the door wider, revealing a room full of people.

I follow Annie in, dipping my head again to Todd as I pass, and continue to trail her as she snakes through the room.

We walk through the living room first, a room with two couches and maybe a chair or two, though it's hard to tell with people standing around, their chatter echoing from the walls and blending with the house music playing over a speaker. I keep my head down.

The kitchen is in the back of the house. When we get there, Annie greets James, pulling them into a hug.

"You're here. Late, but here." James teases Annie, shoving her shoulder gently.

"I said I'd make an appearance, didn't I?" Annie grins and my heart stutters, seeing her liven up around people she loves.

"James, meet Zayn. Zayn, James."

James reaches out their hand toward mine, so I lean forward and shake it. "It's nice to officially meet you," James says.

I slowly nod and form a thin-lipped smile.

"So, how does Todd know Zayn?" Annie looks at me now, and I'm about to answer, but Todd slides in between her and James, throwing his arm around them.

"Young Actors Association. I joined as the event manager after I stopped working at Flora."

"Why do I not remember this?" Annie asks.

"Because you never hang out with us outside of work, little bird. Hard to keep you updated," James says.

Annie's face falls, but she picks it back up with a smile. "I'm working on it. Why aren't you going to the gala tonight?" Annie turns to Todd.

"They don't need me. My team has it handled. It's a smaller event, so I'm not worried. This was the only weekend we could have our celebration event before we enter the busy fundraising season."

I look around the kitchen, trying to spot something to drink or maybe something to snack on. Anything to keep my mind off of Todd, and the Young Actors Association, and Annie. Also the fact that we are severely overdressed, and I don't need to give more people a reason to look at or talk about me.

"Well, lucky you." Annie loops an arm through mine and I stiffen, not expecting the touch.

I glance down and find her eyes soft, watching my reaction. Her breath hitches at the same time mine does, and for a moment I wonder what it'd be like to take her on a proper date. The moment is quickly squandered when she continues talking and I'm reminded why we are here.

"We are going to grab a drink and mingle a little before we head out. I'll find you before we leave to give hugs."

Annie starts walking, and since we're intertwined, I follow. She hands me a lemon seltzer, takes one for herself, then guides me back to the living room before turning to the left and heading into a room off to the side.

This room must be their library. Books are stacked on a coffee table in the center of the room, a couch behind that, and then two giant bookcases on either side of the room. Annie flicks on the light like she's done it a million times and takes a seat on the couch.

"I figured this room might be a bit quieter," Annie says as she pops the tab on her seltzer.

"Didn't you want us to mingle?" I open my drink and take a sip, plopping down next to her.

She shakes her head. "No, I want to ask you some questions. You can mingle with me."

I want to do a hell lot more with her.

"A question for a question," I propose, figuring it's a good time to learn a little bit about her on my terms.

Annie sizes me up like she's wondering if I'm serious.

"Fine. I'll go first," she says. "Why are there so few interviews with you from the past year?"

Starting with a basic question, easy. "I didn't want to be interviewed and stayed away from events. How long have you worked at Starlet?"

She takes a sip, then licks her bottom lip. *Fuck.*

"Three years as a paid intern. Why do you stay away from events?"

"My ex attends them. How serious were you and Dan?" If she's going to inquire about my personal life, that gives me permission to do the same.

"Serious enough to move in together, I suppose." She barks out a laugh before shaking her head. "But not serious enough apparently. Are you two close?"

I ignore the urge to pry for more information. "No, haven't been for a while. No real reason, we just don't talk much."

"Ah," Annie says, leaning back into the couch.

I do the same, turning slightly to face her.

"Are you with anyone now?"

"Are you coming on to me, Zayn?" Annie flutters her lashes, exaggerating each blink.

"You can't answer a question with a question," I say.

"No, Zayn, I'm not with anyone. Do you think my job allows time for someone in my life?"

I shrug. "I don't know much about your job. Why did you become a publicist in the first place?"

She shifts her knee to rest on the couch, leaving only a few inches between us.

"I like to help others," Annie says, her eyes falling to her lap. "It's different with celebrities though. There's a lot of attention on them, and they need someone in their corner to help guide them through the wave of the media. Sometimes it's calm, and they're able to tread water on their own. Other times it's a massive storm, where I need to help reel them in and bring them to safety."

She smiles as she talks and I find my own mouth twitching to do the same.

"Sorry," she chuckles. "I'm blabbering on. Why did you become an actor?"

I pause, thinking of *why* I do what I do. "I was shy when I was younger, and there was a play at my high school. I was a sophomore, I didn't have a lot of friends and I happened to be walking past the room they were having auditions in. Something pulled me in there, and the rest is kind of history. I landed a part, then started acting classes, got involved in the Young Actors Association."

"And you love it?"

I nod. "Don't you love what you do?" I ask, already knowing the answer.

"Am I going to have to worry about you breaking someone's camera tonight?" Annie asks, and I know she's joking, but the question frees me from whatever grasp she has me in.

"Not if you do your job."

"What's that supposed to mean?" she asks.

"Nothing." I avert my gaze to my can, not having anything else to say, knowing I've already ruined whatever moment we've had.

When I look back to Annie, her lips form a thin line, then she stands up from the couch, not bothering to glance my way as she exits the room.

I run my fingers through my hair and drop my arms to my knees. This night has gone from okay to awful, and I just want to be home. I don't want to be forced to talk or smile at people that want to write a shitty article about me.

When Annie comes back to the room she hollers at me to join her, then proceeds to walk out the door.

"Annie," I yell, standing up from the couch, then increasing my pace to reach her. I grab her wrist and tug her to a stop.

"What?" She yanks her arm out of my grasp.

Yeah, what? I shake my head and mutter, "nothing."

"Great. Let's go, I already said bye."

She walks to the car and goes to open the door, but I surpass her and open it instead. With a few grumbles, she slides inside. I shut the door and take half a second to center myself. A few more hours and I'll be home.

"I have some pointers for you to go over." Annie says to me on our way over to the venue. She grabs her clutch, clicks the top open, and reaches in to grab a stack of notecards.

I take them from her with a weary glance. This is a lot of fucking notecards. Has she been carrying these all night? They're like the kinds of flashcards you make when studying for a test. Question on one side, answer on the other.

"I know it's a lot," she adds.

"You think?" I peer up to find Annie biting her lip.

Fuck, when she does that I feel bad for my attitude. It's easier this way. The less feelings involved, the better. I don't have to give her any part of me that she can't physically see. I don't want her to care.

"These are questions that I've seen past reporters ask. I watched a few videos from this kind of event and took note of any relevant questions."

She did research? Did she know about my involvement with the association? Surely she had to. If you googled "Zayn Barnes" and "Young Actors Association," you would find articles and videos of our past partnership.

Except that's a different version of me. Someone who enjoyed being around others and was genuinely happy.

The old Zayn would have donated money and time to tonight's event or would have spoken at the dinner. This organization introduced me to some of my closest friends, even if I don't talk to anyone anymore. The old Zayn would have done something besides ignore the fact that the event is happening, which is what I was planning on doing before this whole PR stunt.

After shuffling through the notecards, skimming over a few, I realize there is no reason to spend my energy on these. I don't plan to talk with anyone. Avoiding people is something I'm good at, and tonight will be no different.

"I don't need these." I extend my notecard-filled hand toward Annie, who grabs them from me. Should I tell her thanks? Maybe, but I didn't ask her to do this. I didn't even want to go to this damn event.

Annie shoves the notecards back in her clutch and snaps it shut. She doesn't reply and instead shifts her body to the right. Her hands lay on her legs while she peers out the window.

"You're going to have to let me help you, you know. I'm just trying…" A sigh escapes from Annie's mouth. "I'm just doing my job."

For the last thirty minutes of the ride to the venue, we sit in silence. Every few minutes, I look up from mindlessly scrolling on my phone to sneak glances of Annie. She's crossed her left leg over the other, causing her dress to ride farther up her thigh. Internally I'm groaning every time I look over and realize it's an inch higher than before.

When the car approaches the venue, I realize I didn't think about needing to walk on the red carpet. The driver listens as I tell him to drive to the rear in hopes of sneaking Annie and myself through the back door.

"Afraid of the photographers?" Annie glances up from her phone.

"Not afraid, I'd just like to avoid them."

"That's kind of the whole point for tonight, Zayn." Annie gives me her best side-eye.

"Well, Annie, if it's a photo of us you want, I can arrange that."

"As if." Annie mumbles under her breath, speaking mostly to herself.

"What was that?" I ask, wanting to push her buttons.

A glare in my direction tells me enough.

The driver stops and I open my door quickly, trying to walk fast enough around the car to get Annie's door. She beats me to it. By the time I round the trunk, she's already standing, moving out of the way so she can shut the door.

Time stops as she turns to face me. I slow to a walk, stopping a few feet from her. Annie's face is rosy. Is she angry? Or maybe upset?

"If you were embarrassed to be seen with me or worried about your brother seeing us together, you just had to tell me. You are the one that forced me to come tonight. I put on this damn dress for you and thought we would have a good time. But you know what?" Annie breathes in deep, shaking her head. She's hesitating, and when she looks at me again, there's sadness in her eyes. "Never mind. Enjoy your night, Zayn."

She walks toward the door, picking up the right side of her dress to not get it wet in the puddles that line the ground. When she reaches the door, her hand hovers over the handle.

Her head turns to me one last time. The light from above the door highlights her expression. Her cheeks are flushed a deep red, showing me that she's bothered from our conversations. She blinks slowly, keeping her eyes closed for an extra second. I watch as her chest rises and falls, her eyes open, then as she opens the door and walks through it.

I'm left standing between the car and the door, wondering what the fuck to do. Tonight is already worse than I anticipated. I pinch the bridge of my nose, closing my eyes, and taking a deep breath. When did everything go sideways?

7

ANNIE

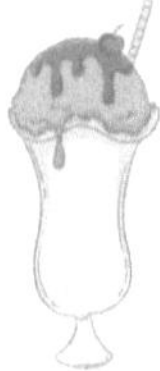

Walking through the back door of the venue was not how I predicted making my entrance.

There were no cameras, no reporters, nothing. Just a dark hallway, a kitchen with confused staff, and a kind woman who helped lead me away from their inventory room.

If I wasn't distracted by how immaculate the venue was, I would have been more angry with Zayn. Or with myself.

I'm the one that put me in this situation.

The lights in the venue sparkle as I move through the grand hall while soft music plays in the background. People filter in through the front door and I find my feet moving me to where the seating chart is posted.

"Excuse me, miss." A voice comes from behind me as I reach the entrance. I turn to find an elderly man with his date.

"Oh, I'm sorry, I don't—" I start to say before he interrupts me.

"Do you know where I can find my table? I'm afraid I've lost the email." The smile he gives me is innocent, and I can't tell him no.

"Of course. What's your name?" I smile back at him, and as soon as I tell him I'm able to assist, there's relief in his face as he takes a moment to look at his date.

Somehow I get stuck helping people find their tables for the next fifteen minutes. Every time I'm about to step away, I see someone else coming. I could walk away, let people help themselves, but they see me helping others and assume I can aid them.

I don't mind the distraction. It's helping me avoid thinking about Zayn. The conversation we had, the way he looked at me, it's all starting to be too much. My chest hurts when I think about the past and how things ended with Dan. I've done my best to take steps to forget about how he hurt me, but sometimes I find myself staring at the wall a little too long or smiling to myself when a random memory pops into my head.

"You don't seem like you're here to work." A voice comes from my left.

I turn to find a very tall, very handsome, very well-dressed man. His dark hair is buzzed, and his eyes are a deep, dark brown, adding to the mystery.

"I—I'm not, but people needed help," I say, suddenly aware of my heart beating faster the longer this man stares at me.

"Well, if you're helping others, can you help me find my table?" He puts his hands in his pockets, the picture of relaxation unlike the rest of the people I've seen tonight. His date isn't in sight, but they could be mingling, which I should be doing.

"Oh, um, of course. What's your name?"

"Ethan."

"Ethan…" I drawl, already knowing I'll need his last name to find his seat.

"Matthews." He smirks, and I look away before my cheeks flush from the attention.

I find his name fairly quickly. "You're in the front, table four."

"Care to show me?" he asks, and for a moment I hesitate. In the back of my mind, I see Zayn's stern face and his cute smile and his tousled hair and no matter what I do, I can't seem to shake him from my head.

"Sure," I smile, hoping that maybe this will help.

It certainly can't hurt.

Ethan talks the entire way to the table, and I wonder how he's able to take breaths in between telling me about how much money he's donating tonight and explaining the business ventures he's investing in. Every time I try to get a word in, he talks over me, so I resort to smiling and nodding.

It's robotic, the way I'm interacting with him. But I'm not with Zayn, and to be honest, at least this guy is smiling. He seems to like being here, supporting the young actors.

"Well, this is your table." I turn to him, forcing my lips to turn up in a smile.

"Care to sit for a moment? Keep me company? My date couldn't make it this evening," Ethan says. He pulls out a chair at the table and hovers next to it.

I'm sure his date decided to not associate with him, due to his lack of conversation skills, but I can't bring myself to say no. Have I rejected anyone this evening? Well, besides saying no to waiting so Zayn could stay on his high horse and open the door for me, I've said yes to pretty much everyone.

Zayn is the only person I don't care to please. I don't seem to force myself to be someone else, someone who is always willing to help. Zayn finds ways to push the right buttons to get me to burst.

An agonizingly slow hour passes as Ethan talks to me and our table mates about his latest investments. My head hurts from constantly nodding, and my cheekbones are on fire from being raised in a smile for the duration of this one-sided conversation. I am not built for long-form communication with people who don't care about anything other than themselves.

"Do you want to dance?" Ethan leans over to whisper in my ear.

No, it's not my first option, but I have nothing better to do.

"Sure." Anything to get me out of this conversation. Anything to get me closer to being able to leave.

Ethan grabs my hand and leads me onto the dance floor.

I thought dancing would mean less conversation, but I was wrong. Ethan talks, and I let him. I laugh when I'm supposed to and chime in "hm"'s and "wow"'s every few minutes to show I'm listening when truthfully, I'm looking around the room for Zayn as we twirl in a slow circle. Even with the lights low, I can see the tables. But with so many people, and being in the middle of the dance floor, it's hard to find him in the sea of bodies.

His brother broke my heart and yet I find myself wanting to give Zayn a small piece of it. Maybe it's the familiarity, or maybe it's feeling something pulling us together. And even though we've only recently reconnected, I have this feeling that this time spent together will have an impact on my life in more ways than one.

8
ZAYN

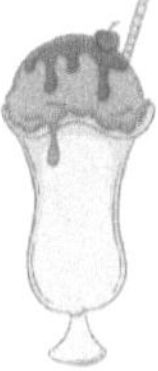

Not having anything better to do and needing to keep up appearances, I enter the venue. I snake my way through the back hallways, keeping my head down, and finally find my way to the large room where the event is being held tonight.

I've managed to avoid anyone with a camera or microphone. So far, so good.

Peering around the room, I don't see Annie. She perhaps found someone she knows, or maybe she's checking out the opposite side of the venue.

I requested a seat at the back, not wanting to get any attention, and my request was granted. Logan let me know ahead of time, so I head straight to my table. As I approach I notice that it provides me a better view of the dance floor than the stage, but I don't mind. I wasn't going to stay the entire time, anyway; I'll likely leave within the hour. The firm never said how long I had to stay, just that I had to make an appearance. If no one sees me, that's not my fault. Entirely.

Over the course of the next hour, people file into the hall and I have the pleasure of people watching. Each person is dressed to the nines in every color imaginable and accompanied by a date. No one walks in alone. Besides me. I'm still alone. I'm tempted to text Annie, but what would I say? Sorry, again? It's not you, it's me? I can't think when I'm around you, *why did you wear that goddamn dress*? Forest green is officially my favorite color.

At least my table is fairly empty, besides another pair that took seats directly across from me. They are as far away from me as they can get without actually leaving the table. I feel like I was sat at the table with all of the rejects, or the singles. The table that most try to stay clear of, especially at an event like this. The type of event where your name isn't just known in this city, but across the state, maybe even the country.

The servers circle the table, bringing dinner and refilling drinks, and I still don't know where Annie is. I don't think she's at a different table. At least, not that I can see with the lowlights of the venue. My gaze ping-pongs from my plate to the room whenever I hear someone speak, thinking it may be Annie finally coming to find me. Except, normally, it's just the couple in front of me, singing alone to the God-awful music the DJ is playing a few tables over. If I roll my eyes one more time, they might just fall out of their sockets.

"Alright, folks, it's time to slow it down. Grab your partner and make your way to the dance floor. Time to loosen up so your wallets are loose later for the silent auction!" The DJ's voice booms over the microphone.

The music slows down, playing some tune I don't recognize, but the dance floor fills in anyway. Couples flock from every direction, grabbing hands and waists, pulling each other closer and beginning to sway. Usually, this is when I'd walk up to the bar, down a shot of tequila, and find the prettiest girl in the place.

Tonight, I already know who that pretty girl would be. I shake my head at the thought. Something must be in the air. My emotions are all out of wack and it's all because of Annie, who smells like a fucking cookie. My mouth waters just thinking of her, picturing her sitting in the chair next to me.

Instead, she's not...

Wait...

Annie is on the dance floor. Dancing.

Some random man's hands are on Annie's waist, a little too low, if you ask me. A growl escapes my mouth. I thought I wanted more eyes on her, but what I'm wondering is if I meant only my eyes, not anyone else's. She should not be dancing with some random person she barely knows, she should be dancing with...

Me? Fuck. No, she shouldn't dance with me. She barely knows me, and I'm the last person she wants to see. Except I can't just sit here and watch her dance with him. If anyone's hands are going to be around her waist, it should be mine, not his.

I waste no time scooting back my chair. The screech from the legs on the hard floor gets the attention of my table mates, both of their heads whipping toward me with their jaws dropped. It's like they planned that. Refraining from rolling my eyes at them, I keep my mouth shut in a thin-lipped smile. My head dips in a brief nod before I storm toward the dance floor.

Lights in the shades of blue and purple bounce off the tiles, helping lead my way to Annie. She is smiling, laughing at some joke this guy must have told her. Am I going to be the asshole and interrupt her time? She clearly seems to be enjoying someone else, actually having a conversation with them, being her normal, happy self.

But I know better.

She's hiding. The smile, it's not real. Want to know how I know? Well, easy. When she smiles at me, truly smiles, her eyes get a little crinkle on the outsides. Her smile is so wide that it even manages to crinkle her nose, just a little bit. And now, she's distant. Sure, she's smiling, but it's small. Barely more than a smirk. Her eyes are down, rarely meeting his gaze unless he says something to her directly.

It's only been a fucking week since we reconnected, and I'm realizing I know her better than I want to. That's a problem I will think about later. Right now, we're going to dance.

"You're dancing with my date," I say loud enough for the guy to hear me and know I'm directing my attention at him. I don't know him, but he knows me. I can tell by the way his eyes widen when he turns around, and by how quickly he hands Annie off to me without a word.

Annie hesitates, looking around the room to see if she can run. But she can't, not without people noticing. She wraps her hands around my neck, standing as far away from me as possible. Her fingers are barely snagged around me. Both of my hands find their place on her waist. I apply a small amount of pressure, silently begging her to move a little closer, to wrap her hands even tighter around me. She gives me an inch more, which I accept.

"What do you want?" Annie looks up, but her eyes barely meet mine.

"I..." I did not think this through.

My brain is thinking about Annie, but more of what my hands would do to her if I had her dress on the floor instead of snapped on her body. "I wanted to say I'm sorry." I grimace at the words. I haven't apologized to anyone since Marissa, not giving two shits about anyone other than myself. And Kiley, obviously I've never been mean to my sister, just closed off.

"Sorry?" Annie's brows raise, not believing my apology.

"Yes, I, um, am not embarrassed to be seen with you or worried about my brother seeing us together. You didn't deserve for me to treat you that way, and I hated watching you walk away angry." The words come out choppy, but at least they are honest.

Why am I suddenly wanting to impress this woman? Someone my brother dated, mind you. What about her gets under my skin? Annie is the type of woman you bring home to your parents. Someone with a great smile, a nice attitude, and someone who would show you love, unconditionally. In some ways, I'm triggered by my past relationship, having been with someone for twelve years.

Marissa was my high-school sweetheart. We didn't have a perfect relationship, but we were on again, off again for twelve years. Throughout that time, there were multiple long breaks where I wasn't sure if we'd get back together. When I turned twenty-nine, I finally felt like it might be time to settle down. We had conversations about our future, the kind of house we'd want, having kids, and any other major topic you can think about when you think about a married couple. So, I did what was next in the evolution of our relationship. I proposed.

I created a scavenger hunt to all of our first locations, a note at each one with a clue to the next spot. It all ended on the beach, the place where I first told her I loved her. The beach is now my least favorite place to go because that's also where the proposal ended with her telling me no. Apparently she forgot to mention in all of our many, many, conversations that she wanted to travel more and felt like marrying me would hold her back. A decade and some change gone, just like that.

Then, here comes Annie. The instant I met her at my parents house, I felt a spark, a small connection from just her smile, and I thought it could have been the universe giving me a sign. Maybe I needed someone like this, someone the complete opposite of anyone I've ever been with. When I found out she was dating Dan and wasn't just there to hang out with Kiley, I instantly shut myself off from the connection.

The constant thumping in my chest when I look at her should be enough to warn me that nothing good will come from being around her. She's too nice for her own good, smiling and acknowledging anyone around her. When Annie is around, you feel... lighter. As if her presence helps extinguish any negativity.

And now, her soft curves entice me to trail my fingers around the natural shape of her body.

With each song, Annie steps slightly closer. Closing the gap between us, inch by inch.

"I am sorry, Annie. I, um, don't apologize often, so I guess I also apologize if this apology sounds terrible." A nervous chuckle escapes my lips.

"It's not as bad as you think, Mr. Barnes." Annie's head makes contact with my chest, her ear resting on my heart. Can she feel the effect she's having on me? We continue to sway, mimicking the beats of the song. The dance floor isn't as packed as it was, but there is still a decent crowd sheltering us from wandering eyes.

"I'm not used to having people..." I hesitate, not wanting to erase the small amount of grace she's given me, but I'm also trying to practice honesty. "I'm usually alone. I choose to be alone and I don't think a PR firm can just fix me, make the media all of a sudden like me. If it were up to me, I would do this alone."

Annie lifts her head from my chest, stopping the sway of our bodies. "Is that so?" Her head tilts to the side, her brows furrow. I feel her hands slip from my neck, trailing down my body until they are at her side.

"Fuck, that's not what I meant."

"You wouldn't have said it if you didn't mean it." Annie retorts, crossing her arms over her chest, pushing up her breasts. That's not the kind of distraction I need right now.

"Annie, I—"

"You know what, Zayn? I was giving you the benefit of the doubt, but you're just like your brother."

My brother? What did he do to her? I know his character, so I'm sure he wasn't the best to be around, but I'm not like him. He's heartless, shut off, and thinks only about himself.

I'm...

All of those things.

But, I wasn't always like that.

"I—" I start to say something, I want to say something, anything to salvage tonight. Except, what good would that do me? Isn't this what I want? I don't need her pity, or her nice attitude. What I need is to appear happy to the outside world, smile at the right people, and land my role. That's my priority and the only thing important to me.

Annie shakes her head, turns on her heel, and walks away. This time, she doesn't look back.

9
ANNIE

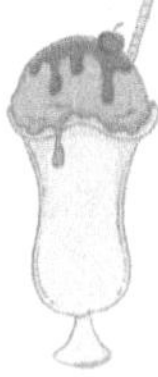

EATING A BLUEBERRY MUFFIN should solve all of my problems, right?

No?

What if it's freshly baked, with cinnamon crumble on top, and some sort of glaze that melts when you take a bite?

Not even then?

Last night was a disaster. I have whiplash from Zayn's polarizing behavior. I didn't know if I should slap him in the face or tug him closer and slam my lips against his. My mood is all over the place when I'm around him. He makes it hard to keep my mask up, to be the nice Annie everyone knows.

If Mary told me they didn't have blueberry muffins today, I think I would have lost it. That would be the final straw, the universe clearly telling me a sign that the rest of the year is destined to be shit.

I take a seat at a table near the front window, basking in the sun while I wait for Cassie. After last night, I knew I had to talk to her. Flora is my favorite coffee shop in the area, my safe place. It is always packed, so I make an effort to get here early if I know I'm wanting to sit for a while. The cafe is painted a bright pink, with pale yellow accents for the trim. There are numerous shelves hanging from the wall, covered with pothos and other types of trailing plants. Fresh flowers sit in the middle of every table, simple, yet enough to brighten my mood. It's a little further from my apartment than I'd like. I'd give anything to be able to walk here at any given moment.

I take a deep breath, closing my eyes, taking in the smell of the cafe: caramel from my latte that I splurged on, the sweet smell from the rose in front of me, and the freshness of the air fill my nose.

"Long night?"

I peek open to see Cassie taking the seat in front of me with a "Flora Coffee" pink mug in hand. The pink dress she's wearing blends into the rest of the cafe and her hair is done up with small waves. Even though Cassie is recognized most places she goes, the people inside Flora always tend to leave her alone. We will get the occasional interruption, someone asking for a photo or a signature, but for the most part fans let her drink coffee in peace.

"Not a long night, but an exhausting one. How was your night?" I take a sip of my latte.

"Oh, fine. Emmett and I just stayed in, nothing too exciting. Why was your night exhausting?"

"I went to a gala last night," I say.

"Oh, right, Anns! I forgot about your new client. Who is she?" Cassie sips her coffee, keeping both hands on the mug.

"He is Zayn. Zayn Barnes." I grimace.

Cassie's jaw drops and her hands unravel from her mug, finding their way to her lap.

"Wait, your first client is Zayn? And you went to a gala with him? Why is this the first time I'm hearing about this?"

"You don't need to sound so distraught about it. Yes, I went with him. And I've been busy? I don't know. It honestly came as a shock to me, so I've been trying to accept my fate with having him as my client."

"I don't mean to. He just..." Cassie sighs, leaning in toward me. "He has a reputation, and not a good one," she whispers.

"I'm well aware, Cass. That's why I'm hired, remember?" I tilt my head down, raising my brows.

"Yes, yes, I know. I just never figured it'd be someone I know. So, tell me about last night."

"Well, I—" I start explaining, but am distracted by Mary walking toward us. Her focus travels from her phone to me and back before she reaches our table.

"Hi, Annie! Hi, Cassie. This is going to be random..." Mary says. "But, this is you, right?"

Mary flips her phone around to show us something that is on her screen. I half expect to see Cassie, since she's now used to being in the spotlight. But as soon as I catch a glimpse of the screen, I see a familiar shade of dark green.

Cassie and I exchange a look.

"That's me, from last night," I confirm. It's a photo of myself and Zayn on the dance floor at the gala before I stormed off.

"I thought so, but I wanted to double check before I go off on people in the comments." Mary pulls back her phone. "This photo is everywhere. I can't scroll social media for thirty seconds without seeing someone post about it. Everyone seems shocked that he's with someone again after all the bad press about him this year."

"Bad press?" Cassie asks since she doesn't read articles anymore, not after she was almost involved in her own photo scandal a few years back. I glare at her, but she just keeps smiling at Mary. What a great sister.

"Yeah, did you read the article where he broke someone's camera just for asking how his day was going? Or the one where he threw a plate of food on the floor? Or—"

"We are hoping the bad press is behind us." I smile at Mary. The fact that she thinks we are together should send red flags my way, but instead ideas are churning in my head. If there's one thing I've learned on the job, it's that you need to be prepared to seize an opportunity when it's in front of you.

Zayn isn't a person I would choose to be associated with, but my stomach is in knots over the thought. There's always been a spark between us, and if I'm honest, I don't *hate* it. I want to, but thinking of his arm wrapped around mine, thinking of his smile directed at me and no one else, has me wondering if this is all happening for a reason.

"Well, I'm rooting for you. He's hot and so are you."

"Thanks, Mary." I chuckle. Mary waves and says bye, then pockets her phone and heads back to the bar.

I turn my body back toward Cassie.

"What?" I ask, matching her glare.

"What do you mean, what? You can't let that poor girl assume you're dating him. She's already thinking about him in a different light and if the story gets squashed, you won't be helping him." Cassie explains.

Not true. I don't think it would be terrible, or harm his image anymore than it is right now. Stories like this don't disappear—they get picked up by other outlets and spread like wildfire. This is my fault. I'm responsible for the public's persona of him. I'm the one who let him get to me, which is why he came to apologize. I think I may have a plan. This is an opportunity, and I'm going to seize it.

"Oh, no. I don't like when you have that look on your face." Cassie peers up at me from her coffee mug.

"Well, it might be a little insane, but I think I have a plan to help improve Zayn's image."

"Don't say by dating him."

"By *pretending* to date him."

Cassie rolls her eyes. "Annie... are you sure that's a good idea? You haven't been with someone since..."

"Dan?" I fill in the blanks, my mind clouding with too many memories from the past.

"Yes, that bloke. You were with him for two years and instead of telling you he loved you, he cheated on you. He was the worst, never supporting you and always asking me if I landed any roles." Cassie shivers talking about Dan, and she's not wrong. He was always trying to find the failure in someone, always trying to one-up them. And yes, the last year we were together, he was cheating on me. It started shortly after we moved in together.

I look at my latte, grabbing the cup with my right hand and swirling it around until the foam blends with the milk. I'm slowly thawing from the numbness of the past.

"Well, Zayn is Dan's older brother. Remember? I know what I'm getting myself into." I glance up with just my eyes to find Cassie stunned, once again.

"Oh fuck," Cassie drawls. "Anything I knew about that man and his family has been erased from my brain."

"Yep. Complicates things in a way, but nothing I can't handle. He needs me just as much as I need him," I explain, not sure if I'm trying to convince myself or Cassie more.

Complicated doesn't begin to explain what Zayn and I are. We are nothing. He won't even agree we're partners, just two people forced to be with each other at random times during the week.

"And you're sure this is the only thing you can do? What about just pushing out an article that says you two are just friends?" Cassie cringes at the thought.

"Would likely look like we are trying to cover up the fact that we are dating," I say, using quotation marks around the word dating. "Besides, it's not like I'm dating anyone right now anyway." Or ever.

Cassie just stares at me. Glares is likely a better way to describe the way she's looking at me with her narrowed eyes and her arms crossed over her chest.

"I'm not happy about it, but you're going to do what you want."

"Yup." I emphasize the 'p' and take a sip of my coffee.

I get two seconds to think about the decision I just made before she asks me more questions.

"Any update on apartment hunting?"

I peer up from my cup. "Nope."

"How much longer do you have?"

"At least two months," I guess. "But I'll find something. I have a few leads," I lie and hope Cassie doesn't push me for more information.

"Oh, that's great. I'm sure one of them will work out." Cassie grins, and I smile back. She's optimistic about things as of late, so I'll let her believe everything will work out and I'll magically find some apartment that doesn't cost more than two thousand dollars. Cassie would give me money, buy me a loft, help me in any way possible if I asked. But she also knows I would never ask and would never accept a hand out.

After finishing coffee with Cassie, I let her know I'll text her with any updates. I have to go home and do a bit of planning before suggesting this plan of action tomorrow with Logan and Zayn.

Greg texted me about the photo when I was with Cassie, and I told him I had a plan, to just show up in the office at nine a.m.

tomorrow. He asked a few follow up questions, but by the end of our conversation, I had him convinced I had it covered.

I need to make a PowerPoint. People love slide decks to view information. Maybe I'll grab donuts too, or some variety of pastries. I need it to be perfect. This is my first proposal and change to the contract, and I'm going in blind. No one is going to approve or suggest changes. It's all on my shoulders.

I need to make sure they have no other option but to say yes.

10
ANNIE

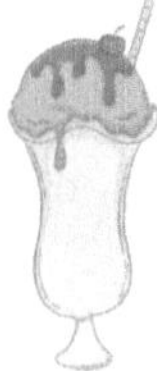

IN THE OFFICE ON Monday, I wait for Logan and Zayn in the conference room with Greg. I'm wearing a dark green v-neck wrap dress with short sleeves; it's not as sensual as the one from Saturday, but I'm hoping it brings Zayn back to the dance floor. If he remembers more good memories than bad, it might play to my advantage.

The ding from the elevator echoes from down the hall, signaling they have reached our floor. My fingers drum on my legs. Judging by the clacking of their shoes, they're almost here. My breathing accelerates, and I feel as if my entire body is a kick drum. When the door clicks open, my cheeks blaze as I meet Zayn's eyes.

I wonder what he's thinking when he sees me and what he thinks about Saturday. What is on his mind when his eyes pierce mine? Is he thinking about me as much as I'm thinking about him?

"Greg, thank you for extending the offer to host us at your office. We are eager to hear about the plan you have." Logan takes a seat across from Greg and waits.

Zayn, on the other hand, sits across from me, mimicking our first meeting. His eyes haven't left mine. A small smile appears on his face, which I hope doesn't turn into a frown as this presentation gets underway.

"Actually, Annie is the one with the plan and will be giving the presentation today." Greg leans back in his chair, crossing one leg over the other, waiting for me to begin. I can't discern if he thinks I'm going to give a good or bad presentation, but I bet he's hoping for the latter. It'd give him more ammunition for this trial.

"Thanks, Greg. Right, so I have a proposal. Think of it like an addendum to our contract." I stand, grabbing the pointer for the computer to advance my slides.

Zayn's eyes travel my body, pausing on the shortness of the dress, the small slit on the left side. I watch as his chest rises and falls, then as he shifts in his seat and crosses his right leg over his left. When his eyes meet mine, his cheeks flush from being caught.

I click the remote to kick off the presentation.

Slide one features the photo from Saturday night.

"Here you'll see the photo that was taken of us, dancing at the gala on Saturday. We were just playing a part, you see, it's a harmless photo, but that's not how the media took it."

Click, next slide.

"The photo has been picked up by various magazines and news outlets and it's not slowing down. In fact..."

Click.

"I found that 'Zayn Barnes girlfriend' and 'Zayn Barnes next movie' are trending in search queries and topics."

Click, almost done.

"From the data, you can see that people are responding well to Zayn having someone in his life. It's proving good for his image."

"What are you proposing?" Zayn asks.

Flustered, I click again. The slide reads "PR RELATION-SHIP" in caps and bold.

"No." Zayn shoots the idea down immediately.

"Actually, I think that's a great idea." Logan breaks his silence.

Zayn's head whips to face Logan. "What do you mean it's a great idea?"

Logan ignores Zayn and looks at me. "Annie, what are your terms?"

"Unbelievable," Zayn mutters, but I choose to ignore him.

Click.

"As you can see, we have until the second week of December to get Zayn's perception up, since they are finalizing roles in the third week before the holiday. I propose we date and keep up appearances until then. When Zayn signs the role for the contract, we break up. The media will be so focused on the movie, that they won't care about our silly little breakup."

"That's brilliant. And I know this isn't a typical PR strategy, but I think it will work." Greg beams.

"I agree. Send over the updated paperwork, I'll see to it that it's signed." Logan adds.

"Don't I get a say in this?" Zayn huffs.

"You did, you chose to put your hands around her waist, which led to this problem, and now we have to deal with it," Logan argues.

I smile. For once, Greg is on my side. I'm surprised that Logan would agree without Zayn's full consent, but I'm sure they need to talk alone.

Zayn acted how I predicted, for the most part, though. I didn't expect his eyes to remain glued to me for the entire presentation. He is the most confusing person I've ever met. I can never read what he's thinking.

He has the worst attitude and most people shy away from him, yet his eyes are on me in front of the others in this conference room.

Logan moves closer to Greg to work out some details. I sit down at the end of the conference table, farthest away from everyone, and shuffle my notes.

"Are you out of your mind?" Zayn's whisper gets my attention. I find him perched in the seat next to me, rolled awfully close to my legs.

"What do you mean, Zayn?" I bat my eyelashes at him. "I'm just trying to solve our *little* problem." I return my gaze to the papers, not necessarily paying attention to them, but I'm trying my best to ignore Zayn.

"Zayn, come on. We're leaving," Logan says from the other side of the room.

I look up to find Zayn a foot away from me, still sitting in his chair. He leans closer. "This isn't over, Princess."

I bite my lip to suppress the smile trying to make its way to my face. I knew Zayn wouldn't be happy with my plan, but it's in his best interest. He hasn't specifically told me, but from his whole vibe, I gathered that he's not looking to date.

If anything, he should be thanking me. He'll do a lot better with the media if I'm by his side. I can smile, talk him up, and flirt with the reporters on his behalf. Zayn can sit there, be his moody self, and the media will love him again.

"Great work today, Annie," Greg says with a smile. "I was nervous about your plan since I didn't get to see it beforehand, but it's a solid one. I look forward to seeing how the media perceives him now. I will submit an official statement to the news on your behalf. I have a few requests for comments in my inbox already."

I shove my papers into my bag, stand up from the chair, slip the handle over my shoulder, and walk out of the conference room and down the hall. I stop a foot from my office. The door is ajar, which is odd because I always keep it closed. It's possible the cleaning person left it open, or maybe James was in here trying to find a pen.

I shrug.

After walking into the room, I turn to shut the door. When I spin back around, I'm frightened by a certain someone standing in the middle of my office.

"Ah!" My bag slips off my shoulder, hitting the floor with a loud thud. My hand grasps my chest. "Jesus, Zayn. What are you doing in here?"

I don't wait for him to respond. Leaning over to reach my bag, I grab the handle, slip it back over my shoulder, and walk toward my desk. I feel Zayn following me.

"We need to talk." Zayn takes a seat in the chair in front of my desk. Okay, I suppose he's staying for a minute.

"Weren't you leaving? What if I don't want to talk?" I take a seat behind my desk.

"I need to talk to you, so too bad. We *are* dating now, don't you remember?"

"Fake dating, and that doesn't mean I have to talk to you. No one is here to witness this conversation," I counter.

"What happened to you and my brother?"

He wants to talk about this now? "None of your business."

"Seriously?" he asks.

"Seriously."

Zayn rolls his eyes, taking his right hand to pinch the bridge of his nose. If I'm lucky, this conversation is giving him a headache and will force him to leave so I can get some work done.

"Okay, well. Can you explain why you think that this," Zayn gestures between our bodies, "will help make a difference? I guarantee a few nice interviews would have sufficed."

"What? You don't think I'm a catch?" I ask, pushing his buttons. Zayn readjusts in his chair, uncrossing and recrossing his legs.

"No, that's not..." Zayn lets out a sigh, dropping his head into his palm. "I just don't see how this is going to get me my role."

"Well, you're just going to have to wait and see. I am a professional." I wink, then glance down at my papers. "If that's it, I have some work to do."

Zayn's sigh lets me know I've won, even if it's momentarily. I don't look up as he leaves, only knowing he's gone from the click of the latch on the door.

My phone buzzes not even thirty seconds later.

Zayn

> My place. Tonight at 6. We need to set ground rules.

Oh, right. I suppose we need to do that. What does one allow their fake partner to do? Hug? Kiss? Am I going to have to kiss Zayn? Do I *want* to kiss Zayn?

I didn't think this all the way through. What I imagined we would do is go to a few parties, show up to some events, and look like a couple. Matching outfits, holding hands, maybe even a kiss on the cheek.

It's too late for me to cancel, once again. First the gala, now the fake dating. And what makes this worse is that I'm the one that suggested it. So, naturally, I can't have an issue with it. I've taken my stance.

11
Zayn

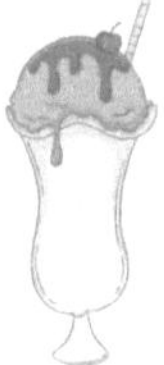

WHEN I GOT THE call from Logan to go to Starlet PR's office on Monday morning to talk about the photo, I thought they might give me a new publicist. If they thought that people would talk about us being a couple, it might end up looking bad for them. I would have understood, even preferred, if that was the plan.

Instead, Annie suggested we date. Fake date. I somehow managed to keep my jaw from dropping during her presentation while I stared at the way her dress rounded her perfect ass. She's infuriating.

Yet, I can't keep my eyes off her. She was trouble the moment I met her, and it's only making me respond to her with more of an attitude.

I should have left, should have kept walking out of the office, but I had to see her and talk to her before I went home. I didn't have anything to talk to her about, so for some reason I thought it was a good idea to bring up my brother.

I hardly talk to Dan these days, but I know that he and Annie were together for two years before breaking up. The few times I saw Annie, she *looked* happy. And it's eating me up that I don't know what he did to her to have her compare me to him.

Even though our paths rarely crossed, I wouldn't forget that face, those lips, her gorgeous blue eyes.

During one of my longer breaks with Marissa, I had a run-in with Annie. It was late in my parents' house, and I was hungry, which is normal. What might not have been so normal was me sitting in the dark kitchen without a single light on.

Annie didn't see me when she walked in. So, I watched her. She was wearing a sleep set, pink and so short, and her hair was in a messy bun. She was my brother's, but I couldn't look away. Couldn't stop my eyes from grazing her entire body.

I stood up from my chair before I comprehend what I was doing. Annie was reaching for a snack in a high cabinet, too high for her short frame. When I approached, she froze but didn't turn around. I pressed against her, reaching up to grab the box of cereal she wanted. Her body stayed frozen, but her breath hitched as I wrapped my arm around her to set the box on the counter. I stayed for a moment, calm as she inhaled and exhaled, and then I left. I went to my room, stayed in there until they left the next day and then avoided her whenever possible.

The night she and Dan broke up, I almost looked her up. And when Marissa broke my heart, I almost looked her up then too. I truly didn't think I'd see her again, so I don't know what to think now that I'm seeing her more than ever.

It's right after six when I hear a knock. Annie.

I walk to the door to let her in.

"Hi, Zayn." Annie greets me as she enters.

My eyes drift the length of her body. Annie decided to replace the dress with a pair of black leggings and a cropped t-shirt. To make things worse, she bends over, giving me a full view of her ass, as she takes off her shoes.

Before she stands, she peers around her leg and catches me looking. A smirk blooms on her mouth.

Fuck. She's doing it on purpose, likely paying me back for being a pain in her ass. One point for Annie.

"I have dinner for us." The table is currently set for dinner, and a candle is lit in the middle. It's not a date, but I wanted her to feel comfortable.

"Great. You'll be excited to know I took time to write down a list of rules for us."

Of course she did. Annie would come to this prepared, with a list and all.

We walk into the dining area, where the pasta I prepared waits. "I, um, hope pasta is okay. I wasn't sure what you'd be hungry for." I palm the back of my neck.

"I like pasta." Annie smiles, then walks to the other side of the table to take a seat.

"Alright, let's get this over with. Tell me your rules and I'll tell you mine." Once I come up with them.

"Right now?"

I nod, stuffing a bite of pasta in my mouth to stop myself from saying anything I shouldn't.

"Okay, well. I just have three rules." Annie takes a piece of paper out of her pocket, unfolding it twice before continuing. "One, you can't be seen with anyone else. This needs to be exclusive. Two, we treat this like a partnership, which means we work together to prepare for events and interviews. Three, no kissing on the mouth. Cheeks and forehead are fine."

"No kissing?" Why is that the first thing I ask? Maybe because I can't stop thinking about those damn lips and what I'd do to have them pressed against mine.

"It complicates things. Haven't you seen what happens in the movies?" Annie takes a bite of pasta, trying her best to glare at me but doing a terrible job.

"Afraid you'll fall in love with me, Annie?" I smirk and drop my head to rest in my hand as I stare at her.

She shakes her head. "Nope, I think you'd be the one to fall in love with me."

It's my turn to shake my head. "No way, I'm closed off for good."

"That's what they all say, Barnes."

"And I mean it," I reiterate. "Okay, my turn."

Annie nods at me to go on.

"One, no more notecards for events." I pause, scrambling to think of more. "And I think that's all..."

"That's all? Just no notecards?"

"If I think of more, I'll tell you later."

"Great." Annie smiles and my heart surges with joy, but I leave my poker face on.

When we're done eating, she gets up from her chair, leans over to grab my empty plate, and stacks it on top of hers. She walks to the kitchen and plops the dishes in the sink, spraying them down before loading the dishwasher. Every time she bends over, I have to clench my jaw to stop myself from moaning at the sight.

She's only been in my apartment for a half hour and she's already making herself at home. It feels normal to have her here, helping with domestic chores.

"Annie, sit. I can clean up," I say, standing from my chair.

"I don't mind." Annie walks toward me with a towel to clean the table.

"I do."

"Well, I don't." Annie rests one hand on her right hip, shifting her weight to that side. "I don't remember you being this stubborn."

"You're impossible. Do you know that?" I ask, swiping the towel from her to wipe down the table. Her challenging me is turning me on, which is not what's supposed to be happening.

"And you're irritating. Do *you* know that?" Annie grabs the towel back from my hands. A growl escapes my mouth.

Annie walks to the table, leaning over to wipe it down. Not thinking about my actions, I follow. Standing behind her, I lean over, reaching around to grab the towel from her. My cock is hard in my jeans, pressed into her back. The tension and the fighting is turning me on more than I'd like to admit. Plus the memory of the moment in my parents' kitchen, and I'm losing my composure.

"My house, my rules, Princess," I whisper into her ear.

She gives up, letting me take the towel from her. I stand back up, confused at why I just put myself in that situation, especially when she's wearing skin-tight leggings. I haven't been able to take my eyes off her all night.

Slowly, Annie rotates 180 degrees, resting her butt on the table. "You need to not do that."

"Why, all hot and bothered?"

Her cheeks fill with a sweet pink. "Zayn. I'm serious. I'll add a rule."

I roll my eyes, not promising anything. I'll have to go to the gym or something to help with all of this built-up tension.

"Well, I should go." Annie says, walking toward the door.

"Let me drive you back."

"I can get an Uber," Annie says.

I don't answer and instead walk over to grab my keys from the hook by the door. Then, I proceed to bend over and slide on my shoes. Finally, Annie sighs and tromps over toward me, putting on her shoes.

We stay silent the entire drive, but I don't mind. There's normally someone that drives me, so this is a nice change of pace. Being able to be behind the wheel, be in control of where I'm headed, and having Annie with me is somehow making my evening better.

Why do I feel the sudden urge to flirt with her? It's like Annie enters my presence, and bam, my hormones shoot up and I try everything in my power to get as many eye rolls and blushes as possible.

I want her to lower her guard, show me the feisty side hiding underneath. She's shown it to me a few times now: at the gala, in her office, and tonight. It seems as if I'm affecting her as much as she's affecting me. She tries to hide too, I can see it. She avoids my gaze, tries to take deep breaths, tries to reset herself. Instead, I push her past her breaking point and the mask falls away.

I may have decided to not pursue any romantic relationships, but that doesn't stop me from looking and thinking about a certain woman. No one over the past year has captured my attention the way Annie does.

I'm used to everyone smiling at me, like she normally does, except they don't speak back to me. They typically just nod or leave me alone. Not Annie. Annie does the opposite, talking to me with a matching attitude and facing me head on.

When we get to her complex, I get out of the car and follow her toward the door.

"You don't need to come with me." Annie peers over her shoulder as she types in a passcode to the building. "I'm not inviting you inside."

It's not the worst building, but it seems outdated. No broken windows, but a few cracked ones, and the brick needs to be repaired in many places. It may be dark out, but I already don't like where she's living.

"I want to make sure you get home safe."

"Well, I'm home safe. Good night." Annie goes to shut the main door behind her, but I put my foot out to catch it. I expect her to say something, but she doesn't. She just keeps walking and starting to climb the stairs to the second floor.

"Shit," Annie says when we get to her apartment.

"What?" I ask.

Annie sighs, opens her apartment door, and walks in. And instead of shutting it, she leaves it open.

So, I follow.

Her apartment is small. Smaller than I expected. There's a kitchen to the left that has an island with two stools. In the middle of the room is a giant pink floral couch. That's where she plops down, dropping her head in her hands.

After shutting the door behind me, I realize I'm in Annie's apartment, her personal space, and my fingers are itching to snoop. What records are next to the player on the bookshelf? What is her latest read on the coffee table? What's behind the closed door on the other side of the room?

"You don't have to just stand there," Annie says, her head still drooping.

I clear my throat and walk toward her, sitting on the opposite end of the couch. "I, uh, realize I shouldn't have come in."

Annie shrugs in response, then sinks further into the couch.

"I'm getting kicked out of my apartment in thirty days," Annie says with a look to the ceiling.

"You didn't know you were getting kicked out?"

"I did, but I thought I had more time. Apparently I missed the previous notice, and this is a casual one-month reminder."

"Hm," I grumble.

"Yup," she says.

"Where are you going to go?"

"Fuck if I know." Annie barks a laugh. "Marcy—" she pauses, bringing her eyes to me before she continues with, "you know Marcy, right?"

"I know Marcy."

Annie nods. "Well, she offered me to stay with her. She lives in this fancy studio, which is ironic since her building is across the street from this place."

"And you don't want to live with her?" I ask, confused.

"Oh no, I'd love to live with Marce." She shifts, bringing her knees on the couch and her eyes back to me. "But she just doesn't have room, and I don't want to impose. Even though she says I wouldn't, I just don't want to disrupt anything, you know?"

I don't *actually* know. "Sure. And your sister?"

"Ha, no. I'd rather not stay in Emmett's office with walls as thin as a piece of paper. So yeah, that leaves me with a hotel? An airbnb? Fuck, I'm screwed."

"You could—"

"Zayn, don't."

"You don't even know what I'm going to say. How am I the grumpy one? You won't let me talk."

"Because I know what you're going to say, and I don't need your pity."

"It's not pity, it makes sense. We can make it part of the contract. Move in with me as my fake girlfriend while you try to find a place to stay. It might look better to be seen leaving my house. After not being with anyone for a year, it will look odd to just be seen together at events. You must know that, I'm sure you've googled my past."

Annie blushes, caught.

"Move in with me, Annie. I promise I'm a good roommate."

"You drive a hard bargain, Zayn. But know that I am only saying yes because you're within walking distance of Flora, which means I can have blueberry muffins for breakfast any morning."

"You can have muffins for lunch and dinner too. I'll make sure the apartment is stocked with them," I say.

"Don't be nice to me now, Zayn, you'll ruin your whole..." Annie looks me up and down. "Vibe."

"Oh, I won't, Princess. Nothing will change besides you invading my every waking moment." I fake a smile to show my sarcasm.

"Ha ha, very funny. I *was* trying to spend less time with you, you know," Annie counters.

"Yeah, yeah. We can text this week about moving details?"

"Oh, I suppose, Z. Looks like this whole fake dating thing is about to get even more complicated."

And she doesn't even know the half of it. With this small crush blooming, I wonder if I'm going to regret my offer. At least our time together boils down to a transaction and nothing more. She helps me land this role, I give her a place to live and she receives contacts based on our success. If only I could keep her off my mind, that would be one less distraction I need to worry about, because I'm not looking to be with anyone anytime soon and definitely not with the girl I'm pretending to date.

12
ANNIE

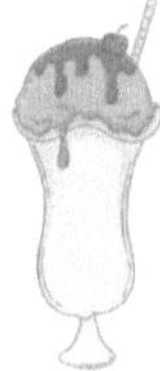

"You're doing what?" Cassie yells into the phone.

"I'm moving in with Zayn." I pace around my apartment as movers pack my things, making sure they are handling everything with care. I can't have my favorite mugs getting broken.

"Yeah, no, I heard that. But, why?"

"Well, the building will be torn down in a few weeks and I'm out of good options for places to stay. Zayn has a spare bedroom, so I'll hardly see him."

Cassie's laughter echoes through the phone.

"Okay, one, you will see him. He's not a ghost. And two, you could have stayed with Emmett and me."

"Sis, I love you. But, your spare bedroom is Emmett's writing office. That wouldn't work."

"Does this not cross some sort of line?" Cassie asks, and I grimace. Would I choose to live with my ex-boyfriend's older brother? On a normal day, no. But this isn't normal, and I can't help but wonder what it's like to be around him more. The push and pull between us is enough to dredge up old memories with Dan, and I'm finding it hard to keep what happened to myself.

"Oh, it crosses a line. But Zayn was with me when I found the notice and I couldn't find a reason to say no to him. Plus, we are dating now, so it kind of makes sense from a media standpoint."

"Fake dating, Anns."

"Same difference," I argue. I lean against the wall and watch the movers as they finish packing up the last few boxes. I thought I'd be more emotional about this. I've lived in this apartment since I came to LA, but I find myself ready to take that next step, at peace.

"No, not the same. Are you sure you're not in too deep already? I just don't want you to get hurt again after—"

"I know what I'm doing. And there's no way I'd ever like someone like Zayn. One brother was enough for me, okay?" What Cassie doesn't need to know is that I'm already nervous that I'm in over my head.

"I trust you know what you're doing. Just, promise that you'll text me if you need anything. And don't forget, if you need money or something—"

"You know how I feel about that. I'm okay, I promise. Love you." Cassie never shoves money down my throat, and I know it takes a lot for her to bring it up, but she also knows I would never accept it. I can do this on my own.

After hanging up, I send Zayn a text to let him know I'm leaving and to meet me outside his building. Since he's going to help move, and the media will be at his apartment at noon, I need him to be ready to fake it.

It's a short drive to his apartment, but following the moving truck there takes a few minutes longer than I estimated. Zayn's waiting for me outside.

"You're late." Zayn looks at me, arms crossed. He's wearing a white henley, with the first few buttons undone. His outfit is super casual, yet I'm drooling at the way the shirt grips his biceps and chest. Has he always been this good looking? It's alarming how much *more* I'm attracted to him than I ever was to his brother.

"Shush. I'm late by like..." I glance down at my phone momentarily. "Three minutes." My eyes snap back to his.

Zayn walks toward me, pausing for a moment, then leaning in. He hovers his mouth right above my ear. "That's late in my book, Princess," he says in barely a whisper, his warm breath sending a wave of small goosebumps over my arms.

I give him a playful shove. The thought was to give us a bit more distance, but it comes off more flirtatious than intended. "Go grab a box, Z."

Zayn walks away, but not before playfully rolling his eyes while a smirk dances on his face. Every time I'm around him, I find myself chipping away at that exterior. I know we need to talk about his brother, but I don't even know what I'd say. I'm not about to tell him that his brother is the reason why I push myself hard at my job, to prove myself to everyone around me.

For the next hour, I help Zayn move boxes.

"Okay, I regret this plan. Why does it look like we haven't made a dent in this truck?" I say, sitting on the edge of the trailer.

Zayn decides now is the perfect time to shed his shirt, leaving him bare-chested. This is what my hell loop would be.

"Might want to pick up your jaw, Annie, otherwise you might embarrass yourself." Zayn raises his brows. What he doesn't know is this is the second time my jaw has dropped due to his shirtless chest. He jumps next to me on the truck bed, offering me a water bottle he got from I don't even know where.

"Shut up," I grumble. Out of habit, I bite my lower lip and look down at my feet. He makes me nervous, and I'm starting to feel a little flutter in my stomach, which is awfully annoying. I need to throw water on this fire, and I know just the way.

I shift my attention back to him to find him already staring at me. An unsettling chill darts through my body, knowing he was already looking at me. Watching me.

"Are you close with your brother?"

Zayn shakes his head. "Far from close. We don't talk much. I'm much closer with Kiley."

"Mm," I respond as a speck of dirt on the moving truck's floor catches my attention. Our body language has officially gone from borderline flirtatious to two teenagers talking at a school dance.

"I know I said some things before about your job, and..." Zayn starts.

I turn to face him again. He runs his right hand through his blonde locks like he tends to do any time he's nervous, dipping his head down, before meeting my eyes.

"I'm not like him. I don't want to be perceived as like him. Your job is important and will help me land my dream role. And that alone is not a small task." Zay's apology catches me off guard. He's always been a mystery to me. Whenever Dan talked about him, it was always surface level facts or about the latest film he was in. And when I did see Zayn, it was as if he was already closed off. I want to ask him about his past, his relationship, know more about it.

It has to be more than what the media led everyone to believe. I know first hand what it looks like to cover up a story and fake a new one. Zayn looks like he lost all joy from his life and has shut himself out from everyone. If what was in the media is true and his previous relationship ended amicably, he wouldn't be like this. He wouldn't need me.

It's almost like everything happened for a reason. Has fate truly brought Zayn and I together? For what purpose? To ensure a new trilogy gets made and a new fandom is born? Doubt it. I'm not sure why the universe would decide to throw my ex's older brother in my path, but I'm starting to not hate it as much as I did last week.

"It's okay," I say. Zayn raises his eyebrow at my sudden forgiveness. "I mean it, water under the bridge."

Zayn grumbles and he's back to his grumpy self. He shifts a little closer to me on the bed of the truck so our legs are touching. Next, he throws his right arm around me, and I tense up. I forgot he wasn't wearing a shirt.

This is supposed to be friendly fake dating, limited touching should be required.

Zayn's upper body leans closer to me, his mouth doing that thing again where it hovers right above my ear. "It's showtime, Princess."

13
ANNIE

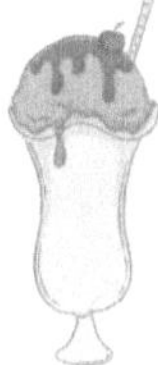

MY EYES DART UP and widen as I spot a camera off in the distance. Quickly I remember I shouldn't look like a deer in headlights. That would not paint a positive picture. So, I turn to Zayn, smiling. I'm not used to being in front of the camera, so this experience is new for me.

"Think they got it?" I ask, trying to read the fine lines on his face.

"I'm not sure. Think we're convincing enough?" Zayn asks.

My gaze trails back toward the camera, second guessing again if this was the right decision. I'm not great at dating, who was I kidding? I don't know the first thing about PDA and what a normal couple would do. What's too much? What's too little?

Zayn leans in again, and his breath mingles with mine. My whole body is hot, and my breaths come faster. "You think too much," he whispers.

He grabs my jaw with his left hand, gently tugging my attention back to him. Before I have the chance to ask what's next, his lips are on mine. The same pair of lips I could not take my eyes away from. Always wondering, what would it be like? What would it be like to kiss Zayn Barnes?

Our kiss is done as quick as it started, but for that brief moment, I forgot where I was and who I was with. After, the sounds of passing cars and birds disappear and the only thing I can hear is the rising beat of my heart.

"I'd say that was fairly convincing," I whisper, looking into his eyes. "Although, we just broke the rules."

"Rules are there to be broken, Princess." Zayn's attention dips to my lips. His own mouth opens, as if he wants to say something, but then his jaw shuts and he hops off the truck. Did I want him to kiss me again? "Alright, let's finish moving you in, then we can get some dinner."

For the next two hours we move and unpack. If I were to wait until later, I would never move out of the boxes. Clothes are sorted into the dresser and hung up in the closet. The room that I'm staying in looks like it came out of a Crate & Barrel catalog. It doesn't look like anyone has ever stepped foot in here. The bed is immaculate, queen size with crisp white sheets and a pink pillow for a pop of color. The furniture is matching dark brown wood. There is only one bathroom, in the hallway, but that is about in the same condition as the bedroom, and I know Zayn uses that. At least he's cleared me a drawer in the bathroom and has bath towels, which I assume he bought for me as well.

I'm sitting on the floor of the bathroom, putting away a few toiletries, when I hear Zayn walking down the hallway. He appears in the doorway, leaning to one side to rest for balance. "How much longer will you be?"

"Not long," I reply, already over the mood switching.

"Not long as in five minutes? Fifteen minutes? What time frame are we talking?" Zayn pesters.

I roll my eyes. "Five minutes? I don't know?" I swivel to face him. "Want me to give you a play by play?" He brings out this side of me that I've never seen. I don't think before I speak when I'm near him, I just say what's on my mind, and it's freeing.

"Five minutes," Zayn mutters before storming down the hallway. Okay, maybe not storming, but he's not a very happy roommate.

Exactly five minutes later, Zayn walks back into the bathroom. I'm done but decided to sort my drawer a little more to make finding a few items that I use on a daily basis easier.

I stand up from the floor. In the mirror, I see Zayn behind me, arms crossed, staring. I turn around and lean on the counter. "Can you try to be less grumpy?" I ask, even though I know the answer.

"No. Are you staying for the show or are you leaving?" Zayn asks, his hands already gripping the band of his pants.

My eyes travel down his chest. Heat circulates through my body, and I'm this close to staying, to see how aroused he is around me. I let my gaze stay there for a few seconds before I peer back at him, knowing I should leave.

"I'd rather watch paint dry."

When I shut the bathroom door, I hear him chuckle from the other side. One of the first laughs, if you can even call it that, that I've heard from him. The only emotions he wears outwardly are his smug face and the occasional smirk. Today, when we kissed, that was new. But I didn't get to read his emotions very well around that situation. Also, it was staged, fake, for the cameras.

I shouldn't be thinking about our kiss.

But I can't stop thinking about our kiss.

I'm supposed to not like Zayn. I don't like Zayn. He's the complete opposite of me. Not only is he the grumpiest person I've met, he only cares about himself. He doesn't seem to care about wanting to get to know anyone past a surface level, and he only cares about landing this role.

I'm his ticket to that.

Well, at least I'll be with him all of the time to help coach him when needed. My phone buzzes as I walk to the kitchen to try and find something to eat.

"Hey Marce." I hold the phone between my ear and my left shoulder, opening the fridge with my right hand. It's stocked with multiple types of beverages including my favorite sparkling water, as well as fresh veggies and fruit, and a dinner ready to go in the oven. He even has the blueberry muffins from Flora on the counter. I take the prepared dinner out and wander over to the oven.

"How's the bachelor pad?" Marcy asks.

When I told her I was moving in with Zayn, I wouldn't say she was thrilled, but she didn't question my decision. It's only temporary, which helps, so we didn't talk about anything about this deal other than the basics of the arrangement. She wanted to make sure I had my own room.

"It's not very bachelor pad-ish? Marce, his fridge is stocked." I click the preheat button on the oven, then turn around to rest my butt on the edge of the counter. "And not like with a few things. Every shelf has something on it and everything is prepared. Which now that I talk about this it does kind of sound bachelor pad-ish... and my room *was* extra clean..."

"Definitely giving bachelor vibes," Marcy says.

"Well, he is thirty and single, which is kind of the definition of a bachelor." Looking around for a place to sit, I notice the stools by the island. I walk over to take a seat in one, sinking into the leather and leaning back to give myself a moment to relax. "But, it's cute. I did just get here though, so maybe I just haven't uncovered his hidden shrine for me."

"You joke, but from interacting with him, Zayn must have some secret side to him that convinced you to do this whole thing." By whole thing, she means fake dating to increase his likability in the media.

With a sigh, I press the speakerphone button on my phone and set it on the counter, not worrying about Zayn overhearing since he's taking a shower. That is one thing I'm desperately trying not to think about.

"This whole thing was my idea, not his. Come on, I'm the mastermind here."

"Oh, trust me, I know you're behind it all. I just mean he used to look so..." Marcy trails off.

"Happy? Enjoyed his life? Loved his job? Want me to continue?"

Marcy chuckles. "Yes, Anns, all of that. I just want you to be careful."

I lean my elbows on the island, hovering over my phone. "No need to warn me, there's nothing to be careful of. It's not like that."

"Sure it's not. Not yet. Did the media successfully see you two today? Did you give them a good shot?"

Flashbacks to a few hours ago appear in my head like a daydream. His sweaty body. His smile. The kiss. "Yeah, we did."

"Fuck."

"What?" I ask, confused at Marcy's sudden expression.

"You two kissed, didn't you?"

"How in the hell—" I start, wondering how on earth she would figure that out. "You know what, never mind." I shake my head even though she can't see my hesitation.

"Damn, you two look good. I can't believe I'm going to say this, but I wish he was cupping my face the way he's cupping yours."

"Wait, is there already an article?"

"Articles, babe. Plural. Just sent it to you. Gotta go though, need to run a few errands for the studio. Text me with any updates! I want to know everything!"

I chuckle as the line goes dead. Sure, Cassie may be my sister, and I'm glad we live in the same city again, but Marcy is my best friend and ride or die. When I moved here for college and only knew Cassie and Emmett, they quickly took me in and introduced me to their group of friends at the studio. It helped my transition to know a few people while meeting some of my own. Marcy and I clicked immediately, bonding over our love for Emmett—mine more of an obsession I was trying to get over since he was now married to my sister and he wasn't just a hot LA actor to me anymore. Every week we would meet for coffee to talk about any of the latest studio gossip. Then, we started getting dinner or running random errands together. Now, she's like a second sister to me.

I pick up my phone and google Zayn. Sure enough, there are a solid twenty articles already out from this afternoon's charade. The cover image of every single one is one of three variations of Zayn and I. The first is the one Marcy mentioned, us kissing with him gripping my jaw. The second is us standing in front of the trailer, which is the most boring of them all. The third, my favorite, was taken right after we kissed. Zayn's head is tilted down toward me and I'm looking slightly up at him. Both of our faces are flushed, which could have been from the moment or the heat or the fact that we were moving boxes. He's still gripping my jaw, our eyes locked on one another. Frozen in time. A photo shouldn't turn me on as much as it is at this moment.

"Shit, they work fast." A shiver runs down my spine. I drop my phone, face down, and turn my head to the left to see Zayn inches from me.

"Told you so."

"Pretty sure that was because of me." Zayn leans away from me and walks around the island. The oven is yelling to let us know it's preheated.

I follow his every action, watching his hands as he grips the oven door and pulls it toward him. When he leans over to place the tray on the rack, I'm rendered useless. Utterly useless. My stare makes its way to his perfect ass, and I notice he's wearing gray sweatpants, which are every woman's weakness. To pile on top of my suddenly horny state, he's decided to wander around without a shirt, leaving his full, toned body on display.

Needing something to occupy my mind, I slide off the stool and look through cabinets to find the plates. On the third try, I find the plates and grab two small ceramic ones. I turn around, getting ready to go set them on the island or the table, when Zayn appears mere inches away from me. When he's this close, it takes everything in me to not reach up and rub the stubble on his chin, to pull his mouth to mine. My eyes blink uncontrollably, unnerved with the way he's making my body feel.

"What are you doing? You're in my bubble." I glare at him.

"I'm not sure, but I find that I like finding ways to make you squirm."

"Well, can you stop it?"

Zayn takes a step closer to me, and I grip the plates tighter against my chest. They're his plates, it's not like he's going to steal them from me. Almost touching, Zayn leans toward me. Once again, hovering in that same spot makes my toes curl and my heart beat fast. "Do you want me to stop? Or are you hating the fact that I turn you on?"

"I—"

"I think we should talk about the rules," Zayn leans to whisper in my ear. With his right hand, he tucks a piece of hair behind my ear.

"What about them?" I whisper back.

"How do you feel about throwing them out? Just letting whatever's going to happen, happen? Isn't that something you want?"

He's baiting me, but I can't help but give in, even just a little bit.

"I don't know," I say.

"I think I know what you want," Zayn says and begins to trail his fingers down my face, my neck, stopping at the top of my chest. "But you're not going to let yourself have it, are you?"

His fingers move again down my torso and end on my hip. He stays there, his face still close to mine, his chest echoing the rise and fall of my own.

"That's too bad," Zayn whispers one last time before he pulls his face away from mine and removes his hand from my body.

Once again rendering me without words, Zayn steals the plates and walks toward the dining room.

14
ZAYN

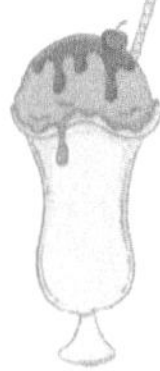

Every now and then, I make a decision that seems great, but as time passes, I find out how awful it actually is. This is one of those times.

Annie is everywhere.

She's in the living room, lounging in her matching pajama set. Shorts so fucking short that I can't stand to be in the same room.

She's in the kitchen, wearing the same said outfit, reaching into a high cabinet for a mug to drink tea. Every time my mind flashes to my body pressed up against hers that first night we met. I've since moved the mugs to a nice spot on the counter. No reaching necessary.

She's in the bathroom, showering, and all I can think about is how soft her tits must be and if she'd let me kiss that damn mouth again.

I'm losing my mind.

Every morning, I wake up before her to work out. The gym is conveniently downstairs, so I spend the first hour or so of the day there. When I get upstairs, she greets me in the kitchen with an already-made pot of coffee.

Annie doesn't even drink regular coffee most mornings. For her it has to be an Americano or tea.

She's been making it for me since hearing me mutter about having to wait too long for a cup after a long workout one morning. She was in the kitchen wearing those damn shorts, and I complained about needing caffeine on my way to the shower. Every morning for the past week, a pot of coffee is on with a mug already set out next to it.

Trying to ignore her is pointless because she's everywhere I look. And when I close my eyes, she invades my personal thoughts and daydreams.

We have been on "dates" the last two Friday evenings. Each to the same ice cream spot, which has now been dubbed as "our spot" by the media. Annie wants us to keep going because she heard they were at risk of shutting down and thought helping a local business might bode well for my public appearance.

She's also made us go to Flora on more than one occasion, to the point where I also order a damn muffin every time.

This morning, I'm having Kiley over while Annie is working for a few hours. I figured it would be easier to catch up with my sister if Annie wasn't around, since that would lead to more questions and conversations I'd rather avoid.

"It smells so good in here." Kiley looks around the living room. She sets her bag on a hook, then struts over to the couch to take a seat. "Are you burning a candle?"

How do I tell her that my roommate just happens to smell like a freshly baked chocolate chip cookie? And that I'm losing my mind over my fake relationship?

"No, neighbors must have baked something." Choosing to lie is easier. "How's everything going with the new job?"

"It's just a new department, but it's been good. My boss can be a little grumpy sometimes, and I'm not quite sure how to read him. I'm trying not to let his mood swings get to me, but that can be hard when we work together on projects."

"Well, that's good." Suddenly self aware, I realize that's how I appear to many people. Unapproachable and grumpy.

"Zayn, you wouldn't believe what—" Annie comes barreling through the front door. "Oh, Kiley!" She walks over to Kiley, embracing her in a hug before walking to the kitchen. Annie grabs a mug, which I can only assume means she's going to make a cup of tea.

Kiley follows her. "I didn't know if you'd be here or not. I have to admit, after seeing you two plastered all over the internet, I wasn't sure if this was real or not."

"Of course this is real, Kiki. That's what I texted you last night," I say, annoyed that she would even think that. I get that I haven't been the most open and honest big brother, but I feel like this is believable.

"Oh, I know. I'm just kidding. I was just shocked by it all. To see you a year ago with one brother and now to see you with my other brother. Small world right?" Kiley chuckles.

Annie lets out an awkward chuckle. "Right, Zayn and I. We *are* together." She looks at me with a raised brow, slightly concerned at the fact that my sister thinks we are actually dating.

I stand up from the couch and meander into the kitchen.

Walking over to Annie, I lean down and give her a peck on the cheek. It's the first time I've touched her since our interaction two weeks ago. The hand holding on our dates doesn't count. I chalk the day of our kiss up to being high on testosterone and unable to control myself. The extra touches, the glances, the flirting... It was all too much.

"I didn't expect you home already," I say, walking to sit in a stool on the other side of the island.

"I felt like surprising you on our three week anniversary." Annie winks at me, and I'm grateful to be sitting down, for that wink alone causes my cock to harden. Not something I'd like to publicize.

"Aw, you two are adorable," Kiley says, her eyes darting back and forth between Annie and me. "How did you reconnect anyway?"

I look at Annie. Annie looks at me. Neither of us know what to say as we haven't practiced this before.

"We, um, reconnected at the studio," Annie says, taking a sip of tea.

"Yes, one day at lunch when she came to meet her sister," I add, surprised how believable this is.

"And the rest was history." Annie shrugs and leans against the counter behind her.

"And you've been together all this time?"

"Not too long," I say. I don't want to act like the two of us are endgame and lead Kiley to believe she might have a new sister-in-law.

"Yeah, we hung out as friends for a while, then he took me out on our first date. And that's pretty much how it happened."

"And the gala was an accident?" Kiley asks, looking at me. "Why was that when you two were first seen together?"

"I couldn't resist not having my hands on her any longer..." I glance longingly at Annie.

"Gross." Kiley makes a gagging sound. "No offense Annie."

"None taken."

They both laugh and I glance between the two, seeing for a brief moment what my life might look like if I had Annie for real. She blends in with my family so well, and maybe before she was attached to the wrong piece of the puzzle.

Kiley stays for another hour badgering us with questions. Annie and I alternate answering, and by the time Kiley finally decides to leave, I'm glad to be done with the interrogation.

"Okay, I'll let you two have some time." Kiley walks toward the front door, already grabbing her purse from the hook.

"Oh, you don't have to do that, Kiley," I call after her.

"Z, it's fine. We can catch up during a call this week! Bye love birds!" Kiley yells, walking out the front door.

Annie lightly punches me in the left arm, and I whip around to face her.

"You didn't tell her this was fake?" Annie demands.

I shrug. "I didn't feel the need to disclose that information."

"What the fuck, Zayn? Why not?"

"I do what I want, Princess." I stare at Annie, begging for a fight, an argument, something to take my mind off the fact that I want to bend her over this island and fuck her from behind. "You should know that by now."

Annie does the opposite of what I desperately want. She rolls her eyes, signature Annie response, then grabs her second cup of tea off the counter, and she walks away without saying a word.

A heavy sigh escapes my lips. It's not that I want to fight with Annie. I just don't know how to react when I'm around her. She always has something witty to say to bring out more of my grumpy-ness when I'm trying to be a little better around her. I want her to be able to tolerate me. We have to live together for the next four months.

But what would tolerating me look like? Shared breakfast? Me making her tea? Friendly conversations in the hallway? That wouldn't make my attraction to her go away. It would make it worse, which I don't need.

I need to focus on practicing for the role I'm going to land, not fantasizing about a civil relationship with Annie.

A few hours later, I'm in my room trying to figure out what to wear for our date. We're going to Sunshine Scoops and a pumpkin patch. I can't remember the last time I was at one of those. All I can picture is people in flannels, but it's still warm outside, and a flannel is the last thing I want to wear. I reach for a plain white tee as a knock comes from my door. I slip on my shirt as I answer it and find Annie on the other side, her gaze locked on my bare skin.

"Enjoying the view?" My tone is laced with playful curiosity.

"Mhm, it's quite nice. Are you ready to leave?" Annie takes her time meeting my stare, trailing up my chest slowly. What I'd give to know the thoughts inside her head.

"Are you like this with everyone?" There's this hidden side to Annie that is revealing itself to me the more time we spend together. It's bubbly with a hint of irritability. As if she's not letting herself give into what she wants to say, but she's comfortable enough with me to explore this side of her.

"What do you mean?" Annie trails behind me as I grab a few things from my dresser, shoving my wallet and keys into my back pocket.

Yeah, what do I mean? I want to know the way she carries herself when she's alone, when she's around me, and when she's around a group of people. I want to know who she is.

"You're just hard to read, Annie Mitchell. I never know which version of you to expect. Sometimes you're optimistic about everything, giving a glass half full vibe to any situation. Other times, you're..." My feet move toward her. I give her a playful shove, and she lands flat on her back on my bed. "Unpredictable."

Annie sits up, crossing her legs under her like a pretzel. "And which version of me do you like better, Zayn?"

"Neither. I like this version of you. This version of you, full of attitude and excitement, I might like a little bit too much."

"Well, if we are being honest..." Annie's feet unravel from under her and plop on the floor. She stands, walking toward me, and my eyes widen as I wonder what her next move is. "I don't *not* like you anymore." A wink escapes before she walks past me and out my door. "We leave in five, Mr. Barnes! Ice cream waits for no one."

15
ZAYN

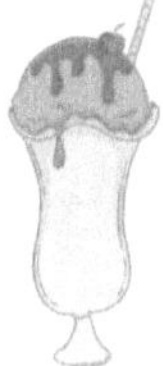

THE ICE CREAM SHOP is packed when we arrive. This is our third week in a row going, and people around town are starting to take note. Groups of people wait outside and around the shop, stealing glances at Annie and I as we make our way toward the front entrance.

Annie loops her arm through mine, stitching us together as we walk the final stretch across the parking lot. She's smiling at people, waving, showing the side of her that people expect to see on the arm of an actor. I try mimicking her. A thin smile graces my face as I give out a few nods here and there until we finally reach the door.

"Wow, it's packed in here," Annie notes. She's not wrong, nearly every seat is taken in the small place. The booths and stools at the bar are all occupied by groups of teenagers.

"Annie, glad to see you!" The worker behind the counter greets her as if they are long lost friends. He's here nearly every time we are, yet I can never remember his name.

We walk up to the counter, where I pretend to look at the ice cream in the display case. Every week we order "Summer Bliss" out of habit. Annie and I both tend to get hyper fixated on something, like her with blueberry muffins. For me, I figure, if I like it, why would I change what I order and risk not liking it as much and regretting it?

There's a new tag next to the giant tub of ice cream. Leaning closer to the glass to try and get a better view, I see the worker shuffling in front of me to aid me with any questions.

"What's the tag mean?" I ask.

A look of shock appears on his face, wide eyes and all. "Well, Mr. Barnes, you see, well—"

"Call me Zayn." I'm grateful this kid has manners, but damn, him calling me Mr. Barnes makes me feel old.

"Right, Zayn, okay." A smile appears on his face, followed by a bit of confidence. "Mr. Jones, the owner of Sunshine Scoops, was planning to shut this place down at the end of the season. And well, with you two stopping by as often as y'all do, we don't have to anymore. Or at least, that's what he tells me, and you two only ever order this flavor, which I get why, it's so good, I also like this flavor, it has the perfect balance of sweet and nutty with a bit of—" His hand goes to his chest, as if he's trying to calm his heart. I'm used to nervous rambling, having been involved with a lot of youth in the past at the Young Actors Association. The kid shakes his head, recentering his thoughts. "Anyway, this is now our best seller. Well, kind of only seller, so we put a tag here to honor the two of you as a way of public thanks."

Huh. The tag reads "Zayn Barnes and Annie Mitchell, favorite ice cream" with a few graphics of an ice cream cone and suns with faces. Seeing our names together, even on a silly printed label, sends waves of heat through my body. I feel like the Grinch; my heart is growing larger and larger the more I'm around Annie. Everyone gravitates toward her.

She radiates pure fucking sunshine.

"That's amazing, Liam." Annie beams. I smile too, a little bigger than usual. This smile is real, and it's all because of Annie.

"Here you two are." The worker, Liam, hands us our normal ice cream.

We pay and hover by the end of the counter. Both of us look around trying to find a place to sit but come up with nothing. A couple tries to get up to offer us a seat, even though they still have what looks to be most of their ice cream, and I politely decline.

Turning to Annie, I can see her brain churning. Her eyes dart around the room, but she's trying to be inconspicuous. The ice cream cone currently on its way to melting is being passed back and forth between her hands like a basketball. She's trying to figure out the plan, or what plans B and C are. Sometimes I forget these nights together are technically work for her. The success of all of this doesn't only fall on her shoulders, but she is the mastermind behind this whole fake-dating ruse.

"Do we have time for a short walk on the beach?"

Annie turns to me, a smile blooming on her face. "We have a few minutes."

"After you, Princess." I add a wink for extra points, and for the reporters that seem to be moseying about.

A few patrons also have cameras out, likely recording or trying to get a picture of the two of us. We haven't had a lot of people stop us for interviews, which I attribute to the scowl that still remains on my face. Just because I'm out in public doesn't mean I want people to interrupt our time together.

I'm used to people around me taking photos, though the amount of cameras ebbs and flows depending on what movie or campaign I'm promoting.

When I'm able to step outside my complex and take in the sounds of the city, when I hear the noises of birds chirping and cars beeping, that's when I know it's going to be a good day. When I'm able to walk down the street to Flora and know that when I stroll inside I won't be asked for a photo or an autograph. It's my favorite time of the year, when I'm able to be slightly invisible to others around me. Once the photographers show up in the busier months, I stop those walks and stay indoors as much as possible.

There was a time when I wouldn't have cared as much, still gone outside knowing I'd be bombarded by the media. Marissa always took control of the narrative. She could talk to a reporter for me, letting me stand there watching as she handled the interview. I didn't know it at the time, but I *let* her define our relationship, my feelings.

But, Annie, she's the opposite. Sure, she may have the same friendly persona, but she doesn't speak for me. She stands there, lets me have my say, and squeezes my arm to show my support. She doesn't need to answer questions for me and certainly doesn't care that the camera isn't pointed to her.

The difference is that Annie isn't Marissa. The more time I spend with Annie, the more I open up. The wounds of my previous relationship fade, chipping away until they are simply scars. Still visible, still present, not going away, but merely a reminder. My past is starting to be simply that, a memory of what was and how I'm better because of it.

It's because of Marissa that I lack trust in others and can never tell if people are telling me the full truth. It's the reason why I ended up alone and the thing that holds me back from developing relationships with others.

Annie leads the way out of the shop while I process these thoughts.

"I haven't been on the beach in a year," I say.

Annie reaches for my free hand, lacing our fingers together. We walk, our other hands holding our cones of ice cream.

"We don't have to talk about what happened if you're not ready to tell me," Annie mutters, masking her curiosity with empathy.

I hesitate. No one has cared to offer me any semblance of respect like Annie has. She could push me, ask me questions, but she doesn't. And if she does, I believe she would know what is the right thing to ask to not push me further than I'd want to go.

I want to tell Annie what happened. I want her to know me on a deeper level, to understand why I am the way that I am. Someone I loved chose not to love me back, and I wasn't prepared to handle that.

Instead of telling her, I give her hand a squeeze. It's my way of saying thanks for letting me open up on my own terms and not being forced into telling her something if I'm not ready.

"We should turn around." Annie peers behind us and to the right up the bank of sand. Besides a few people lounging on towels, we are practically alone, the reporters that were around us nowhere to be seen.

Our ice cream is gone, and I realize that I'm leaning too close to starting to feel something for Annie, so I drop her hand like it was suddenly burning me. Her gaze drops down to where our hands were just laced. She clasps hers together and lets out a small sigh. I watch as her chest rises and falls, breathing in the salty air of the ocean.

"Let's go pick some pumpkins." Annie smiles, but it stops short from reaching her eyes. Where little crinkles should form, smooth lines remain.

I know I caused that. Let her down somehow with my lack of intimacy, but this is fake. It's best if we both remember that.

16

ANNIE

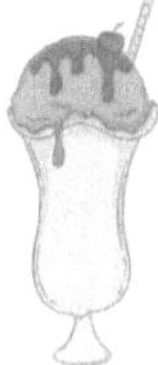

I'M STARTING TO LIKE Zayn, which doesn't bode well for this whole fake dating thing. My career isn't in a place where I can let someone else in. I'd be worried I'd lose focus on myself and what I've been working on over the past three years. Not to mention, I'm still not over the fact that his brother is the sole reason why I have a messed up relationship with my performance at work.

During our first year together, Dan was supportive and loving. He helped me study for tests and attended local events with me. It seemed as if he was rooting for me, but that all changed when we moved in together a year into our relationship. He became distant, even with us living under the same roof. When I tried to talk to him about my internship or ask if he'd come to an event with me, he'd make up an excuse or tell me he was busy that night. Then, one day when I came home early from an event to surprise him for his birthday dinner, I found him with a coworker in our bed.

It was at that moment that I vowed to put myself first, to make sure I am proud of myself for the career I've made. It's why my first real client is so important. It's what will set me up for success in the future, and I don't want feelings or whatever is going on to get in the middle of that.

The car ride over to the pumpkin patch is silent; not even music plays on the stereo. Just the sounds of the interstate and road noise echoes in the car. We're in the back seat of a black sedan and sitting what feels like miles apart.

Zayn has his nose in his phone the entire time, never putting it down or sneaking glances my way. I, on the other hand, have my notebook out. Checking and double checking the agenda for tonight's event.

When I researched Zayn after our initial meeting, I was shocked to see how involved he was with the Young Actors Association. I'm not just talking about monetary donations. He was a speaker at events, teaching classes to students, mentoring new actors that just landed roles. Then, he just quit. It wasn't a gradual stop either, it was as if he was never involved.

Tonight's event is a fundraiser of sorts. All I've told Zayn is that we're going to pick pumpkins, which isn't a lie, it's just not the full truth. Maybe I was scared that if I told him, he wouldn't want to go. When Logan reached out about the event, he told me that this fundraiser would be great media coverage. After a few calls, and a good word from Todd, I was able to get Zayn an interview.

January Studios and the Association have a great relationship. The Association is the reason why Zayn began acting at the studio. Him starting there has helped evolve their partnership and this fundraiser tonight will help bring new classes and mentorship opportunities to kids who think they might want to be actors.

This interview comes at the perfect time because I need the media to talk less about our relationship and more about his acting.

Step one of this fake dating ruse was to get the media to notice Zayn again. That was easier than I thought it would be. Who knew that everyone both loves and hates that Zayn is in another relationship? Teenage Annie would be freaking out, knowing that someone like Zayn is dating someone like me. To the rest of the world, we look happy as can be. Every photo that's taken looks natural. I would have had a field day on gossip sites, trying to figure out this mystery gal and stalking their every move.

The sound of the tires on the gravel road fills the car, breaking my attention from my notes. Looking up, I find the pumpkin patch in front of us. There are people everywhere. Kids are running around, chasing each other. When the car stops, I move for the handle of the door, getting ready to open it, when I hear Zayn from behind me.

"Don't move."

My chest tightens. When Zayn gets commanding, I don't know how to handle it. I'm half turned on and half frustrated.

But I stay put. Knowing it would lead to some sort of argument or disagreement if I were to open the damn door myself, and I can't have him getting mad before he finds out why we are actually here.

In mere seconds, Zayn has walked around the trunk of the car. Once he has my door open, he reaches for my hand.

I hesitate, letting him stew for a moment. Teasing him is my new favorite hobby.

"Don't make me wait, Princess." His eyes darken as he thrusts his hand out again.

"Or what?" I tease. "What if I want to see what trouble you incite, Z?" The driver is probably irritated with my flirty tone, but he's being paid by the hour, so he can deal.

A growl escapes from Zayn when I call him by his nickname, or maybe it's from the teasing.

"I didn't know when I met you that you'd be so much trouble."

Finally, I place my hand in his. "There's a lot more than meets the eye, Zayn."

He tugs hard. It's enough to send me flying into his chest. Using my free hand, I brace myself on his bicep. Being this close to him, I can feel his chest moving, his breathing deep from the tension between us.

"You need to stop." Zayn takes a step back, increasing the space between us and dropping my hand. It's the same warning I gave him when we were first in his apartment.

I shut the door, letting the poor driver leave. When I turn back to face Zayn, he's still staring at me with his darkened eyes.

"I don't know, I kind of like pushing you. I like seeing how far you bend." Taking a play from his book, I lean toward him and stand up on the tips of my toes, my hands finding his shoulders. I hover my mouth right below his ear and whisper, "I want to know what it takes to break you."

Zayn's hand moves to my hip, lightly gripping me in place. He slowly guides my heels back to the ground, then turns his head toward mine, echoing my previous move. His breath is hot, leaving chills down my spine. "Annie," he says, his voice barely above a whisper, "you alone are enough to break me."

Zayn takes a step back, his hand moving from my hip to my hand. He interlaces our fingers and turns around. "Let's go," he says.

I'm still trying to come back down from the high his words gave me. *You alone are enough to break me.* My stomach is in knots. The line between us has blurred, and even though I know it's not what my brain wants, I can't help but follow my heart. At least give in a little bit because I'm painfully attracted to him and when he says things like that, I don't know how to respond.

We walk toward the entrance of the patch. I give my name to the lady working and she lets us know where to find the tent for the event.

As we walk, the sun reflects off of the metallic playground equipment randomly dispersed into small areas for kids to play on. Various birds, goats, a horse or two, and some chickens are grouped together in a small petting zoo. Ahead of that is the tent where we are supposed to go.

Before we get there, I pull Zayn to a stop.

"What?" He turns to me, tilted head and all.

"I need to brief you on what we are walking into."

"Right... work... okay, lay it on me."

"This event is for the Young Actors Association, which I know you're familiar with. And, you have to do a small interview." I grimace, bracing myself for his response.

His eyes narrow and he turns to fully face me. "An interview?"

I nod, my bottom lip disappearing under my teeth. His eyes snap to my mouth for a moment as he follows my actions before he meets my eyes again.

"Okay."

"That's it? You're not mad?" I ask, wondering why he's suddenly okay with this. The thought of him not agreeing was the whole reason I didn't tell him ahead of time.

"If you think this will help, I trust you. But next time, you need to tell me." Zayn tugs on my hand once again, pulling me into his chest. His free hand grips my jaw, moving my face closer to his. At the last moment, he turns my head slightly to the left, bringing his mouth to my ear. I have never been so turned on in the middle of a pumpkin patch. "Otherwise, this partnership, as you like to call it, won't work. We need to be on the same page. Got it?" He hovers. His breath feels hotter than the sun.

"Yeah, Z, I got it." I call him by his nickname again, knowing what it does to him.

The grip on my jaw tightens by a fraction before he puts the slightest bit of pressure for my face to be aligned with his. We are so close, our noses almost touch. With the small height difference, Zayn is looking down at me, his forehead resting on mine. Just when I think he may kiss me again, we're interrupted.

"There you two are!" A man's voice comes from behind me.

Zayn peers up. Whoever he sees causes his eyes to briefly close and a heavy sigh to leave his mouth. The moment is over as he removes his forehead from mine but not before giving my hand a light squeeze, which I perceive as him feeling whatever tension is between us too.

Turning around, I find Logan grinning, walking toward us from the opening of the tent.

"It's almost time for the interview," he says, handing us both a sheet of paper with an agenda on it. We missed some of the earlier activities, but we still have the interview, followed by a small photoshoot, and then free time to do any activities here.

"Here, this has a few of the specifics on it," I say, turning to Zayn and handing him a piece of paper from my bag.

"No notecards?" Zayn asks, and I shake my head. "I'll find you after," he says with a chuckle, then leans forward to plant a kiss on my forehead. He looks at me one last time, seemingly shocked that he just did that, but we don't have time to talk about it. He smiles, then follows Logan toward the tent.

For the next few minutes, I wander, glad I decided to wear my sneakers. The last time I was at a pumpkin patch had to have been when I lived in Indiana. Picking pumpkins and carving is a Midwest spooky season tradition and something my mom loved to do with Cass and I. Since moving to California, I haven't done anything in the traditional fall sense. Blame it on the heat or maybe me just not having time, but it hasn't been on my mind. Now, I'm finding myself wanting to show Zayn more about me, about where I've come from, and that has me feeling even more confused than this morning.

There is a small concession stand next to the event tent, so I stop by to grab something to drink. They have apple cider slushies, which are surprisingly tasty. Not too sweet, with a hint of cinnamon.

Behind the tent, there are a few benches and picnic tables. I sit at one of the tables, with my back to the tent. In front of me is a maze with a sign that reads "California's largest corn maze." Huh. I never would have expected there to be so many cliche fall activities here, but then again, I haven't gone out of my way to look for them.

People meander around the area, pointing to the surroundings. A few tractors are loaded with families, taking their kids around on a ride. It reminds me of home, so I sip my slushy and smile at everything around me. Today is going to be a good day.

The buzz of my phone radiates on the bench beneath me. I wrap my arm around my back to grab the phone from my pocket. Marcy is calling, probably to check in and make sure Zayn's behaving.

"Hi, Marce." I rest my elbows on the table.

"Do you need rescuing yet?"

"I'm actually sitting by myself right now. So, I think I'll be okay," I reassure her.

"Why are you sitting alone?" Concern comes through her voice.

"Z had an interview."

"Z?" Marcy asks.

Shit. Marcy and I don't talk about Zayn much, because there isn't much to talk about. He doesn't like me any more than he has to, or at least I don't think he does. But occasionally I get confused due to moments like we had earlier, and I do dumb things like call him by his nickname.

And Marcy is the type to overthink something—which means even though she's not going to ask me any questions about it, she's already thinking we are in love.

Which I *would* argue against because most days Zayn doesn't seem like he wants to be around me. Even though I make him coffee every morning, he still beelines past me. We hardly spend time together outside our events.

"It shouldn't be long, and then I think we may go into the corn maze." I decide on the spot, ignoring Marcy's remark.

"Oh, corn maze? I forgot that we had those here," Marcy echoes, which is funny because she's from here. Northern California, but still California.

"Right? Well, what are you doing today?"

"Not sure. Ed has someone he needs me to meet. Someone that's starting to work with us for the next film. I think he's a producer or something, so he'll be my new boss."

"Oh, interesting! You'll have to fill me in," I say, knowing full well I will receive multiple voice memos and text messages after this meeting.

"I will, I will. You know more than my own sister," Marcy jokes. "Alright, well I just wanted to check in, but since you're obviously fine and not being murdered, I'll just text you later."

"I love you Marce, but you're ridiculous. Talk to you later." I chuckle, then remove the phone from my ear to end the call.

After sitting and people watching for a few more minutes, the crunching of the few almost-dead leaves causes me to turn my head to see who's behind me. Zayn. It's hard not to stare. He looks nothing like his brother. Zayn's blonde, where Dan has brown hair. Zayn's eyes are swirls of milk chocolate and his stature is toned and extremely him. That's the only way I know how to describe it. Dan was twenty when we dated, practically a baby. He acted like one too, and I missed all the red flags.

"If you don't stop staring, I might get the wrong idea, Annie," Zayn says as he approaches. He throws his legs in between the bench and the table, taking a seat next to me. Our knees brush, but neither of us make it a point to move.

"How was the interview?" I glance at Zayn, trying to see if I can see any of his typical signs that he's annoyed or frustrated. But, I don't see any. No furrowed brow, no slight turn down of his mouth, nothing.

"It went well. Photoshoot was quick too. Do you want to do that?" Zayn points in front of him.

"The corn maze? I would love to." I grin, which earns me a small smirk from Zayn.

He reaches for my hand under the table, lacing our fingers together. I haven't seen a lot of cameras around, but I assume he's doing this just in case we get caught together. We need to look the part of the couple. We need to be convincing.

We walk toward the maze and I look to my left at Zayn to find him biting his lip. I would ask what's wrong, but I choose to leave it for right now. If he wanted to tell me something, I would hope he would say it.

"Okay, ready?" Zayn asks.

I nod.

"How hard can it be?"

17

ANNIE

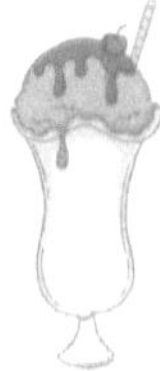

WHAT FEELS LIKE FIVE hours later, we come to another dead end. It's just a wall to some building at the end of this route with corn on both sides.

"Fuck, another dead end." Zayn kicks in front of him, hitting a few stalks of corn.

"It's fine. If we can't find our way out, we can just walk through the corn." Thinking it might be helpful to offer a solution, I keep a smile plastered on my face. Even though I need water and am exhausted from walking in circles.

"It's not fine." Zayn glares in my direction.

I walk over to the wall, turning my back toward it. Just a little bit of rest is all I need. "Mhm, fine. We will find our way out." I close my eyes briefly, trying to calm my nerves.

"Don't do that."

My eyes snap open and I roll my head to the right to look at him. "Do what, Zayn? Please enlighten me," I bark back.

"Don't pretend like you're in a good fucking mood right now."

"I'm not pretending, I am having a good time," I retort, plastering an even bigger smile on my face.

Zayn's eyes narrow. "Liar," he mutters.

"I'm sorry, what was that?" I shift my weight, hoisting my left leg up a few inches to rest the bottom of my foot on the wall behind me. "I can't hear you, Zayn."

Zayn's a few feet from me, and it only takes a handful of seconds before I feel his body on mine. His hands are on either side of my hips, resting on the wall behind me. His head leans toward mine as he gets ready to whisper something into my ear. My knees are weak just thinking about it.

"You're doing this on purpose."

"I don't know what you're talking about, Zayn."

A low growl escapes from his mouth. "If I didn't know any better, you wanted us to get lost in this maze. You want people to see us, to keep telling yourself that whatever this is isn't real."

I lift my hips slightly, putting pressure on his lower body. A slow moan echoes in my ear.

"What do you want from me, Princess?" Zayn's whisper is a plea and is so unlike anything I've heard from him.

He asked the million dollar question. Zayn is not someone that I should be provoking in the middle of a pumpkin patch.

He hardly sees this thing we're doing as a partnership. The only person he thinks of is himself.

Then why do I find myself staring at him and wishing he would care about me? Just a little bit. Looking into his eyes, I feel like he does, but it's only temporary.

His eyes search mine, waiting for an answer. His gaze dips to my mouth again, and I know he's waiting for me to make the next move.

Finally, I release a sigh, a small whimper with it. I look down at his mouth, then back up to his eyes.

"Kiss me," I say, maintaining eye contact, putting the ball in his court.

My first thought is that he's not going to do it. Zayn is staring at me, not muttering a word. My second thought is that we shouldn't do this. We've already kissed once, and I can't get that off my mind. Before I'm able to think of a third thought, Zayn closes the gap and presses his lips to mine.

When our lips connect, he's still hesitant. There is still space between us that I'm internally begging to be closed. Our kiss isn't as deep as I want it. I want more. I *need* more from him.

I find his neck with my right hand and pull him toward me, tilting my head to let him in more. Zayn's left hand finds its way to my hip as his right hand moves to grasp my jaw. His tongue explores mine; they dance like we've done this a million times before.

His left hand trails up my body, landing on my breast. Using his palm, he massages over my shirt. A small moan finds its way out of my mouth. Zayn shifts the hand that was gripping my jaw to the back of my neck, somehow finding ways to deepen our kiss even more. And it's in this moment that I realize that

I'm ruined. Zayn is leaving me utterly ruined because nothing can compare to this. The passion of his lips pressed against mine, the fire between us, it's nothing like I've experienced before. And because of that, I don't want to stop, I don't want to let him go.

Zayn pauses, separating his lips from mine. Our breathing is labored. Our cheeks flushed red. He rests his head on mine once again.

"Why can't I resist you? The moment we are alone and you look at me like that..." Zayn says, his eyes staring directly into mine. "I find myself drawn to you," he adds with a whisper.

"Like a magnet," I say, my face warm from the blush creeping up my neck.

Zayn takes a step back, creating a bit of breathing room between us. He chuckles and runs his right hand through his hair, his gaze momentarily dropping to the ground. When he looks back up at me, he smiles. A real smile. I take a mental picture. This is the first time I'm getting a peek into the real Zayn Barnes.

"Tell me something about you that I don't know," Zayn says as he takes my hand in his and pulls me along.

"There's a lot about me you don't know," I say. We've barely spent time together.

"Start at the beginning." Zayn looks at me and my stomach does a tumble. I *truly* wish it'd stop doing that.

"Um, okay. I grew up in Indiana with Cassie and my mom. We didn't live too far from the city, but we hardly traveled there. I had a typical childhood, but my mom wasn't around a lot. Cassie helped raise me." I shrug and keep my eyes trained on my shoes.

"What was high school Annie like?"

"Embarrassing." I laugh. "I spent too many nights obsessing over gossip articles and stalking actors on social media."

Zayn looks at me with raised brows and I have to shake my head and cover my mouth with my hand to stop myself from full-on giggling. "Don't look at me like that, it's the whole reason why I'm here."

"With me? In this corn maze we can't find our way out of?" Zayn teases.

I bump my shoulder into his and throw him off balance. "No, in Los Angeles, Z."

"I can picture younger Annie." Zayn shrugs while his lip turns up in a smirk.

"Oh, yeah? What was high school Zayn like?"

"I also spent too many nights obsessing over gossip articles," he says with a straight face.

"Oh, someone alert the media, Zayn has jokes."

Zayn pulls on my hand to bring me closer to him as he spins toward me to wrap his other arm around my waist.

My breath is stolen as I meet his chest and look up to see him staring at me with a look that I can't quite read. It's almost like he's surprising himself.

"High school Zayn would never imagine he'd be walking through a corn maze with the most beautiful woman he's ever met."

My mouth parts, and I know I should say something, anything, in this moment. But I can't find the right words to express how all this is starting to feel like something more and how much I'm leaning toward wanting it to be. Does he say these things to rile me up? To lead me on? Or is he starting to feel the same way as me, starting to feel that us fake dating may be getting complicated if feelings are involved?

Zayn's hand moves from my waist to cup my jaw, and he runs his thumb up and down. I lean into him and close my eyes for a brief moment, relishing his touch. There's the sound of rustling corn husks near us. He drops his hand from my face, takes a step back, and clears his throat. His cheeks are flushed once more. I'm glad to see that he's affected just as much as I am.

"Come on, let's find our way out of this maze and go home."

18
ZAYN

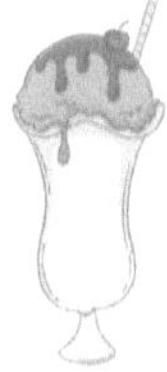

"WELL, I'M FUCKED, AND I blame you."

Ever since kissing Annie in the corn maze, I've been a mess. We haven't spoken about it, just decided to pretend it didn't happen like the last kiss, and I need someone to talk to about it. I'm pacing around my apartment, making figure eights between the living room and the kitchen. Logan is over because he's the only person that's been with me for long enough to know me. We may not be close, but I consider him a friend. Even though I think he's an asshole.

"I didn't suggest you two move in together," Logan says. He's sitting on the couch working on his computer. He doesn't even bother looking up.

"Well, no, but you sure as hell don't help the situation."

Logan peers up, sighs, and closes his computer. "I'm in a tough position."

I stop in front of him, throwing my hands up in the air. "You're in a tough position? I'm the one falling for this fucking girl, and I'm in a goddamn fake relationship."

"Falling, huh?"

"I... I don't know. I don't know what's going on. I'm confused. I'm trying to be better to get this role while everything is getting complicated. I don't know why I thought coming to you would be a good idea when you're half of the reason why I'm in this mess."

Logan was there when everything happened with Marissa. He was the one that suggested we hide all negativity around the breakup. I trusted him. I think it was the right call, but I had to suffer and grieve in silence. Whenever anyone saw me, instead of sympathizing with me about the situation, they mentioned that they loved how we ended things amicably. They would tell me they thought we were endgame and I had to stand there and hear all of it. I couldn't say anything to anyone. Eventually, it wore on me enough that I stopped leaving the apartment. Whenever someone brought up my past relationship, I'd either say something I shouldn't, or I'd shut down and ignore them.

All of this has led me to this moment with Annie. If I would have just controlled my anger at that first gala, we wouldn't be here. I'd be doing boring interviews or attending events I'd rather not be at. But I also wouldn't be feeling like this again.

My heart has been slowly mending itself and I can already tell that if I let Annie in, fully in, and something happened, then all of my bandages would slowly unravel until I'm broken again. I didn't think I'd be interested in anyone ever again.

Nothing can happen. Nothing should happen between Annie and I. She would wreck me.

"Listen, Zayn. I've known you for a while, and I just want to comment on the fact that no one has gotten under your skin like Annie has." Logan stands, his bag already packed and hanging over his shoulder.

"Your point?" I walk into the kitchen and lean over the island, resting my elbows in front of me, while glaring in his direction.

"I—" Logan sighs and walks backward toward the door. "Just don't think about it too much. Let whatever it is happen. It doesn't have to be a thing."

"You're the worst at giving advice, you know."

"You're the worst at listening to advice, you know." Logan counters, hand on the doorknob. "So listen when I tell you it's okay to keep things casual, figure out what you want. Your contract ends in a few months with Annie and this whole fake dating thing will be over, you'll have signed this new movie deal, and then you two can go your separate ways. I have to go, but don't hesitate to text me if you need anything." Logan pauses before opening the door, waiting for me to respond.

"Bye, Logan." I wave, standing up from the island and turning my back to him. I hear a chuckle as the door closes.

I glance at the stove. Annie will be home in a few hours, and then we have another date. Logan wasn't wrong when he said Annie is weaving her way under my skin. It's little by little, like a damn parasite. I use bickering as a defense mechanism, but it only makes it worse; Annie seems to feed off of my grumpy moods. She gets more vocal and flirty, which has led us into some dangerous territories.

I've thought about talking to Kiley about all of this, but I'm not ready to tell her it's all fake. She was heartbroken, maybe more than me, about how my previous relationship ended. Marissa was like a big sister to Kiley, and when everything happened, Kiley lost her too.

Granted, Kiley is older now and has thicker skin, but that doesn't mean this wouldn't hurt her.

The fact that it's with Annie actually makes things worse. Kiley and Annie have a relationship, even if it's just surface level. They know each other because of Dan. Out of the billions of people in the world, I manage to fake date a girl that's gone out with my brother. What are the odds?

I'm in the living room when I hear the front door open. Annie rushes through with the biggest smile on her face.

"Zayn, I think Greg might have a prospective client for me to interview next month." Annie doesn't even bother taking off her shoes before she walks into the living room, taking a seat next to me on the couch. Not that it bothers me, but she always takes her shoes off at the door.

"What does that mean?" I lean my elbow on the back of the couch, resting my head in my hand as I stare at Annie. When she's excited, she moves her hands a mile a minute and her smile never fades. My heart stutters just taking her in.

"Well our contract ends in two months, and I'm going to need money in order to live in a new apartment." She's looking at me like it's obvious. Her jaw is slightly open and she shakes her head quickly a few times. "That is, if Greg decides to hire me full time."

"You can stay here if you need to. Longer, I mean." Why did I offer that? And why am I feeling my chest tighten with rage over her mentioning the end of all of this? That's still over two months away. We are barely into the month of October.

Annie purses her lips and narrows her eyebrows. "I don't think that'd be such a great idea..." She trails off at the end.

A moment of silence washes over us. This is ending. We both know it.

"Well, are you ready for our fake date tonight?" I ask, overemphasizing the word fake.

Annie peers over at me and nods. "Mhm, we can leave whenever." The tone of her voice is slightly lower, disappointed almost.

"Okay, I'll go get ready, then we can head out." I push off of the couch to stand. When I turn to face Annie, she's already looking up at me, watching me. A small smirk plays on her lips before she nods and hops up from the couch.

"Alright, Z, let's get ready and go get some ice cream. I'm excited."

I roll my eyes and give Annie a playful shove. She lets out a chuckle, pushing me back. I shake my head and give her one last glance before I walk away and head toward my room.

Small moments with her remind me what it was like to have someone in my life. I forgot what it was like to want someone to laugh at your jokes or to get excited to tell you something happened that day. Being with someone for twelve years is a long time, and I took it for granted. I thought I had forever, but instead it all crumbled in a single evening.

Maybe that's the real reason, deep down, that I told Annie to move in. It's possible I've been craving more human interaction since I've shut myself off to the world. It's been different since she moved in. I figured she'd be in her room most of the time, or simply not here. Instead, she's in the kitchen in the morning, or lounging on the couch in the afternoon, acting as if this is her home too. And because of that, I want it to be her home.

"I'm ready! Hurry up! If we don't get there soon, they may sell out of our ice cream," Annie yells through the door.

"I'm coming, I'm coming," I respond as I fasten the last button on my shirt.

When I reach the living room, Annie is leaning over the counter and my mind dreams up the ways I can make her moan like she does when taking a bite of ice cream. She's wearing high-waisted jeans that are tight in the ass, but taper off into a more straight leg pant paired with a light pink crop top that hugs her tight. I resist the urge to slap her on the ass when I pass by.

Instead, I walk past her to the front door. My jacket is hanging from the hook to the left, so I lean over to grab that, in case it gets cold. I also grab Annie's white bomber jacket, thinking she might want it.

"Annie," I announce.

She's busy staring at her phone, likely checking in on the latest press about us or some email from Greg.

She glances up at me and nods. Then, she leans off the island, shoving her phone in her back pocket. In a few steps, she's next to me, wearing a smile on her face. If Annie was left on a desert island and could only bring one food item, it would be the ice cream that we are about to consume. She loves it that much.

When we get to the shop, it's the same routine. We see Liam, and he and Annie spend ten minutes catching up on his week. Okay, maybe not ten minutes, but it's enough time for me to get tired of smiling and nodding after everything they say. I try my best to pretend to be engaged in the conversation when I'm actually just staring at Annie the entire time.

I've never been around someone who brings out joy in others like Annie does. Whenever she starts a conversation with someone, her smile and enthusiasm is enough to cause the person she's talking to to smile. It's contagious. She radiates happiness and everyone around her feeds off of it. She cares what others have to say and goes out of her way to show them. Annie makes them feel heard. Even if it's Liam updating her on his coin collection.

We opt for a single cup this time, two spoons. Normally we sit across from one another, but this time Annie slides in the booth next to me.

"What are you doing?" I peer at her out of the corner of my eyes.

Annie snuggles in further. Her knee brushes against mine. She moves her right hand to rest on my leg.

"Switching it up." She shrugs.

My eyes dart to my leg. The weight of her hand is like a massive brick, the warmth of her touch spreading up my thigh making it impossible to think of anything appropriate for a family ice cream shop. What are our rules? Are we still sticking to them? *Fuck*.

The sound of Annie moaning enters my ears like a fucking symphony. I try to even my breaths, but they get deeper by the minute.

"Can you not?" I twist my head to the left, giving Annie my best glare to match my stern tone.

"Do what?" The flirtatious notes in her voice are followed not breaking eye contact as a spoonful of ice cream enters her mouth and exits in a leisurely manner.

"You know what…" I mutter, redirecting my attention back to her hand that hasn't moved from my thigh.

Inch by inch, her hand trails farther up my leg. Just when she's about to touch my dick, the pressure disappears as she moves it to her chin.

"You know, I've lived here for five years and this is the most time I've spent at the beach," Annie says.

She's looking at the waves out the window to my right. A sigh escapes her lips, then her eyes close for a moment as she takes her next breath. My eyes drift to her chest, watching as it expands and contracts. My breath mimicking hers.

"Why haven't you been here?" I ask, curious to know her answer.

"I just haven't had the time. I've been so focused on my job, my career, giving all my time and energy to the firm that I rarely make it out here. Plus, it's always better when you're with someone, you know? Someone to share the memory with."

The sounds of the waves fill the silence. I know exactly how she feels, it's a similar reason why I haven't been to the beach. I haven't had someone I wanted to share memories with, past and present.

"Why don't you like the beach?" Annie's voice drags my gaze to meet hers.

"I never said I didn't like the beach."

Annie picks her head off her hand, twisting toward me just enough for her knee to touch mine again.

Her eyes flutter, moments pass as she contemplates what to say next. "Why can't you tell me one honest thing?"

"Why would I do that?"

"Why would you—" Annie sighs again, but this time it's exaggerated and loud. "I can't with you."

Annie scoots out of the booth, turning toward the table to grab our trash. On her way toward the door, she turns back to me and leans to one side, popping her hip and resting her hand for added sass.

"Coming, Z?"

With a shrug, I follow Annie out of the ice cream shop and as soon as the door closes behind us, my hand interlaces with hers.

Out of the corner of my eye, I can see Annie glancing at me, surprised by my gesture. If she were to ask, I'd tell her it was for the cameras. Nothing more. She doesn't need to know that when she stopped touching me and walked away, my chest sank with an emotion I haven't felt in a long time. Longing. A burning ache to pull her back toward me.

We walk in step around the shop and onto the beach, letting our feet sink in the sand, the whooshing of the waves calming my nerves.

I turn my head to the left to look at Annie to find that she's already looking up at me with a small, apologetic smile on her face. The innocence of her gesture goes straight to my heart.

"You were right." I break the silence.

"Hm? About what?"

She's going to make me spell it out for her.

"I don't like the beach."

Annie begins to respond, but I cut her off.

"But, I don't want to talk about it," I say.

"Before us, when was the last time you were here?"

Letting this one question slide, I respond with, "A year ago."

Annie hums as we walk down the beach, politely smiling and nodding at any person we pass. A few photographers take photos, probably in hopes of posting yet another article about our relationship.

"Well, what do you want to do now?" Annie asks.

Honestly? With her hand in mine, I can't stop replaying our kiss from the maze. Her small touches along my back, the taste of her lips, the smell of a fucking bakery radiating from her body.

"Why are you blushing?" Annie prompts me with another question.

Instinctively, my free hand flies to my cheek, and I give Annie a side-eye.

"I'm not blushing."

"Hm, must be the heat."

"Must be," I drawl.

"Do you want to go home?"

"And do what?" I ask, turning us around to walk back toward the car.

"We can do anything you want."

"Anything?" I tease.

Annie rolls her eyes. Unexpectedly, she lets go of my hand, gives me a playful shove, then starts running away.

Running. Not walking fast. Not jogging. Fucking running, right next to the water. Her hair flows behind her and she has the biggest grin on her face every time she peers back to see if I'm still just standing there. So, what do I do?

I chase after her.

19
ANNIE

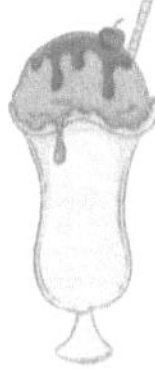

THE MOMENT I STARTED running away from Zayn, I knew it'd lead to trouble. I just knew. Which is why, the moment I feel sand kick up in my direction, I don't have to look back to know he's chasing me.

"Annie, stop," Zayn yells over the sound of the crashing waves.

"Make me," I yell back, twisting my head to wink in his direction.

I continue running, my laughs blending with the sounds of the beach. It only takes Zayn a few more strides before he catches up with me.

His arms wrap around my waist and he pulls, twisting us around in a circle as our momentum slows. Laughter escapes both of us, the feeling of bliss pouring out as my feet touch the soft sand.

"I told you to stop." Zayn's breath is warm against my skin, sending shivers down my spine, even in this summer heat.

I twist around in his arms until my chest faces his. Looking up, I can see the specks of green in his hazel eyes and the soft lines on either side of his mouth. A smile rests on his face. It's a look I haven't had the pleasure of seeing so far.

"You're a mystery, Mr. Barnes." I instinctively wrap my arms around his waist, feeling him tense under my touch.

"You're..." Zayn hesitates, pulling me closer to him until my head meets his chest and his head rests on top of mine.

"I'm what?" I try to pull away, but it only encourages him to hold me closer.

Finally, after what feels like a million hours passes, he lets go of me and takes a step back. My arms fall back at my side.

"You're more than what I originally thought." And with that, he grabs my hand and starts walking us toward the parking lot.

"And that was?"

"I thought you were a people pleaser."

I chuckle. "Yes, and?"

"And I thought you smiled too much, which isn't a bad thing. You're just the opposite of me." He explains, shrugging as he drags me toward the car.

"You mean I'm not grumpy? Or frown all the time? Or storm out of rooms? Or—"

"Yes, but you definitely are something else," Zayn interrupts, glaring at me, squeezing my hand a little tighter. The urge to say fuck it grows and grows with each tense touch, and I'm having a hard time keeping my hands to myself.

"Care to elaborate?"

"Not at this moment," Zayn responds, reaching for the handle to the car door to let me in. "Get in the car."

"What happens if I don't?" I tease.

"Annie..." Zayn pleads.

I pout for a moment, but then decide to appease him.

"Fine, fine."

After getting in the car, I take a deep breath to center myself. Every time I'm near Zayn, I can't stop thinking about our kiss. Is it terrible of me to want to do it again? It's mutually beneficial, after all, and at this point, our rules are basically non-existent.

The entire car ride home, I catch Zayn stealing glances at me without him realizing I'm paying attention. Every red light. Every stop sign. Every opportunity that he can take his eyes off the road, his gaze lands on me. And when I look in his direction, it's as if he senses he's about to be caught because his head snaps forward and a light shade of red grazes his cheeks.

When we finally reach his apartment, he turns off the car but doesn't move. Both hands stay on the steering wheel, his knuckles turning white from his grip.

"Zayn, what—"

"I don't know if I'm going to be able to keep my hands off of you when we get inside, and I'm not sure what our rules are." His chest rises and falls at a rapid pace as he keeps his attention on the wall in front of us.

"So don't. Fuck the rules."

I reach my hand across the console, placing it on his thigh like I did at the ice cream shop. Starting above his knee, I inch my hand up his leg, stopping when I get to his groin. Zayn allows his chin to drop to his chest. His eyes close as if trying to maintain the little bit of restraint he has left.

There's no going back at this point. I've laid all my cards on the table. I move my hand again, this time reaching his length. A hiss escapes Zayn's lips as I rub him over his jeans.

"Fuck, Annie. You've hardly touched me and I'm close. Do you see what you're doing to me?" Zayn says as he throws his head back and lets out a groan. "Do you see how much you affect me?"

Barely a minute later, the ringing of my phone startles me, and I jerk my hand away from his pants. Zayn straightens his torso while running a hand through his hair. I dig in my bag, trying to find my phone amid various pens, a notebook, my wallet, and other random items.

"You should answer it," Zayn prompts, gesturing to my phone.

A thin-lipped smile and a small nod is all I can muster in response. I hit accept on the screen and step out of the car. Zayn and I walk to the door together, heading toward the elevator.

"Hi, Marce," I say, trying not to sound like I was just rubbing my fake boyfriend's dick in a public parking lot.

"Anns! What are you up to? Want to come over tonight? Give yourself a break from Mr. Grumps?" Marcy asks. The sound of pans clashing resonates through the phone, indicating that it's nearly dinner time.

"I, uh—" Out of the corner of my eye, I can see Zayn watching me as we ride up the elevator. He has his bottom lip tucked under his teeth, which just adds to my pent-up sexual frustration. "I'm actually busy tonight." Taking this window of opportunity, I glance at Zayn and although he's shifted his gaze to his feet, there's a small smile on his face and that alone sends a tornado of butterflies through my stomach.

"Busy? Doing what? What can you—oh, I see, you're planning on fucking Zayn." Marcy's loud voice echoes from my phone speaker to the four walls of the elevator.

"Marcy Lynn," I whisper-yell, knowing Zayn heard every word. How do I know? Well, as soon Marcy said those words, the elevator dinged, and when I looked over at Zayn, his eyes were wide and his cheeks were flushed. Incredible timing.

"I'm just being a good best friend and calling it as I see it. Be safe. Love you. Okay, bye!"

Marcy immediately hangs up, leaving me in the entrance of the apartment unsure of what to do. We had a moment in the car, but what if it's gone now? What if we snapped back to reality and Zayn realized he doesn't want me like that? Or that we shouldn't cross the line?

The door closes behind me as I try to shake the thought from my head. My stomach feels like a giant pit just opened and I'm fidgeting, moving my hands, blinking too much, staring at the ground. I'm not feeling like myself: confident, happy, sure of the situation that I'm in. Not knowing if Zayn is reciprocating how I feel has me unsure if my advances were too much.

With caution, I turn to Zayn, expecting him to be growling in my direction, back to his grumpy self. Instead, he's staring at the ground, avoiding eye contact. I knew I went too far.

"I'll just be in my room for the night, you don't have to worry about me," I say, taking a step toward the hallway.

"Annie, wait."

I pause, but I don't turn around. I can't. I'm doing everything I can to hold back tears right now after embarrassing myself.

"It's fine, Zayn. I get it."

"Get what?"

I sigh. "I know this is all fake, okay? I let my emotions get ahead of me. I went too far."

Zayn's hand wraps around my wrist. He tugs, just a little, to try to get me to turn around. I comply, not wanting this situation to escalate. But I keep my eyes on the floor.

He keeps pulling me toward him until his other hand finds my waist.

"Annie, look at me," Zayn commands, and my knees feel like jello from the deep tone.

I lift my eyes, then lower them. Then lift again, as Zayn starts moving me, spinning us until I feel the hardness of the door on my back. His hands trail from my waist to either wrist, holding on to them with a gentle grip. Slowly, he moves my hands toward the ceiling, stopping when they are both above my head.

"Look at me," Zayn repeats, softer this time. His voice is almost a plea and a gentle reminder that this version of Zayn is one that I've met briefly and have been hoping to meet again.

My cheeks are rosy. Heat radiates my entire body from his touch, his stare, his presence. I meet his gaze, the tears in my eyes no longer wanting to escape. My embarrassment fades until all that is left is my feelings for Zayn. My feelings, confusing as they may be, are real.

"Now, answer me this..." Zayn uses his knee to wedge in between mine, encouraging them to part. He then shifts his body, flushing his chest against mine as he leans closer to my face. Hovering next to my ear, his breath sends shivers down my spine as he whispers, "Does this feel fake to you?"

"I'm not sure," I mutter.

"Not sure? We can't be having that," Zayn whispers. He removes his hands from my wrists and begins slowly moving them down my arms, causing goosebumps to follow in his trail.

I adjust my hands, wanting to touch him.

"Keep them there," Zayn says in a low growl.

My hands freeze, and for a moment I'm in my head, wondering what's about to happen. Here I am, with a man that I hardly know, and I'm pinned to a door. My chest rises and falls at a rapid pace as Zayn cruelly takes his time bringing his hands down my body.

His hands pause at the button of my jeans. "This doesn't mean I like you."

"Good, because I don't like you either. I'm just using you for your body," I tease back, knowing full well it's a lie.

A chuckle escapes his lip at the same time as he begins sliding my jeans over my hips and pushing them down my body.

"I'm okay with that, as long as you let me use yours." He travels down my body now, peppering soft kisses on my chest, my torso, my hip. "You drive me insane," Zayn admits in a whisper against my skin. "What was I before you?"

"Sane. Ten times more grumpy. Left alone with the company of your hand," I reply, letting amusement and sarcasm lace my tone.

More chuckles as he pulls my underwear down, leaving the lower half of my body bare.

"I'm going to make you feel good and then maybe you'll be nice to me. I'm not grumpy now, am I?" Zayn inquires, resting the palm of his hand above my most sensitive area, causing me to squirm. "Patience, Annie, all you have to do is ask nicely."

"Please, Zayn," I practically beg, needing him to touch me. To feel something other than his breath. To know that he wants this as bad as I do. That the weeks leading up to this means something. That all of our small interactions weren't just for show.

I'm rewarded with a small movement to his palm, allowing his thumb to rest on my clit, pausing for me to ask again.

"Are you going to make me beg for it?" I ask.

"I'm debating, although I'm already on my knees and that feels like it would be a waste of effort on your part."

"I'm starting to wonder if you know what you're doing down—oh," I gasp as Zayn brings his mouth to where his finger was.

"What was that?" Zayn says in between kissing me where I need it most.

My hands fall down and land on his shoulders, but he doesn't comment on them. Not when he's working on giving me the pleasure my body has been aching for.

Zayn's hands wrap under each leg, prompting me to wrap them around his shoulders. If anyone else pinned me against a wall, begging to go down on me, I would have wanted to be more comfortable, go to a bed or a couch or a counter, but for some reason, Zayn's touch forces me to ignore all rationality, leaving only thoughts about him circling around my brain.

More, more, more. Like a chant, my thoughts echo in my head. My hands tug at his hair, partly for balance but also to convey the passion I'm feeling for him at this moment. Within seconds, I'm falling apart, my breathing ragged from the exhilaration of being with someone that should be forbidden. But also that exact same someone bringing down every last barrier, who sees the masks I wear to maintain my positive appearance.

Zayn, although grumpy in nature and unapproachable, has a soft side to him. One that I've only seen a few times, either through passings inside our home or small glances while we are on our dates.

"I'm close," I whisper, tugging harder at his hair as I focus on the rising pressure within me.

Zayn quickens his pace, pulling the hand that was stabilizing me away from my thigh and inserting two fingers into my folds, only causing me to arch my back at the sudden pressure. My legs shake both at the pressure Zayn's applying and the fact that my feet have not touched the ground since he started.

I gasp his name as I finish, my fingers loosening in his hair. Zayn removes his fingers and his mouth leaves me, his thumb replacing where his tongue was a moment ago moving in slow circles as I come down.

Slowly, using his hands, he helps my legs lower to the ground. Once I'm safely planted, Zayn stands up, moving his hand to grasp my neck toward him until our mouths clash. We kiss in a fury, reveling in what just happened and the line we just crossed.

I move my hand down his torso until I land on his cock.

"No," Zayn mutters. "This was for you. I'm okay."

"You don't feel okay."

His lips meet mine again. One of his hands grabs mine and moves it, interlacing our fingers.

Zayn moves his head backward, his gaze never wavering from mine. "Let's watch a movie."

"A movie? That's what you're thinking about right now?" I glance down to the ground, my lower half still exposed.

"I'm thinking about you, if you must know, and I'm not trying to cross too many lines tonight. One is enough."

"What are we doing, Zayn?"

"Hm?" Zayn mutters, his eyes tracking my hands as I pull up my pants. I gesture between us with my hands.

"This. This complicates things. I need to know what this means to you." What I mean to him.

"I...I just want to take advantage of the time we have. Explore whatever is between us. Make you feel good..." Zayn's lips meet mine again. "More than once, if I have the choice."

"I don't see why not. What harm can having a little fun for a few months have? We have until December after all..." I say, knowing the looming deadline of our relationship is still a little while away.

"Exactly." Zayn wraps his arms around me. "We don't have to label this. It can be what we want it to be. Then, come contract end, we end too. No hard feelings."

Zayn pulls me closer to him. No hard feelings? I don't know if I can promise that, but I nod my head into his chest anyway. I'm fairly certain I'm fucked and this isn't going to end well, but I'd rather spend time with Zayn and grow to love him than ignore the pull between us and go back to what we were.

20
ANNIE

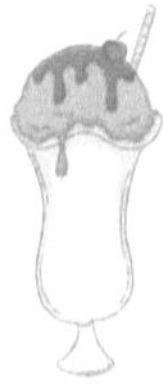

"He did what?" Marcy yells at me as we sit on her couch.

"Don't make me repeat it," I say, throwing my head into my palms. Last night was... different. Zayn and I watched a movie and snuggled on the couch like we were a real couple. Not fake. Not doing it for someone else or for cameras. It was just us. We ended up falling asleep, then woke up this morning to Logan knocking on our front door because Zayn was late for their meeting to talk strategy about an upcoming event.

"And you didn't sleep together?" Marcy gives me her best side-eye.

"No, no. He had to go and be selfless. The complete opposite of what he's supposed to be. I'm not supposed to like him, Marce. It's all fucked up now."

"What's wrong with having a little fun?" Marcy raises her eyebrows.

"Having fun with a deadline isn't fun." I'm starting to wonder if I want this to end at all.

"Well no, if you think about all the negatives, you won't think it's fun. But, from my point of view, you two like each other enough to not only live together and fake date, but to also have multiple intimate moments."

"I don't know if I'd call them intimate," I mumble, pulling out my phone. Greg texted and asked me to pick up some coffee on the way to the office this afternoon.

"I know you have to go soon, but why don't we focus on the positives. I only know Zayn as the douchebag at work, always so grumpy and never talking to anyone, so tell me what you like about him," Marcy prompts.

"You're supposed to be on my side. Team no-Zayn. I shouldn't be thinking about the things I like about him. It's only going to make me want him more." I stand and move toward the front door to gather my things to head to work.

"That's not a bad thing, you know. You should like him a little, give into the temptation, make the most of your time with him. So, come on. Let's hear it."

A sigh escapes my lips and my eyes shut from the weight of what I'm starting to feel for Zayn. It doesn't help that I can't avoid him and only see him for publicity. Every morning, we cross paths in the kitchen, grabbing coffee and awkwardly shuffling around one another. Every evening, the same dance occurs. Except, as the weeks pass, it's getting less awkward. Now my heart stutters when I know I'll see him.

"I, uhm, like that he never is shy around me," I admit.

"What do you mean?" Marcy asks.

"Well, he pushes me to the point where I snap at him. He's the only person that I do that with, outside of you and Cass. It's like he's allowing me to be myself, just by being *him*."

"Yeah, I can see that. You do tend to put up walls to people you just meet."

"Yeah, I know," I say. "And also, he's surprisingly fun. Like, I know he has this grumpy shell and all, but when I get him to laugh or smile... I don't know. It feels like I won the lottery." I'm getting bashful now, my cheeks warming in embarrassment from opening my heart to Marcy.

"Oof, Anns, I don't think it's possible to be team no-Zayn because you're down bad for him. And before you say anything, it's not a bad thing. You, my friend, are allowed to have fun. Your job sucks anyway, might as well make the most out of it."

Marcy might have a point.

"You always know the right things to say. Just promise you'll be here when my heart breaks at the end of it all." I grimace, looking at Marcy with a sheepish smile on my face.

"I'll have ice cream and movies ready to go." Marcy grins.

"I'd be lost without you."

"I know."

She walks toward the door, holding it open for me. "Now, go on, I know if you're late you'll never hear the end of it."

She's right.

"True, true. I'll text you later."

"You better." Marcy closes the door after I walk out.

After stopping at Flora, which thankfully had a blueberry muffin, I feel better. My chest is lighter, my head doesn't pound from the constant struggle to keep thoughts of Zayn out, and I'm hoping that by the time I get home tonight, I'll know how to approach him.

We still haven't talked about his breakup that happened a year ago, nor have I told him what happened with me and Dan.

I'm content to focus on what's happening currently between us while still remembering that everything will end. We are using each other to get to the next level of our careers, and choosing to have a little fun. That's it. Right? Why does thinking that make my heart ache and my stomach feel uneasy?

Luckily, the office gives me other things to occupy my brain than endless thoughts about my not-love life.

I march into the main conference room and set Greg's coffee in front of him as he types away on his computer, humming a song to himself. James enters a few minutes later. They hand a clipboard to Greg, mouth to me that we will talk after, then leave the room.

A sigh escapes Greg, and he shuts his laptop. "Ah, Annie, thank you." He grabs the coffee I set next to him ten minutes ago, brings it up to his mouth, and takes a sip.

"Of course." I force my lips to form a smile that resembles my normal attitude. "What did you want to talk about today?"

"Oh, right, let me look at my notes." Greg puts the coffee back down and flips through his notebook for a few moments. He could have included the reason for this meeting in his message, or on the calendar invite, but that wouldn't be very Greg-like.

"Ah, here we go." Greg chuckles to himself, proud of his findings. "I have a lead for a future client should everything go well, but let's talk about the Rising Star Gala first."

I nod for him to continue, clicking my pen and opening my notebook to write down important details.

"This gala acts as the first event where Zayn is speaking in front of a crowd." Greg tells me details I already know because I'm the one that landed him that speaking spot, but I bite my tongue. "You'll not only be Zayn's date, but you'll be representing this firm in a more public eye than you have before. Any future client will be watching any posted interviews, so be sure to keep a tight lip."

"I understand." Play the doting girlfriend, make sure Zayn talks to the right people. Easy enough.

"Great, I knew you would. And no need to worry about what future clients will think, with you playing both roles and all. To everyone else, your relationship is as real as it gets." Greg dons a smile, and I don't know where all of this anger is coming from, but him downplaying my capabilities makes me want to throw my notepad at his head. "And for the future client, it would require you to relocate to New York, to our other office."

"New York?" I parrot, confused why the client would be located in New York. Is Greg trying to get rid of me? Are there really no other celebrities here that need PR help? I doubt it. I'm stunned. Confused. Angry. Sad. Most of all, I'm *terrified*.

Everything with Zayn is going great, or at least is on the path to being something good. And now? With the possibility of having to move across the country? Well, then there's no way things with Zayn can be anything more than temporary.

"Yes, would that be a problem?" Greg asks, shaking me from my initial shock. It's as if he's stunned at the possibility that I might not want to move to New York. When have I ever given this man the thought that I might want to relocate?

"Well, respectfully, I've never thought about moving to New York," I say, hoping my tone comes across as polite.

"You should, as that might be the only client that would fit your..." Greg pauses like he's unsure what word to use to describe me. "Capabilities and all." I'm at a loss for words, so I simply nod again and try my best to form a smile, disappointed when all I can muster is a thin-lipped version.

"Great, well, have fun at the gala and I'll keep you up to date if we have any local clients that I feel would be good for you, assuming things with Zayn continue the way they are." Greg stands, gathers his items, and leaves before I'm able to mutter a response.

Fine by me. I don't have anything to say anyway. If he wants to push me out after I have a successful campaign with Zayn, because it *will* be successful, then fine. I'll do what I always do, smile my way through it.

"Sweetie, are you okay?" James scares the shit out of me when I enter my office a few minutes later.

My hand slams to my chest and I almost drop my coffee.

"I was before you almost made me give myself a third-degree burn," I exasperate, strolling over to my desk. "Everything is great." I smile, knowing it's a mask to hide the fact that all I want to do is curl up in a ball and cry.

"You know you don't have to do that." James walks over to my desk, taking a seat in the only other free chair in the room. "You don't have to hide yourself from me."

"I know," I mumble, half to myself, half to the floor.

"Why don't you tell me a little bit about what's going on? Is it Zayn? Do I need to pay him a visit?" James tries to furrow their brows together to show me they are serious, but I just end up giggling.

"It is, but not for the reason you think." I glance at them to catch their reaction, grimacing when I realize I'm talking about my feelings with someone who isn't my sister or my best friend. I've gotten so used to keeping everything to myself that even though James has turned into a good friend of mine (and is eternally grateful to me for finding their soulmate), I've never been the type of friend to offload my problems on someone else. I don't need someone else telling me terrible things about myself.

"Well you did move in with the guy..."

I begin to roll my eyes but catch myself, not wanting to show my attitude. "I did, yes, but it started with good intentions."

"And now?"

"Well, James, to be honest, I'm a bit fucked." I squint my eyes and shrug.

James' jaw drops. "Annie, I think that is the first time I've heard you cuss in the three years I've known you."

I roll my eyes for real this time, letting more of me out. The side of me that only certain people get to see, Zayn being the most recent. "Get used to it because I need advice. Greg told me I might have to move to New York for my next client, and I don't know what to do about my boyf—Zayn."

"Oh, shit. That sucks, Annie. I'll keep my ear out for any other opportunities," James says, and I know they mean it. They'd gossip with Nancy if I asked them to. "As for your *boyfriend,* do you like him?"

I refrain from reacting to James picking up on how I almost called Zayn my boyfriend, my *real* boyfriend, and nod instead.

"And does he like you?"

My mind flashes to last night. I nod again.

"Then I don't see the problem here. Just have some fun! What's the harm in that?"

Why does James have to say the same thing Marcy said? It would be nice to have one person tell me that I'm making a big mistake, to knock some sense into me, but I'd be lying if I said I wasn't glad people are rooting for us.

"I suppose you're right," I admit. It's not like I'm going to be able to avoid Zayn for the next couple months. And I'm not going to ignore his advances, if he even still wants to have me in that way.

"So, what's the plan?" James asks.

I ponder for a moment, tapping my feet together under my desk. "Have fun for a few months and try to avoid heartbreak when it ends." I grin.

"Not a fail-safe plan, but I think you'll be happy where it leads. Regardless if you two stay together or part amicably."

"I hope you're right. Otherwise, I'll be sending you my therapy bill."

James chuckles. "I'd expect nothing less."

After James leaves, I'm heads down all day. I research topics for the gala this weekend, try to find a dress (when did they get so expensive?), and text Zayn about dinner. He texted me a little while ago, asking if I had plans, and then told me he's cooking dinner. I said no, even though I could have lied and went to Marcy's. But I want to see Zayn. I haven't seen him all day and… I miss him. Actually miss him.

Thoughts swirl in my head about New York and the chance that I'll have to move away from my sister, my best friend, and the guy I'm starting to fall for. When all the pieces of my life are starting to come together, this is when a tornado decides to rip through and destroy it all.

If I didn't move to New York, I could stay here and see what happens with Zayn. Maybe we wouldn't end it, maybe we'd dissolve the end date and decide to date for real.

But also, I'd be starting over with my career. I wouldn't have a solid place to land since no one wants a publicist with no solo client experience, and I'm not sure James could even be a reference for me if I wanted to find a different role.

I'm going to have to choose Zayn or my career, and at this moment, I'm not sure what I'm going to do.

21
ANNIE

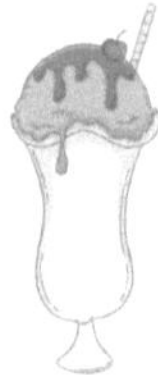

WHEN I ENTER THE hallway outside the apartment, I smell something burning. Then, I hear a grumbled string of cuss words from the man inside.

"Zayn?" I open the door and find him waving a towel over a burning casserole dish. He doesn't turn around.

When I reach him, I place a hand on his shoulder.

He tenses at my touch before his eyes meet mine and his posture softens. He must not have been expecting me home yet. His cheeks are flushed red—from embarrassment, maybe? Or from the heat of the stove?

"Annie, I, uhh—" Zayn ping pongs his gaze between the stove and me. "I…" He lets out a loud sigh.

"Hey, it's okay. We can order in." I try to make it better, try to show that I wasn't expecting anything.

"I wanted this to be perf—" Zayn pauses. He rakes his hand through his hair as he looks to the floor. "I wanted this to be perfect."

"Who are you and what have you done with Zayn?" I tease.

He chuckles and playfully pushes at my shoulder. "Shut up. I should punish you for that comment." His tongue swipes against his lower lip.

"If you think I deserve it." My heart flutters at the possibility.

His eyes darken, pupils widening at my advance. "Annie."

"Zayn."

"Annie."

"Zayn."

"Stop," he commands.

"Make me."

Zayn's eyebrows narrow. He releases a low grumble with each exhale.

"Do you need me to make the first move?" I twirl a stand of my hair between two fingers.

"I don't need you to fucking do anything."

"You're extra grouchy tonight."

Two steps later, I'm pushed against the island. Hard. Zayn's hands block me in.

My neck instinctively tilts to the right as he slides his mouth up my throat.

"You want to know why I'm extra grouchy tonight?" Zayn's lips pepper kisses on my neck, slowly, passionately, deliberately. I moan as he switches from the left to the right side. "I wanted to do something nice. For you. I never want to do anything nice. I'm selfish. Fuck. And you. You, Annie. You just... get under my skin. I can't. Resist. You."

My eyes roll to the back of my head. A soft sound, barely a moan, leaves my lips. "Don't start what you can't finish."

"Is that a challenge?" Zayn's stubble grazes my neck, my chin, and it's too much. My legs tremble and I grasp at his shirt, trying to close the remaining gaps between us.

"I need you," I whisper into his ear, nibbling on the bottom before I pull away.

"We need to eat dinner," Zayn counters, still kissing me everywhere except the places I ache for him the most.

"Dinner can wait." I'm about to get on my knees and beg, *beg*, him to keep going. After yesterday, he's all I've been able to think about. I'm not going to tell him that though; that's a secret for me.

"I had a special night planned, Annie."

Zayn pulls back. His doe eyes stare at me with a secret message hidden in them that I can't quite understand.

"This is important to you." I take a guess.

He nods.

"Alright, Z. Your plans first, then mine."

I expect him to say something, or maybe cancel tonight, realizing we are getting too close. But he doesn't.

"It's a date."

22
ZAYN

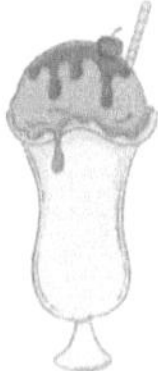

"So, THINGS ARE GOING well?" Ed asks, pacing circles in the trailer. It's been busy at the studio, and although I've been here three days a week to help actors run lines, Ed hasn't had time to check in.

"I think so," I admit.

After I finally convinced Annie to eat dinner last night, we spent the rest of the night doing things you typically wouldn't do with the person you know is only around you temporarily. The person you shouldn't let get under your skin.

Whatever I do, I can't stop thinking about Annie. It doesn't help that she slept in my bed. It's all too much. Her touch. Her smell. Her fucking smile. *Her.*

"Looks like you're thinking pretty hard."

I look at Ed, scrunching my brows. He doesn't need to read my mind to see that my mood has improved, and I haven't decided if that's a good or a bad thing.

Ed's reason for not offering me the trilogy right off the bat is the whole reason Annie is even in my life.

"I just have a lot on my mind. Any news on the movie?" The couch catches me as I lean back, bracing myself for a negative response.

"Not the news you're wanting."

I knew it.

"But keep doing what you're doing and I can promise you that it'll all work out. You have the gala this weekend, where you'll be speaking. Do that well, talk about your acting, show me you still want this."

A nod is all I can muster. I don't think I have the right to be disappointed or angry, it's just that I was hoping Ed would have said something positive by now. He knows I'm not auditioning for other roles right now, that I'm banking on this trilogy working out. I'm keeping it my main priority.

I've been trying, genuinely fucking trying, to be better. The tabloids show me in a positive light, I've been smiling in photos, and I haven't complained once about attending these galas. Annie even made us go to a movie premiere, and a restaurant opening, and some other charity event to show the media that I'm out there trying to make a difference.

It's not good enough. Not yet. But it will be if I have anything to say about it. I'm not going to fuck this up because that would also mean I fuck up Annie's career, and I care about her. Too much. And that's terrifying.

As soon as Ed leaves, I take the time to call Kiley. I've been avoiding her calls, her requests to come over and hang out with

Annie and me. I hate lying to her. She deserves to know that our relationship is fake and has a set end date. But whenever I'm about to bring it up, I chicken out. The way she reacted to the news of Marissa leaving makes me want to protect her from any heartbreak.

"Z, hi, I was starting to think you were ignoring me." Kiley greets me with a sassy tone.

"I'm not ignoring you, just busy. You know," I reply.

"Yeah, must be, if you don't want to hang out with your only sister. I want to see Annie and you."

"I know Kiki, I just don't know when we'd make that work. She's also busy." Busy with me, that is. My mind flashes to pinning her against the counter last night and that is the last thing I need to be thinking about right now.

"What about tonight?"

"Tonight?" All the other times that she asked about hanging out, it's been over text. I haven't had to audibly tell her no. Little siblings have a way to be persistent and get their way, always.

"Yes, tonight, you can pick me up."

"I could send a car, I suppose." I give in. One night can't hurt, can it?

"I knew you'd say yes."

If I had to guess, Kiley is beaming right now, trying to resist the urge to bounce with excitement.

"You're hard to say no to. Plus, Annie would love to see you." I think. I hope so.

"Yay, great. Well, text me what time to be ready and I'll see you later Z, love you."

"Love you too, Kiki."

When the line goes silent, I move the phone away from my ear and open my messages. Knowing Annie would like to be prepared, I send her a text and let her know I'll order carry out. The bubbles showing she's typing immediately dance across the screen, then disappear, then return, then disappear, then she finally sends me a smiley face and a heart emoji.

My own heart stutters at the small, yet notable, notion. Does it mean something? Maybe. Maybe not. Either way, the grin that I can't hold back any longer comes out in full force.

That's the moment I know I'm truly fucked.

Liking Annie is as easy as waking up in the morning. The way her body reacts to my touch should be a crime, a fucking crime. No two people should mold together the way we do, our banter feeding off each other, only fueling the fire between us.

A knock on my trailer door tears me away from my dangerous thoughts, and I've never been more thankful. Although opening the door to Emmett is a surprise.

"Oh, hey man," I greet awkwardly, waving a hand even though he's on the other side of the threshold.

"Mind if I come in?" His tone doesn't even hint at the reason for this visit, so I'm not sure what to think. He is Annie's brother-in-law, after all.

"Sure, yeah, sure." I step back and to the left, getting out of the way for Emmett to come in. "What's up?"

"I, uh, do you mind if I take a seat? This is going to be awkward already, and I'd rather not have to stand here while I do it."

I nod for him to move to the couch, but instead of sitting next to him, I sit on a stool near the kitchen.

"I know we haven't talked much lately, even though we share an agent, and I didn't come here on Cassie's behalf, but I just wanted to talk to you and try to understand what's going on between you and Annie. Even though you've been ignoring me, I still want to make sure everything is okay."

"Nothing's going on between us," I say carefully. I desperately wish I had a drink or something to fidget with. My nerves are doing all they can to escape my body.

"Right, just like nothing was going on between Cassie and me when she started working here." Emmett dips his head, clearly seeing through my bullshit. "We were also just friends for a while before it turned into more."

"It's—" I drop my gaze to the floor, not wanting my emotions to show like oil on water. "It's complicated."

"I'm not here to threaten you, but I will say that if you need someone to talk to, I'm here. You don't have to keep all this to yourself. I know what happened a year ago couldn't have been easy. The guys miss you at lunch."

"I don't need anyone. Did Annie tell you I needed someone?" I snap, knowing full well that it's no longer true. There was once a time where I wouldn't have even let Emmett into the trailer. I wouldn't have even opened the door. I would have never let someone enter my life and play my heart like a fiddle, to risk it breaking again. But here I am, in so fucking over my head.

"Clearly you're doing so well on your own. And no, Annie didn't. But I see the way you're changing and Cassie has noticed the change in Annie, so I'm just trying to be a friend," Emmett snaps back.

"Well, thanks, but I've got it covered. Is that all you needed? I have somewhere I need to be."

I hate the look in Emmett's eyes. They started full of hope and offering of a friendship, yet now they are lifeless, unforgiving. I know that because it's what I see when I look into the mirror every morning. I recognize the look of disappointment.

"Yeah, that's all." Emmett tosses me one last look, which has now turned into pity, and he's out the door a moment later.

I gather my bag, sling it over one shoulder, and shoot Annie a text before I leave. The car I called is already on its way to pick up Kiley, so she should arrive shortly after I do.

When I reach our floor of the apartment building, I know that the smells of vanilla and caramel are coming from our kitchen before opening the door.

"Ah, Zayn, you're home." Annie's smile greets me from across the room as she places cookies onto a tray. "I thought I'd make us a treat since Kiley will be over tonight, and I haven't had a lot of time to bake recently. I'm excited to see her."

As if Annie could weave herself any deeper into my life, she goes and bakes because my sister is coming over. I try my best to not smile, to stop giving into whatever is going on between us. The best I can do to avoid that is to avoid her eyes and make some gruff noise to know I heard her.

I walk straight to my room, but she follows me. After last night, giving her the cold shoulder isn't what I want, but it's what I need to do. I'm getting too fucking attached. If Emmett has to come to my trailer to talk to me about Annie, that means she's getting attached too. Something neither of us can afford.

"Is everything okay?" Annie stays at my door, one foot crossed over the other, and leans her body onto the frame. Her bottom lip is tucked, and she won't meet my eyes.

Fuck. What am I doing?

"Yeah, Annie, everything is okay. Come here." I gesture for her to sit next to me.

She saunters over slowly, hands clasped in front of her. "I thought we were past this," she says, sinking next to me. I can tell she tried to sit further away, but her body gravitates toward mine, clashing our legs together.

"Past what?" My eyes meet hers, challenging her to say what's on her mind. Encouraging her to push me, even though I know I should be doing the opposite.

"Past you..." Annie pauses, exhaling before shifting her gaze to her hands that are still clasped in front of her. "Past you hiding from me," she finishes, her voice barely a whisper.

My hand reaches for hers without my brain realizing, weaving its way in between her clasped hands. "Emmett came to visit me today," I mutter.

"He what? Why? I swear I haven't said anything to him." Annie glances at me, searching my face, trying to read my reaction.

"I wouldn't think you would, it just made me realize how deep I'm getting with you."

"Too bad you're not deep *in* me." Her voice is soft, but I hear the playful tone.

"Annie," I growl, letting my emotions show for her, trusting that whatever this thing is that we are doing will fix itself in the end and I'll be able to heal from whatever slashes she takes at my heart.

She lets out a chuckle, and she's lucky we are about to have company, otherwise I would keep my word from last night and punish her, nice and long and hard, for that.

"He just asked me what was going on between us."

"Isn't that a good thing?" Annie grimaces, biting her lip again. "Doesn't that mean the PR is working?"

"It means that I'm getting too close to you," I mumble, retracting my hand from hers.

"No, you don't get to do that now." Annie reaches for my hand, pulling it back. I let her. "We agreed, fun, casual, until December."

"Is this just fun and casual to you, Annie?" I want to push her, to break her down into telling me that she likes me. Even just a little bit.

"It's fun and casual, but it also means a lot to me. You mean a lot to me."

"Be careful Annie, I may think you actually like me."

I'm falling over on the bed before I know it as laughter comes from both of us.

"Well, I hate to break it to you, Zayn, but I think I am starting to like you," Annie says.

"Doesn't that make things with us less casual?" I ask.

Annie shrugs and says, "Maybe."

I reach out and grip her jaw. "Well, if it's any consolation, I kind of like you too."

She leans into my touch and her eyes flutter closed. We stay there for a moment, reveling in the silence after the small confession. I like her a lot more than I let on, but she doesn't need to know that. Right now, I'm content with what we have going on if that means she ends each night by my side in bed.

I stand, reaching out my hand toward Annie, hoping she will take it. "C'mon, Kiley will be here soon."

23

ANNIE

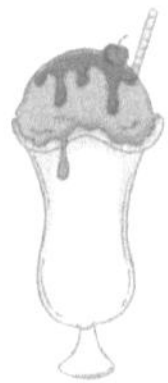

Placing my hand in Zayn's feels too right. I shouldn't feel butterflies in my stomach, or weak in the knees, or hot in my cheeks. It's not supposed to be like this. I can't like him, not after everything. I know he's not his brother, but I still can't let someone in. Not again. Not when my career is finally starting. And I worry that if I were to succumb to the way I feel for him that my career would be put on the back burner and I wouldn't feel the need to make it a priority. I need to make sure I feel stable and secure, even if I bring someone into my life.

I let go of Zayn's hand when a knocking comes from the front door.

"I'll get it," Zayn mumbles as he walks over to let Kiley in.

The door is barely open two inches when she comes barreling in, coming straight for me.

"Annie, I'm so glad to see you. Zayn wouldn't let me come over." Kiley tosses a glare over her shoulder before enveloping me in a hug.

"I never said that," Zayn quips, walking to sit on the couch.

Kiley moves to sit next to him, giving him a side hug as a way of forgiveness. "I know, I know, you're just busy," Kiley says.

I grab the cookies from the kitchen and set them on the coffee table before moving to sit in a chair next to the couch.

"Oh, my gosh. Annie, sit here." Kiley quickly gets up from her spot and points to it, leaving Zayn to just stare at me with raised eyebrows that say "*I told you so.*"

Right, I have to play the doting girlfriend here, as Kiley doesn't know this is fake. Perfect.

"Thanks Ki," I say, plopping next to Zayn. A little too close. Our legs, hips, and shoulders are brushing, but it'd be too obvious if I moved away, so I stay.

Zayn's hand finds mine, intertwining our fingers. If I think about it too much, I'll start overthinking, which is not good. Luckily, Kiley came prepared to chat our ears off.

"So, I went down to that ice cream shop that you two always go to," Kiley says, snatching a cookie off the tray and taking a bite.

"Sunshine Scoops?" I take a sip of my tea, trying to keep my tone intrigued.

"Yeah, they say it's where you two fell in love."

My tea leaves my mouth before I'm able to process what I'm doing. I immediately start coughing, wondering why the universe had me take a drink at the worst time.

"You okay?" Zayn whispers in my ear, and it does not help one bit, the warmth of his breath leaving a tickle along my ear.

I peer at him for a moment and nod before looking back to Kiley, wondering if he's going to say anything. He doesn't. Maybe he's processing the information just like I am.

"Anyway, how is it being Zayn's girlfriend and publicist?" Kiley asks.

"Sometimes I forget, if I'm being honest." I chuckle. "The only time I'm his publicist is when I need to schedule events for him or make sure certain reporters will be around. And so far, it's actually helped that Zayn is with me. The media seems to like that we are together."

"I like that we're together too," Zayn says. He leans into me and presses a kiss to my forehead.

"I still can't get over the fact that you two are together. Does Dan know?"

Where Zayn appears calm and collected, I feel like a stiff board. His hand tightens on mine and helps bring me back to this moment.

"Unless he lives under a rock, then I'm sure he knows. But no, I haven't personally told him."

"Z, you need to tell him."

"We never talk, Kiley." Zayn's hand tenses, and I move my other hand to rest on top, rubbing small circles to smooth his anger. Slowly, his grip loosens.

Kiley doesn't push the issue any further, thankfully.

"Well, Annie, what have you been up to since I saw you last?" Kiley asks.

"Working, and more work," I say with a laugh. "It's pretty much consumed me."

"Well it seems to have landed you in a good spot, I'd say. You must be good at what you do!"

She doesn't know how good it feels to hear that. I'm so used to proving myself to others, to show that I can do the work, and Kiley simply complimenting me based on who my current client is speaks for itself. Yes, it's her brother, but Zayn is also a B-list actor. When he gets this trilogy, it'll put him in A-list territory. He's the type of client that should require someone with years of experience to run his PR strategy, not someone like me, fresh out of their internship.

"Thanks, Kiley. I think I landed in a good spot too." I twist my head to look at Zayn, who's already looking at me, of course, and I smile. I'm thankful for him, truly. He's not only helping heal my past wounds and showing me that I'm good at what I do, but he's also there for me.

"And how are things for you?" I look back at Kiley.

"Oh, I was telling Zayn the other week that my boss is the literal worst, but it's okay. I'm a marketing manager, so I spend a lot of my time with clients and such. So likely similar to you."

"I'm here if you ever need to rant about something." I smile warmly, and I know Zayn is staring at me without having to look at him. Kiley means the world to him, so I know me offering that means something to him.

After an hour, Zayn asks for the tenth time if she's ready for the car. Okay, maybe not the tenth time, but after all the questions, I think he's ready for her to leave.

"Okay, okay, I'll leave you two lovebirds alone," Kiley says while gathering her things. I made sure to put a few cookies in a bag for her to take on the road.

When she pulls me into a hug she whispers, "I know my other brother didn't deserve you, but Zayn does. And you make him happy. Thank you." She doesn't give me time to respond, simply hugs Zayn and leaves.

I stand there, facing the door, shocked. Trying to process what she said, what she thinks is going on. Kiley is already getting attached to this relationship, and it's not even real.

"Annie?" Zayn's voice pulls me out of my thoughts.

"Yeah?" I look at him, knowing that my eyes aren't as bright and my mouth forms a thin line.

"What did she say to you?"

"Oh, it was nothing."

"You look like someone delivered bad news to you. It couldn't have been nothing. Tell me."

"What if I say no?"

"Then I'll ask again later." Zayn is nothing if not persistent.

I sulk over to the couch, letting out an exasperated sigh as I sit down. Zayn follows, sitting next to me, grabbing my hand.

My gaze remains on my lap as I mutter, "She said your brother didn't deserve me, but you do."

For a millisecond his hand tenses, tightening around mine, before he releases the pressure.

"I don't deserve you either." He doesn't say he doesn't want me, or that she's right, but he says this as if we are together, a real couple in love.

"You deserve more than your dick of a brother does." I grimace, realizing how that sounded. "Sorry."

Zayn brings a finger under my chin, tugging my face toward him, begging me to meet his stare. "Don't ever apologize for him."

I try to tug out of his grasp, but instead his fingers hold me tighter, not letting my head detract from his grip.

"I mean it, Princess. Nod if you understand."

I do as he asks, and he lets go immediately. He takes his free hand and rakes it through his hair, throwing his body back. His other hand still caresses mine.

"He cheated on me for most of the last year of our relationship," I start, knowing there will never be a good time to tell him about Dan. "And we were both so busy with work that I never noticed. When I came home early from an event to surprise him, I found him with someone else. And he didn't even apologize or feel sad for what happened. He just told me it was about time I found out. Then he proceeded to tell me he didn't believe in me; he told me that he couldn't see himself supporting me if I continued on this path. That if I wanted him to choose me, I would change careers. Do something more safe, less me. He said I was too much, that I let things get to me too easily, always too emotional."

"You're not too much. And fuck him for cheating on you, you deserve one hundred percent of a man's attention. You deserve someone that you can trust."

The sound that comes out of my mouth is barely a laugh, humorless. "You hardly know me and you think that?"

"Look at me."

Something about Zayn's commanding tone always gets me to do what he says.

"He was one person and hardly in a place to say anything to you considering how much of a fuckup he is. You are doing the damn thing, making a way for yourself in your career. You should be so fucking proud of yourself because I know I am. I may have lost some time with you, but I feel like I've known you my entire life."

It's too much, too soon. Tears streak my face before I realize what's happening. Zayn lets go of my hand and brings both of his to cup my cheeks.

"You are incredible, Annie. Don't let anyone cloud your sunshine."

The moment his lips touch mine, my shoulders relax, my breathing lightens, and I savor the time we have left together. Our perfect little bubble.

"He doesn't deserve your tears, your sympathy, your thoughts... fuck," Zayn mumbles against my lips. "You're mine, and you deserve to be treated like the fucking princess you are."

"Zayn," I say, sighing into his grasp. He tugs me closer and I oblige, settling myself over his lap, doing everything I can to be closer to him. "If I'm yours, truly yours, then you're mine."

My arms rest on his shoulders, and I pull him closer, trying to show him how much I need him right now. Zayn's tongue traces the seam of my lips, tantalizing me. Again, I let him in, my head tilting to welcome his kiss, deepening the connection between us.

A moan escapes his lips as his hands caress my back, switching between tracing light circles and grasping me with everything he has. "Need. More," he growls, his voice reverberating through me.

I know he's asking me to make the next move, to take the next step. Even though he might seem like a grumpy asshole to everyone else on the planet, he's turning out to be the opposite in the comfort of our home. *Our home.* Here, he is soft, encouraging, flirtatious, and supportive, but still commanding when it matters. Like now.

Our relationship may have started fake, as something neither of us wanted, but we've crossed the line into reality, and there's no going back.

I take my shirt off and throw it behind me.

Zayn lets out a hiss before dipping his head down to take my breast in his mouth. "You weren't wearing a bra under this shirt all night."

My head falls back, my eyes close, and I let out a low moan.

"What to do with you..." Zayn trails off, his lips enveloping my other breast while a hand comes to pinch the other nipple.

"God, Z."

"Only me, Princess."

"Fuck me," I hiss as Zayn bites my nipple, then uses his tongue to soothe the pain.

"Is that a request?" His lips move up my body, pressing small kisses everywhere: my breast, my collarbone, my neck, my jaw.

My hips move slowly as I nod.

"Words, Annie. I need you to use your words and tell me yes."

"You're the worst, do you know that?" I tease, getting an eye-roll from him.

"Consent is necessary for what I'm about to do to you."

"And what might that be?" I tease again, moving my hips at a more deliberate pace, enjoying the grumbles and growls and hisses that leave his mouth.

A tug on my hair is all it takes for me to shut up, to remember who I'm with.

"Just say yes, Princess." He presses his lips onto my exposed neck, biting and sucking, until I'm left with no other option.

"Yes," I say, the word more of a moan more than anything.

"Fucking finally."

He lets go of my hair, moving both hands to cup my ass. I've never been the type to let someone pick me up, but this time, I don't give it a second thought. I would not let go of this man.

"Do you know how long I've wanted this?" Zayn whispers into my ear.

"Since you chased me on the beach?" It's a good guess, one of the first moments I felt his barrier truly come down.

He shakes his head. "When you gave that damn PowerPoint presentation, wearing that fucking dress to tease me."

"I did not wear that dress for you," I stammer too quickly, giving myself away.

"You wore that dress for me, and I wanted to tear it off and fuck you over your desk."

"I wouldn't have let you. I didn't like you, remember?"

He tosses me on the mattress when we make it to his bedroom. The minute my back touches the bed, Zayn climbs on top of me. He takes the hem of my pants and pulls down, revealing the lace I wore for him.

His head drops and shakes as a small chuckle leaves his mouth. He leans down and presses kisses where the band of the lace meets my skin, taking it in his fingers and pulling them down with my pants.

"Do you *like* me now?" Zayn stares at me, his head positioned in between my knees, his hands on either side.

"Maybe a little bit. Do you like me?"

Zayn pinches my side and I yelp, trying to wriggle out from under him, but he pins my legs down hard.

"I like you so much I don't know what to do with all these feelings. It's *overwhelming*."

I want to know if he will still feel that way in the morning, if he will still want me to remain his. When he gets a reminder that none of this should be real and our deadline is coming quickly, what then?

"Stop thinking so hard and enjoy this." Zayn's voice rumbles against my inner thigh.

"Hard to enjoy this when nothing is—" I'm cut off by my own moan. Zayn's lips find my center, his tongue darting out to draw circles around my clit.

"What was that?" He removes his mouth, which has me whimpering for more.

With my right hand, I tug on his hair downward.

"As my princess wishes." He trails off, bringing his mouth back to where I need relief the most. I don't even have the energy to laugh at how often he's using my nickname or the fact that he's literally on his knees for me.

Zayn doesn't let up. He increases his pressure when he notices my breath hitching, switches his movements when he notices my hips move a certain direction.

He's always noticing.

"I need more," I whisper, digging my fingers into his hair, grasping for him to be closer, not caring what he thinks of me, of this.

He inserts one finger, then another, into my folds. He starts by pushing them in slowly, unbearably slow, to the point where I'm about to tell him I need more yet again, but then he pushes them all the way in. Hard. When he pulls them back out, he drives them in again. Over and over, until my back is arching and I don't know how much more I can take.

"Come for me, Annie, you're such a good girl. Look at you."

That's all it takes to have me coming undone. My moan echoes through the room, bouncing off the wall and reverberating back into me. Zayn slows his hands and tongue to match my breathing.

"Oh, shit, I'm sorry," I say. My fingers loosen on his hair as I realize I was holding him extra tight, harder than I should have.

"Don't be."

I can't hide my smile as Zayn trails his mouth up by body to meet mine.

When our lips collide and I taste myself, I moan, again. God, what is this man doing to me?

"Every time I think I have you figured out, you surprise me." His stubble brushes against my chin as he kisses my jaw, my chin, my mouth. It's as if he's also savoring this moment, this little bubble that we are in.

"I'm a woman of wonders, what can I say?" I tease, knowing it's a default response to hide how I actually feel. I want to tell him I'm scared. I don't know what's going on, what this is, what will happen, and it terrifies me. I don't want to ruin our evening though, not when it's going so perfectly.

Luckily, Zayn chuckles. Not being able to read my mind is a plus.

"Are you sure about this? You can tell me no and we can stop now. I wouldn't mind."

"I'm sure."

"Let me grab a condom." He presses a light kiss to my cheek before sauntering off to fetch it.

"That's not a convenient location to have those stored," I yell to him as he fumbles through drawers in the bathroom down the hall.

"I haven't needed them," Zayn says as he comes back to the bed.

"You haven't—" I start, but Zayn cuts me off.

"I haven't been with someone in over a year. I haven't let anyone get close to me. No one."

"Why me?" I ask before thinking. His shoulders tense. I shouldn't have asked; I don't want to come across as needy.

But after being chosen second for my entire life with my own mother and her fling of the week and then Dan, it means something to have someone choose me.

"Why you?" he asks, his shoulders relaxing, thankfully.

I nod.

"God, Annie, is it not obvious?" Zayn opens the condom and rolls it over his length. "You showed up, over and over. You continued to be there for me. Not giving a damn about my attitude. Not asking questions about my past. Giving me the attitude and sass you keep tampered down." He takes this time to rub his cock up and down my center, teasing me. I let out a soft whimper, both because I need him and because I desperately want him. "Fuck. You're amazing and you don't even know it."

He slams his entire length into me, and I scream. It's the kind of scream where I'm surprised, shocked, and all my sensors are going off at once, blinking and telling me there's an error somewhere, because this shouldn't feel this good.

"Fuck, Zayn."

"That's right Princess, say my name."

I reach a hand down to press on my clit when one of Zayn's hands slaps it away.

"Mine." And then a finger finds its place where I want it, slowly circling as he thrusts. "*You're mine.*"

Our breathing becomes ragged. My fingers scratch at his back to pull him closer, and I can feel myself about to orgasm again. I've never had this happen.

"Come with me, Annie," Zayn rasps.

My entire body reams in pleasure, and I'm having trouble coming to terms with what's happening right now.

"Annie, with me."

With more pressure from his finger and an increase in pace from his thrusting, I come like he asks. He captures my moan in a kiss, tangling our tongues together in a slow pace to match our breathing coming down from the high.

"That was..." Zayn starts to say, the biggest smile I've seen from him plastered on his face.

"Incredible."

24
ZAYN

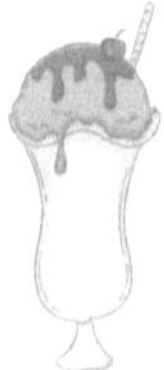

I'M HAVING A HARD time ignoring Annie. After the other night, I find myself moving toward her like a moth that hovers around a light post. If she's in the kitchen making tea, I'm right there next to her making coffee. If she's lounging on the couch in the shortest fucking shorts that make my dick hard immediately, I'm sitting next to her.

Another thing is I can't stop touching her. I reach for her hand when we are next to each other, and she lets me. I give her shoulder squeezes, hugs in the morning, kisses on the cheek.

I know I need to find a way to pull back. My heart is already breaking as I'm convincing myself none of this is even fucking real. On top of that, we have to attend a gala tonight, so I'm busy getting ready.

"Zayn?" Annie's voice echoes from the doorframe of my room.

"Hm?" My gaze lands on her and my jaw drops. Damn. This woman.

She's wearing a floor length royal blue dress with a slit up the right leg, taunting me with the little bit of bare skin. It hugs her hips and breasts, showing off her lovely curves. The straps of the dress lay on her shoulders, leaving the perfect amount of cleavage on display.

Her breath is heavy, and I find myself lost in the rising and falling of her chest. Mesmerized by this temptation, unable to look away.

"Zayn." Annie stares at me with a knowing glare, but she knows what she looks like.

"You look like a fucking goddess."

Small crinkles appear around her eyes and mouth as she dips her head and chuckles, swiping away a piece of hair that falls in front of her face.

"That's quite an upgrade from a princess." Her head is still tilted forward, but her eyes look up to meet mine. Her cheeks are a dusty shade of red, and I can see a smile on her face as she starts to turn around, showing me her back. "Can you zip me up?"

"Ye-yeah," I stutter, unsure why my voice decided to wane. It's not like I've never seen a woman in a dress before. Hell, I've had women use dresses like this to their advantage, teasing me with the slits and the dips of fabric.

When I reach Annie, I take her hair with my hands and sweep it out of the way. I lean forward and kiss the back of her neck, slowly, letting the moment last a few seconds longer.

"*Fuck*, you are beautiful." I kiss her again as my finger finds the zipper. Slowly I move it up, until it's at the top and my work here is done. "I can't wait to tear this off you later."

"And if I say no?" Annie twists her head and shoulders back to see me. As she turns fully around, I shift my hands to rest on her lower back.

"You wouldn't."

"You don't know that."

"Then let's make a bet." My hands move to her butt, grasping firmly and pulling her toward me. I laugh when she lets out a soft moan.

"Alright, Mr. Barnes. Let's make a bet. If you win and my dress comes off by your hands, and your hands alone, then you can have your way with me."

"God, Annie, do I like the sound of that." I lean in to kiss her on the neck, but she starts to talk again.

"But if I win, you need to rejoin the Young Actors Association."

Moment killed.

I move my hands to her waist.

"Okay." I don't know if she's asking this of me because she cares about me or her job, maybe it's both, but I was already planning on rejoining the cause after the gala tonight.

After attending multiple events for the association, I find myself missing the community. And Todd has tried to reach out a few times, asking if I'd consider rejoining. I helped out a lot with the young actors that were planning for their first auditions, and I miss that.

"I don't see a world where you win, though, so good luck." I plant a kiss on her forehead and remove my hands from her, stepping back to grab my wallet from the dresser.

"I don't know Zayn, I can resist you."

"We'll see." I smile and thrust my hand out to her. She grabs it, smiles, and follows me out the door.

When we reach the venue, there are lights flashing everywhere, ricocheting off the black interior of the car. Mumbles of chatter are outside the door; it's going to be hard to make it to the entrance without having to stop and talk to someone.

The me before Annie wouldn't choose to be here, but if I was, I would have kept my head down, pretended I didn't hear any of the reporters or paparazzi, and made it to the front door within seconds. I wouldn't have given anyone the light of day. They didn't deserve to know anything about me. I didn't owe anything to anyone.

But it's different now. I owe it to Annie and myself to smile, chat with the reporters, talk about my movies, and show myself in a better light. I need to prove to Ed that I have the image it takes to lead a trilogy.

"Ready?" I look over to Annie, who is staring out the window at all the people.

"Ready as I'll ever be." She gleams.

With that, I open the door, and the night begins. Flashing lights come at me from all angles, shouts from reporters and photographers follow, and I do my best to look friendly while walking to the other side of the car.

I reach out for Annie and she grabs my hand with a squeeze. When her body is close enough to mine, I lean toward her, place my lips above her ear, and whisper, "I can't wait to tear this dress off later and fuck you until you scream my name."

Annie playfully pushes at my chest, which sends rockets into my stomach. I chuckle as I pull her back to me, wrapping my arm around her waist. We walk toward the door, but a reporter stops us almost right away. And because I have Annie by my side, I feel calm and ready to answer questions from the media. There's no anger.

"Zayn, can you tell me who you have with you tonight?"

"This is Annie, my girlfriend." I look down at her and smile, beaming because she's mine in every way it counts.

The reporter smiles back and nods before saying, "And I hear you have a speech tonight. Any spoilers on what that's about?"

"Good try, but you'll have to wait and see like everyone else." I almost snarl but hold it back when I feel a pinch at my side. *Annie.*

He laughs and all is forgiven. "Alright, alright, can't wait."

I offer a nod before continuing to walk, only needing to stop two more times. Once for a photographer to get a few shots, and once for another reporter looking to ask questions about my upcoming movies.

Annie proceeds to fill me in as we walk into the venue. "Okay, so you'll go up to talk about the organization and how people can give money before we eat dinner. So we have some time right now to mingle."

I nod along as she shares the agenda for the evening, putting on her publicist hat. She smiles and greets everyone that passes as we make our way to our table at the front of the room. My heart swells as I watch her do her thing, and I'm so proud to have her by my side.

Every table is lined with silver satin tablecloths, low hues of purple and blue lights illuminate the area, and light jazz music that reverberates off the wall. This room is full of people that care about young actors who are trying to find their place in the industry. Mostly everyone has gathered at their tables. My speech will start things off before the donations and the dinner.

When we get to our table, Todd greets us.

"Zayn, glad to see you made it," Todd says, shaking my hand. "And Annie, glad to see you in my world." He pulls Annie into a hug and I remember that they know each other through her coworker. The night of his wedding party feels like it was ages ago at this point.

"It is." She smiles, and it goes straight to my heart. And my dick. But luckily there are enough people around to calm down the thoughts in my head that should be saved for later.

"Are you looking forward to your speech?" Todd faces me again, taking a sip from his glass.

"I figured I'd just wing it."

Annie slaps my chest. "You what?"

I grab her hand and give it a squeeze. "I'm kidding, Annie," I wink in her direction before turning back to Todd. "I have notes."

"Wouldn't be the first time you had to wing a speech. Remember the event we did with the city a year and a half ago?" Todd asks.

"The one when you called me on stage at the last minute to save your ass? Yeah, I remember."

We both laugh, and it feels good. My heart is mending, piece by piece.

"Okay, it's showtime." Todd clasps his hand on my shoulder.

"Good luck, Z." Annie leans over and plants a kiss on my cheek. I twist to look at her, giving her a smile that I hope shows her all the words I've left unsaid. That I'm so grateful for her. That I wouldn't be here without her. That I don't know how I'll let her go.

The walk up to the stage is short, and by the time I get in front of the microphone, I've forgotten what it's like to be in a room full of 300 people. The heat of the spotlight shines on me as I reach for the notes in my jacket pocket with sweaty, shaky hands. The microphone is at the right position, thankfully, because I'm just realizing that I didn't rehearse this ahead of time. I didn't even think about it.

"Um, hello everyone. I'm Zayn Barnes." I let out a chuckle. My nerves are threatening to overtake me, and my brain is telling my feet to move and get off stage and brush this off. But when I look down, I spot the only person that calms me. Her smile is enough to have me breathing normally again and ready to give this speech.

"I know I haven't been around lately, and that I am sorry for. But I'm not here for me, I'm here for the kids. The Young Actors Association means a lot to me and many others, and we wouldn't be here tonight if it wasn't for all of you. Every donation matters, every volunteer hour counts. Before you leave here tonight, I encourage you to write your name down to give money or commit a few hours to help kids who just want to be given a chance. I'm thrilled to announce that I will be donating $50,000 tonight and have accepted a position on the board. I look forward to talking with each and every one of you. Thank you."

Cheers and applause echo in the room. I didn't even look at my fucking note cards, but I didn't need to. I knew what I had to say and I wanted to keep it short. Deliver the news, make sure the people know to donate, and hope that it's received well. The idea to donate came to me in the moment, but I'm thrilled about the decision when I find Annie in the crowd with the largest grin on her face. As I approach the table, her eyes crinkle and there's a look of wonder, admiration maybe? She's still clapping with the rest of the room, and I feel like I won an award for best movie of the year.

The cheering dies out as dinner rolls around and I take a seat.

"What was that?" Annie lightly punches me in the arm.

I exaggerate a wince and put a hand to the spot to tease her. "What was what? Was it not a good speech?"

"You—" Annie stammers, shaking her head. "Did you know you were going to be on the board when I told you what I wanted if I won our bet?" She crosses her arms, trying her hardest to be mad at me. The pout on her lip only makes me smile more. God, I never used to smile. What is this woman doing to me?

"I might have known, yes."

"Why didn't you tell me?"

"I knew I was going to win anyway." I lean in closer until my mouth is hovering over her ear and whisper, "I can't wait to rip this dress off and fuck you later."

"Zayn," she accosts me, playfully pushing me away. I laugh it off, knowing she's loving every second of it.

"Let's eat, Annie, and then we can have some fun."

The rest of the evening is uneventful. There's no dancing, just lots of talking and more talking. It's impossible to leave the room. Every step is interrupted by someone new. They thank me for the donation, then tell me some story about a family they knew that was affected by the organization. Or they're appreciative that I'm back on the board, knowing how much impact that made. They also ask me about my future films. Those are my favorite questions to answer, and I know Ed will be thrilled to know that this event has gone better than we both expected.

As the night goes on, I steal many, many glances at Annie. She has this side of her that draws conversation out of people.

She can be meeting someone for the first time, but by the time they are done talking, she knows the names of their entire family and where they are going on their next vacation. Her confidence is the hottest thing. She doesn't care that she doesn't know a soul in the room besides me and Todd. She's the one leaving the most impact, helping me encourage more donors and keeping me comfortable through it all.

"You doing okay?" I squeeze Annie's arm. For the past ten minutes she's started to look distant, like she's thinking about something, or maybe there's something bothering her. "Annie?" The music isn't that loud in here, but maybe she didn't hear me.

Her head snaps in my direction. "What?"

"I asked if you were doing okay."

"Oh, just tired I think. It's been a long day." She puts on a soft smile.

She's holding something back, but I'm not going to push her. Instead, I stand and grab for her hand. She doesn't fight me, which I'm grateful for. We say bye to Todd and a few others we pass as we walk toward the exit to the car waiting for us.

The sky is pitch black, flooded with clouds, barely a star in the sky. I reach for the door handle and pull it open for Annie, letting her slide in before shutting it and moving over to my side. When I sit, I reach for her hand, cupping it in mine. Annie's face is lit by the glow of the streetlights as we drive home. I let us sit in silence, not wanting to make whatever is going on worse.

When we reach the apartment, Annie moves to open the door. Damn her independence, I want to be there for her. "Stay," I grumble.

I give her hand a squeeze before exiting the car, walking over to the passenger side to open Annie's door. Is her face more pale? Why is she breathing heavily?

"Are you sure you're okay?" I ask again. She glares at me. Figures.

"Yes, let's just get inside."

Okay, whatever she says. I steal glances as we walk, not knowing what to say or what to do to bring back the Annie from an hour ago. The apartment door is barely open when Annie goes staggering down the hallway, into the bathroom, and shuts the door.

To give her space, I stay in the kitchen. I make us both tea, since it's the evening and I don't need coffee right now. Then, I grab some pre-portioned cookie dough that Annie made out of the fridge, place them on a tray, and plop them in the oven. The least I can do is make sure she still has a good evening.

When the cookies are done, there's still no sign of Annie. A loud noise comes from her direction, and I drop everything and run.

When I throw open the bathroom door, I see Annie sitting on the floor with her knees curled to her chest. She's still wearing that damn dress. She raises her head from her hands and looks at me. Her cheeks are stained with tears and mascara.

"Who did this?"

"My uterus," Annie jokes, but she doesn't move. If anything, she curls more inward.

"Your uterus?" I ask with a cocked eyebrow, confused at what that would... oh. That explains why she is hunched over on the ground, irritable, and moody. I have a younger sister, I should know these things.

"Fuck, Annie," I say, rushing to kneel in front of her. I cup her cheeks and press a kiss to her temple. "Is it bad? Can I get you anything? I made tea and cookies. But I don't know if that will help. I can run out to the store? Or send some—" She places a hand in front of my lips to stop me from chattering on.

"I'm okay, I promise. It's not that bad, I swear. I just thought you…" She sighs, looking down at her lap again.

My hand lifts her chin back up.

"Thought what?"

"I thought you would be mad at me for ruining our night. I'm trying to be there for you. I know it's not going the way you expected. You won the bet, after all. God. This is stupid."

She tries to throw her head back in her hands, but I catch it, making sure she's looking at me when I speak next.

"Annie, I don't know what kind of men you are used to, but I would never be mad at you for telling me no. For any reason. I'm not doing whatever the fuck this is for that alone. It's just an added bonus. You are what's important. You being here—" I wave my hands around the room before I continue, "—is being here for me. I don't need anything else from you. Do you understand?"

She nods, and a single tear streams down her face. I lean forward, pressing my lips to catch it, using my hand to smooth over her hair and show her that I'm not mad.

"C'mon, let's get you into something more comfortable and let's go eat a few cookies before bed."

25
ANNIE

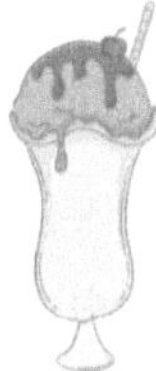

THERE'S BEEN A SUDDEN change in the apartment with Zayn. He's still his normal grumpy self in the morning, sulking around until he's had his coffee and some sunshine. But he's also leaving notes on the counter when he's gone to the gym, touching my waist every time he passes, and planting kisses on my forehead almost every time we are near each other.

His touch is addicting. I crave him in all the ways that matter. He still hasn't told me about what happened one year ago, but he's let me in more and more each night. I'm waiting, choosing not to ask, letting him tell me when he's ready. Our routine is my favorite: dinner, talking, movie, sex. Sometimes it's just sex and then we realize we forgot dinner, but it's starting to feel normal. As if we are a real couple doing real couple shit.

Which is why I'm having my girls over tonight. After the event a week and a half ago, Cassie practically threatened to show up at my doorstep if I didn't invite her and Marcy over. I think they miss me. With everything going on, it's been impossible to find balance. If I'm not working, I'm here with Zayn. And since I like him and all, it makes it hard to want to do anything else.

Zayn is at the stove when I walk into the kitchen, making breakfast for us before work. When he sees me enter, his face lights up with the kind of smile that tells me he's grateful to see me and that he's the luckiest man in the world. His smiles always make me feel like a teenager falling in love for the first time. I hardly remember what it was like to converse with grumpy Zayn.

"Morning." I smile back and take a seat at the island. "What are you making?"

"Eggs. That okay?" He turns around, spatula in hand, and I am doing everything in my power to not picture him spanking me with it. He then slaps the spatula into his palm and I jump. Only a little bit, but enough for him to chuckle. "Picturing something, Princess?"

"Hm? Oh, um, nope, I'm not. Just, nope, never mind," I stammer. My palm rises to my cheek and damn, it's already hot to touch.

"Alright," Zayn sings, turning back to the stove. He plates our eggs, prepares me a mug for my tea, and comes to sit next to me.

And in Zayn-like fashion, he throws his fork down, grabs the seat of my chair, and pulls me toward him. And I'm not talking a gentle pull, where I gradually slide over to him. No, this is a full on tug, like he's trying his best to win at a tug the rope contest. I barrel into him. Hard.

"Zayn! I could have stabbed you by accident." I press away from him and point my fork in his face. "I could have hurt you, you idiot."

He just laughs, of course, throwing his head back at the notion. "Annie, you've already hurt me. Just by being here..." He pauses, dragging a hand down my chest, to my thigh, and up toward my hip.

My breath hitches as his fingers make small circles on my inner thigh. He lets out a groan as his fingers slip beneath the thin layer of fabric.

"Fuck, Annie. I knew it. You've been sitting here, wet for me, and you didn't think to tell me."

I grab his shoulder as he pushes two fingers into me, pulling him closer to me, forgetting all about the breakfast we were eating.

"Cancel your plans today. Hang out with me," Zayn whispers into my ear, moving his other hand to rub small circles around my clit. Fuck, the pressure is too much. My heartbeat echoes in my ears, I can hardly hear what he says next. "Please."

My hips move on their own accord, following the rhythm of his pumping fingers.

"Come for me, Princess. Let the neighbors hear who makes you feel this fucking good."

That's enough to send me over the deep edge. Shocks of pleasure wash over me like a wave crashing into the sand. He presses forehead to mine, pulling his hand out of my shorts. Our breathing syncs as mine slows.

"That was fast," Zayn whispers with a chuckle.

"Would you believe me if I told you I was thinking of you doing that?" I whisper back.

His hand finds my chin and he brings my lips to his, kissing me once slowly. He pulls back to look me in the eye. "I'd believe anything you told me, Annie."

"I can't cancel though. Cassie, Marcy, and Lucy are coming over."

"I know," Zayn replies, pressing a kiss to my forehead. He pulls the hair from around my face and tucks it behind my ear before separating our bodies and going back to his breakfast.

"She, um, Cassie, asked if maybe you want to go over to her apartment?" I ask cautiously. It was her idea, not mine. Zayn already told me he'd go to the gym or something to give us the apartment.

Zayn looks at me with his fork still in his mouth. "Why?"

"Well, Emmett will be there and asked if you wanted to. And I think the other guys will be over, so... I mean, you don't have to, I was just... you know never mind, it was a dumb idea." I turn back to face my plate, picking up the fork to stuff food in my mouth before I say something I'll regret.

"Don't do that. Don't belittle yourself and your opinions. I'll go, that sounds fun," he says, like it was an easy decision to make and not something that feels like a chore. The old Zayn would have never agreed to doing this.

"You don't have to, seriously, I don't want to force you to do anything."

"You're not forcing me to do anything, Annie. But you could force me down on my knees in front of your pretty pussy and I wouldn't blink twice. You could force me to watch as you pleasure yourself, knowing that I can't do anything but sit there and watch. You could force me to do a lot of things, Annie, and I'd be happy to do all of them. I don't mind spending time with the guys, it might be nice."

Words. Need to say words. Also, I need to shut my mouth since my jaw has been hanging wide open since he started declaring surprisingly dirty things to me.

"What happened to Mr. Grumpy? Who are you?" My eyebrows furrow as I wait for him to answer. Wondering if he's going to give me a truthful answer or play it off.

"Mr. Grumpy found a princess who is healing him bit by bit." He stands from his stool, planting what feels like the tenth kiss on my forehead. "Now, I'm going to get ready and head out so the girls can come over. Finish your breakfast before it gets too cold." His eyes dart to my plate that still has most of my eggs on it before he patters down the hallway. I like to picture him grinning the entire time.

I text Cassie to let her know Zayn will be coming over and also send him the address so he has it. I'm excited to have the girls over. My old apartment was small and dated, so girls' nights were always at Cassie's since her apartment is larger and centrally located. Sometimes we'd go to Lucy's, since her and husband (and Emmett's best friend) Tyler just bought a house. Cassie and Lucy have been best friends for nearly a decade.

And now everyone is coming here. To our home, Zayn's home. And I already know I'm going to be asked a million questions, and I don't know what I'm going to say. I just know that Zayn will likely get hounded worse, knowing that group.

"Alright, text me if you need anything. Otherwise, I'll be back later tonight." Zayn hesitates by the front door. He looks down at the floor for a moment, still contemplating something.

"Everything okay?" I ask, concerned with the fact that he's just standing there, not making a sound.

His eyes snap to meet mine. He takes five steps toward me, grasps my head with both hands and slams his lips into mine. I'm overwhelmed by the pressure of his hands, his lips, his presence. The kiss slows, lessens, until he pulls back from me and rests his forehead on mine, his eyelids closed.

"What was that for?" I ask, realizing how out of breath that one kiss put me. My heart stutters from the confusion of this and the tension of wanting him.

"I don't know," Zayn admits, taking one step back.

"Okay," I say. I don't know what it was for either, but I don't want him to think I didn't want it.

"I'll, um, yeah, I'll text you when I get there. Have a good time, Princess." He leans back in, pressing his lips to mine one last time, then smiles at me before walking out the door.

Somehow, I finish getting ready. It's hard to focus on the task at hand when I can't stop replaying that kiss. A goodbye kiss. A see-you-later kiss. An I-want-to-kiss-you kiss. The line between this being just fun and being something else is blurring. I'm glad I'll have a distraction tonight.

A half hour later, there's a knock at the door as I'm pouring a bag of chips into a bowl. "Come in!" I holler.

Cassie, Lucy, and Marcy come barreling through the door. They stop in the entryway, all of them looking around the apartment.

"Damn, Anns, this is better than my apartment," Marcy says.

"Seriously, this is where you've been, and we are just now getting an invite?" Cassie asks.

Lucy comes over and wraps me in a hug. "Nice to see you, Annie."

"I can't wait to hear all about the honeymoon," I say to Lucy, smiling as she beams with excitement.

"Oh my gosh, yes, we will get to that. But we will be talking about you tonight." Lucy squeezes my shoulder as she passes me on the way to the fridge, snagging beverages for everyone.

"I can promise you all that I am not that interesting." I grab the snacks and walk over to set them on the coffee table, before plopping down on the couch.

"You're dating one of the country's most talked about actors. You're now being talked about. That's by far the most interesting thing," Marcy says, pointing at me like she's disappointed in me for even thinking that. "No offense Luce."

Lucy playfully rolls her eyes. "No, no, I get it. I had my time to be interesting when I started dating Tyler. Now I'm just married and boring. Just like Cassie!"

"Hey! I am only one of those things." Cassie glares at Lucy, and Lucy replies by blowing a kiss.

When Cassie first moved to Los Angeles, Lucy was her roommate. They worked together, became best friends, and then fell in love with people in the same circle. They were secretly dating in tandem, but everyone knew they would end up with the other person. It was just a matter of time.

Is that the same thing for Zayn and I? Is it just a matter of time until we get together for real? Why do I want that?

Marcy turns to me and says the one thing I was dreading tonight.

"Okay, so tell us about you and Zayn."

26
ZAYN

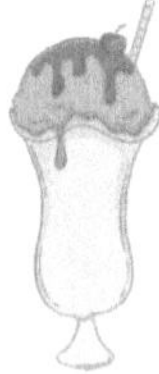

"You're going where?" Logan screams through the phone.

"Why are you screaming? Where are you?" I roll my eyes, already regretting that I called him.

"I'm at the club," he says as if he's annoyed I asked. It's only seven o'clock on Wednesday night.

"I'm going to Emmett's." I sigh into the phone.

"And you're calling for pointers? Why? You know everyone." Logan counters.

And that's true. Emmett is married to Cassie, and they both work out of the studio with their giant group of friends. The same group of friends that I kind of started to hang out with when I was with Marissa.

"Yes, I know. But I didn't know if there were any updates I should be aware of."

"Tyler and Lucy just got back from their honeymoon. Max and Lane are both still single, I think. That's all I know. They aren't my clients."

Tyler, Max, and Lane are best friends with Emmett. They've all been friends for close to a decade. Tyler leads catering at January Studios and Max and Lane lead casting. Ever since Emmett stepped away from acting and into writing, it's like they run the studio with Ed.

"Thanks for your help Logan," I say sarcastically.

"Why are you even going over there?"

"Annie asked me to," I admit before wondering if I should have kept that to myself.

"Fuck, dude. You're in deep." Yep, should have kept that to myself.

"Bye, Logan." I hang up the phone before he responds.

A few minutes later I'm at Emmett's apartment. It's in a gated complex, with plenty of large trees that line the property. They already have fall decorations on their door, probably due to Cassie's midwest upbringing.

Two knocks is all it takes before it swings open and Emmett appears on the other side. I didn't know what to wear tonight, so I'm glad to see that he's also in casual wear. Women talk about being insecure over outfits all the time, why can't guys? When was the last time I hung out with a group of people where I had to make an impression? I don't have friends anymore, not since my breakup took everything and everyone from me. Some my doing, some the natural ebb and flow of friendships dividing.

"Glad you made it, man." Emmett steps to the side to let me through the door.

"Um, yeah, me too." I awkwardly agree, feeling overwhelmed and unsure why I came.

Emmett points out the kitchen in front of us, the living room to the left where the others sit, and bathroom down the hall if I need it at any point. Tyler, still blond and six-feet tall, sits on one of the couches staring at whatever is playing on the TV. Max waves at me, his short red curls bouncing as his head turns back to the front of the room. Lane is sitting next to him, and I can see that he still wears outfits to match his black hair.

I don't know if I should apologize to Emmett or let what happened between us last week in my trailer be in the past. I wasn't the nicest and here he is, opening his home for me because of Annie. Letting me hang out with his friends, because of Annie.

"Hey, I'm sorry about the other day. I wasn't in the best mood." I immediately feel like a weight has been taken off my shoulders.

"It's water under the bridge," is all he says.

"Thanks. But I just want to say it because I care about Annie."

Emmett gapes at me.

I add, "It's not just casual for me. And I want you to be able to trust me with her since she's your sister-in-law."

Emmett nods while I talk.

"You know, I reached out after things with Marissa ended," he says. "You could have come and talked to us. That's why we are friends, Zayn, we help with the heavy shit."

"Yeah, I know." I tousle my hair and avert my gaze. It's not that I didn't want to talk to them, or anyone else, I just didn't know what to say. I was supposed to appear okay on the outside, yet I was desperately hurting on the inside. "I guess I didn't know how to handle it all, first heartbreak and all." I laugh, because even though I was twenty-nine when it all ended, we were together for a long time. Marissa was my longest relationship and the only one to break my heart.

Also, guys are supposed to be tough, keep all feelings inside. My dad gave me a pat on the back when I first saw him about the breakup and told me I'd find someone else. He never bothered to ask about how I was feeling. Because of that, it made me not want to open up to anyone. If I kept the feelings bottled up, then they would eventually go away.

"Well, we are glad you're here now. Let's go sit," Emmett says.

I follow Emmett and sit in between him and Tyler.

"So, what's up with you and Annie?" Max asks. Lane shoves him. "What?"

"I said to give him at least ten minutes before asking," Emmett says.

"It's fine, I figured I was coming over for an interrogation." I try to joke, hoping that it lands well. Thankfully it does, everyone laughs back. "Annie and I are... dating, but not? It's complicated. But I like her."

"Well no shit, anyone can look at a photo of you two and see that." Tyler glances over again, rolling his eyes in the process.

"I don't know what you're talking about," I say, trying to defend the little bit of secrecy I have left.

Lane speaks next. "You're always looking at her when she's looking at the camera. I've seen that same look on Emmett. Even in the first time he and Cassie were photographed together by paparazzi."

"You two were photographed?" I look at Emmett and he nods.

"Yep, outside a club for my thirtieth birthday party. Except her face wasn't in it, so I didn't have to pull whatever stunt you and Annie are trying to do."

"Trying? I think the media would say that we are meant to be," I reply, throwing a knowing look in Emmett's direction.

"Well, let's just say it's not exactly a stunt. I care about her, but it's going to be over at the end of the year. That's what we agreed on," I tell them for some reason. And my chest feels lighter, like I can breathe, having told someone something that I've been holding in for the past few weeks.

"Shit man," Emmett says. He doesn't push me for more, which I'm glad about. We all sit there for a moment, the sound from the TV filling the silence.

"Anyway, enough about me, I need to hear some shit about you all. Who's first?" I ask.

"Tyler just got back from his honeymoon," Emmett comments.

"Oh, yeah?" I ask.

"Yep. We spent fourteen days traveling up and down the west coast. I even convinced Lucy to camp off the Pacific Coast Highway, which I think was my favorite stop. Camping right on the cliff, overlooking the ocean." Tyler closes his eyes for a moment. "And of course we had lots of sex, which is always great."

"Fuck, man." I shove him and he just laughs. Glad to know that Tyler hasn't changed over the years. Still as blunt and talkative.

"Hey, just being honest." He shrugs.

"Mhm, honest," I say and we all laugh.

"The casting business is going well," Lane comments.

"Yeah, we started taking on work for a second studio that mostly focuses on smaller indie movies. Emmett writes and directs some of their short films sometimes," Max says.

"Oh, that's awesome. So writing is going well?" I turn to Emmett.

"It's keeping me busy. I haven't been able to act much all year. My dad is not the biggest fan of that."

Emmett's dad was an A-list actor before he retired.

"Ah, still hurt that you chose writing over acting? Hasn't it been like three years?" I grimace.

"Four, but I don't think he'll ever get over it . He and my mom still attend every red carpet event. And they love Cassie. So I can't complain."

"Well, that's good," I say.

"And how's acting stuff for you? Any update from Ed on the trilogy?" Emmett asks.

"You're trying to land the trilogy role?" Tyler asks, grabbing Lane and Max's attention.

"Yes, that's kind of why I've been working on my image. But you probably haven't noticed because it was great to begin with," I joke.

"Yeah, destroying the reporter's camera did great for your image," Tyler chides.

"And don't forget cussing out that one reporter for looking at him wrong," Max jokes.

"That's not—" I press a palm to my forehead and laugh. "You guys must have missed me, huh?"

"We've been waiting for you to come back and give us all the juicy gossip now that you have a publicist for a girlfriend." Tyler says it so nonchalantly that I just grin and shake my head at how ridiculous they all are.

For the next few hours we play video games and watch a movie.

"Shit, it's late," Lane comments.

"Yeah, Cassie just texted me to let her know she's on her way back home," Emmett says, nose in his phone.

"Cool, I'll head out. Thanks guys for inviting me. This was..." I hesitate. "Fun."

"Aw, don't go soft on us now Barnes." Tyler punches me in the shoulder. "Kidding, please hang out with us again. I'm getting tired of these guys." He points to Emmett, Max, and Lane and they all laugh.

"Thanks, man."

On the drive back to the house, I can't stop thinking about how my life is so different from six months ago. Six months ago I had no Annie, which means I had a quiet house, no media or press to worry about, and no one to talk to besides family. And Logan. But he doesn't count. Now, I have a roommate that I'm falling for, people that I can see myself being friends with, and a future in acting. My dream is coming true and it's all because of the woman waiting for me back at home.

27
ZAYN

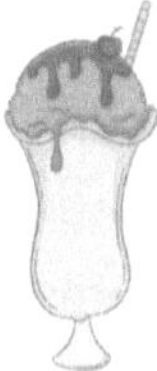

"ANNIE?" I CALL OUT when I enter our apartment. I'm used to her waiting in the living room, book in one hand, tea in the other.

"In here," she calls out from down the hallway.

I drop my bag by the door and make my way to my room.

"What are you wearing?" I ask, easily recognizing one of my old college t-shirts.

She looks down for a moment, apparently forgetting that she borrowed something that didn't belong to her. When she looks back at me, her cheeks are a beautiful shade of red. Her bottom lip disappears and she averts her gaze again.

"I wanted something cozy," Annie says.

"And if I wanted you to take it off?" I lean against the frame of the door, crossing one leg over the over.

"I can't do that, I'm busy painting my nails, Zayn." Annie holds her hand up to me in a *duh*-like fashion.

"It's almost midnight, why are you doing this now?"

"Who are you? The nail polish police?" She goes back to painting her nails, folding one of her legs in front of her so she's sitting in a half pretzel. She's not even wearing any pants, this fucking woman. Teasing me in my own house, in my own shirt.

I hold both of my hands up in front of me. "Hey, don't get sassy with me. I just got home."

"Oh, right, how was Emmett's? Come sit."

I'm not going to say no to that. I walk to the other side of the bed and sit next to her, leaning my back on the pillows.

"It was good. Different. I haven't hung out with anyone in a while."

"Since something mysteriously happened a year ago?" Annie peeks at me for a moment, gauging my reaction. I just nod and she goes back to painting the next nail.

"Why haven't you asked me what happened?"

"You'll tell me when you're ready," is all she says.

"No one ever gives me the space."

"You haven't let anyone in, Z, in a long time it seems like."

She's not wrong, I haven't. Not even my family.

"I want to tell you because you deserve to know."

"As long as you want to tell me, that's all that matters," Annie says.

"You don't want to know?"

"Of course I want to know, Zayn." Annie puts the nail polish down. "I want to know everything about you. It kills me to not know what happened, to not know how she hurt you when everything seemed perfect from the outside."

"It did seem perfect from the outside, didn't it?" I ask. "It seemed perfect to me, too. I thought everything was going well. I know we had a bumpy few years and had a few breaks."

"Weren't you on a break when..." Annie trails off.

"When I came on to you in my parents kitchen, even though you were with my brother?" I finish the sentence for her.

"Yes," Annie whispers, her cheeks flushing deep red.

"Yes, we were on our longest break then. That time was six months, and I wasn't sure we'd get back together. But we did, and I don't know. I thought she was the one. But she's not."

"How do you know that?" Annie says, still painting her nails like she's trying to be placid about this conversation.

"Because I've realized that she never got under my skin to the point that I wanted to pin her to the wall and show her who's in control. I never found myself missing her every time we were apart, regardless of how long. And I especially didn't feel the same way about her as I feel about you."

I'm out of breath by the time I'm done confessing what's in my heart, what's been driving me crazy.

"Oh," Annie says, her eyes still on her nails. But then she looks my way, meeting my eyes, and says, "I've never felt like this before either."

I refrain from pulling her toward me because I still haven't told her what happened.

"Well, that makes me extremely happy," I say, because it's true, and we both chuckle. "But I want to tell you what happened if you want to know."

"I want to know."

"A year ago, on the beach that we visit practically every week, I proposed to Marissa. She said no, told me I was holding her back from chasing her dreams."

She shakes her head, then looks at me with wide eyes. "What?"

"Yeah."

"She didn't deserve you."

"I know that now, but for the longest time I hated myself and everyone around me." And now I don't.

"Thank you for telling me." Annie blows on each nail carefully, trying to dry the polish.

"I've wanted to tell you for a while, it's just hard to talk about. A lot of articles had to be covered up and taken down, it took Logan and my team weeks of nonstop work to make sure that nothing negative was in the press. And I became the asshole that the press couldn't stop talking about anyway. Then you came along." I lay a hand on her knee, squeezing once.

"Then I came along and rocked your world." Annie winks.

Damn. I love this girl.

Fuck.

28

ANNIE

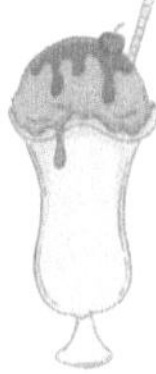

"How are you feeling about our date tonight?" Zayn rolls over on his side to face me.

We have been waking up like this for days, his arm wrapped around me.

"Should I feel a special way?" I ask, furrowing my brows.

Zayn slaps a hand to his chest and gasps. "Annie, princess of PR, forgetting about our two month-a-versary. I'm disappointed in you."

I shove his shoulder, forcing him to roll onto his back. He starts laughing and pulls me closer to him. I let him, snuggling my head into the nook of his shoulder.

"Does this mean you're doing something special for me?" I look up at him.

He runs his hand through my hair, twisting the strands as he makes his way toward the bottom, then starts over again. All of these intimate touches are enough to keep me in this bed all day.

"Maybe." Zayn presses a kiss to the top of my head. "Now, let's get up. I'm going to make you breakfast."

"Or you can bring me breakfast in bed." I grin and squeeze him a little harder.

"Nice try, Princess. Get up." Zayn has the audacity to pinch my butt, causing me to squeal and jerk toward him.

"Fine, fine. What are you going to make me, anyway?" I ask as we walk to the kitchen.

"French toast. That okay?" Zayn moves through the kitchen, grabbing bread, sugar, eggs, and a few more items from the pantry.

"Of course. Want me to help?"

"No, you can sit there and watch."

"Are you going to tell me what we are doing today?" I lean my elbows on the counter, catching my head in my hands.

"Nope, it's a surprise."

A surprise. Okay. After Zayn told me about his ex last night, I feel like we are a little bit closer. Just a little. He knows my past, I know his. It's more than either of us expected to admit to one another, but we didn't expect any of this to happen.

"What are you thinking about over there?" Zayn calls over his shoulder. I suppose I am being quiet.

"You," I admit sheepishly.

Zayn looks at me, eyebrows raised and a smirk on his face. "Oh, is that so? Care to tell me what about?"

"No."

"C'mon Annie, give me something," he begs, picking up the bowl of batter and bringing it to the island to mix in front of me.

"I was just..." My head falls further into my hands. I'm all of a sudden embarrassed at opening up to him.

"You were just..." Zayn pokes at me.

I peek between my fingers and catch a glimpse of him biting his lip, staring at me, mixing the bowl of batter. His arms work in circles and my mind flashes to last night, when he was drawing circles on my body.

"I was just thinking about how all of this is unexpected. You and me."

"Oh, yes, except I knew you wouldn't be able to resist me when you moved in." He leans over and places a dollop of batter on my nose.

I roll my eyes and grab a napkin to wipe it off, laughing all the while. "You did not. If anything, you are the one that couldn't resist me," I tease; everything we have done has always been mutual, a pull from both of us.

"That's true." He glances at me and holds my gaze before looking back down. His eyes look so sincere, full of truth in what he just said.

"Well, let me at least make us coffee while you make those," I say, hopping off the stool.

For the next little while, Zayn flips the toast, I make coffee, and we just talk. It's so domestic, so normal, so us. Everything he tells me makes me laugh, from little jokes to stories from his childhood, it all shows me glimpses of him. Who he used to be. Who he can be again, if he wants to be.

"Alright, eat up." Zayn smiles at me before sticking a piece of French toast in his mouth.

29

ANNIE

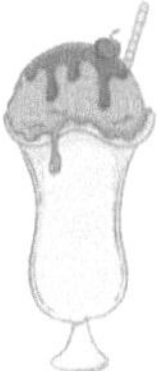

"Are you honestly not going to tell me what we are do-ing?" I ask Zayn when we get to the beach a few hours later. My arm is around his back, and he stiffens at the question.

"I planned a date for us."

"Oh. Should I tip the media so they send photographers?" I look up at him as we reach the ice cream shop.

He shakes his head and opens the door for me. "No photog-raphers, Princess. Just us."

Oh. Again. What is this supposed to mean?

I stumble a bit walking into the shop, almost falling over myself because my thoughts are elsewhere.

"Hi, Annie! Hi Zayn!" Our favorite employee, Liam, greets us. "The usual?"

Before I can answer, like I normally do, Zayn talks. "Yes, one cup, two spoons. Thank you." He hands his card over, and I'm frozen in place. What is going on?

"Thanks man." Zayn takes the ice cream, grabs my hand, and walks us over to the bar.

We sit on stools today instead of our typical booth. He scoots close enough for our legs to intertwine, placing a hand on my knee. It's warm and heavy, and my gaze drops to it.

He squeezes once, then moves to tilt my head up so my eyes meet his.

"Everything okay?" he asks, searching my face to see what's wrong.

"I think so," I whisper.

"You think so? Talk to me."

"It's just not our normal Friday, and we are at the ice cream shop. "

He chuckles. "Well, today isn't a normal day, Annie. I wanted to spend a day with my girlfriend, is that so bad?"

His girlfriend. He's never called me his girlfriend in private. Not only that, but he leans toward me and plants a kiss on my cheek. Something he never does in public.

"G-girlfriend?" I stutter.

"It is our two month-a-versary."

"Yeah, but you never call me that. At least, not when the media isn't around." I take a bite of the ice cream, hoping if I occupy my mouth, I'll stop saying everything I'm thinking.

"But I'd like to."

"You would?"

Zayn takes a bite, pondering my question for a moment. He laughs to himself, running his hand through his hair as his gaze drops to the floor.

"We already established that you are mine."

"Are we doing this?" I ask.

"We are *undoubtedly* doing this."

"Oh." It's the only thing I can think to say.

The last thing I ever thought would happen is Zayn admitting his feelings, or something along the line of his feelings, and us moving into something more than fake dating. Except that's exactly what we did, and for some reason, my mind is just now catching up.

"Let's play a game. Tell me three things you like about me."

"Hm, three things?"

He nods in response.

"Okay. One, you always make me breakfast in the morning. Two, you ask me questions about my day. Three..." I take another bite of ice cream, thinking about what else I want to tell him. "Your smile is my favorite thing to see when I wake up in the morning."

"Who knew you could be so nice?" Zayn teases.

"Hey!" I shove his shoulder. "I am the nice one in this relationship."

"So, you admit this is a relationship." He raises his brows in a challenge.

I chuckle.

"My turn for you. One, you have a habit of twirling your hair and it drives me insane. Two, whenever I see you, you're always smiling. Three..." He pauses, then leans over to the right before smirking at me and saying, "your ass."

"There he is, the Zayn I know and love." My heart stops. I did *not* just say the 'l' word. Have I fallen in love with Zayn and just openly admitted that to him?

Zayn doesn't say anything. He just leans toward me and plants yet another kiss on my forehead. I'm starting to become addicted to them. These kisses might be small and brief, but they are intimate and impactful.

"Let's finish our ice cream, I have plans for us, remember?"

"Oh, I remember. I'm excited." I smile and take spoonfuls of ice cream until the cup is empty.

"Okay, let's go." Zayn grabs my hand, and I follow him out the door.

I thought we might turn left out of the shop to go back to the car, but instead he turns to the right, toward the beach. After what he shared with me about his ex, I didn't think he'd want to spend any more time at the beach than he had to. I understand what it's like to have bad memories in a place. You don't want to be there, or near there. You don't want to remember what you felt like in that moment when grief took over.

I know what it feels like to be heartbroken, to have someone that leaves and you have to pick up the pieces. It's no wonder he shut everyone out.

We walk in silence, only the sounds of the waves crashing, the birds above, and the occasional song from a person on the trail breaking the silence. His hand still grips mine, his thumb moving on its own accord, almost comforting in a way. I'm not sure if it's for me or more for himself.

I think he's nervous. Wherever he's leading me, it's not far, but far enough that we have to walk for ten minutes. His gaze keeps bouncing between the water on the left, me, and the street to the right.

Finally, I see an umbrella in the distance. It's bright blue, hard to miss. The closer we get, the more I can see. A white floral picnic blanket is on the ground, with a basket on top of it.

He planned a beach picnic for us.

I don't know how much of my heart to give him. He already has too much.

But maybe that's okay? Maybe we weren't meant to be forever, but only for now. Maybe the world put us together to heal, to help each other when we both needed it most.

When I look at him, I no longer see the man I first met. The furrow in his brow is no longer permanent. It's a small line that only appears when he's actually upset or angry, or sometimes in his flirtatious moods when he's trying to remain serious. That's my favorite. He no longer looks sad. His mouth isn't always turned down, his eyes no longer cast downward, his posture no longer sulking.

Now, he's brighter. You can look at Zayn and see that he is happy, or at least happier than he was. He smiles back at you, he waves, he remembers your coffee order, he cooks for you, he texts you every day, he asks you questions, he cares.

He's still the same Zayn, still grumpy at times, but he's happy and he's mine.

30
ZAYN

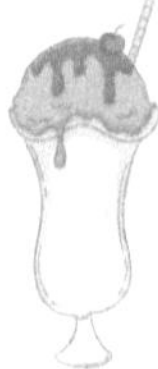

When I first started planning this day for Annie, I knew I couldn't do it alone. I didn't know the first thing about what all should go into a date, or whatever this special day is supposed to be. So, I did the only thing I could think of.

I contacted Marcy.

Since we both work in the same place, it was easy to find her. Although she's still getting used to me. Every time I see her, she glares at me, doesn't wave, just continues walking. But that's typical Marcy. So I had to yell after her.

When I told her I needed her help with something for An-nie, that finally got her attention. She stopped walking for long enough to tell me a few of her favorite foods. I already planned on the beach, I knew it had to be there, but I had no idea what to get. I didn't know her favorite snacks, since Annie buys groceries without me, and that's something that you need for a picnic.

"You did all of this?" Annie asks, walking up to the picnic blanket lying in the middle of the sandy beach.

"I might have asked Marcy a few questions, but yes." I let go of her hand so she can continue looking around what has been set up. I had to hire a company. Did you know that there are companies that set up picnics? I didn't, but now I do.

"But why the beach? Isn't this the last place you want to be?" Annie looks up at me, concern in her eyes. She's thinking of me, even now, when this day is for her.

"I figured it was time I made new memories. Better memories. Ones that make me smile when I think of the beach." I shrug, trying not to make a big deal out of it. But it is a big deal.

This beach holds a lot of negative memories, but every time I'm here with Annie, new memories pile on top and the past starts to look smaller. I remember the bad times less. They're still there, like a scar that will never go away, but it doesn't hurt. It's there as a remembrance of who I was and what I thought I'd lost. In all honesty, I never lost anything. If I loved Marissa back then, then what I feel for Annie is ten times the amount of that.

"I love it, Z."

"Good. I was hoping so. Open the basket," I say, taking a seat next to her on the blanket.

"Oh my god, Zayn. You didn't." She opens the basket and a hand shoots to her mouth. "Did Marcy tell you about all this?" She looks at me, still awestruck by the contents of the basket.

"Yeah, is that bad?"

"Bad? Oh, no, this is great. I can't believe you went to all this effort."

"It wasn't any effort at all, Annie. I did this because I like you. Remember, I don't need to do anything. I wanted to."

Annie starts pulling out the items in the basket. A packet of peach rings, crackers with goat cheese and raspberry jam, dark chocolate covered pretzels, a dark chocolate bar with caramel, popcorn, a blueberry muffin, and her favorite non-alcoholic wine.

"Zayn, you're going to make me cry. No one has ever done something like this for me." Annie looks at me and her bottom lip is formed in a pout.

"Come here." I reach out for her and she moves to me, wrapping an arm around my back and snuggling into my side. "You deserve so much more, Annie. You deserve to be treated right."

"You sure there aren't any photographers? You're being awfully nice to me," she teases.

"No, Annie, this moment is just for us. There might be a few stragglers, but I haven't seen any cameras." I place a hand under her chin and tilt her head back until she's close enough for me to press my lips against hers.

Annie relaxes into me. I'm seeing the way my words affect her. She's smiling more, laughing, and it's not because she's trying to impress me. It's because she wants to be here, and I love that she's giving me more of her.

We spread out the food around us and start snacking, alternating between the crackers and the sweet treats. We finish the first bottle of wine, so I'm grateful I packed two. It's still only mid-afternoon and we have a bit of time before we will head home. I plan to spend the next little while just chatting and getting to know Annie.

"Will you tell me about your mom?" I ask.

"My mom? Oh, um, there's not much to say. She wasn't the biggest fan when I decided to follow Cassie out here five years ago. It's always just been the three of us, so when she didn't support Cassie moving out here, I didn't know how she'd take me moving. It was rough for a little while, but she came around. Once she knew I'd be with Cassie, *and* they made up their relationship, *and* when she found out Cassie was in a serious relationship, she actually started making an effort. She comes out here two or three times a year, otherwise we just catch up on the occasional phone call or text."

"Does she support you now?"

"Yeah, she says she's proud of me and all the things parents are supposed to say. Does it mean anything? Not sure, but yeah, she doesn't think I've thrown my life away for a useless career. It's been nice to repair our relationship over the years and to show her how much progress I'm making with my job," Annie says, taking a bite of a peach ring. She closes her eyes and lets out a soft moan.

"Good?" I ask, laughing.

Her eyes snap open and she joins my laughter. "Yes, it's been a while, okay? Don't make fun of me." She tries to push me backward into the sand, but I grab her wrist for stability and hold myself close to her. I plant a kiss on her forehead for good measure. "How are your parents?" she asks.

"They are fine, I think. I haven't talked to them much since last year, but I'll be visiting over Thanksgiving." My parents always saw Marissa as a daughter, and I think when we broke up, they felt like they lost a child. They always assumed we'd get married, they became best friends with her parents, and they didn't know how to talk to me when I didn't have her by my side anymore.

"You're going there for Thanksgiving?"

I nod in response.

"Alone?"

"Yes, I didn't think you'd want to come with me."

"Why?" Annie asks, her head tilting in confusion.

"Well, my brother will be there."

"If you asked, I would go to be there for you, Zayn."

"Well, do you want to go, Annie?"

"I would love to." She smiles.

"It's a date." I reach over and squeeze her shoulder. "You don't have to worry about Dan. You're mine. You'll be there with me, and I'll make sure to let him know you'll be there ahead of time."

She just nods, and I know she's worried or maybe just anxious, but she needs to trust that I have her.

"If he says anything to you, I'll punch him," I say.

"You wouldn't do that."

"I would. Don't you know by now that I would do anything for you?" I plop a peach ring in my mouth.

"Yeah, I do," she says, her voice practically a whisper.

This time at the beach is different. It's not just because there are barely any photographers either. The air feels lighter around us, our bodies naturally draw together, and I can't stop feeling the urge to touch her. Touch her anywhere: her shoulders, her hips, her knee, her arms. It's like there's a magnetic pull from her that keeps attracting me, and no matter what I do, I keep coming back. Again and again.

We stay at the beach for another hour, talking, watching the waves, just enjoying each other's company. Today is already starting to replace the bad memories of a year ago, and it's all because of Annie.

"Want to get out of here?" I lean over, drawing her chin to mine to plant a kiss to her lips.

She leans into me and uses a hand to grab the side of my face to pull toward her. She kisses me slow and deliberate, savoring the time alone we had.

"Yes."

31
Zayn

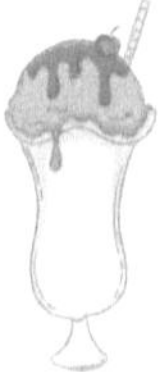

As each day passes, it gets harder and harder to tamper my feelings. I'm fully in this relationship, and I know Annie is too, but it feels like we still have an end date when our contract ends. The bubble we are in is perfect. This time together has been so special for us both, but I worry that if we fully commit and negate the end date, the bubble will pop. And what happens if I lose Annie too?

I'm grateful to have the distraction of work today. Being at the studio helps keep my mind occupied on other things, even though it is Saturday and they aren't as distracting as I want them to be. The prospect of landing the role I desperately want looms over me.

For the past hour, I've been in my trailer, trying to rehearse lines for a short film that Ed casted me in recently. It's enough to keep me busy, but I'm finding that I lack the mental energy to memorize the script right now.

My phone buzzes on the counter next to me, so I reach over to pick it up.

"Logan." I greet, still not happy with him about the other day.

"Zayn, how's it going?"

"Good, I suppose. What's up?"

"I have a meeting scheduled for us with the PR firm in a few days. I'm going to text you the details, but I wanted to make sure it won't be a problem," Logan says.

"Why would it be a problem?" We haven't met as a group for a while, but there are still a lot of emails going back and forth between Annie, her boss, and Logan. I see them because I'm cc'd on every one.

"Well, we are talking about the transition. Annie's contract will be ending within the next two months, and we need to align on a few things prior to that."

"Okay, I don't see why I need to be there. Can't you do that without me?" I don't think I want to be in the same room when they discuss our time being over. I'm not ready.

"No, I need you to be there. It will look better if you are there. This is a team effort. I thought things between you and her were going well?" Logan asks. He grumbles in the background, and I can only assume that he's driving somewhere or walking down the street. It doesn't take much for him to be angry at people.

"They... are. They are. I'll be there."

By the time we hang up, it's time for lunch. I still have an hour until I need to be on set, so I decide to head to the cafeteria.

Normally I avoid it like the plague, getting food delivered to my trailer or grabbing a quick bite to go. The desire to sit and converse with others is rare for me, but today I need to get Annie and this whole "end of our contract" thing off my mind.

As soon as I enter the cafeteria, I see the guys in the corner of the room. Lane and Max sit on one side, facing the door across from Emmett and Tyler.

"Mind if I join?" I ask as I approach the table, already forgetting to grab the food I came in here for.

"Not at all," Emmett says, pointing to the seat next to him. I take it.

"You look like shit," Tyler comments while shoving some fries in his mouth.

"I feel like shit, so, makes sense," I say.

"Want to talk about it?" Lane asks, but it's muffled as he's also scarfing down a burger.

Do I want to talk about it? Talk about my feelings? I've never had someone, besides Kiley, ask me to talk about things. I've been raised to just shake it off, ignore them, it'll go away. But I don't think shoving everything down is working. It's how I ended up in this place to begin with.

"I just, um, don't know what to do about my situation," I admit.

"Have you seen a doctor about it?" Tyler jokes, then gets shoved by Emmett. The entire table bursts out in laughter. At least they know how to lighten the mood.

"Have you made a pros and cons list?" Max asks.

I shake my head. "I already know there aren't a lot of cons."

"What even is the situation?" Emmett looks at me, and I find myself anxious about saying anything because he is Annie's brother-in-law. He could rush to her sister at any moment and spill all my secrets, and she would tell Annie.

But, for some reason, I trust him. Maybe it's the fact that Emmett is this well-known actor and writer and has non-celebrity friends, or maybe it's just a gut feeling. Either way, I feel comfortable saying what's on my mind.

"Well when we started dating, we knew it wasn't going to be for forever," I say. "We had until the end of December, when I hopefully get signed on for the trilogy."

"But you don't want it to end anymore, I'm assuming?" Emmett asks. His tone is curious, not laced with any mal-intent.

"No. I don't. But I'm also worried it'll be different if we decide to continue. My last relationship didn't end great, and I just don't know if I'll ever be able to give someone else one hundred percent. I don't know if I have that much to give."

"Fuck, man. This is heavy shit for this early," Tyler says.

"Yeah, I know. I don't need advice, it just feels good to talk about it. I haven't, um, had anyone to talk about it with, so I guess thanks?"

"That's what friends are for," Emmett says, slapping a hand on my back.

I smile in his direction, appreciative of what he said. Being brought into this group of friends is something I didn't see coming, but something I've always wished for. To have a group of friends to just listen to me, not necessarily give advice, but know that they have my back. Now, if only I could figure out what to do about Annie and me, then I'd have my life back on track.

32

ANNIE

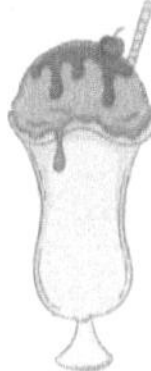

"So, everything's kind of messed up?" Cassie asks.

"Yep, kind of," I mumble.

Zayn is gone at work today, so I invited Cassie to come over to the apartment. After the other night, the date, the picnic on the beach, and the knowledge of Zayn's past, I needed someone to talk to.

"What are you going to do about it?"

"Nothing," I say. What can I do? With how things ended for him and myself in previous relationships, I can't talk to him about what's next for us. Everything is going so well right now. We are having fun, just like we agreed. Sure, some feelings might be there now, but they'll go away. Right?

"Oh, Annie," Cassie says, turning to face me on the couch. She places a hand on my shoulder and squeezes.

"You sound like Mom." I roll my eyes, knowing she'll hate that I said that, but it's true. "I just wanted to talk about it and hope that if I keep talking about it, then my heart will get the message. I know things are ending. I know it. So, if I keep reminding myself, maybe it'll hurt a little less? Or maybe these feelings will just go away before then?" I sigh and throw myself back on the couch. My eyes close and I take another deep breath because I know my feelings won't go away. Not when we still have two months left of doing this.

"I think I know what I'm talking about. I did have a similar situation, if you remember."

"Yes, I know about your love story. How can I forget when you had a million articles written about you?"

"It was not that many." Cassie's response is defensive.

I dip my head and raise my eyebrows, giving her *the look.*

"Okay, fine," she concedes. "It was a lot. But still, it's not much different than the situation you find yourself in. I don't know how we both fell for celebrities..."

"Yeah, I don't know." I lift my head from the back of the couch.

Cassie's eyes widen and a hand shoots to her mouth.

"What?" I ask.

"You just admitted to me that you've fallen for Zayn."

"I did not," I spit out. I can already feel my cheeks getting warm from knowing that I just told a lie.

"Annie, I know when you're lying. You're not looking at me, your knee is bouncing, and you're fidgeting with your bracelet."

Fuck.

"I don't want to talk about it, okay?"

"Okay, okay. Just know I'm here if you need someone to talk to, okay? You shouldn't have to carry all of this on your own. And I know that Zayn feels the same way. Well, not actually, but I can assume the way he looks at you is the way that Emmett looks at me."

"Thanks, Cass." I smile.

"Would you two want to double date with us tonight?"

"Tonight is our typical date night, so we can come after ice cream?" I ask.

"Or we can meet you there? I still need to try your flavor."

"Yeah, we can do that," I say. It'll be nice to have Cassie and Emmett there.

"Great! Well, I'm going to get out of here. Just text me when you're planning on leaving, okay?"

I nod, then stand from the couch, walking with Cassie to the door. She gives me a hug.

"Love you, sis. It'll all work out, okay? Maybe it doesn't have to end. You should talk to him."

"I'll think about it. Love you, too." I smile because it's all I can do.

While I wait for Zayn to get home, I figure I can take the time to catch up on some work. Over the past few weeks, it's been busy. A lot of my primary communication from Greg comes through email, as does every correspondence with journalists, photographers, and any other contact. I'm grateful to have a job that is flexible and enables me to work from anywhere, but some days it can get overwhelming.

My music is at full blast in my ears, and I'm ready to get some shit done. For the next few hours, I sit at the island and catch up on anything I missed over the past few days. Being around Zayn is distracting, and I'm used to doing a lot of these admin tasks at night. That's how it was when I first moved in. Now, we spend most nights cuddled in front of the TV, and my laptop stays plugged in in my room.

The light dims in the apartment as the time passes, the natural light filtering out as the sun starts to set. It feels good to be back doing things, even if the rest of my life is all fucked up. At least I have this one constant. For now. If Greg makes me consider moving to New York to keep working for his company, this will change too.

I'm about to switch over to researching new jobs when I feel a light tap on my shoulder. I scream, throwing my headphones off my head, and my body starts falling the opposite way, off the stool. Two strong, capable arms catch me. Hot breaths tickle the exposed skin of my neck.

"Miss me?"

Zayn. Immediately, my body relaxes in his arms, slacking at the fact that it wasn't a robber or a damn spider coming to get me.

"I hate you," I mumble as Zayn helps me get down from the stool. He doesn't let me go though, just turns me around to face him, moving his hands to cup my jaw.

He leans down, makes sure I am meeting his gaze, then leans a few more inches toward me, taking his time to plant a kiss on my lips. "I hate you too." One more peck, then he lets me go, circling around to the other side of the kitchen. "What's on the agenda for tonight?"

"Besides being scared half to death by my boyfriend?"

Zayn chuckles, cracking open a sparkling water.

"We're still going to the ice cream shop, but Cassie and Emmett are meeting us there."

Zayn stops mid-drink and says, "Oh yeah? Double date?"

"Apparently," I say, plopping back down in the stool to close out the tab open on my computer.

"Why do you not sound happy about that? You don't want to be seen with me with people we know?" Zayn raises an eyebrow.

"No, it's not that." I shake my head. "It's just... it's different now that we are *together* together."

"Do you not want me to touch you?" Zayn stalks closer, leaning over on the island. He slides a hand over to cup mine and draws circles with his thumb. The rhythm is enough to send me into the memories of the other night.

"It's not that," I whisper.

Zayn walks to me, placing his hand on mine inching it toward my shoulder.

His face is close to mine, his mouth hovers over my ear in his signature position, as he whispers, "Do I make you nervous?" He nibbles at my ear before dipping his head to press a kiss on my neck.

"Sometimes," I admit, my voice still a low timber.

He moves my hair to the opposite side and his lips to the other side of my neck.

"You love it." Not a question, a statement, because he already knows.

His teeth dig into the skin, softly, enough to feel the bite, and a whimper creeps from my mouth.

"Oh, how I'd love to leave a mark on you, Princess. Let the whole world know you're fucking mine, no one else's."

"I dare you," I say.

"No, I can't. Not when we are about to go on a double date where I'm going to have to impress one of the only people in this world that means something to you." He kisses me again and again.

"We can cancel," I suggest.

"Not an option. I look forward to our date nights, and I need this time. I need this time with you." One more kiss and then his hands replace his mouth, massaging my shoulders. I didn't realize how sore I've been from hunching over all afternoon.

"Fuck," I say.

"That good?"

I don't have to see Zayn to know he's smirking.

"That good," I mumble.

"C'mon, let's go get ready." He plants a kiss on my head, then grabs my hand for me to follow him.

33
ANNIE

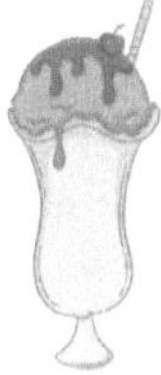

"Is there anything I should know about your sister before we go in?" Zayn looks over at me in the car. We parked a moment ago, and Cassie and Emmett should be here any minute.

"She's like me? But older? I don't know. Don't you know her?"

"Very helpful." Zayn rolls his eyes. His hands tighten on the steering wheel. "Yes, I've met her before, but we don't cross paths a lot."

"Zayn, are you nervous?" I tease, pushing at his shoulder.

He tries to give me his best side-eye but ends up smiling anyway. "Stop looking at me like that."

"You're the hot actor, you shouldn't be nervous to talk with someone you likely see more than me."

"You think I'm hot?" Zayn's head dips to the right, and damn, the way he's looking at me takes my breath away.

"I think you're very hot, is that not obvious?" I lean closer to him, my arms resting on the center console.

"For the record, I think you're very hot, too." He grabs my chin and pulls me all the way to him before pressing his lips against mine.

My head turns to the left to deepen the kiss, bringing us closer together, but a bang on my window causes me to snap back into my seat. My hand goes to my chest as my heart rate climbs.

"Fuck, what was that?" I see something out of the corner of my eye.

Cassie. And Emmett. I shake my head while they stand outside the car laughing.

Zayn opens his car door to get out and join them.

"Have fun without me! I'm going to stay here so I don't die from embarrassment." I sink into my seat as my door opens.

"Oh, I was just having some fun. Taking advantage of your back being turned, you know." Cassie grins, proud of herself for catching me off guard.

Growing up, we would take turns jumping out of dark bedrooms or hiding in closets, just to scare one another. It first started by accident. Since I'm five years younger than Cassie, I didn't realize how creepy it would be to sit in a dark room waiting for her. From that moment, she got me back, and then we would do whatever we could to scare one another. I learned to keep the lights on and my chest to the door ever since.

"C'mon, Princess." Zayn's in front of me, holding out his hand, waiting for me to grab it.

Cassie catches my attention, her eyes wide, which I can only assume is because of the nickname. The one that's meant to be private, for us. Ugh. I can't even hide the fact that it makes me blush every time.

I press my hand into his palm, and he wraps his fingers around mine and tugs, pulling me out of the car and into his chest. He presses a kiss on my head. I'm officially sure that Zayn's love language is physical touch.

Either that, or he just genuinely enjoys it.

"Annie, Zayn, you brought friends!" Liam calls when we enter the shop.

I know Liam is a huge fan of Emmett from the few times he's worn shirts with sayings from his movies. And I know what that's like because of how celebrity obsessed I was at a young age. If Emmett was in it, I not only watched it, but I purchased it, found merch, memorized lines, made collages, made friends in message boards, and bothered Cassie a billion times when she first started working at January Studios.

"We did," Zayn says before I get the chance.

When we first started coming here, he wouldn't say anything. He'd just sulk and be his grumpy self. But piece by piece, he's started opening up and acting more full of life. And Liam especially loves when Zayn talks to him.

"We heard you have the best ice cream." Emmett walks up to the counter to inspect the buckets of ice cream.

"We do, sir, would you like to sample one? Or two? Or five? Well, maybe not more than five, because that is basically one scoop." Liam rambles, out of breath from trying to impress Emmett.

"Call me Emmett, and I don't need samples." He turns to Cassie and says, "Want to split a cup of Summer Bliss? Apparently that's their flavor." His eyes flicker to us and his eyebrows raise, before he looks back at Cassie.

She nods.

"Alright, Liam, two scoops of Summer Bliss, please."

"Same for us, Liam. Thanks man," Zayn chimes in.

Liam smiles to himself as he scoops our cups. After we pay, I look around for a seat. It's packed in here, like normal, but we find a booth to sit in.

"Is it always this busy? I wouldn't think an ice cream shop would be this busy at the end of October," Cassie says.

Zayn just chuckles. "Pretty much. All because of Annie."

"It was not just me, it was a team effort." I beam at him, and he smiles back before plopping a spoonful of ice cream in his mouth.

I turn back to Cassie and Emmett. "They were going to shut this place down, but when we started coming here and bringing the press, everyone else started coming here. They had to enforce the capacity of the building in the heat of the summer. That's how busy it got."

"Wow, seems like you two make a great team. Saved the ice cream shop, pulling in tons of donations for the Young Actors Association, who knew?" Emmett comments.

"Yeah, who knew." I don't have to look at Zayn to know he's smiling at me. I can feel the heat of his gaze as I take another bite of the ice cream.

"What projects do you two have next?" I ask, switching to a subject that takes me out of the spotlight.

"We, um, are taking a break." Cassie smiles at Emmett. He gives her a nod, signaling something silent.

"You two never take breaks," I say.

The most time they've taken off is a month, and I thought Cassie was going to go crazy from not working.

"We will have our hands full in a few months." Cassie's expression changes. Her cheeks turn red, her eyes soften, and Emmett's hand moves to her belly.

"Are you serious?" I ask.

"Serious."

"Oh my god, Cass. Em." I reach to wipe a tear from my eye.

"Congratulations. You two are going to make amazing parents."

"Thanks, sis. We are excited."

"Well, look at me. I'm a mess. These photographers are going to wonder what's wrong because I'm a crying mess," I say, frantically wiping my tears with a napkin.

"A beautiful mess," Zayn says, barely a whisper.

34
ZAYN

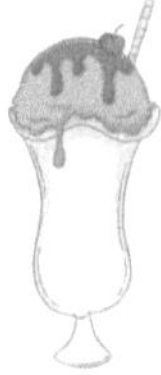

"Annie, we need to go," I yell down the hallway.

We are meeting Greg and Logan this morning to talk about the end of the contract since it'll slow down a lot when we get to December.

"I'm coming, I'm coming." Annie comes out of my room, *my* room, wearing the same dress she wore when she gave that damn presentation, and I'm weak in my knees all over again.

She saunters over to me, presses her hand to my jaw and says, "You dropped your jaw, Z," then kisses my cheek.

She moves past me, getting coffee or tea I can only assume, but I'm able to slap her ass before she gets too far away.

She screeches and jerks forward, snapping her head to me. "Zayn Andrew Barnes, did you just slap my ass?"

I take two steps and pull her toward me, gripping her ass with both hands. "I couldn't resist."

She can't help but let out a small moan when I grip her tighter and close the gap between us. I dip my head and press a kiss on her lips, feeling grateful I can do this whenever I want.

"I thought we needed to go," she mumbles against my lips.

Shit. We do.

I groan, letting her go. "Why do we need to be responsible adults? Can we call in sick? That's a thing, right?"

Annie places a hand on one hip and leans to that side. "We can't do that, Zayn. They would know we're faking it."

"I don't know Annie..." I say, walking past her to fill a to-go mug for her, since I distracted her enough that she forgot. "I feel like we are great at faking things until they are believable."

Her expression drops. The smile that was there turns slightly down.

Fuck.

"Annie, that's not what I meant—"

"No, it's okay. You're right. Let's go." She grabs the mug from my hand and rushes to the front door to slide on her shoes.

What do I do? Do I give her space? Do I run to her? Talk and try to get her to understand that none of this is fake? That I'm fucking falling in love with her and I'm trying my hardest not to? In my previous relationship, we didn't communicate. If we had issues, we let them simmer until they went away, and all that was left were grudges and lots of bickering.

I don't want that again, so I do what my gut is telling me to do.

"Annie." I rush over to her, cupping her face with both hands. "Look at me, please."

Her eyes snap to mine, and I can see water already pooling in her tear ducts. I fucking caused that.

"I didn't mean it."

"Zayn, it's fine. I'm okay," Annie says, clearly trying her hardest to convince me. Her eyes blink over and over again to keep her tears from falling.

"Sweetheart, this is..." I sigh. "This is new to me. I'm trying. I have a lot to learn. But one thing I do know is this... this," I point between us, "is far from fake. Okay? This is real, as real as it fucking gets. I'm crazy about you."

"You're crazy about *me*?" Her eyebrows narrow, and she has the cutest pout on her face.

"Have I not made it obvious? Have I not shown you that I worship the fucking ground you walk on? God, Annie, you've brought me back. My princess." I pull her head toward me, pressing a kiss on top of her forehead.

"Well, you should know that I'm equally as crazy about you. It hasn't been fake for me for a while."

"Is this when I get to bend you over and fuck you over the island?"

Annie laughs, and the sound travels straight to my heart, sending sparks through my body and joy to my brain. This girl. I'm a goner.

"Let's get this meeting over with."

I groan loudly, making sure I follow it with an exaggerated eye roll. "Fine, but we are stopping for blueberry muffins."

And when she smiles again, it reaches her eyes, and I know in that moment that I've found my way to her heart.

We reach the office within the hour. The sun shines bright today, so I'm hoping that means this meeting will go well. I grasp Annie's hand as we walk toward the office.

"This okay?" I ask, noticing that her gaze tracks our hands as I interlace our fingers.

"I mean, yeah, but if we walk in there like this, they might get the idea that..." She trails off.

"That we are together?" I raise an eyebrow.

She nods.

"Good." I pull open the front door of the building for us to enter.

"Good?" Annie asks.

"Yeah, Princess, good. I want the whole world to know you're mine." I lean to the right to press a kiss onto the top of her head. "Now, let's go get this over with." I tug her toward the elevator.

Greg and Logan are already here, waiting for us in one of the conference rooms.

"Ah, Zayn, Annie, good morning," Greg says when we enter the room.

"Hi, Greg. Logan." I greet them with a nod. I pull out a chair for Annie, then settle next to her. My hand finds a place on her leg.

Logan has an eyebrow raised. "This for real?"

I look over at Annie, her gaze pinned on me as her lips bloom into a smile.

"Yeah, Logan, this is real." I return my eyes to him, and he just nods in response. But I see him smile even as his head turns down toward the table. I can see that he's happy for me.

Greg doesn't comment. We start with an overview of the articles that have been published recently and how I'm trending in the media. All positive things, thankfully.

"There's been speculation about what you're doing next, which is great. We want people to wonder what you're doing because it will draw attention to the studio," Logan comments.

That's great. It's what I wanted, but I can't help but feel this sinking feeling in my stomach. I'm close to getting what I want, yet the future with Annie is unknown.

"And Annie, I have an update on your prospective client that would have you relocating to New York," Greg says, eyes trained on the papers in front of him.

New York? She's thinking about moving to New York? She hasn't mentioned anything. I look over at Annie to gauge her reaction, but it's unreadable.

"I didn't realize it was moving forward," Annie says, her voice slightly trembling. Her hands fidget on her lap. I move the hand that was on her leg and grasp one of hers, squeezing.

"It's close, and we will need to talk about it to decide if that's what you want to do. But as a reminder, it is the only option at the moment."

Only option? That can't be right. This city is overflowing with people who need PR help, and not just celebrities. There are plenty of restaurants and public figures that could use Annie's brain.

Annie doesn't respond, doesn't ask questions, just nods. A smile is plastered on her face, but I know it's fake. The mask she wears is back on, and she's back to playing the role of a people-pleasing employee.

"Zayn, are you feeling good with the progress Annie has made? If this…" Greg looks to Annie, then back at me before continuing, "relationship is a distraction, we can find a new publicist for the rest of the contract."

He wants to give someone else the credit that Annie's earned? I'm only in this spot because of her. She brought me back to life, gave me the chance to work through my shit and realize that it's not worth being angry over something that happened in the past.

"I don't need a new publicist. Annie is perfectly capable of doing her job," I tell him, narrowing my brows in his direction.

He has every right to be intimidated by me. If this goes well, and it will go well, people should be fighting to have Annie as their publicist.

That's why I don't understand why New York is the only option.

Greg simply nods, quickly looking at the paper in front of him. He grumbles to himself, but instead of paying attention to him, I look at Annie. Her eyes are also looking down at her lap, her hands still fidgeting. I squeeze her hand to get her attention and when she meets my gaze I mouth, *"I got you."*

She's been here for me; now it's my turn to be there for her. If New York truly is her only option, then I need her to know that I support her. I won't be the one holding her back from chasing her dream, not when she's so goddamned good at it.

"Logan, is there anything else we need to discuss? Or are we done here?" I don't want to be in this room any longer. The air is stiff from tension, and it's silent enough that we can hear people from down the hall.

"There are a few other things we need to talk about, mainly a few upcoming events." Logan pushes a piece of paper my way, and I pick it up, holding it so Annie can read it with me. Logan continues, "There is another gala this weekend, followed by a charity event at the Moonlight Club, and finally a holiday charity event, which will be the last public event for the two of you."

My grasp on Annie's hand tightens. If I have anything to say, this will not be the last public event we attend, fuck, didn't Logan just confirm that this was real? Didn't I say yes?

"It won't be the last public event, just the last one on the contract," I state, briefly making eye contact with Logan.

"Right, yes."

"Who arranged these events? Why was I not informed?" Annie asks, her voice timid.

"I wasn't sure if you could handle it, so I took care of the inquiries on your behalf. The emails came directly to me, so I didn't see the need to forward them," Greg replies, and I want to punch him in his face. Maybe then he'd get the hint that he's a shit boss.

"Zayn is my client," Annie says. She lets go of my hand and shifts forward. "If there are events where reporters will be present, I need to be made aware."

Greg is silent for a moment, likely just as stunned as I am that she spoke back to him. He's used to her being complacent, nodding, and doing whatever he says. He takes a deep breath before saying, "Annie, I know you've interned with us for the past two years—"

"Three," I correct.

"Yes, right, three years. I know you've been busy with everything, so I wanted to lend my help. I know the next client in New York is low profile and won't require as many events."

This time Annie doesn't say anything back, not a peep. She just nods, and nods again, like she's trying to comprehend what's going on here.

"Great, so that's settled," Greg says, standing up from his chair. "Keep Logan and I updated on the upcoming events, and Annie?"

"Hm?" Annie looks to Greg now, her eyes blinking as fast as she curls her lips inward.

"Think about New York. Let me know by the end of December. Your contract would begin January fifth, but we would need you out there by the first."

"Oh, okay." Annie nods again and smiles softly.

Greg leaves the office first, followed by Logan, who grips my shoulder and gives me a pity smile on the way out. Annie stands, says nothing to me, and starts to walk out of the conference room.

"Annie, wait," I call after her, but it's no use. She's already halfway down the hallway, speed walking her way to her office.

I take larger steps, forcing myself to move quicker to catch up to her. I make it through the door just as it's about to shut.

The door latches, and Annie throws herself into my arms, letting out the tears she was holding back for the last hour.

"It's okay, Princess," I say, running my hand through her hair. "We'll get through this."

35

ANNIE

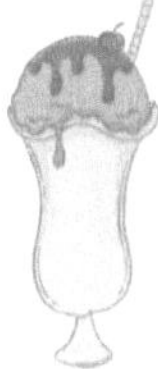

NOTHING IS GOING THE way I expected. I've somehow wasted the past three years working for a company that doesn't even believe in me. What if Dan was right? What if this career is a dead end and I'm just wasting my time?

"It's going to be okay," Zayn whispers into my ear, trying to calm me. "We'll figure it out."

It only makes me cry more. When was the last time I cried? Have I been holding in all these emotions for this long? Trying so hard to please others that it just became a part of me? Going through each day with a smile for so long that faking it became real?

"I got you." Zayn kisses the top of my head and I melt further into him, if that's even possible.

"I don't know—" my words come out in between sobs, "what I'm going to do."

"You don't need to figure that out right now."

"But—"

"No. Stop trying to fix everything. You don't need to be perfect around me." The sobs keep coming. Zayn rubs small circles on my back while trying to reassure me that everything will be okay. That we will figure it out together. Together. I don't know how we can be together when I might have to move to New York, but I try to do what he says and not try to figure it out right now.

The tears slow and my breathing follows. Zayn pulls away just enough to wipe my cheeks, leaving kisses on either side.

"You are incredible at what you do, Annie. Don't let anyone convince you otherwise, okay?" His hands grasp my face and he presses his lips to mine. He kisses me softly, and I know in this moment that I've fallen for this man. This wonderful, grumpy man.

How can I not? He's here, for me, always. He stands up for me, encourages me, believes in me.

"Let's go, yeah?" Zayn asks.

I can't find the strength to say anything, so I nod. He picks up my bags, interlaces his hand with mine, and pulls us toward the door to go home.

Well, at least I thought he would be taking me home. Instead, he keeps driving and pulls into the ice cream shop. It's only eleven in the morning. Are they even open this early?

"Annie, Zayn! This is early for you," Liam greets us as we enter.

They're open, but there's only one other family here. I know it's still warm in November, but I suppose being from the

Midwest, I always associate the fall with getting cold and not wanting cold things. Some people can drink iced coffee any time of the year, but not me.

"Hi, Liam. Can we get two cones to go today?" Zayn steps up to the counter, pulling out his card from his wallet.

"Yes, yes, of course. Coming right up," Liam says.

If my face is splotchy and red, he doesn't say anything. Liam just scoops two heaping spheres of ice cream onto two cones and hands them to us.

"On the house." He smiles.

"Thanks, Liam." Zayn puts his card away and takes the cones from him, handing one to me.

"Thanks, Liam." I smile.

An ice cream shop was the last place I thought I'd be a regular, but now I wouldn't want it to be anywhere else. There's something special about going somewhere and being recognized and remembered. It's simple, but the way that Liam remembers what we order or asks us questions about Zayn's movies, warms my heart.

And then I look at Zayn.

"Yes?" he asks.

I shake my head and smile. "Nothing, just thinking."

He holds the door open for me, then brings his hand to mine, pulling me to the right toward the beach.

"Walking on the beach? How romantic," I tease, pressing my shoulder into his.

"Well, this is kind of our thing, isn't it?" Zayn looks at me and winks.

"I suppose it is."

We stop talking for the next few minutes and just walk while eating our ice cream. It's empty at the beach, since it's early and a weekday. There are a few clouds in the sky. The crash of the waves is soothing, meditating, and I wonder if that's why Zayn brought me here. To a place that has become "our thing."

"I'm feeling better already, thank you," I mutter, trying to make sure I lick my ice cream fast enough before it melts.

He squeezes my hand. "Good, I thought this might help. Lately, the beach helps me get in a good mood too."

"Yeah?"

"Yeah. And you, of course. It's kind of a package deal for me." Zayn chuckles.

I want to ask him about us, about what's next, but I don't. Whatever is happening with us is perfect; it's the only thing in my life that I feel like I have some control over. And that's not saying a lot, considering I don't know when all of this will be over.

"How are you feeling about everything?" I ask.

Zayn looks at me with a smile on his face, and I remember when the sight was rare.

"About the movie? Or us?" Zayn asks, his eyebrows raised.

My cheeks turn red and I move to look in front of us before I answer, "Both."

"Well, I feel good about the movie. It seems like everything is trending positive. Even Ed has talked to me a few times about it. I'm fairly confident I'll get it."

"Yeah?" I beam at Zayn.

He nods, then leads us over to a trash can so we can throw away our cone wrappers. We turn around and walk back toward the car.

"Yeah, Annie. And..." He leans toward me, pushing into my shoulder playfully before continuing. "It's all thanks to you. And speaking of you, I like you so much."

"Yeah?"

"Is that the only thing you're going to say to me?"

"No..."

Zayn pushes me again. My feet touch the water this time, and I squeal as I jump back toward him. He just laughs.

"I know you like me too, it's okay," Zayn says.

"So sure of yourself, huh?" I ask.

"You *are* my girlfriend."

"What if I can't stand you? Ah! Zayn—"

Zayn tugs at my hand, slamming my chest into his. He grips my shoulder with his free hand so I don't fall backward, and leans his head toward mine. His lips near my ear, and his breath sends shivers down my spine. There's a jolt of pain on my ear as Zayn bites and tugs before he lets go. I let out a soft moan, the sound blending with the waves crashing to shore.

"Doesn't sound like you can't stand me." Zayn's hand moves from my shoulder, down my back, and finds its place on my butt. He squeezes, hard, bringing me closer to him.

"I hate you, *boyfriend*." I nip at his neck.

"I hate you right back." Zayn removes his hand from mine and brings it to my face to cup my jaw, pulling my lips to his.

Hours could pass and I would know no difference. Being here with Zayn feels like a fairytale dream, and I don't want to wake up. There's a slight breeze in the air, but I'm surrounded by the warmth of Zayn's arms. The sounds of the birds and water echo around us, transporting me to a different place.

When our lips disconnect, Zayn leans his forehead on mine. Our chests rise and fall in tandem.

"You definitely are something else," Zayn reminds me.

"Are you going to elaborate this time?"

He pulls back, interlaces his fingers with mine again, and walks us toward the car.

"When I first met you, I wanted to know you so bad. I can't explain why. Maybe deep down I knew you were already connected to me, or maybe it's because you're the opposite of me and I wanted that. You're like gravity, pulling people toward you, until they are stuck in your orbit. That's me, stuck in your orbit."

"I suppose that means you're stuck with me," I say.

Zayn reaches for the car door to open it for me. "I suppose I am."

He kisses me on my forehead before letting go of my hand and walking over to the driver side.

Zayn holds my hand for the entire ride back to our apartment, and every time his thumb swipes back and forth or he squeezes, the butterflies in my stomach flutter. Damn butterflies, don't they know I'm not supposed to feel like this? The heart wants what the heart wants, even if my brain is trying to remind it to be realistic.

"I have to go to set for a few to work on some scenes for the short film, are you going to be okay?" Zayn asks once we're parked.

"Will I be okay in our own apartment?" I ask.

He rolls his eyes in a Zayn-like fashion, then tousles his hair. "Yes, Annie. I can call off work if you want me here."

"You never call off work." Zayn is notorious for always going to set. It's always his priority.

"I would for you."

"Going soft on me, Barnes?" I wink for added sass.

"Fuck, no. I just, ugh, why are you making this difficult?"

"Because I can."

"You're changing me into a better man, Annie, get used to it. Call me if you need anything. Seriously. Even if you need a fucking loaf of bread, you call me."

"Why would I need a loaf of bread?" I ask.

Zayn lets out a frustrated sigh. "A loaf of bread, a latte, anything your heart can desire."

"And what if I just need you?"

"Then I'll be there."

I lean over the center console and press a slow, soft kiss against his lips. "I'll see you in a little bit."

"In a little bit," Zayn repeats, kissing me one more time before I get out of the car and head into the apartment.

By the time I sit down on the couch, my mind is busy going through a million different scenarios of what my future could look like. Will I be with Zayn? Will I not? Will I still work in

PR? Where will I work? What if I get a job feeding dolphins? Shit. I need to talk to someone.

As if the universe can sense my distress, my phone rings.

"Cassie!" I greet, realizing my tone reflects a bit of desperation.

"Hey, sis. How did the meeting with Greg go?"

"How do you know about that?" I ask with a tinge of confusion. It's been a few days since I talked to her, and I don't believe I mentioned it.

"Someone might have texted me that you might need someone to talk to."

Zayn.

"Of course he did." I sigh, leaning back on the couch.

"What is going on with you two?" Her tone is curious.

"We are dating? He calls me his girlfriend, and we've both agreed that whatever is going on isn't fake anymore. But I'm not sure what's going to happen in a few weeks when our contract ends."

"Will you stop sighing? It can't be that bad."

I roll my eyes even though Cassie can't see me. "It is bad, especially when apparently the only job available for me after Zayn's contract ends is in New York."

"Seriously?"

"Seriously. Greg says there aren't any other options here."

"That's so not true," Cassie says.

"Maybe I'm not doing as good a job as I thought I was."

"That's not true either, Anns. It's because of you that Zayn is thriving in the eyes of the media. He's going to land that trilogy role and it's all thanks to you. If Greg doesn't see that, then maybe it's time to look for a new company to work at."

Could I even do that? I'm fairly certain that if I started looking for jobs, Greg would find a way to put me on a *Do not hire* list.

"Just think about it, please," Cassie pleads after many moments of silence.

"I will," I lie.

It's not like I haven't thought about it. I have. The search history on my computer will prove that I've looked into any PR firm within a thirty-mile radius of Los Angeles. Even though I interned for a firm, most companies still want at least three years of experience. That's why it was a blessing for me to get hired on after my internship. I was able to prove my abilities without having to know someone. But I must not be that capable if Greg is trying to push me to New York.

When I hang up with Cassie, I figure I should get out of the house. I need to move. There's all this anxious energy built up inside of me and I need to do something to get rid of it. The perks of living in a city is you can walk outside and find most things you need within a ten minute walk.

I grab a book, my bag, and head out the door.

I reach Flora Cafe and order an Americano, then sit down with my book. If my mind keeps going in circles about what I'm going to do, maybe immersing myself in a fairytale land will distract me.

It does. Two Americanos, a blueberry muffin, and an iced tea later, my phone starts buzzing.

"Hello?"

"Annie, where the hell are you?" Zayn's voice is frantic.

"Zayn? I'm at a coffee shop."

"Why didn't you text me?"

"I didn't expect to be gone so long. I kind of got lost in my book," I explain.

"Stay there, I'm coming."

"You don't even know what coffee shop I'm at."

"Yes, I do," Zayn argues.

"How?"

"Annie, I know you. Blueberry muffin? Americano? See you soon."

36
ZAYN

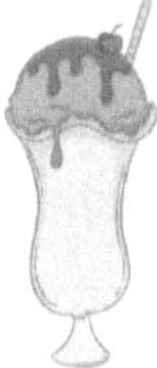

WHEN I GOT HOME from work, I expected Annie to be waiting for me like she always is. I'd open the front door to find her hunched over her computer at the island or watching something on TV.

Except that's not what happened. She wasn't there. In any room. When I texted her that I was picking up dinner and coming home and she didn't text me back, I thought she was just busy. Imagine my surprise when I opened the door and she wasn't there.

And why am I reacting like this? I have no fucking clue. Annie can leave whenever she wants. She could be at the grocery store or with a friend. Fuck. But knowing the type of morning she had, I flipped.

Annie answered her phone the third time I called. One more try and I would have checked every place in a ten-mile radius and called Cassie to help me find her.

As soon as Annie told me she went to get coffee—the damn coffee shop, I should have known—I left the apartment and headed there.

"Thank you," I say to the person holding the door open for me.

When I walk into the coffee shop, I'm hit with the smell of coffee and cinnamon. If only I could spend all day here. There's plenty of seats, low lighting, lots of snacks, and great company. And by great company, I mean Annie, who is currently hunched over her book in the back corner of the shop.

I move toward her but am stopped before I get to her.

"Zayn, hi, huge fan. I was wondering if you could sign this?" a man says to me, holding out his receipt. Is that all he had on hand?

"Uh, sure, do you have a pen?" I ask, flicking my gaze to Annie for a moment to see if she notices me, but nope. She's still nose down in her book. Must be good.

"Oh, um..." The man pats his pockets, all ten of them (he's wearing cargo pants), but no pen.

"Here, I'll ask the barista," I offer, growing painstakingly impatient as the minutes pass.

Luckily, I don't have to talk to anyone at the counter. I just grab a pen from a jar and walk back over to the man.

"Who should I address this to?" I ask.

"Jeremy. My wife's not going to believe I met you here."

I grumble some nonsense in return, then hand the receipt back to Jeremy.

When he moves out of my path to Annie, two more people replace him.

And that's how I get stuck signing random pieces of paper, coffee cups, and anything people have on hand.

When I finally finish with the mob of people, one more person stands in my path.

"I'm sorry, I have to—" I start to say, but the words die on my tongue as I look up to find Annie standing in front of me.

"Hi, Z."

God, she is fucking gorgeous. I grip her shoulders and pull her into a hug, breathing in the familiar smells of cinnamon and vanilla. My own personal dessert.

"Did you miss me or something?" Annie chuckles against my chest. I squeeze her tight one more time before letting her go.

"Or something." I smile. "I'm sorry, for, uh, freaking out." My hand tousles my hair.

Annie grabs my hand and leads me to where she was sitting when I first came in.

"Why did you?" Annie asks once we sit.

"You had a bad morning, I didn't know where you were. I wanted to make sure you were okay."

My gaze meets hers, and I do my best to portray that I'm serious. That she knows that I would do anything for her. She means that much to me.

"I'm okay. I promise." Her smile isn't convincing, but I don't want to push. Not here, not now.

Instead, I throw my arm around the back of the booth and tug her closer.

"Come here," I say.

Her body relaxes into mine as soon as her head rests on me.

"We will need to talk about New York, right?" she asks.

"We will, but we don't have to today. I thought we might do something fun instead."

Annie lifts her head. "You? Do something fun?" she teases.

I roll my eyes and playfully shove her away. "Come on, let's go."

I stand up and grab her hand, hoping that this will help improve her mood. One car ride and twenty minutes later, we arrive.

"What are we doing here?" Annie asks, standing outside the door of the shop.

"Well, we have a gala tomorrow and I think you need a new dress."

"I don't need a new dress, I can wear one of Marcy's."

"I want to buy you a new dress," I tell her, walking forward to hold open the door.

She entertains me by at least entering the shop.

"Hi." The store worker greets us. "Let me know if I can help you find something your size."

"Thank you," Annie says, smiling. Then, she turns to me. "What now?"

"Let's find you a dress." I smile back, loving that she's letting me spoil her.

It only takes us a few minutes to have a rack full of dresses for her to try on. All different colors, lengths, and styles.

Then, my favorite part, watching her try on all of them. Slowly, her smile starts to reach her eyes, and I know that this is working. She's beautiful any day of the week, but today she sees it too.

"Z, I need your help," Annie calls from within the dressing room.

Fuck, when she calls me Z, all blood rushes straight to my dick. Something about her saying it gets to me.

"Okay," I reply, twisting the knob of the door to open it.

"Can you come in and close the door?" Annie whisper-yells.

The trance I was in dissipates as I shake my head and take two steps forward so I can close the door. Annie is dressed in a dark green dress, a similar color to the first dress she wore with me. It has a deep v in the front, thicker straps, and the back... Dear God, the back droops *so* low.

I have to clear my throat before speaking. "What, uh, what do you need help with?"

She smirks, knowing what she's doing to me.

"I think this is the one and wanted your opinion. And I need your help zipping the side."

"I also think this is the one." I allow my eyes to slowly take her in. I move toward her, hovering barely a foot away. "You are beautiful." I lean forward, planting a kiss on the back of her left shoulder as she watches me in the mirror.

With one finger, I trace the side where the zipper has yet to be closed, feeling her smooth skin. She shudders and her eyes shut. A short breath follows as I plant my lips on her body again. I find the zipper and move my other hand to help hold the dress in place as I zip it up. Inch by inch, I move the zipper while planting kisses on her shoulder, her neck, her arm. Annie's breathing becomes more ragged by the minute.

"You are fucking delicious. Fuck, Annie." I let go of the zipper once it's all the way at the top. My lips not leaving her shoulder, my eyes flick forward to see her staring at me, her cheeks flushed a deep shade of red. "So delicious," I say and then I bite. Not hard, but enough to leave a mark, sucking on her neck as she leans into me.

"Best be quiet, Princess. We wouldn't want anyone to hear. Think you can do that for me?"

Annie nods once, quickly.

"I need words, Annie. Tell me no and I'll stop. Tell me no and I'll be done. But fuck, tell me yes, and I'll make sure to make you feel good."

"No," Annie says.

I immediately remove my lips from her shoulder and take a step back, temporarily confused by her decision. Annie turns around to face me, her back now toward the mirror.

"I mean no, don't stop. I can be quiet," she whispers.

"Are you sure?"

"Don't make me beg, Z."

My eyes roll to the back of my head as I picture her on her knees, but this moment is for her. I step back toward her and twist her around so she's facing the mirror again. When I was zipping her up, I realized this dress has a slit on the left side, perfect for what I need.

"Watch me fuck you with my fingers, Annie."

I press long kisses to her shoulder as I trail my hand down her body, my other hand wrapping around her waist to pull her close to me. The slit of her dress is high enough for my hand to reach without having to search for it, and I wonder if she chose it with this in mind.

"The answer is yes," she whispers again as my hand pushes past the layer of fabric and back up her thigh.

"Fuck, Annie, are you—" I pause, catching a breath before continuing, "are you not wearing any panties?" My finger teases her before landing on her clit to rub small, gentle circles.

"No," she moans. "I didn't want lines."

"You did this and then asked for my help, hoping it'd land you here in front of me. Is that right? You wanted me to fuck this pussy with my fingers."

"God, Zayn. You've got some ego," Annie says.

"Oh, do I now?" I pull back my hand, but Annie's hand clasps over it. "Be nice to me, otherwise I might choose to keep you on edge for the rest of today."

"You wouldn't." Annie's gaze meets mine.

"I would. But you're lucky I like you a little too much and that you're just a little bit tempting. You smell like a goddamn bakery and I can't resist." I quickly find her clit again, this time rubbing harder, faster, and Annie whimpers.

"Remember, you need to be quiet. Or I stop," I remind her.

The store is ours for the hour. I made sure no one would bother us, but she doesn't need to know that. I need her to feel safe, with me, in this moment.

Annie nods and bites her lip, then leans her head back on my shoulder. I can feel her getting close as the minutes pass. My lips return to her neck and my other hand moves to her breast, pinching her nipple through the fabric.

"Fuck, Annie, you are so beautiful," I tell her again. "Coming undone for me like this, knowing that when you wear this dress you'll be thinking of this exact moment."

"I'm coming, Zayn." She moans, and I follow the pace of her breathing with my finger.

"That's it, Princess," I praise her, slowing down my pace as her body begins to relax.

I remove my hand from under her dress and wrap both of my arms around her, resting my head against hers. We make eye contact in the mirror, both of our faces flushed from a mix of the heat and what just happened, and start laughing.

"So, that was..." Annie starts before laughing again, bringing a hand to cover her mouth.

"How is everything fitting out there? Can I get you a different size in anything? Need help zipping anything up?"

Annie jumps at the sound of the store worker outside the dressing room door.

"No—no, thank you."

"I'm helping her, don't worry," I say, winking at Annie in the mirror.

"Great!" the worker says before we hear her steps dissipate.

"I hate you," Annie says, but her face says the opposite.

"Yeah, I've heard that before."

"Didn't last too long."

"Nope, sure didn't." I kiss the top of her head. "Let's buy this and get out of here."

Annie nods and takes off the dress after I help her unzip.

"Zayn."

"Hm?"

"This is too much. This dress equals my three month salary." Annie holds up the tag for me to see like I care what it costs.

I might not have been in a lot of big-name films, but I have plenty of money to spare. More than I know what to do with.

"I already bought the dress, so I can't exactly return it." I shrug.

"What do you mean you already bought this dress? I tried on like ten dresses. What happened if I chose a different one?"

"You wouldn't have. I know you, remember?"

Annie smiles and doesn't say anything, just removes the dress and changes back into her original outfit.

Annie could have chosen another dress. I bought them all. They are all her. All colors I've seen her wear, all cuts of things I've seen her save to her Pinterest board when we lounge on the couch at night together, all styles that scream "Annie" to me.

She'd look beautiful in anything. All I care about is wearing her on my arm.

37

ANNIE

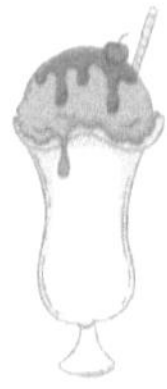

Zayn told me he bought all the dresses. That man. I made him return all the other ones since there is no way I need to own as many fancy dresses as Marcy. I don't need my own *27 Dresses* closet.

"You look stunning," Marcy says, sitting on the edge of my bed.

She's helping me get ready before the gala tonight. With all the past dates and ramping up to the end of the contract, we haven't seen each other as often as we normally would.

"You have to say that, you're my best friend," I say over my shoulder as I look at myself in the mirror. This dress is out of my comfort zone. It's lower in the back than I would normally like and the way it hugs my stomach is just enough for me to notice it. The urge to pull at the fabric piles up, but I take a breath, try to push it down, and remember why I chose this dress.

When I tried it on, I knew nothing would compare. It immediately reminded me of the first night with Zayn, attending as his fake date to our first gala. The event that truly started this insane relationship. Then, when Zayn entered the dressing room and his eyes fell on me, it made me feel like I was being seen, truly seen. Not just as people-pleasing Annie, but real-me Annie.

Marcy walks up to me from behind and hugs me. "You look stunning, I swear. And you're going to have the best night. Okay? Don't think about work."

"This is kind of work, though. That's going to be hard."

"You know what I mean." She squeezes me once before letting go. "I'm going to head home since you'll be leaving soon. I can't wait to see pictures. I love you!" Marcy yells as she leaves the room.

I return my attention to the mirror, sighing again at the sight. I know I look good, I do, but I'm also... overwhelmed? I don't know. It's all a lot. My job. Zayn. Tonight. My future. Everything.

I don't even realize I'm crying until Zayn's appears and swipes a tear off my cheek.

He presses a kiss where the tear was, and all I can do is stare at him in the mirror and let more tears fall.

"I can call to cancel, we don't have to go," Zayn whispers in my ear while pushing strands of my hair behind the other ear.

"We do, it's work. It's important."

"You're important," Zayn argues, pulling me into his arms.

I pause and breathe him in, his presence alone calming me.

"I want to go. I want to dance with you."

"We can dance right here, Princess, we don't need a fancy event for that." He presses a kiss to my forehead.

I don't know why his ex decided to say no to his proposal, but I'm thanking the universe she did. How did I find someone who not only encourages and supports me, but also is willing to do whatever to make me happy? And what am I going to do when this is all over? Because it has to be over, right?

"But," Zayn continues, "if that's what you want, then we can go."

"Just give me a few minutes to freshen up, okay? Then we can head out."

"Okay, I'll make us a snack for the road." My stomach grumbles as soon as he says snack, and my hand moves to cover the noise.

Zayn presses one more kiss on my forehead and whispers, "You're beautiful, no matter what that voice says inside your head," before walking to the living room.

It only takes me a few minutes to calm myself, and I spend a few more touching up my makeup. After one more look over, I decide that it's good enough and head out to the living room.

"Okay, I'm ready," I say as I approach Zayn, who is hunched over the island.

When he stands to face me, I see what he's wearing. I don't know how I didn't see it before. The dark green three-piece suit is beautiful.

"We match," I say, smiling at his appearance.

"I don't want anyone to mistake you for someone else's," he says. "You sure you still want to go? It's not too late to back out."

I nod. "Yes, I'm sure. It's good that we are going. Plus, Todd might miss you if we aren't there."

Todd and Zayn have been meeting regularly since he rejoined the board. It's been nice to see Zayn excited for something besides the trilogy. I think that him joining the board gave him a renewed purpose and Todd has helped tremendously with the transition.

"He'd live," Zayn says. He hands me my coat. "But I am excited for tonight, surprisingly. It's been a while since I've felt like this."

This meaning what's going on between us? This meaning the gala? This meaning what? Instead of asking, I smile at him, wrap my arm in his, and pull us toward the door.

"Cassie and Emmett will be there too," Zayn says as we reach the car.

"Really? She didn't tell me that," I say, surprised because Cassie tells me everything.

Zayn nods and says, "I thought it'd be fun to do another double date kind of thing."

"A double date kind of thing?"

"Don't make me regret this," Zayn says, holding open the door for me.

Zayn slides in after me and immediately laces our hands together.

"Thank you," is all I say, not knowing how to show that him thinking about me in the slightest means everything.

"Anything for you, Princess." He squeezes my hand and gives me a look that says a million words.

When we get to the venue, Zayn holds my hand as we walk down the red carpet. Lights shine on us from every direction, from cameras to streetlights.

"Zayn, Zayn, care to answer a question for us?" A reporter yells as we walk.

"Sure, what's up?" Zayn stops, switching to have his hand around my arm instead of interlaced with mine.

"There are rumors that you may be cast in an upcoming trilogy."

"Is there a question in that?" Zayn asks, and my eyes widen in horror at how he just responded to the reporter. But luckily they both laugh it off and my shoulders ease. Just a little bit.

"Yes, yes. Do you feel like you have a chance in landing the role?"

"Yes," Zayn answers immediately. "If you would have asked me four months ago, I would have told you the same thing, but it wouldn't have been true. I didn't deserve the role then, but now... now I have something worth fighting for."

I meet Zayn's gaze and my thoughts swirl in my head, wondering how I'll be able to let him go when I've fallen hard for him.

"Great, thank you, and Annie, question for you if you don't mind?"

"Oh, uh," I look at Zayn to see if I should answer the question or just say no, but he simply nods. "Go ahead."

"It seems that you are great at what you do if you brought Zayn back to the living—no offense." He looks at Zayn.

"None taken, it's true." Zayn shrugs.

The reporter continues, "Do you have any idea what's next for you? Who would be lucky enough to have you in their corner?"

"I'm not sure yet, but when I do, you'll be the second person to know," I tease, trying not to show that the fact that I might have to move to New York is looming over me.

"Great, thank you both."

We both nod, then Zayn pulls me toward the front door of the venue. The inside is decorated with a mix of auburn and burnt orange. A live band plays soft jazz as everyone finds their seats.

It doesn't take me long to spot Cassie and Emmett because Cassie is running toward me as Emmett trails behind.

"Look at us, our first event together." Cassie beams, pulling me into a hug.

"We have been at plenty of events together," I note, rolling my eyes as she pulls me toward our table.

"Yes, but you were always working."

"I am working tonight, too," I argue.

Zayn pulls out my chair for me to sit down, which I don't think anyone has ever done for me before.

"It's a different kind of work," Zayn says as he plops down next to me.

"That is true, it doesn't feel like work."

"See," Cassie chimes back in. "So, this is different. I hope they have ginger tea, because I am feeling a little meh tonight."

"Tonight?" Emmett quips.

"Most nights." Cassie shrugs.

She's about two months into her pregnancy and she's been texting our group chats with updates that I would have been better off not seeing to begin with.

"Anyway," I say. "I love that you two are here, with us."

"Us too." Cassie smiles.

Eventually, dinner is served and the conversation starts to flow. Emmett moves to sit by Zayn, the two of them laughing and catching up on some topic while Cassie updates me on all things baby.

"They are getting along well," Cassie whispers to me, nodding to the boys.

"Have you two never talked to Zayn on set?"

Cassie shakes her head. "No, not on set. We talked over lunch sometimes when he'd sit with all of us. And even though everything he was cast in did well, especially the indie films, we didn't cross paths. We typically worked out of different areas."

"And Zayn and Emmett connected because of Logan?" I would have assumed having the same agent would have led to some sort of connection between them.

"Kind of. Logan was the reason why Zayn first landed a role at the studio. But after that, Emmett and Zayn hung out a little bit on set or at lunch, like I said, but when they started to get closer, that's when everything happened with Zayn. "

That makes sense, I suppose. But still, it makes me sad that Zayn didn't feel like he had anyone to talk to about anything. And that the people he was mutual friends with because of Marissa, abandoned him when he was at his lowest.

"He's lucky to have you, you know." Cassie grabs and squeezes my hand.

"She's right," Zayn whispers in my ear and I almost, almost, jump and hit him because I did not know he was listening.

I swivel around to face him and grab his face, pulling his lips to mine in a kiss.

When we pull apart, I keep his stare as I whisper, "I'm the one that's lucky."

Zayn is about to respond but is interrupted by Todd.

"Zayn, I'm glad to see you two here."

Zayn pulls away from me and stands up, shaking Todd's hand.

"We are happy to be here."

"You'll be at the club event, right? I thought I saw an RSVP come in for that."

"Yes, wouldn't miss it," Zayn confirms.

"Will James be there?" I ask.

"Of course. James wouldn't miss it, and they'll be excited to hear that you'll be there. They've told me you haven't been around the office much lately. I think they miss you," Todd says, enveloping me in a hug.

"Well, tell James I miss them too, and we'll catch up soon."

"I will," Todd says with a warm smile, then glances around the room. "Alright, I should go mingle. I'll catch you two later."

Zayn says goodbye and sits next to me.

"You look beautiful," he leans over to tell me.

"You've already told me that." I glare in his direction.

"And I'll keep telling you, so get used to it." Zayn pinches my side, causing me to squeal and jerk to the right.

"Are you two doing anything for Thanksgiving?" Emmett asks.

Oh, shit. I forgot Thanksgiving is next week. We have the charity event and then fly to see his parents the next day for two nights.

"We are going to my parents," Zayn says.

"Will your siblings be there?" Cassie asks, pretending her question is innocent.

"They both will be, yes."

"Ah, interesting," Cassie drawls.

If it wouldn't be obvious, I'd roll my eyes and shove her shoulder just to show how annoyed I am that she asked that. She will be texting me later about it, I can almost guarantee it.

I'm thankful when dinner arrives because that means less interrogation. I know Cassie is trying to look out for me and play the part of older sister, but I need her to let me handle all this. I don't want to know if she's judging me for my actions or disapproves of Zayn and I. I don't get the feeling that she does, but it's hard to talk about how I'm actually feeling because no one truly understands.

If I told Cassie about my dilemma, she'd be on my side. She'd want me to take the job in New York, but she'd also want me to try and make it work with Zayn. And I don't know how that's possible. I couldn't do that to him, not when he's starting to find himself again. Our schedules would never align, with him starting to act in the movie and me needing to go to event after event for a new client. I know how busy I am with Zayn. So, when I picture that times two, I don't know how I could manage that and fly across the country each time.

If we did try long distance, I could see us making it a little while. Having dates over video calls and sending gifts. But over time, one of us would resent the other, or we'd slowly unravel because we don't have time for one another. It's not that we wouldn't make the other a priority, but there's only so many hours in the day and when we are hundreds of miles apart... we'd never make it.

And that's why I wear a smile for the rest of the night when secretly my heart is shattering into a million pieces.

38
ZAYN

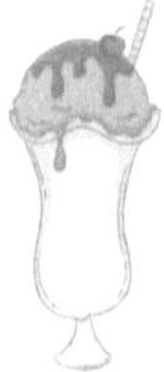

IF SOMEONE TOLD ME going into this contract with Starlet PR that I would end up finding the person that was made for me, I would have laughed in their face, gave them the middle finger, and left.

This year has changed me. Annie has changed me. Now I'm not sure what's going to happen in the next couple of weeks, but I almost want to pretend that nothing will and that we will continue to be whatever we are to each other.

I want to pretend that we are in this forever and no distance can stop that. I'm afraid if we start to talk about the end of our relationship, we risk losing what we have. If we acknowledge this is almost over, the anxiety of that stop date would consume us like a wildfire. If New York is the only option for Annie, she needs to take it. I'm not going to be the one to hold her back. I won't do that to her. After Thanksgiving, we will talk about it. But for now, we have a great Sunday night ahead of us at the club.

I'm glad this is the last event before a short week. Part of me forgot that becoming part of the board for the association includes attending one or two events a week during the spring and fall fundraising seasons.

Tonight's event is different from the gala last Tuesday. Typically a charity night consists of dinner, entertainment, a silent auction, and maybe dancing. There's a large guest list, lots of reporters, and many pictures taken because of that. It's more of a marketing event to help future charity nights.

Tonight is the opposite. It's a smaller, more intimate list. That's because of how much each ticket costs. Each person pays $10,000 minimum, with the option to donate more. Overall, the event will bring in close to one million dollars and fund the next round of internships for a group of one hundred kids.

I will mentor ten of those kids myself as part of me being back on the board. It's important for me to go to this event tonight, to show Annie that I'm serious about improving my image and getting back into giving back to the local community.

When Annie was trying to figure out what to wear tonight, I had to give in and show her the closet of dresses that I've been storing.

"Zayn Barnes, how dare you Jane Nichols me," was her exact wording, and I have never been more confused in my life. She told me that our next date night will end with us watching *27*

Dresses and then I'd understand. "You're lucky that all of these are cute at least and not horrendous."

She seemed mad when I showed her the closet, but the sparkle in her eyes told me a different story. For tonight, she chose a floor-length satin blue dress, no slit this time. She paired it with a simple rose gold necklace that rests right on her collarbones. Her hair is pinned half up, letting a few curled pieces frame her face. Then, to top it off, she's wearing a red lip, which is my kryptonite.

I picture those red lips wrapped around my cock. Her head moving slowly up and down my length. Her pretty eyes meeting mine with every stroke.

"Ready?" Annie looks at me, pulling me out of my fantasy.

The car just pulled up to the club, and I already hear the chatter of cameras and fans outside. The closer we get to the end of the year, and the more articles are published about Annie and I, the more I've noticed people around just to see me.

"Ready." I grin.

"I didn't expect this many people to be here," Annie says once we get inside the club.

Lit with various shades of red light, Moonlight Club is known for hosting private events for celebrities.

"Todd has a lot of connections around the city," I say.

"And I'm sure you rejoining the board has helped," Annie says, smiling and waving at people as we make our way to the bar.

My hand is pressed on her lower back, guiding her. We stop twice to shake hands with top donors.

What should be a one-minute walk turns into a five-minute walk, and I'm already grumbling under my breath.

"How long do we need to stay?" I ask Annie as we reach the bar.

"At least two hours."

"Anyone specific we need to talk to?"

"Did you not read my email?" Annie asks, her brows raised.

The bartender comes over, and Annie orders us both their mocktail special.

"I did not read your email." I grimace.

She sighs, but in a way that I know she's not annoyed with me. "Well, we need to talk to Todd. And I want to make sure I say hi to James."

"Right, that makes sense."

"And there's a reporter from the *Daylight Digest* that we need to talk with." Annie takes a sip of her drink and says, "This is good. I think it has lime in it."

"Mm, lime and pineapple? I think? It is good," I say, taking a sip of my own drink. "Anyway, is that it?" I turn around, resting my back on the bar so I can survey the room. The dance floor is mostly occupied.

"That's it."

So that's what we do for the next hour. People like to talk. I don't. With Todd, the conversation is easy. We speak about the holiday event coming up, how the previous event was, how the current event is going, and that's basically it. Annie talks with

James, and every time I look in her direction, she has a wide grin and laughs at whatever they're talking about.

Then comes the reporter. Annie helps answer questions or fills in the blanks when it comes to what I've been up to, how things are going, if there are any upcoming projects. I'm still having a hard time getting back into answering questions about myself since being used to shutting down and shutting people out. It's something I'm working on.

"I think I'm all talked out," Annie says as we find ourselves sitting at a booth after talking to the reporter.

"You're telling me. This is basically my version of hell." I pull at the collar of my shirt, more than ready to take it off.

"I know how to make it better." Annie glances my way with a mischievous smirk.

"Oh yeah?" I rest my elbow on the table in front of us, and my head follows, resting on my palm as I watch Annie. "How's that?"

"Come with me."

Annie slides out of the booth and holds her hand out. "We talked to everyone, and we have about an hour before we can leave without being noticed."

"Okay," I say, not sure where she's going with this. But I'd follow Annie anywhere.

Annie leads us through the clusters of people, not pausing for anyone this time. I thought she might stop on the dance floor, but as we get further to the other side of the room, I'm less sure where she's going with this. Then, she stops.

We're in the back corner of the room, still on the dance floor but as far away from people we can get without leaving.

Annie stands on her tiptoes and leans into me, whispering in my ear, "Let's dance, Z."

The slow beat echoes in my ears as I grab Annie's hand and bring it to my chest. I reach for her other hand and interlace our fingers, one by one, taking my time to feel our pulses merge into one. Annie's head rests on my chest as we sway to the music.

When I'm with Annie, I feel whole, complete, at ease. Even though we may not have forever, I know that I wouldn't have traded these last few months for anything. She made me feel again. There aren't enough thank you cards in the world to repay her.

The slow rhythm continues, pumping into our chests, playing alongside our heart beats. The music shifts into a faster beat, and I pull away from Annie, lifting our connected hands in the air.

Annie twirls in a circle and I tug her back to me, moving our hips more quickly than before. A grin blooms on her face, and I've fallen in love all over again. I lift our hands and she twirls, this time twice.

Laughter explodes from us as we collide. I grab her other hand and continue dancing with her, pulling us in opposite directions, twirling her in more circles, pretending like I know what I'm doing.

She doesn't care though. She's here, laughing, being an awful dancer alongside me. The heat of the club rises around us as the music plays, and we dance until we are both out of breath.

For some reason, when I pictured dancing with Annie again, I thought of something more slow and sensual. But this is better than I could have dreamed. Seeing her eyes crinkle, the small dimple that appears as she grins, and the way she bites her lips to stifle more laughter is enough for me to know this is a core memory.

When I pull her back to me, I kiss her forehead, lingering for a moment longer, not wanting to let her go. Not wanting tonight to end. Not wanting to leave our small bubble and visit my family in a few days. But, there's no avoiding that. It's time I confronted my brother.

39
ANNIE

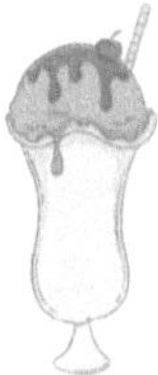

I NEVER IN A million years would have predicted going to my ex-boyfriend's parents house for Thanksgiving. This is normally the time of the year where I like to stay home, order a pre-made meal for two, and eat nothing but turkey and mashed potatoes for the entire weekend.

For the past few years, I've spent Thanksgiving evenings with Cassie or Marcy, but the rest of the time is for me to relax. There's enough traffic in Los Angeles around holidays to convince me to not leave my apartment. Everything is delivered, most conversations are held over FaceTime, and if my mom wants to visit, we plan to do that a few weeks before whatever holiday.

Zayn has been pacing the apartment all morning, checking in on me, making sure we have everything we need.

"Zayn, we will only be there for two nights," I remind him.

He's acting like we are staying there for an entire week, packing multiple suitcases.

"I just want to make sure you have everything you need."

"I already packed my one bag, Z, I don't need anything else."

"Nothing else? Are you sure?" Zayn's standing in his closet, his hands full of different shirt options.

Why does this man care so much about this?

"Yes, I'm sure." I walk toward him, take the shirts off his hands, and place them on the bed. "Is everything okay? Are you having second thoughts about us going?"

Does he not want to bring me home anymore?

"No, no, not that at all." Zayn shakes his head. He pulls me toward him, enveloping me in a hug. "I just want this to be perfect for you. I'm already stressing out about my brother and I'm just not wanting it to be a bad few days for you."

"Oh," I say. "We will get through it together, right?" I pull back, meeting his gaze.

His brother is only one person. I can handle him.

Zayn nods. "Guess I don't need all of this stuff then, right?" he asks with a sheepish grin.

"Nope, I'll help you put it all away."

We barely make it to the gate at the airport. After spending an hour putting away the clothes and hitting the road, we got stuck in traffic. I should have known, should have been better prepared. I know what LA traffic is like, especially going to the airport. If it says it's only going to take a certain amount of time, you might as well triple that. At least.

Zayn's hand wraps around my knee as we take off, stopping it from bouncing uncontrollably. It's a short flight, but I'm nervous. My heart won't calm down, I can't focus on a single thing, and my mind is wondering who won season 42 of *Survivor*. There's that many seasons right? I don't even watch *Survivor*, why am I thinking about that?

Anything to keep my mind busy, I suppose.

"It's going to be okay," Zayn whispers into my ear.

"You're supposed to say that." I glare at him.

"I'm not *supposed* to say anything."

"You can't guarantee anything. I haven't seen your brother since everything happened," I say.

"I know he didn't treat you well, but I'm glad you ended up with me."

"I am too," I say, looking up to meet his gaze. "You're nothing like him, you know."

I need Zayn to know that. That I trust him and know that he would never hurt or belittle me like Dan did.

I shift closer to him, brushing my lips against his. "You're something else," I mumble against his mouth.

"That's my line," Zayn says, chuckling.

"Our line."

Zayn presses a kiss on my lips, then on my forehead, before leaning back in his chair.

"I got you. I'll never leave your side. And if I do, Kiley will be there."

I smile at him and nod, knowing that he's telling the truth. But, I know that it's time I confront this and find some sort of closure. I don't know if it will do anything, but I need to show Dan that I'm doing well for myself.

The plane lands an hour later, and we take a taxi to his parents house. Nestled in a neighborhood and lined with tall trees, Zayn's parents live in a typical Californian family home. Even though Zayn is famous, his parents work normal jobs.

His mom is a banker in town, and she's been there for over thirty years. She has many stories, and apparently could talk my ear off for hours. His dad is an insurance agent, and even though I know nothing about insurance, I know he is a huge fan of music, so we can talk about that if things get awkward.

And Kiley will be there today, which I'm glad about. Between her and Zayn, I shouldn't need to talk to anyone else for an extended period of time.

Then there's Dan. Dan is apparently bringing his current girlfriend, but Zayn couldn't remember her name. They won't be there until tomorrow. He's still working some office job, still an asshole.

"Last chance to turn around," Zayn quips as the car slows in front of his parents' house.

"I'm fairly certain the last chance to turn passed back at home."

"I would buy us tickets to fly us back home," Zayn teases.

His home feels like my home.

"You don't need to spend more money on me, Z."

"I'm sorry, I didn't hear you. Can you say that again?"

"I said, you don't—"

"Oh, Annie, we should probably get out of the car, sorry, you can tell me later," Zayn interrupts, winks for getting his way, then exits the car.

I follow his lead, helping him grab a bag, then following as we walk up the sidewalk to the front door.

He rings the doorbell and we wait.

"Zayn!" Zayn's mom, Darla, appears on the other side of the door. She's dressed in a burnt orange midi-dress, which is stunning and complements her dark brown waves. When she smiles, I see where Zayn gets most of his facial features.

"Gosh, where are my manners? Come in, come in." She waves us inside and pulls me into a hug. "Annie, I'm so excited to see you again. It's been too long. I was surprised to hear about your relationship, but I'm loving all the new images and articles about you two. It helps me stay up to date since Zayn doesn't like to call me anymore."

"Mom, I'm busy, you know that," Zayn says, rolling his eyes in her direction.

"Well, either way, I'm glad Zayn could drag you here." She beams at me, her excitement pure.

"No dragging necessary, she came willingly, Mom," Zayn retorts.

"She must like you, then," Darla comments, and I smile at their banter.

"Or she just puts up with him." Kiley's voice comes first, then I see her round the corner. "Hi, Annie!" She hugs me too.

"Hi, Ki! I was excited when Zayn told me you'd be here," I say.

"I wouldn't have missed it." She turns to Zayn to say, "Dad is in the family room."

"Great. We'll go put our stuff down and then come hang out for a little before we settle in for the night."

"Okay, sweetie. That sounds good. Again, Annie, I'm so excited you're here," Darla comments.

Zayn grabs my hand and leads us down the hall. The last time I was here, I was in Dan's room, which is one door down. I never snooped in Zayn's room, but I remember thinking about it. After feeling the way his body morphed around mine, I found myself curious about what he hides in there and what's behind his mysterious demeanor.

"Is this weird?" Zayn asks as he plops the suitcase on his bed to unpack for the two nights we're staying.

"A little?" I shrug, snooping through the books on a shelf in his room. "But not as weird as I thought it was going to be."

"Explain..." Zayn looks at me with a sly smile.

"Well, before it felt like I was intruding? If that makes sense. Like, I was here with Dan, but I didn't feel like he wanted me here. I felt like an obligation. Almost like because it was a holiday, it was expected of him to bring me here."

"And now?"

"Now it feels different. I don't know how to describe it." I sit down on the bed next to the suitcase, fidgeting with my bracelet.

"Can you try?" Zayn steps in between my legs and grabs my hands, soothing me with small circles from his thumbs.

"It's you, Z. You make it different. Being here with you feels right? Like I belong, which is something I'm not used to. And even being here, in your childhood bedroom." I huff a laugh as I take in the random trophies around the room and music posters on the wall. "I'm just extremely happy, and because of that, it makes me feel calm and wanted and safe."

Zayn lets go of one of my hands and cups my jaw. "I'm glad to hear that. You are wanted and safe with me. Always."

He leans over and presses a kiss against my lips.

"Gross you two." Kiley's voice comes from behind Zayn, and I giggle into my shoulder.

"Kiley," Zayn grumbles.

"Don't hate the messenger. I'm just here to remind you that our parents want to see Annie, and you're hogging her."

"She *is* mine."

Every time he says that, it sends chills up my spine. I'm his.

"C'mon, Zayn. Let's go mingle. We'll have time later to chat more." I push him back slightly to give me room to stand, then saunter over to Kiley.

Zayn follows, and we all make our way to the family room. Their dad looks the same as the last time I saw him; he still dresses in athleisure and has a shaved head.

"Hi, Jerry." I smile as he stands up from the couch.

"Annie," he says as he pulls me into a hug. "Not sure how this happened, but I'm glad you're here."

"It's a long story." I chuckle and move to take a seat in between Zayn and Kiley on the opposing couch.

Darla chimes in. "Give us the basics. We are extremely curious."

I look to Zayn to see if he wants to tell them or if he wants me to.

"Well, you guys know how this past year hasn't been the best for me..." Zayn starts, and I reach over his lap to grab his hand. He looks my way for a brief moment as he interlaces our fingers. "Annie was hired to be my publicist after we reconnected at the studio. She didn't know I was the client at first. Things just kind of evolved from there naturally."

"Yep," I say with a grin, not feeling the need to add anything else.

"And you two live together, right?" Jerry asks.

"We do. And we know it's quick, but we didn't want to spend time apart."

"Aw, that's so sweet," Darla comments.

"Agreed. You two fit so well together," Kiley says.

"I agree, Kiki," Zayn says and he squeezes my hand.

My heart swells from all the compliments and how well this day is going. I know tomorrow will be different with Dan arriving, and I hope he doesn't cause any problems. We just need to get through dinner tomorrow when he arrives and then we get to go home the next day. I know Zayn has my back. He will be there to help me through any uncomfortable moments, but I'm still nervous. For now, I smile to myself as I look around the room, knowing that the man I love is sitting next to me and there's nothing that can change how I feel about him.

40

ANNIE

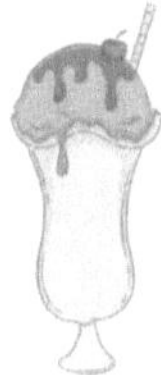

THE NEXT DAY I try my best to not be anxious. To keep my thoughts from wandering to what's going to happen when Dan gets here. We spend the morning with the parents and Kiley eating breakfast, then when they prepare for dinner, Zayn and I go to the backyard to wait and get some alone time.

Kiley joins us later, and we just hang out. I read a little bit. Zayn and Kiley spend some time catching up. With all the recent galas and date nights, they haven't had their normal weekly calls.

This trip has been so nice, to see this side of Zayn. He's calmer, his shoulders relaxed. He laughs more, and I'm realizing that he's just slowly opening back up. It's as if he was a flower that was moved to a dark room and closed up because it was missing sunlight. And then because of me and the support he's getting from friends, he's starting to bloom again. Starting to brighten from all the light around him.

"Kids, it's time for dinner," Darla hollers from the house.

I put my bookmark in my book, then follow Zayn and Kiley inside, placing my book in our bedroom before heading into the kitchen.

Zayn holds out a chair for me at the table and I take a seat, thanking him.

Sounds of laughter and chatter travel from the front of the house. It's time, and I know I said I could handle this, but my stomach is starting to feel like a storm on the ocean.

"You say the word and we leave this dining room, you understand?" Zayn says, and I only have time to nod before Dan stands before us.

Not much about Dan has changed except the woman on his arm. His hair is still buzzed, he sports a clean-shaven face, and he still wears the same bland color of tan. The woman with him is the opposite, dressed in a brightly colored patterned dress. She smiles, not knowing who I am, not knowing what is about to happen.

But I do.

Because I know Dan. And even more, I know Zayn.

"Zayn, I forgot you were bringing leftovers," is the first thing Dan says to greet us.

My hand is tugged up by Zayn's and I tug it back down, making sure he doesn't punch his brother already. The night has barely started.

"Hi, I'm Annie. I'm Zayn's girlfriend," I say across the table, making eye contact with Dan's date, choosing to ignore his comment.

"I'm Carrie." She smiles, the discomfort apparent on her face.

"I was thinking you might change your mind and come alone." Dan tries again, this time a little more subtle with his remarks.

"I wouldn't have left Annie."

"Right, girlfriend is it?" Dan takes a sip of the wine that was placed in front of him. He's ignoring his own date at this point.

"Yes," Zayn grits.

Dan opens his mouth, about to dig himself into an even deeper hole, when his parents come into the room.

"Alright, who's ready to eat?" Darla smiles as she takes a seat.

Let's get this awkward dinner over with.

41

ZAYN

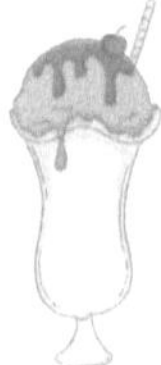

I was *this* close to jumping over the table and tackling my brother. If he says anything like that again, I will. He cannot talk about Annie like that and get away with it.

Dinner remains mostly silent besides the few questions my mom peppers in. Perks of being close to home is she mostly knows everything going on, or at least the highlights.

We manage to avoid any bloodshed, thank you parents for acting as buffers, and once dinner is done, Annie and I retreat to the living room first.

"Are you sure you're okay?" I ask her for what feels like the tenth time.

"Z, yes, I'm okay. I promise." She presses a kiss to my forehead. "Let's just enjoy the time with your parents."

"Okay, if you insist. We only need to hang out for a few, then we can go to the bedroom."

We take a seat on one of the couches in the room. I pull her hand to mine, feeling the need to protect her more than normal.

"So, Annie, Zayn tells us here that you're working for a well-known firm in LA?" Mom asks.

"Yes, I am. You could say it's a childhood dream come true," Annie replies.

Dan rolls his eyes, and part of me wonders if he's acting like this because Annie is with me and not him. I don't know much about their relationships, but if you are with someone for two years, you have to feel something. There had to have been a point where it was good between them, maybe even great.

Even thinking about that aches my heart, thinking about Annie being with anyone but me.

"I'm going to grab a drink," Annie says in my ear.

"Let me," I say, getting ready to stand up, but she places her hands over mine.

"I'll be right back, promise. I know where it is." Annie smiles. It's hard for me to say no when she's looking at me like I hung the moon from the sky. Bright eyes, wide smile, all mine.

I nod, then switch my attention to the room.

Dad updates us on work. Mom does the same. The girl that Dan brought, I can't even remember her name, talks to us about her work. All of it is boring, but I do a great job (I think) staying engaged.

"Where'd Dan go?" Dad asks.

Dan isn't where he was next to his date. When did he leave the room? I wasn't paying as close attention as I thought I was.

Fuck.

And Annie's not back yet.

Fuck.

"I'll find him," I say, shooting up out of the couch.

A pair of voices reach me before I have eyes on the kitchen.

"What do you mean you miss me? You can't fucking say things like that."

Annie's voice barely reaches me as she whisper-yells.

"Look, I'm sorry, okay, but you can do better than Zayn. Look at him."

"He's your fucking brother. I get you two don't get along, but I'm his," Annie says.

"Good luck picking up his pieces because he's a goddamn mess if you haven't noticed."

"He's picked up the pieces himself, he doesn't need me to do that. And you need to accept that we broke up a year ago and you have no claim on me anymore."

When I finally reach the kitchen after what feels like a prolonged minute, I catch Dan wrapping his hand around Annie's wrist, stopping her from moving. I don't think, I just move.

One step.

Two steps.

"Zayn, what are you—" Annie gasps.

My right fist connects with Dan's jaw.

"Fuck, Zayn." He stumbles back, hitting the counter.

Pans clash and clatter on the floor, alerting the rest of the family.

"Don't ever fucking touch her again. And don't dare speak to her like that. Do you understand?" I ask.

"You can't tell—"

"Do you understand?" I stand tall in front of him, looking down at his current hunched state.

He's gripping his jaw, but I can still see the nod.

"Come on, let's go." I grab Annie's hand and walk us out of the kitchen, pushing past my family waiting in the hallway. They can hear what happened from Dan.

Annie is my priority.

"Zayn. Zayn, slow down, please. Talk to me. Zayn, shit, you're shaking." Annie grasps both of my hands and stops me from walking in circles in front of my bed. "Sit down. Breathe."

I listen to what she says, taking a deep breath in and exhaling a long, deep breath. And I do it again. And again. And again.

"Good, that's good." Annie rubs small circles up and down my back, further pushing me to a more calm state. She places a hand over mine and I tense, just now realizing that maybe punching someone wasn't the best idea when I have no experience in the matter.

My hand is red, not bruised, but throbbing with a dull pain.

"Let's take care of this," Annie says. She stands up and grabs my other hand, interlacing her fingers in mine.

My body willingly follows her to the attached bathroom. She guides me to sit on the toilet and I am at her will, too exhausted to put up a fight. To tell her that I don't need help, that I can do it on my own.

Because that's what I'm used to. It's what my life has been for the past year. Not needing anyone, not relying on anyone, that's been my safety net. People don't leave your life if you don't let them in. People don't let you down, hurt you, lie to you, if you never give them the chance.

"I'll be right back," Annie says, and I find myself not being able to focus enough to answer her or think about what she's doing.

My focus stays trained on the floor, my brain running through the entire scene with my brother. Am I shocked that he did something? Kind of? But I should have expected it with the comments he was throwing her way earlier.

"This should help," Annie hands me a bag of ice.

"Where did you—?"

"Kiley." Annie smiles, her bottom lip tucked slightly inward.

I just nod, knowing that Annie would have gone out to the kitchen if I needed her to. She would have faced Dan, my family, if it meant helping me. That's how incredible she is, always thinking of other people before herself.

"You didn't have to punch him, you know." Annie looks at me from the now-shut door. She walks over to the shower, turning the knob to let the water fall.

"I did. That was the second time tonight I wanted to. I wasn't planning to let him walk away from me a third time. He deserved it. "

"Maybe so, but I can protect myself." Annie begins undressing. Not in a way that's sensual, but intimate. Like she's her most comfortable self when around me.

"You can, but I want to. I want to be the one that puts others in their place. You don't ever deserve to feel little again. He's already made you feel that way once, I wasn't planning to let him talk down to you like that again."

Annie walks over to me, nude, and situates herself in between my legs. "And I like you a whole lot for that. Feel free to join me, or go lay down. Either way, I'm here for you, too." She presses a kiss on my forehead and then gets in the shower.

It's an obvious fucking choice that I follow her. What better way to relax?

***

The next morning, we walk into the kitchen and Mom lets me know that Dan left last night. That's one less thing we need to worry about. We were leaving today anyway, so it wouldn't have mattered much, but the last thing I needed was an awkward goodbye, or eating an uncomfortable breakfast. Mom wasn't mad at me, but she was furious with Dan. I'm sure it's not easy for them to be in the middle of this feud. They likely don't know the things that happened between Dan and Annie. I don't expect Dan to apologize anytime soon.

"Keep us updated on everything, okay?" my mom says, and I nod.

Annie and I exchange hugs with my parents. Kiley walks us out to the car.

"Sorry again about Dan, Anns. If I knew that was going to happen, I would have uninvited him from dinner last night. You're better company." She pulls Annie into a hug and they stay like that for a moment.

And fuck, if I wasn't getting emotional looking at my baby sister hugging the woman I'm in love with. It's not everyday where you look around and everything just feels perfect. The sun is shining, there isn't a cloud in the sky, everyone has smiles on their faces, and the future is looking great.

Well, maybe that last part isn't set in stone yet, but I know what I want.

"Ready?" Annie looks at me, outreaching her hand toward mine.

"Ready. Bye Kiley, I'll call you this week. Love you."

"You better. Love you."

Kiley waves as we head to the Uber waiting for us in front of the house. Just a quick flight back, then we are back home.

We both need to be back at work tomorrow, back to reality, back to figuring out what our next step is.

42

ANNIE

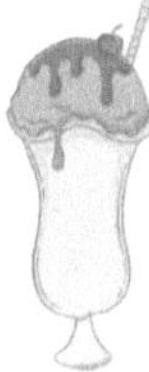

THREE MORE MINUTES AT the coffee shop and I would have been late for my meeting with Greg this morning. After getting back from our Thanksgiving trip, I checked my email and saw that Greg requested we meet to talk about my next client.

The contract with Zayn ends in three weeks, and I need to figure out what I'm going to do next. And what we are going to do next.

I shake my head and arms to flush out all negative thoughts as the elevator dings on the firm's floor.

"Meeting with Greg?" James asks.

"Yep. Do you know anything?" I ask, curious if they have any insider information.

"No. No Nancy gossip, but you know I'd tell you if I did."

"Yeah, I know. We can chat after?" I suggest, hoping that they will talk me off the cliff I know I'll be on.

"Of course, it's a date." James winks as they turn around and head back to their office.

The usual silence of the office is foreboding today as I walk past the closed doors of employee offices. Most of our work requires us to be out and about at events, traveling, doing groundwork, so hardly anyone is here. My heels clack on the floor as I near the conference room, and the closer I get, the more my stomach feels like a bottomless pit.

The door creaks open to show Greg sitting at the table with his computer open and a stack of notes to his left.

"Ah, Annie, perfect timing. This shouldn't take long."

"Great," I say, taking a seat across from him.

"How are you feeling about the last three weeks of your contract? Confident that Zayn will land his role?" Greg leans back in his chair and crosses his arms, staring at me.

"I'm feeling great. We have received a lot of positive news from various news outlets and have stirred up a lot of speculation rumors about what he is doing next. More and more reporters are asking for his time when we are out and about, and he seems genuinely happy to talk to them. He will land the role."

I'm sure of it.

I know going into all of this, Zayn didn't want a partnership, didn't want my help. But along the way, he has become him again. It's like he was stuck in a dark tunnel, and he just needed someone to help light the way out. And now, he's different, but in the best way. He's smiling again, making jokes, enjoying being around others. I'm so proud of him.

"Great, I'm glad to hear that. I've been impressed with the work that you've been doing. For your first client, I know it wasn't an easy one," Greg says.

"No, it wasn't. But I loved the journey. That's my favorite part. Helping someone in need and being able to see the change at the end. It's why I do what I do."

"I'm glad to hear that too, because I have your next client offer. You've been doing wonderful with Zayn's campaign, and I'd love to officially offer this to you."

"Oh, um, great." I stumble over my words.

I knew this was coming, but I thought I could receive information via email. Somewhere that I could process the information in private before having to talk to anyone. Even though this is what I've been working for, part of me doesn't want it. I want to stay with Zayn.

Greg slides a folder across the table. I take it and flip it open, finding a profile about the client, some other specifics, and the contract length. One year, New York, for a B-List celebrity, with possible extension if needed.

"As you see," Greg talks as I look over the papers, "we only have lower-level clients in New York at this time. People I believe to be more in your skill set level. They mostly need help with talking at events now that a recent movie they were in has had record-breaking numbers."

"There's no one here? In Los Angeles?" I have a hard time believing that out of the 3.8 million people living here, that there isn't one celebrity that needs our help.

"At this moment, no. All prospects have been taken by more experienced colleagues," Greg says as if I should have known that.

"Oh," I say.

This is when I should speak up for myself, tell him that I think I did an incredible job with Zayn's campaign, that because of me, he's changed for the better. That I did my fucking job and should be rewarded for it.

But I don't.

My eyes drift back down to the papers and I stay silent, shocked, stunned, in a state where I don't know what to say.

"Just a reminder, I need to know by the end of the year if you're going to accept this contract," Greg says, breaking me out of my trance.

"Oh," I say again.

I'm backed into a corner, and I can't find my way out. I want to scream, cry, beg for a contract to stay here. This isn't how my life is supposed to go. All of the puzzle pieces are finally finding their way together.

"Again, I don't need to know right now. Let me know within the next few weeks. Take some time to think it over."

I don't notice Greg leave the room until the door clicks shut. There is an eerie silence; the fact that I could either take this contract or lose my job looming on the horizon has me on edge.

Somehow, I get to my feet and walk to my office, keeping my head down. If I try not to think about New York, I won't cry.

"How did it go?" James' voice makes me jump when I see them, already sitting in the chair in front of my desk.

I slam a hand to my chest and say, "How long have you been there?"

I walk around to the other side of the desk, slamming my bag to the floor and plopping down in the chair. I sulk my head forward, catching it with both hands.

"Not too long, but I wanted to make sure I was here for you."

The smell of roasted coffee reaches my nose, and I peer up to see James sliding me a cup.

"Bless you, I need this." I grab the coffee and breathe in the calming scent, the warmth of the cup bleeding into my hands.

"So, how did it go?" they ask again, not letting me talk myself out of this.

"Not well. He still said the only available contract is in New York. Nothing else is locally available." I offer a wry smile, knowing I don't have much else to give at this time. My body is still in shock from the meeting.

"Seriously? That can't be right."

"That's what I thought. Am I that bad at my job?"

"Annie, no. You are great at your job, and I know that this is your first client, but you've made a huge difference. That's what we do. We pick up someone, put them back together, show the media the same, and then collect the paychecks along the way. I don't know anyone that knows the media like you do, and remember I've been here for a while." James gives me a knowing look, and I know they're not lying to me. They wouldn't.

"Well, I don't know what to do. I either accept this contract, or I'm done working at Starlet"

"Wait, lose your job? Why would you lose your job?" James asks, eyes wide with shock.

"This was only a trial client. I feel like I spent all this time, giving all I had, and now when I need something in return, nothing is coming."

I shift in my seat, leaning back into the chair, crossing my arms over one another. I follow that by taking a huge sigh. My chest is tight, and my heart beats faster than I can comprehend, and I don't know what I'm going to do.

"I'll figure it out though," I say, plastering a smile on my face. My feet plant flat on the floor, grounding me as I lean forward in my chair, changing my posture to not be so relaxed.

"I'm here if you need me. Even if you just need someone to listen to you, I'm here. You know that, right? " James asks. "And if you want me to make some calls or be your reference, just let me know."

"Thank you. I appreciate it." I smile again, but I know James can see through it now.

But they don't push me. They don't ask me to talk about it, even though I wish they would. I wish James would press, get me to talk, even though that's not the type of friendship we have.

Within minutes they're out the door, and I'm all alone in my office. It's just me and my thoughts, which at this time in my life, is never good.

I don't know what I'm going to do, but it's not going to be staring here at my computer screen, waiting for a magical email to hit my inbox with a new job offer. It doesn't work like that. I've wanted this career for as long as I could remember. Hell, just five years ago I was still spending hours on gossip sites and celebrity chat boards. I was obsessed with finding the news from the latest celebrities, and when I landed the internship at Starlet, it was a literal dream come true.

To think that it might all crumble is enough for me to spiral. But before I can dig myself into a hole, there's a knock on my door. Then, a click letting me know it's open, and a click to let me know it's shut.

"Annie," a familiar voice speaks.

My eyes look up to meet Zayn's as he strolls toward me. He's dressed in a casual outfit, a simple t-shirt with a pair of jeans and a baseball cap, backwards, which is new to see, but it makes me smile. He's so different from when I first met him, and I momentarily forget about everything going on.

"Hi, Z."

Then the tears fall, and fall. Zayn kneels down next to me, pulling my shoulders toward him, enveloping me into a hug.

"Shh, it's okay," he whispers, stroking my hair and rubbing my back. "It's okay, sweetheart."

"It's. Not," I cry, my words barely audible between my cries.

"We'll talk about it later. We don't need to talk about it right now. Right now, I'm here for you, to tell you I'm here for you."

"How—how are you e—even here?"

"James texted Todd, who texted me, and I just so happened to already be on my way to take you out to lunch."

I nod and smile in his direction, realizing I should have known that he would do this.

Regardless of what happens with us, I know that I will forever treasure this time we have had together. To have someone I care for so deeply in a short amount of time, to have one person to lean on during a time like this. If things don't work out, if I end up moving to New York, then I know that I will always have had this time in my life where this wonderful man never left my side.

43
ZAYN

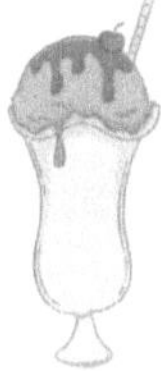

"Zayn, we are going to be late," Annie calls from down the hall.

The week has come and gone too fast, and now it's the second Saturday in December. We have two weeks until our contract is over. Too many events, too many dinners, too many galas—all for publicity.

I'm staring at my reflection in the mirror, making sure I don't have any hairs out of place.

This is our last big event together as a couple, and I want to make sure it's perfect. Tonight is the holiday charity gala for the Young Actors Association. It's hosted at some fancy event space, and there will be food and dancing. Something I'm surprisingly looking forward to.

"I'm coming," I yell back to Annie.

Two hands slip under my arms as I'm doing the final touches and warmth surrounds my back. The pressure of Annie giving me a hug startles me slightly, enough to have her chuckling.

"You look handsome, Zayn." She presses a kiss to my back.

I shift my body, turning around to face her. My hands move to wrap around her waist, and I tug her close to me. Her hands trail my chest, landing next to my collarbones.

I allow my eyes to gaze at her body. What I can see of it anyway. She's wearing a mid-length sapphire blue dress. It dips low between her breasts, and has a smooth, silk like feeling to it as my hands grip her tighter. As I breathe, the smells of her overwhelm my senses and I dive my mouth into her neck.

She laughs again, and it's the happiest sound I've heard. It's music to my ears, enough to make me stop kissing her because I can't stop smiling.

"Zayn—" She laughs again, trying to weave herself out of my arms.

I grip her tighter, peppering more kisses to her skin. She's fucking addicting.

"Zayn, we are going to be late."

"I don't care."

"You should care. You have to talk first."

I groan into her neck and release the tension from my hands.

"Why do you have to be so damn irresistible?" I ask, staring at Annie.

"You're the only one that thinks that."

"Impossible. I don't believe that for one second." I shake my head.

"Believe what you want, Mr. Barnes." Annie winks and turns to walk out the bathroom door. "Let's go!"

A sigh escapes me as I follow. I'm excited for tonight, to be with Annie, but I also know that we may not have many other nights like this. So, for that reason, I'm hesitant to let myself live in the moment, knowing that this could be our last.

***

The clapping in the room tells me the speech that I just mumbled my way through did what it was intended to do: introduce the night, talk about the silent auction, tell everyone to dance and to be on the lookout for news around what I'm doing next. Annie thought it might be good to throw that last piece in there, even though we have no idea if I'll land the role or not. She thought that if we got people talking about it, to be interested in what I'm doing next, then Ed would be more willing to give me the part in the trilogy.

She must be onto something because as soon as my feet hit the ground from the platform steps, I have a few reporters ready to ask me questions.

"Zayn, can you tell us about any of your upcoming projects?" one woman asks.

"Zayn, how do you feel being back and helping the Young Actors Association?" another asks.

"Zayn, we notice a shift in your outlook on life. Can you attribute that to anything particular?" a man asks.

I answer them all, short and succinct, just like Annie taught me. I even throw in a few smiles as photos are taken.

"That was great." Annie beams up at me as I take a seat next to her at the table.

"Were you watching me?" I ask.

"Of course I was watching, and I have to say, you're my star pupil." She winks.

"What can I say? I have the best teacher." I press a kiss on her mouth when I hear someone calling my name.

When my gaze shifts to the right, I see Ed walking our way.

"Annie, good to see you. It's been a while." Ed says.

She smiles and says hello. "I haven't had time to come get lunch with Cass in a while, I've been busy with this one." She nods to me and they both chuckle.

"Yeah, he's a handful isn't he?"

"Hey, I'm right here." I shrug, glaring at them both.

"It's the truth, isn't it?" Ed says, brows raised.

"It was, but not anymore," Annie says with confidence.

"I agree, and that speech you gave was incredible. Think we can chat late next week?"

"Of course," I answer, trying to keep my tone even. Inside, I feel as if my body is turning into mush and my brain is trying to process the fact that next week I will know if I get this trilogy role.

"Great to see you again, Annie. And good luck in New York, Cassie told me about your new job."

Annie's smile falters but returns a second later. "Thanks, Ed." Her voice wavers, but Ed doesn't notice.

I notice. I notice everything about Annie. When she's sad, like now, her smiles aren't as vibrant. They are forced, plastered on. She blinks more often, as if she's trying to tell herself to not cry. She fidgets with the closest item, which right now happens to be a napkin in her lap that she's forming into a ball and rolling between her palms.

But when she's happy, truly happy, her smile is bright and lively. And damn, is it contagious. I find my mood improving around her, as does everyone else. She gets the cutest crinkles around her nose and eyes, and her shoulders are relaxed, like she let go of every tension she was holding on to.

Ed walks away, and Annie turns to face the front of the table.

"You okay?" I ask, not wanting to cause her to think about it, but also wanting to show her I care and am here if she wants to talk about it.

"No, but I will be." She tries to smile, but the corners of her mouth don't lift more than a few centimeters. "Should we go dance?"

Various couples are dancing in circles to the slow jazz music coming from the speakers in the front of the room.

"Yes, let's go dance. Then we might be able to sneak out of here." I smile, grabbing her hand as I stand up from the chair.

Dinner can wait until later. Right now, I need her in my arms. I need to know she's okay.

We walk over to the dance floor and situate ourselves in between the clumps of people. I snake one arm around her waist, and place her other hand in mine. We sway to the beat and she leans her head on my chest. Her chest rises and falls, again and again, letting me know she's trying to calm herself. Hopefully not thinking too hard about it all though, not alone.

She doesn't need to do this alone. Not anymore.

The music shifts to a quicker beat, and I move my hips a little faster. Our hands follow suit, moving quickly in an up and down motion. She giggles against my chest, and I couldn't be happier that between the music and the dancing, that she's starting to feel better.

She leans her head back and meets my gaze.

She doesn't have to tell me she loves me for me to see it in her eyes, to see the longing and ache already settling in. To see that she doesn't want this to end. Because I know my eyes tell her the same story.

With my hand that's resting on her hip, I push her away, lifting our interlaced hands in the air to twirl her in a circle. Dancing with Annie is starting to become my favorite activity. I twirl her again and pull her back into my chest, keeping rhythm with the music.

She's smiling now, enjoying herself, enjoying us in this moment. "You're—"

"Something else?" Annie attempts to finish my sentence.

"No, I was going to say that you're perfect."

"I'm far from perfect, Zayn."

I shake my head as I twirl her in a circle again.

"No, I don't believe that. Your flaws are what make you perfect. You're perfect to me, Annie."

"Stop being so nice to me, it isn't helping." Annie pouts.

"I can't help it, it's who I am now, thanks to someone special." I meet Annie halfway, pressing a kiss against her lips. I want to tell her I love her. I want to tell her, to beg her to stay, to tell her that I'm nothing without her.

But it wouldn't be fair.

I can't do that to her. I can't be the reason she stays. Because her staying would cause her to lose her job, and what if she can't find another one? What if she starts to resent me? Then instead of getting to choose how this ends, we end up in a toxic relationship because neither of us are getting what we want.

"I bet that person thinks you're pretty special too," Annie says, laying her head back on my chest as the music shifts to a slower beat.

We stay like this, swaying to the beats that surround us, ignoring those crowding around. My breath is steady, and I'm grounded. I know what I want, and I hate knowing I can't have it.

But I'm grateful for what I have right now because I don't think I'll ever find a love like I have for Annie. It's not everyday you stumble across the one person that you feel completes you like a puzzle piece, that helps even out the rough edges, that laughs at your bad jokes, and never lets you feel alone. And because of that, I keep us in our bubble, not ready to let it pop just yet.

44

ANNIE

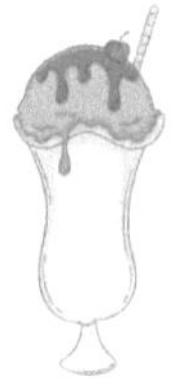

THE GALA WAS PERFECT. From the speech Zayn gave, to the outcome of the auction, to the dancing. Everything in between was magical, letting us have our last perfect event before something happens.

Because something has to happen.

I have to move.

To New York.

If I could find a new job, or even a lead for a new job, I would consider staying. But I've been searching online and haven't found anything. I'm losing hope.

There's one more week left in this contract. One more week of living with Zayn. A few months ago, I was looking forward to this. I couldn't wait for this ending to come, to move on to my next client, to use this as a launch pad for everything else. And yet here I am, still in bed at ten in the morning, replaying dates and talks and Zayn's face over and over and over. Praying

I don't forget any of it the moment I step past the threshold for the last time.

Not that we have talked about this relationship being over. That is one conversation we have yet to have, and I think it's because neither of us wants to admit that this is ending. This perfect, tension-filled, romantic relationship that started as a seed has bloomed into something beautiful. Maybe we are like a weed. Weeds can be pretty, right? But I don't want to cut us down anymore, I want to let us grow, let our love blossom and take shape.

My head tosses and turns on the pillow, which is essentially my tell that I should just get out of bed. Zayn left an hour ago to go meet Logan for breakfast to debrief on the last week before his meeting with Ed. After he left, I left his bed and crawled into mine. Well, what used to be mine in the other bedroom. I've hardly stepped a foot in this room in the past month except to maybe grab an item of clothing. And that's a small maybe because I now have space in his closet, a drawer in his dresser.

Loud knocking echoes down the hallway, interrupting my lingering thoughts. I guess I'll have to pencil in time later to wallow about all of this.

My feet find their way to the floor, sliding into a pair of pink fluffy slippers to match my pink sleep set that I've yet to change out of, and I yawn as I leave the room. You'd think I'd get more sleep the longer I'm with Zayn, that the late nights wouldn't be so...late. Nope. Still late, still exhausted, still pleased. It's the only reason why I'm not grumbling and complaining on my walk to the front door.

More knocks come, annoying me more than normal.

"Hold on," I mumble under my breath, now starting to get grouchy.

When the door opens, I see three of my favorite people standing on the other side, and my frown immediately turns up. Cassie, Lucy, and Marcy all stand outside my front door. Cassie is holding a pink box from Flora. I hope she brought me a blueberry muffin. Lucy has a multitude of drinks in her arms.

"Going to let us in?" Marcy greets, launching herself at me into a hug. "Why does it feel like I haven't seen you in ages?"

"It's been like two days." I roll my eyes as I open the door.

"Two days, two months, same difference." Marcy shrugs.

Cassie and Lucy follow, setting the food and drinks on the counter.

"Decaf?" I raise my brow at Cassie, who now has a tiny bump.

She's not supposed to drink as much caffeine now. That's what the internet told me, at least.

She just glares in my direction and says, "I'm allowed to have a cup of coffee a day, Anns." She takes a sip to prove a point.

I turn to the island and open the lid of the pastry box, searching for the one thing that always manages to brighten my day. Who knew a pastry had that much power?

And there it is, my blueberry muffin, surrounded by various pastry cousins.

"You girls are the best," I say, already getting emotional. And it's because they were thoughtful enough to bring me my favorite breakfast without knowing why I asked them to come over this morning. Since I normally see Cassie on the weekends and we have had to cancel the past couple of weeks, I knew I still had to talk to the girls about New York. I needed someone besides Zayn, someone from the outside looking in.

"Okay," Lucy says, taking a bite of her chocolate croissant, "tell us what the issue is."

"How do you know there's an issue? Everything could be perfect," I say, leaning back on the couch with my coffee and pastry.

"Your face doesn't look like everything is perfect," Marcy says, never holding anything back. "It looks all sad."

"My face? What does my face know?" I try to throw them off, or at least try to pretend that I'm not as sad as I am. I'm shattered inside, but I need them to think that I'm only beginning to crack.

"You're moving in a few weeks, Anns," Cassie says, wearing her own sort of sadness on her face.

It's the way she barely meets my gaze and the way her hands trace her stomach more than normal. It's the way she bites her lip and her eyelashes flutter at a rapid pace.

And that's when the tears fall, landing on my perfectly crumbled topped blueberry muffin.

"I don't—" I catch a breath, trying hard to keep myself together enough to spit the words out. "I don't know what to do." The words finally tumble out of my mouth.

"Can you walk us through it? Help us understand?" Marcy asks. Cassie and Lucy sit in silence, waiting for me to answer. Being patient for me, not pushing for any answers.

"What part?" I ask, wincing at how Marcy and Lucy only know half the story. How they don't know about Dan. Fuck, Cassie doesn't even know what happened at Thanksgiving. I've been plastering this picture-perfect attitude toward my professional life for so long that it's just become me.

"Start from the beginning, Anns," Cassie says.

And so I do.

I tell them every painstaking detail.

Starting with Dan and recounting how we dated and things fell apart.

Moving on to the moment I stopped believing in myself and needed to put on a mask to continue to convince myself everyday that the decision to chase my dream was worth it.

The moment I finally landed the internship and felt like everything was starting to fall into place.

Working my ass off for three years at Starlet PR, making sure that everyone knew how much I loved the opportunity that was given to me and that I would do anything to keep it.

To starting to heal from the hurtful words Dan said, and the opportunity to land a permanent role at the firm, finally thinking that maybe this was all worth it.

That the journey might have been hell, but if it led me to this moment, then it had to be worth it.

And finally, to Zayn. My Zayn. My ex-boyfriend's older brother. Everything that has happened between us over the past few months, from our first kiss, to mornings in the kitchen, to dancing at events, Thanksgiving, and last night.

"So, yeah, I don't know what to do." I finish after having talked for thirty minutes straight, recounting the past few years and forcing them to sit there and listen to me ramble and apologize for not being more open about it all.

"Annie, you can do whatever you want," Marcy argues.

"But I can't. Did you not hear what will happen? I won't have a job, Marce. If I don't go to New York, I get fired. Then what?"

"Then, you look for a new job?" she asks, shrugging.

"No one will hire me. Not only having the experience of one client. And I can't guarantee they won't call Greg to ask about my performance, and if he tells them that I refused a client, that will not do me any favors."

"We could ask around for you," Cassie offers, and I love her for that, but I can't be hopeful for something that doesn't have a likelihood of happening.

"Thanks Cass."

"Have you talked to Zayn about it?" Lucy asks.

I shake my head. My coffee is still in one hand, likely cold by now. My other hand holds my half-eaten muffin, but I hardly have the appetite to finish it.

"Annie, you need to talk to him about it," Lucy says.

"I know..." I whisper. "I know, but I—" I try to continue talking, but it's hard. It's so fucking hard. "I love him. I don't want to leave."

"Does he know that?" Marcy asks.

I shake my head again.

"You need to tell him," she says.

Again, I shake my head. "I can't. Not when he's getting everything he's wanted."

Cassie speaks up. "He's not getting you."

Lucy hands me tissues without me having to ask for them. I smile at her, knowing that the tears will continue to fall until this conversation is over.

"He doesn't need me," I argue.

He doesn't, right? He will move on, find someone who can give him the same company, the same love, the same support. Long distance wouldn't work, not with how busy we both are.

"Annie..." Cassie says, and I hear the pity, the sadness in her voice.

"It's fine, it's fine," I say, wiping the tears from my eyes, begging them to shut off and save any more tears for later. "It will be fine. I knew this would happen, I knew I wouldn't avoid it. It doesn't make it hurt any less, but I wouldn't trade it for anything. You know?"

Marcy scoots closer to me on the couch and throws an arm around my shoulder, pulling me into her, and says, "You're doing what you need to do and I am so fucking proud of you. But know he would do anything for you."

He would do anything for me, and that's exactly why I can't ask him to try to continue this when I move. I don't want to be a distraction, someone who steals his time and attention when he starts the most important role of his career. I don't need to split his love in two directions. He would fly to me every weekend if I let him, I know he would. He's selfless, and fuck, I love him so much.

It's because I love him so much that I know I need to let him go.

45
ZAYN

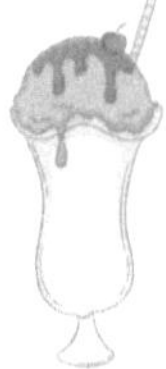

Brunch with Logan went as well as you'd expect. He grilled me about the gala, then grilled me about Annie. After seeing us together this past weekend, I wouldn't have expected anything different.

But I wish he didn't have to talk about her. Not today. Not when tonight is going to be our last date, our last night together. She doesn't know this yet, but it needs to happen. Before she moves out. Before she decides to stay with me, or before I beg her to stay for me. To forget everything she's worked for just to be with me.

And so talking about her with Logan is the last thing I want to do, but I figure I need to get used to talking about her, thinking about her, about us not being an us. So, I put on a smile, and that's what I do.

Does it make my heart hurt less? No, quite the opposite. Any piece of my heart that was previously mending, healing from the past, is no longer.

Does it make me forget that this is happening? That I'll soon be losing her? Also, no. It just reminds me that I don't have more time with her.

I'm grateful when Logan finally receives a call and has to go attend a meeting. It means I'm able to go home. Home to Annie.

When I finally get to the apartment and open the door, I find Annie at the island. She's wearing one of my favorite outfits. It's nothing extravagant, just the shirt she stole from me the first night we slept together over a pair of biker shorts. Her hair is tied in a bun and she's hunched over her computer. She's playing Chappell Roan and swaying from side to side, singing the words. Loud. Loud enough that she doesn't hear me come into the room.

My feet gravitate toward her, like always, and I'm not powerful enough to stop myself. Not that I'm wanting to, but touching her when I'm in love with her and can't have her is not on my to-do list right now. But, my body moves and my hands wrap around her waist. My face nuzzles into the crook of her neck and I breathe in deeply, her familiar bakery scent overwhelming my every sense. She tenses for a moment, barely a moment, before relaxing into my grip and giggling at my nose tickling her.

"Zayn, you scared me."

"Blame the music," I say, not needing to see her face to know she rolls her eyes.

"I thought you weren't going to be home until later? Is everything okay?"

"Yes." No.

My arms untangle from her and she twists toward me. I have a quick second to see her computer screen before it's shut.

"Flights?" I ask, unsure what answer I want.

"Oh, um, just looking."

"Just looking?"

"Yeah, to see how long the flight from here to there is." Annie fidgets in the chair beneath her, crossing and uncrossing her legs like she can't decide which way she wants to sit.

"And?"

"And what?" she asks.

"How long is the flight?"

"I don't know."

"How—how don't you know?" I ask, confused. If she was just looking up flights, she should know this.

"I couldn't bring myself to look." Her gaze drops to her lap and I see a tear fall, darkening the light gray shirt.

I do the only thing I know what to do at this moment. My lips meet her head and I stay there for a minute, maybe five. Annie wraps her arms around me, and it's in that moment that I know we feel the same.

We both want to be with each other.

But we can't.

Because she's moving.

I take a step back and wrap a hand under her jaw, tilting her head up. My eyes meet hers and I kiss the spots where the tears stained her cheek.

"We knew this was coming," I say, hoping that if I say it out loud, it will make this situation easier.

"But it wasn't like this. It was going to be different," Annie says between sobs.

"But it can't be different, can it? You're going to go to New York. And you're going to continue to chase your dream because you're so fucking good at your job. So good. And I'm going to be here, hopefully doing the same. Always being grateful for the time I got to spend with you."

We're both crying now, and I'm glad we are talking about this now, instead of out at dinner. Why did I think this would make a great dinner conversation? I should know that grief and sadness result in a lack of appetite, and we wouldn't be able to have the last few days together before Annie moves out.

"You're not going to beg me to stay?" Annie peers at me with water-filled eyes.

I shake my head slowly, swiping at her cheeks with my thumbs. "I love you too much to beg you to stay."

"You—" Annie says, or at least starts to say, but I cut her off with a kiss.

"I love you, Annie. In every lifetime, I would choose you over and over. The world knew what it was doing when it brought me to you, at the lowest point in my life. I am forever grateful to have met you, to have spent the last few months with you. But no, I will not ask you to stay. You need to go, chase this dream. You know that, don't you?" I grip her face tight, as if I'm afraid if I let her go, she will fade away.

But she nods, and nods again. Her tears slow, likely because she has nothing left to give. She starts to speak, but I stop her again.

"Don't. Please," I beg now, but for something entirely different. "If what you're about to say is in response to what I said, don't. If you do, I can't promise I'll be strong enough to let you go. And I need to let you go. I don't want to, but I need to."

She sits there and stares at me for a few moments. Contemplating, thinking, thinking some more, and finally, her lips curl inward and she nods.

"Okay," she says, her voice barely above a whisper.

"I want tonight to be perfect, for you, for us. I want us to have a few more memories to think of. A few more kisses, to remember you by."

"You act like I'll never see you again, Z." She meets my gaze again, this time with more fire.

"I hope the next time you see me, we are both where we want to be. And I hope we're single, and can try this thing for real."

"Is that a deal?"

I must take too long, because Annie speaks again before I get the chance.

"If the next time I see you we are both where we want and are single, we are doing this thing for real?"

"In every lifetime, Annie."

Then she pulls my shirt with her fist and tugs, her other hand gripping the back of my neck, slamming my lips against hers. We kiss as if it's our last, as if we can't get enough, as if we are trying to memorize the lines of each other before it's too late.

My hands do the same, tracing every curve of her body until I hit the chair she's sitting on. Why is she still sitting on this damn stool?

I firmly slide my hands under her, lifting her off the stool and bringing her body as close as it'll get to mine. Her legs wrap around me as I walk us down the hallway.

"For six more days, you're mine. And I'm going to make sure you remember that," I growl as I toss her back on the bed.

"How do you plan on doing that?" Annie asks, her voice still timid, still weak from just a moment ago, but more of her is back, more of the Annie that I know.

"Where do I begin?" I say, sliding up between her legs, resting my hard length against her. Her eyes flutter shut, her mouth opens, her back arches.

I press into her, harder. "I could begin with this mouth of yours. Always fighting with me, teasing me..."

I kiss her now, lingering.

"Or your neck. I could leave a mark, or two, or three. Something slightly permanent perhaps? Let anyone know who you belong to."

She moans now as my teeth sink into her, then just my lips, sucking and soothing the spot.

"Or maybe your breasts," I say, reaching down to pull her shirt up.

She lifts her back, letting me drag her shirt up, then lifts her head off the pillow so I can take it off. My eyes drop down to her chest, expecting to have to remove her bra, but there's nothing there. Just two perfect breasts, and fuck—her nipples are already hard. A hiss slithers out my mouth as my lips meet each stiff peak, my tongue swirling and my hand grasping at each one.

"But I think I'll start at your pussy. Fuck you with my tongue, for when you're alone and thinking of me, you picture me here, between your legs. Worshiping you."

And that's what I do for the next little while: I worship her. And continue until I manage to have her arching beneath me.

"Fuck, Zayn," she moans, my name continuing to fall from her lips over again as I flick her clit.

She wriggles and moves, her orgasm starting to build. My hand moves from her leg to her stomach, pinning her to the bed. My tongue takes over where my finger was. Faster, harder, and then she's whimpering, moaning my name again as she comes.

I remove my mouth from her and smile, staying in that position, just looking at her. Her chest rises and falls, slowing its pace. Strands of her hair fall around her face while the rest lay on the bed in a messy pile. A soft sheen is on her face, her cheeks are flushed a deep red, her bottom lip red from her constantly pulling it under her teeth.

"Come here," she whispers, and who am I to deny her?

If she asked me to come with her to New York, I'm not even sure if I'd be able to say no. But for now I obey her command and crawl up her body, moving to rest next to her.

"I think I should stay with Marcy starting next week, until I fly out. Just to give us some space. I'm afraid if I stay here, it will be too unbearable," she whispers.

I nod, knowing full well it would be the same for me. "Okay. Let's make sure not to waste any time."

Her hand cups my cheek, and I close my eyes as she caresses me with her thumb. Her lips are on mine before I open my eyes, and we stay like this for a long while. We don't leave the bed for another hour, or maybe two, but eventually both of our stomachs growl and I remember that we were supposed to get dinner tonight.

So, I pull her out of bed, interlacing my hand with hers to guide her down the hallway.

"I thought we were going out?" Annie says, a hand going to her mouth to catch a yawn.

"That was the plan, but I think I'd like to stay in. Just to spend tonight alone."

"I like that plan," Annie smiles. She walks over to the couch to sit down, curling her legs under her before throwing a blanket over them. "Maybe we can watch a movie, too."

"Whatever you want, Anns." I plop down next to her. "As long as I get to be with you, that's all I care about."

46

ANNIE

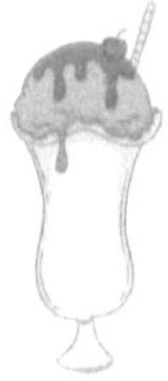

SIX DAYS WASN'T LONG enough. Did they even happen? Or did I dream six perfect days with Zayn? Every morning began with freshly made breakfast, coffee, and tea. We'd follow that with a walk outside, hand in hand, taking advantage of the December air.

I tried not to think of today, of the end. Each step we took, I tried to stay in the present, but I know Zayn was struggling too. Sometimes I'd catch him staring off into the distance and he'd have this glossy overlay on his eyes, as if he were zoning out and getting stuck thinking about the end. It'd be for only a moment, because then he'd blink once to snap out of it and return his gaze to me with a soft smile.

The afternoons were full of watching television, playing games, or just reading together. Actually, most of our time together was meant to be intentional. We both agreed that we wanted the end to be perfect, and that's exactly what it was.

And today, I'm moving out. Well, moving into Marcy's apartment. My stuff will still be at Zayn's for the next few weeks, but he said he will ship it to me when I get settled in New York since I'm getting a furnished apartment.

I'm currently sitting on the bed in the guest room, which used to be my room before I started sleeping with Zayn. My suitcase is packed with all my essentials, and I have a smaller bag with some random items that wouldn't fit. I've been crying on and off all morning and feeling like I'm making the biggest mistake. Am I choosing my career over someone I love? Am I not just doing what Zayn's ex did to him? Or is it different because we are on the same page? We are on the same page, right?

Ugh.

This is not how I pictured living in LA would go when I first moved here. I mean, sure, I thought I'd find *the one* eventually. But that was once my career was solidified and I had time to slow down. I never expected to fall for a client, let alone someone with a promising future like Zayn.

My mind keeps flipping between saying *"fuck it"* and deciding to stay and saying *"you did this to yourself"* because both are true, yet I'm choosing the latter. I did do this to myself. We did this to ourselves.

"Alright, I think you got everything," Zayn says as he crosses the threshold of the bedroom.

I look up and offer a soft smile. It's all I have the energy for at the moment.

"You ready?" he asks.

I shake my head.

"Come on," he says, grabbing both of my hands and tugging my body toward his. "Let's not think of this as a goodbye. Let's think of this as a see you soon."

"That's cliche," I mumble into his chest.

Zayn laughs, his chest rumbling my head.

"Only for you, Princess." He kisses the top of my head, then interlaces his fingers with mine. "Let's get you to Marcy's."

Zayn leans over to grab both bags of luggage. I told him I can handle my own luggage, but he glared at me. Typical Zayn.

I follow him out the door and down to the car in silence. Neither of us are in the mood to talk, but that's okay. I don't know what we'd talk about anyway. He still won't let me tell him that I love him, distracting me with kisses every time I try. But I will tell him. Someday.

"There you are!" Marcy says from the sidewalk when we pull up to her complex. She's standing there as if she's been waiting for the past hour, but we aren't even late. Okay, maybe ten minutes late, but we can blame the traffic for that.

"Hi, Marcy."

"Zayn, thank you for bringing me my best friend back. I've missed her," Marcy says, enveloping me into a hug.

"Marcy, I just saw you," I say with an eye roll.

"Doesn't count, it was a quick lunch." Marcy stands tall, proud even, and I can tell she's thrilled that I'm going to be staying with her for the next two weeks before I fly out to New York. "Here, let me grab those and you two can say bye and kiss or whatever." Marcy grins and winks in my direction as she takes the luggage from Zayn.

Once she's gone and through the door, I turn back to Zayn. He's only a foot from me, so it takes no time for him to close the difference and pull me into a hug. The tears flow again.

"Shh, it's okay, Annie," Zayn says in a futile attempt to calm me down.

"What if I'm making a big mistake?" Trying to be brave, I ask the question that's been haunting my mind.

"We all make mistakes, but you won't know it's a mistake until you make the decision. And remember our deal, okay?" Zayn kisses my head.

"How could I forget?" I somehow bring myself to laugh, the tears slow. I hug Zayn tighter, not wanting to let him go.

This is the last place I expected to see myself, wrapped in Zayn's arms, getting ready to live with my best friend for two weeks before moving across the country.

"You'll call me if you need anything? I'm still here for you, you know. Anytime, doesn't matter if it's three in the morning. I'll be here," Zayn says.

All I can do is nod, knowing I won't be able to bring myself to call him.

That'd be too hard, to stay in contact, knowing that eventually he will find someone to replace me.

Minutes pass and eventually we untangle from each other. Zayn cups my jaw with both hands, meeting my eyes.

"I'm not going to say much because I'd start crying again, but know that you are incredible, Annie. You're going to do great things, I know it. And I'm so grateful to have been included in your story."

He brings his lips to mine, one last time, kissing me slowly. When he pulls away, his hands follow.

"I guess I should leave now, right? Otherwise I think I could stay here for hours." Zayn chuckles as he runs a hand through his hair.

"Yeah, I know. Well, I'll..."

"See you later?" Zayn smirks.

"See you later," I say, wanting that to be true and hoping that this isn't the permanent end of us.

Zayn kisses me one more time on the forehead, then he turns to walk to his car.

I stay standing on the sidewalk as he drives away, waving to him as he passes. And continue to stand there until his car disappears in the traffic and I lose track of him. Then, I turn around to face the apartment complex and head toward the door to go up to Marcy's.

The entire walk to her door, I can't stop replaying the memories of Zayn and I. Like a movie reel, they roll through my head, showing me our dates, our hugs, our kisses, everything. I don't even have the door clicked shut when tears roll down my face again.

Everything hurts. My heart feels like it's being torn apart in a million directions, my head is throbbing from the constant crying, my chest is heavy with sadness.

I don't even see Marcy walk my way when she pulls me into her arms. Hugging me tight.

"I don't want to do this," I sob. "I don't want to leave."

"You could stay, you know," Marcy says, like it's an easy decision.

"I wouldn't have a job. I need a job, Marce. I can't start over."

"Let me make some calls. Maybe Cassie can do the same? We have to know someone in our connections that can help," Marcy suggests.

"Okay," I say, feeling defeated.

The thought that I could get a new job would be great, and it's crossed my mind before. But I didn't want to ask, because I didn't want to feel hopeful, only to get crushed in the end. I know I don't have the experience most firms are looking for, I know that Greg would sabotage any new roles that I wanted to land.

Marcy pulls away, letting me know she's going to call Cassie, and tells me to make myself at home.

So I go to sit on the couch and throw on an action movie, no romance, to try to distract my mind. It works, a little, because I end up falling asleep. And while sleeping, I dream that everything works out in the end and I hope that it becomes a reality.

***

One week has gone by. One week of not talking to Zayn. I don't feel any better. If anything, I feel worse. Marcy has to drag me out of the house. We go for walks and to the coffee shop down the road, maybe the diner up the road. I continue to sulk around, waiting for updates from her or Cassie on any job leads. All my friends have been calling and emailing people they know, and those people have been reaching out to people they know. It's only been a few days, so I'm trying to keep that in mind.

Even though I only have one week until I move.

Today Zayn finds out if he gets the role in the trilogy. The role that was supposed to help transcend my career as well, showing that I can help people get from here to there. I can picture Zayn, in his apartment, on the couch, waiting for the call. And I get sad all over again because I should be there, congratulating him, because I know he's going to get the role.

Marcy told me. She told me in hopes it'd make me feel better, and she wasn't wrong. But this also means our breakup will hit the media, and now I'll have to figure out how to avoid that. No scrolling on social media, unfollow all accounts that report any sort of news, remove my notifications around our names so I don't receive new articles straight to my inbox.

I'm sitting at the kitchen table eating lunch when the door to the apartment swings open. I drop the fork I was holding, having been startled by the door slamming against the wall.

"Shit, Marce, you scared me." I shake my head, rolling my eyes as I pick up the fork from the floor.

"Someone's interested."

"Huh?" I ask, needing clarification.

"We have a lead. There's a new PR firm starting up, female led, focused on uplifting women in the industry."

"Seriously?" I ask, my heart already beating faster, my excitement starting to show.

"Seriously. Pulse PR. Someone from one of the other top firms in the area left to start her own. She wants to meet you."

"Holy shit." I put my fork down now, suddenly not having an appetite.

Marcy nods. "They want to talk to you tomorrow, I gave June, the CEO, your number. She will call you today to give you the place and time. I figured you had nothing going on, so I told her your schedule is wide open."

"I love you. So much," I say to Marcy, grateful to have friends that will bend over backward to help you.

"I would do anything to help you stay, Anns. I'd miss you so much if you were across the country. I want you to stay too, you know."

"I want to stay too," I whisper.

And maybe I can. Maybe I'll talk to June at Pulse PR and they will want to hire me. Maybe I'll love the opportunity enough to say yes and stay. And then if that's the case, then everything will work out. I'll get to keep my career, keep Zayn, and thinking about all of that has me smiling, a real smile.

47
Zayn

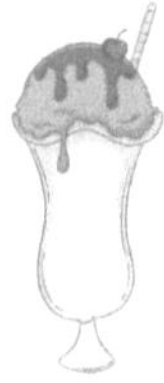

"Zayn, thank you for coming in today," Ed says as I take a seat in his office.

When was the last time I was here? I don't recognize the two dark wood chairs in front of his desk, or the bookshelf that's lining the left wall. I don't remember the two recent movie posters hanging on the right wall. My mind is latching on to everything and anything it seems, as I shouldn't care about these details. I'm not here to hang out with Ed in his office.

I'm here to find out if I got the role for this trilogy. The one that brought me (and lost me) the one person that I love.

"Of course, happy to," I respond, taking a seat in the left chair.

"I won't keep you here long, but I wanted to start by saying how impressed with how quickly your image has improved in the media."

"Thanks," is the only thing I say, because what else is there? It wasn't only me. It was a partnership, a team effort, that led to my name being perceived as anything but grumpy in the media. Before working with Starlet PR, I was on my way to never acting in a blockbuster movie again.

"How are things wrapping up with the firm?"

"Oh, um, fine." I smile, or at least try to smile, hoping that it comes across somewhat genuine. "Everything is good on my end."

I decide that's a good way to say *everything is fucked up but I'm trying my best to hide it.*

"Good, good. Glad to hear it. Alright, so I've already sent the contract to Logan, but I wanted to tell you in person that we'd love to offer you the lead role in the new trilogy that's beginning filming in the next few weeks." Ed has a giant grin on his face as he leans back in his chair, waiting to see how I react.

Except, I don't. Don't react, that is. I'm shocked. Frozen? Am I even happy? I wanted this, right? My fingers are plastered to the arms of the chair, my jaw hangs open, and I want to say something, but all words get choked off.

My chest is heavy, and my heartbeat reverberates throughout my entire body, sending signals to my brain that everything is wrong. I'm not happy, I'm sad. I'm sad that Annie isn't here to celebrate with me.

We did it. Together. Hell, it was more Annie than me, but I sure didn't do it alone. I owe her everything, and she's not even here for me to tell her that. I don't even remember when she's flying out to New York. I tried not to think about it, and my brain seems to have misplaced the information.

"Zayn?" Ed calls my name, leaning forward in his chair to inspect my reaction. His brows are raised in a concerned fashion.

"Sorry, Ed, I'm thankful and happy, I am. I'm just having an off day, I suppose. I'll make sure to get with Logan and sign the contract soon."

"Great, great. I'm glad we were able to chat for a moment before things get busy around here. I'll make sure to send you and Logan the first week's filming schedule shortly once you sign the contract. We also have a kickoff party this Saturday that the cast and crew will be at. You can bring a date if you'd like."

A date? Why did I think I could escape thinking of Annie in my day to day?

"Great, I'll be there. Just let me know the time."

I wrap things up with Ed before he manages to bring up the PR firm, or Annie, or dates for this party. My mind is screaming at me to get out of there, to become a recluse again, to lock myself in my apartment. There's no harm in that, right? I've kept up appearances, now I have the role, I think I deserve a break.

So that's what I do.

For three days, I don't leave the apartment. I get food delivered, I binge-watch movies, and I spend time looking over documents Ed sends over. Logan comes over for an hour Monday night after talking with Ed, and I sign the contract. Tuesday brings me ten emails from Ed with various schedules and film-ing information.

One thing I didn't realize about this role is the need to main-tain visibility in the press, so I suppose it makes more sense that Ed was so adamant with me having a positive relationship with the media before he offered it to me.

Except, thinking about being in the media again is causing too many parts of my body to ache. Reporters will want to know what happened to Annie, why isn't she with me, who am I seeing now... and I don't know how to not punch them in the face or storm away. I have talking points, but they all feel so fucking fake that I can't even picture myself saying them out loud. How can I do this without Annie?

It's hardly lunch time on Saturday when I get a call from Kiley.

"Hi, Kiley," I say, pressing the button to FaceTime her so I can continue to get dinner around. Using a book, I prop the phone up on the counter.

"I'm surprised to see you walking around," Kiley says.

"Walking around my own apartment?"

"Yes, I expected you to be moping on the couch," Kiley says with extra sass.

Little does she know I have been moping on the couch, she just caught me at the time when my body decided to yell at me for nourishment.

"I'm doing fine," I snap.

"Denial is the first step, you know." Kiley crosses her arms and challenges me in a stare.

Two minutes pass, she doesn't let up. If anything, her stare has become more terrifying. Has she even blinked?

Fuck.

"I'm not fine, okay? Is that what you want to hear?" I practically yell at the phone.

"Yes, that's what I wanted to hear. You can talk to me, you know. I'm not little anymore, I know what's going on."

"You're still my little sister," I argue.

"I mean, technically yes, but I'm not naive. I know you love her, and I know she loves you. I don't understand what happened." Kiley goes quiet.

She wants to ask me straight out, but I can tell she's nervous that I'll shoot her down, because that's what I always do.

"You're right," I say, deadpan, looking at the phone to make sure she meets my gaze.

"I'm...right?"

I just nod.

Kiley shakes her head, like she can't believe what I'm saying is true, then says, "But why is she not there right now? And why do you look like shit?"

I give her a look to say "*Really*?"

She just shrugs, because it's true.

"Annie's dream has taken her to New York. I can't get in the way of that." I shrug back, trying to keep my voice even as I talk about Annie for the first time since she left.

"How would you get in the way?"

"The long distance, the missed phone calls, the constant struggle to stay on the same page. There are a ton of things that can go wrong," I say, annoyed that I even have to explain myself.

"But what if things went right? Or what if you asked her to stay and she said yes? It wouldn't have to be her giving up her career. Maybe she could spend more time finding a new job or something if she was given the space."

My jaw goes slack, and I stay silent. Is that something that could happen? Could we find a way to make it work? There are risks that are worth taking, and I think this could be one of them. Why not? I know what we have is special. Annie isn't someone I want to let go, but I thought I was being selfless in doing so.

"Fuck, I'm making a mistake, aren't I?" I run a hand through my hair as I pace the kitchen, my food already forgotten.

"Yup," Kiley says, emphasizing the "p."

"I need to go Ki. I'll call you later."

I hang up the phone before she says anything. A newfound sense of joy rises in my chest as I take in the conversation we just had. Annie and I could find a way to be together, or at least I could put myself out there enough to ask her. If she said no, then I'd learn to live with that.

At least, I'd be able to say I tried. Regret wouldn't be looming over me for months to come.

I grab my keys to drive so I don't have to wait on a car and rush to the bathroom. My hair is a mess, standing up in various ways on the top of my head. Water does little to tame it, but it'll have to do. The mirror shows a stain on my shirt, the one

I've been wearing since earlier this week since I haven't had the energy to change out of it.

Fuck. The shower is calling my name, but I don't have time to spare. I look down at my phone, it's already ten a.m. and I'm fairly certain her flight leaves at eleven. If I leave now, I might make it in time.

I decide to call Marcy, just in case, to double check the time.

"Hello? Who is this?" Marcy answers.

"Marcy, it's Zayn. What time is Annie's flight?" I demand.

"How did you get my number?" is all Marcy replies, demanding right back.

I let out a groan and mumble, "How do you think?"

Marcy just chuckles. It seems giving her back the same attitude is entertaining. "Her flight leaves at 11:30. You waited until the last moment, huh?"

"Should I not go?" I ask, unsure if I want to know the answer.

Annie likely confided in Marcy, and told her how she felt about me. If she wanted me to stay away, Marcy would no.

"You should go. But I'd hurry, you're likely to hit traffic."

And I wish I could say she was wrong. That driving to the airport was easy- breezy and took me the normal twenty-nine minutes. That the interstate had no cars, and that I was shocked to see such little traffic around the city of Los Angeles.

But that's not what happened.

Instead, I hit rush hour. Because everyone knows traffic around the city lasts until eleven in the morning, and if you're trying to get somewhere important, you better plan for it to take two hours to get there. And if I would have figured out earlier this morning, last night, any other day, that this was what I wanted, I would have made it.

I would have made it to Annie.

But, I didn't.

When I get to the airport, the clock reads 11:31 a.m. and her flight has departed the terminal.

48

Annie

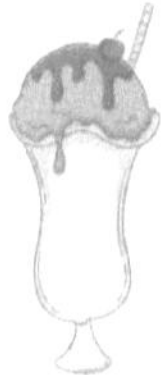

The echoes of voices in the airport surround me as I sit in the terminal waiting for my section to be called. Marcy dropped me off at the airport at nine a.m., barely missing traffic this morning. There was a rush of packing bags last night because I still felt like I was on the fence about moving. Did I want to do this? No. Did I need to do this? Yes. What other options did I have?

There was the possibility of Pulse PR.

After Marcy told me about June at Pulse, I contacted her immediately to let her know I was interested. If I had the possibility to shoot my shot, I was taking it. I didn't know what kind of role they had available for me, but I knew that whatever it was, I would take it.

If it was an internship, I would take it.

I would start at the bottom and climb back up the ladder if I had to, to prove myself. I've done it before, I could do it again.

If I didn't have to work with Greg anymore, or even adjacent to Greg, my life would be so much better.

And I could stay in LA.

With Zayn.

With my friends and sister.

LA has become home for me, and as much as I gripe about the traffic and lack of snow, I would miss it.

When June emailed me back and asked to chat with me in person, I was thrilled. Could this be happening? Could the universe be on my side for once? The past few years I've been giving, giving, giving, and not taking anything in return. Any favor someone asked for, I said yes. Any extra projects, errands, events, I said yes. If no one would believe in me, I was going to do my best job at believing in myself.

I was starting to think it wasn't enough.

But then the interview happened mid-week, and it went great.

"You're exactly the type of person we are looking for," June had said. "We are looking for someone who's looking to grow in their career and is open to taking on the more complex clients and finding ways to help them shine."

Isn't that what I did with Zayn? I helped him find his spark, something to bring him back, to show the media that he's the type of guy that the world would be thrilled to see as the lead in this series.

June continued on to say, "It would be a little slower to start as we build up our clientele, but we want the person we hire to have a say in the processes we take on as a business. It's important to me that everyone feels like a small partner in this venture."

Her words hit me straight in the chest, and I smiled wide. It was a perfect opportunity, one that I've always dreamed of. I've made vision boards of females in suit jackets commanding a room. There have been days that I wondered what it'd be like to work under someone more empathetic, instead of domineering like Greg.

June hasn't called me since, but I know she has a few other people to talk to before they decide on who they will hire. She was impressed with my resume, even though most of it was full of work I helped with during my time as an intern. But in her words it "shows how collaborative you are" and "how willing you are to help your coworkers when they are in a pinch."

I wanted to be the one to be pinched in that moment. Is this real life? That was the phrase echoing in my mind the entire meeting.

And now there's been radio silence, but I'm still hopeful. It hasn't even been a week, something could still happen. But that doesn't help calm the churn in my stomach or the thoughts swirling in my mind telling me that maybe I'm not good enough.

The thoughts are the worst, even with Marcy trying to hype me up any chance she gets. When I returned home from the interview, she had a cake. A fucking celebratory cake. Granted it said "Happy birthday" on it, but it was the thought that mattered. She's been the best best friend, trying to bring joy to my life over these past two weeks away from Zayn.

Some mornings it worked. I was able to go an hour without thinking about the way his lips felt on mine or the way he smiled whenever our eyes met. The ache in my heart dulled just a little. It was less of a throbbing pain, and more of a constant reminder that a piece is missing.

"We are now boarding for Flight 826 to New York."

The voice from the speaker alarms me, and I lurch forward. Then, the throbbing pain returns, in full force this time, reminding me that this is actually happening.

I'm moving.

I'm moving.

I throw my bag over my shoulder, grab the handle to my suitcase, and walk toward the gate. A small line awaits me. Perfect, just what I need. More time to collect my thoughts. All I wanted was to get on the plane, put headphones on, and try to force myself to fall asleep. If I do that, I don't have to spend the entire flight listing out the pros and cons of moving to New York. The cons list would be too long anyway. It would show that there are more on that side of the scale than the other.

But my dreams weigh a lot, right? Even if it's the only pro? I can find friends, new favorite restaurants, a new favorite bookstore. I could even find love, if I wanted to. Which I don't, to be transparent. I want nothing more than to stay here, to continue to fall in love with Zayn, but would I regret that choice? What if I don't give this an honest chance? And I never find my foothold in the industry again? Even one more year with experience would make an impact, and maybe then I could come back. One year isn't too bad, right?

The gate agent grabs my ticket and softly smiles before ushering me along. My suitcase trails behind me as I walk onto the loading bridge. Every step feels heavy. Every breath that I take feels forced. My chest is pounding, aching, tight. I try to take a deep breath as I walk, then push it out. It doesn't work.

If anything, it gets worse. My lungs beg for more, but I have nothing more to give.

"Miss, are you alright?" A flight attendant crowds me, leaning down to ask me the question.

I nod and coerce my lips to curl inward and form a thin line, a polite smile. They don't see past my mask. They don't see internally that I'm struggling with getting on the plane, but why would they? I've perfected the everything-is-fine look.

I picked a seat near the front, so I don't have to walk far. After putting my carry-on in the overhead bin, I plop down in the aisle seat. I would normally prefer the window seat, but I didn't want to watch the city I've come to love fade in the distance.

Before I have the chance to turn my phone on airplane mode, it starts ringing. I get the casual side-eye from my armrest partner, and normally I wouldn't accept a call from a random number, but if this is who I think it is, I have to answer it.

"Hello?" I ask cautiously, hoping it's not a spam call.

"Hi, Annie, this is June. Is now a good time to chat?"

"Hi, June! Yes, of course."

Please be good news, *please* be good news.

"I know you are heading off to New York soon," June starts, and I realize I never told her when I was moving, just that my job was leaving me no choice but to do so soon. I can hear some papers shuffle before she continues, "but I was hoping you might consider sticking around in LA a little longer. We'd love to offer you one of our publicist positions with a small amount of equity. I understand if you need time to think about this."

"No, I mean yes." I stumble over my words. "I would love to review the offer prior to accepting, but I am extremely interested."

"Great, great. I'm glad we caught you before you left. I'll send the offer over now. Email or call me if you have any questions."

I can picture June smiling on the other end as we hang up.

Before I left...*shit*. New York. I'm still on this fucking plane. I need to get off.

I need to review this contract.

Zayn.

I need to tell Zayn.

49
ZAYN

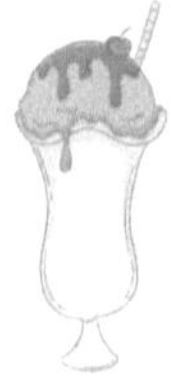

I didn't make it.

Fuck.

And now I have to go to this damn party.

Alone.

Kiley offers to tag along when I call her on the drive back to the apartment, but I tell her I want to be alone. Or at least not have to entertain her at the party. I figure I could use this evening to think about my plan to talk to Annie.

Maybe I'll fly to New York. Maybe I'll just call her tomorrow, tell her immediately that I want to try to work it out. The deal I made with her can be null. I don't want us to wait until we are in the same place. I just want her.

The door to my apartment opens and Emmett strides in, followed by Max, Lane, and Tyler. I'm confused for a moment until I remember I told Emmett we could go to the party together.

"You could have knocked," I say, glaring in his direction.

Even though we are starting to be friends, I still find myself reverting to my old habits. Grumpy, defensive, the opposite of friendly.

"Why would I do that when the door was unlocked?" Emmett smirks, walking to my fridge like he's been in my apartment before.

The rest of the guys huddle around the island, taking up the seats and asking Emmett to find some snacks.

Once everyone has their snack of choice (various types of chips), they all turn to look at me.

"What?" I take my time looking at each of them, glaring in their direction.

I ended up getting home from the airport shortly after one p.m. and luckily had time to take the much-needed shower, so I'm feeling somewhat refreshed after two weeks of sulking around. Having the guys over was meant to be a distraction from Annie, because everything in this damn apartment reminds me of her.

Even these fucking chips that they got out do, because she's the one that picked them out. In every recent memory I have, Annie exists.

"You're just extra grumpy today," Tyler comments.

"Annie did just leave him," Max says.

"She didn't leave me," I say right back, trying to defend her.

"They chose to take a break," Emmett says. He's the only one who knows the entire story, since Cassie keeps him informed.

"Ah, the infamous break." Lane leans back in his stool, slowly nodding at his remark.

"It's not a break," I say, because I don't want it to fucking be a break. "I mean, I don't want it to be a break."

"Then why are you here?" Lane asks, eyebrows raised.

"Because we have this party?" I lean against the counter, crossing my arms. "And I tried to go to her, but her flight already left, if you must know."

Everyone nods and sighs like they are all collectively sad for me. I parrot them, sighing right back and moving my head in an exaggerated nod.

"So, I figure I'll take tonight to think through my plan of action," I say, grabbing my keys from the table.

"You could fly to her," Emmett says.

"Or just call her?" Tyler says.

"Or text her?" Max says.

"Why not all the above?" Lane smiles, wanting a say in this conversation.

"You all are too fucking much sometimes," is all I say, shaking my head, joining them in laughter as the conversation strays to other topics. Topics that I'd much rather talk through to distract myself from Annie.

An hour passes before we decide to head over the January Studios for the party. Everything is different now when I go to my place of work. I have people surrounding me that I can talk to, eat lunch or run dialogue with. This circle of friends is not something I had in the past, but I think deep down I craved it. After Marissa left me, and I shut everyone out, I was lonely.

Maybe I didn't realize it, or maybe I didn't care, but either way I'm smiling now because of everyone around me.

Emmett and Cassie. Tyler and Lucy. Marcy, Lane, Max, and Ed. People that seem to care about me a little bit because of Annie. She brought me back into this world, and I need her here.

"Zayn, you want a drink?" Lane leans over to make sure I hear him over the music in the studio.

They've turned where the sets are built into a makeshift event venue—a dance floor in the middle, two open bars, plenty of seating options.

I nod and follow him to the bar across the room, the one nestled in the back corner.

As the music fills the room, I find myself seeing Annie every time my eyes close. Every time we went to a gala or an event, we danced. I grip the glass in my hand, trying to reign in the memories, but it doesn't work.

They overtake me, so much so that I have to put my drink down. Every song reminds me of my hands on Annie's waist, her head resting on my chest, our breaths mingling with the thick of the air.

I lean against the bar back, taking a deep breath and trying to smile at the people around me when I make eye contact.

I close my eyes one more time and inhale. The smell of cinnamon and vanilla surrounds me, but I don't remember seeing any pastries tonight. Bumps line my arms as I feel the presence of someone close to me. Can't they see I'm trying to stick to myself?

My eyes snap open to find the last person I expected to see.

"Annie." Her name tumbles out of my mouth as a whisper.

My gaze stays locked on hers. Is she actually here right now? Or is my mind playing tricks with me?

"Hi, Z."

Nope, she's undoubtedly here.

Neither of us move. The music and people around us fade into the background until it's just the two of us in this room. I take one step forward, finding her hand with mine to interlace our fingers together.

Two weeks have gone by since I've been able to touch Annie. Two long weeks not being able to see her, hear her laugh, smell her cooking. And here she is, in front of me. Smiling like a goofball, wearing...

Holy shit.

She's wearing the same dress from the first gala.

My eyes rake her body. Dark green, thin straps, slit in the leg. This dress haunted my dreams for weeks after the gala, where instead of her storming away from me, she fell into me and I dragged her off the dance floor for other reasons.

"You're here."

"I'm here," she replies, her voice quivering. "And I'm where I want to be."

I tilt my head in confusion.

"I, um, have a job offer that I'm going to entertain."

"You have a job offer."

"Yes, Zayn, try to keep up." She smiles and the ache in my heart is no longer. It's healed by her presence, her smile.

"And I'm needing a place to stay for a little while," Annie says as she pulls me closer to her, wrapping her other hand around my waist.

"I might know a guy who has a spare bedroom that's hardly been used. Though his last roommate left a bunch of things in there, will that be a problem?"

Closer. I need her closer.

Annie shakes her head, "I need something furnished anyhow, as this might turn into a permanent situation. Do you think your friend would be okay with that?"

"More than okay with that. He'd be thrilled actually."

Annie untangles her hand from mine and slinks it around my waist, tugging me into a hug. She breathes into me, our chests rising and falling at a matching pace.

"I missed you," I mumble into her head.

"I missed you more," she argues.

"Impossible," I say as she laughs. "So, what now?"

Annie lifts her head from my chest and takes a step back.

"Well, I'm here, I'm single, and I'm where I want to be. What about you?"

"Me?" I ask, partially shocked that she's repeating the deal we made to each other just two weeks ago.

Annie simply nods.

"Well, I'm also here, single, and where I want to be now that you're here."

"And you know what that means..." Annie says, smirking. Her eyes smile, a soft red tint blooms on her cheeks, and the way she's staring at me is having me fall in love with her all over again.

"Time to try this thing for real."

50
EPILOGUE: ZAYN

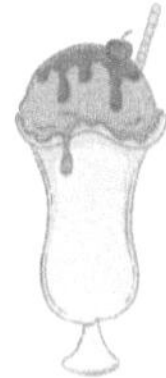

"That's not how you make them," Annie grumbles under her breath.

When she asked me to help make cookies for Cassie and Emmett's baby shower, this isn't what I pictured. I figured we'd go to the store, buy the cookie dough, bake the cookies. What does Annie want to do? Make everything from scratch, of course.

"Princess, I'm rolling the cookies like you told me." I glare in her direction as I roll this cookie into the best fucking sphere someone has ever seen. "See?" I hold it up so she can admire my work.

"That's much better. No more of these oval shaped, lumpy cookies."

"You're bossy."

"It's only because I love you," Annie says, smiling in my direction.

"It's because you love me that you're bossy?" I quip.

She giggles as she rolls the cookie spheres in a cinnamon sugar mixture. "I can't marry you if you can't make cookies. I'm just trying to set us up for success here." She adds a shrug before she waltzes over to me to plant a kiss on my cheek.

"You've already said yes. You can't back out now."

"I wouldn't dare."

Annie beams up at me, and I can tell she's thinking back to a month ago when I proposed.

She moved back in two months prior, and I knew I wasn't going to let her get away this time. Annie is too important to me, and the fact that she came back for me meant that she was choosing me just as much as I was choosing her.

She moved back in the same night of the party at January Studios. We took the time to go over the contract for her new job together, and I even had her talk to my lawyer about some of the details to make sure she was getting the best deal. There was no way my girl was going to regret taking this job.

Everything worked out, and she started a week after. Her first client was a younger actress, barely twelve, who needed help with interviews. Pulse PR got plugged into the Young Actors Association, and now they offer free help each month to our scholarship winners. It's been incredible to see Annie blossom in her role, taking on more responsibilities, and making sure that her voice is heard. She deserves it, after all. Everyone deserves to achieve their dream.

"Okay, I think we're done," Annie says as she scans the counter.

Five dozen cookies lay on cooling racks, ready to be packed and transported to the baby shower tomorrow.

I'm leaning against the counter, watching Annie take it all in. Inspecting a few cookies, and smiling at our work. She saunters over to me and wraps an arm around my waist. I loop an arm around hers and pull her tight against me, allowing her head to rest on my chest.

"This is perfect," she says with a sigh.

"What is?" I ask.

"Just, all of this. Some days I think what would have happened if I was assigned a different client a year ago. Then I wouldn't have all this, I wouldn't have you."

"You don't know that. We might have reconnected eventually," I say.

"Maybe," Annie drawls.

"But I get it because I think about that too. If you didn't come around, I wouldn't be the person I am today. I might have gotten my shit together and somehow landed up getting the role, but I'd still feel like an empty shell. I wouldn't have someone to share these memories with."

"Yeah, you're lucky you have me," Annie says matter-of-factly.

I pinch her side and she squirms toward me.

"We would have found each other though. Even if you were never my publicist, Princess."

Annie lifts her head from my chest to look at me. "You think so?"

"Without a doubt," I say, kissing her forehead. "I would have found you, would have made you mine, in every lifetime."

Acknowledgements

And just like that, January Studios comes to a close. For now. And I'm grateful that you all are here with me, reading my stories, encouraging me to keep writing. I'll never get over it.

When I first started writing this story, I knew from the beginning what I wanted to happen. It might not happen again, but thank you Annie and Zayn for letting me tell your story with ease. It's made this large book easier in a lot of ways, and my editing days were full of laughter and tears.

I want to thank Kristen and Sophie for always writing with me every week. You two have become my ride or dies and are essentially my coworkers. It's your feedback and encouragement that keeps me going on a hard day. Thank you for your accountability and your support.

To Beth, my dear friend and editor. It's been incredible to work with you for this entire series, and I'm so glad that the internet brought us together. Thanks for sticking with me while I finish this dang book and for loving Annie and Zayn just as much as I do.

To Lindsay, this cover is incredible and I'm grateful for the work you do. Thank you for continuing to work with me on this series and to help bring these characters to life.

To Sam, Jillian, Rachel, and Marja—I wish I could fly all over the world and write together in person. Writing with each of you is something I look forward to. Thank you for your feedback and support and love.

To my alpha and beta readers—thank you for the comments and hype over Annie and Zayn. It's always scary to share a new story with so many people, and I'm grateful for all of the help to make this story what it is today.

And finally, to my husband Ryan—Thank you for supporting me on this journey, for encouraging me when I'm feeling down, for listening to me every time I have a new idea, and for believing in me. I love you!

About the Author

Courtney Corlew lives in the Midwest with her husband Ryan and their two kids. When she's not writing, she's reading (like everyone else) and spending time in coffee shops and bookstores around the city. She looks forward to writing many more stories filled with dreams, love, and friendship. To stay up to date, follow her on Instagram @courtneycorlewauthor or visit her website www.courtneycorlewauthor.com.